APACHE LAMENT

APACHE LAMENT

PATRICK DEAREN

FIVE STAR
A part of Gale, a Cengage Company

GALE
CENGAGE Learning·

Farmington Hills, Mich • San Francisco • New York • Waterville, Maine
Meriden, Conn • Mason, Ohio • Chicago

GALE
CENGAGE Learning·

LIBRARY OF CONGRESS CATALOGING-IN-PUBLICATION DATA

Names: Dearen, Patrick, author.
Title: Apache lament / Patrick Dearen.
Description: First Edition. | Waterville, Maine : Five Star, a part of Gale, Cengage Learning, [2019]
Identifiers: LCCN 2018032030| ISBN 9781432855680 (hardcover) | ISBN 9781432855697 (ebook) | ISBN 9781432855703 (ebook)
Subjects: LCSH: Texas—History. | GSAFD: Suspense fiction.
Classification: LCC PS3554.E1752 A616 2019 | DDC 813/.54—dc23 LC record available at https://lccn.loc.gov/2018032030

First Edition. First Printing: March 2019
Find us on Facebook—https://www.facebook.com/FiveStarCengage
Visit our website—http://www.gale.cengage.com/fivestar/
Contact Five Star Publishing at FiveStar@cengage.com

Printed in Mexico
1 2 3 4 5 6 7 23 22 21 20 19

For my wife, Mary,
who walks with me
by the singing waters

MESCALERO GLOSSARY

anee: over there
Bik'egu'indáán: God, Creator
datl'ijee: turquoise
elchínde: children
ént'í: he is a witch
Gáhé: mountain spirits
ga'í: rabbit
góbitseeghálegǫ́líní: rattlesnake
gutaaln: medicine man
guu' k'as: cold
ídóí: mountain lion
idzúút'i: go away
inádlu: he laughs
Indaa: white person, white people
ink-tah: sit down
itsá: eagle
ixéhe: thank you
kunh-gan-hay: fire-place; camp
kuughà: teepee
Ndé: Apache
neeldá: early morning, dawn
nejeunee: friendly, kind, friend
niishjaa: owl
nil daaguut'é: a greeting; how are you?
ntsaa: big

Sháa: sun

shilth nzhu: you're really dear to me; you're close to my heart

shimá: mother

tádidíné: sacred pollen

Tl'é'na'áí: moon

tsé: rock

tseenaagaaí: white-tailed deer

yá: sky

yah-ik-tee: is not present; said of someone dead

yah-tats-an: it is dead; said of an animal

CHAPTER 1

He wondered if Elizabeth's cries still echoed through the desolate pass called Bass Canyon.

Twenty-seven-year-old Sam DeJarnett relived the moment in the Carrizo Mountains of Trans-Pecos Texas as if the gunshot had just now felled him from his horse. The scorching earth under his cheek. The loaded cylinder of the Colt revolver hard against his pelvis. The pain in his temple from the grazing slug that had thrown him flat on the desert floor where the rocky heights on either side hovered closest.

Between a pitaya cactus and a twisted yucca, Sam had found a window into perdition on that May morning in 1880. A runaway schooner careened off-trail to the left and two more to the right, their mule teams in a panic. Rifle muzzles flashed fire and threw white smoke across milling emigrants and fierce, painted riders. And lost and helpless in the mayhem was a stumbling figure in bonnet and blue calico.

The searing sun glinted from a silver locket as she whirled, frantically shouting Sam's name. Then she bolted for him, and the dust rose up thick and bitter when a slumping Apache devil with bleeding breast turned his paint horse after her.

Sam saw it all—Elizabeth's dress flying in the catclaw and her white-ruffled petticoat shredding and the lathered horse running her down. On the first pass its shrieking rider leaned and snatched away her locket, and then he wheeled his mount after her again and readied a stone-head war club with horsetail pendant. But Sam was powerless, paralyzed in a nightmare. He was awake but he was asleep, and he experienced things distantly as if an onlooker and not a participant.

A corner of his mind spoke through his haze, pleading with him to do something with the .45 pinned beneath him. But it had been so much easier to lie there drifting into oblivion and dream and forget Elizabeth and that locket clutched in an Apache hand . . .

Bass Canyon was behind Sam now, eight months by time and a dozen miles southeast across the lowlands by distance. But it was a darker presence than ever on this frigid morning of January 26, 1881, for with every pace of his iron-gray horse through a trampled dusting of snow, he gained on those sons of hell who had taken so much from him.

Mescalero Apaches.

Reports suggested there were a dozen of them, not counting women and children. For months, they had repeatedly spilled blood on both sides of the El Paso road and then vanished into this Chihuahuan Desert complex of six-thousand-foot crags broken by sinuous passes and greasewood flats. US Army soldiers had died at Paso Viejo and Ojo Caliente, and just eighteen days ago this last remnant of Victorio's band had swooped upon the El Paso–bound stage in Quitman Canyon and killed the driver and his passenger.

As heinous as those acts had been, the outrage in Bass Canyon was all that Sam could think about. Good God, why hadn't he done something? He had lost his smoking Spencer carbine in the hard fall, but he'd still had a revolver in reach, so why the hell hadn't he?

Elizabeth! I laid there and just let it happen, damn me to hell!

How many, many times, through mornings breaking as gloomy as his sleepless nights, had Sam wished that the grazing bullet had struck him flush.

You's here for a reason.

His father's long-ago words always competed with the ghost of Bass Canyon, and they invariably came with a memory of the warm clasp of hands before a dog-eared book gracing a hand-hewn table alive in lamplight. But as comforting as his father's conviction had been in Sam's childhood, he recognized it now as founded on an utter lie.

Or maybe not. If no additional significant snow came out of the dark-gray clouds, at least he and the other nine Texas Rangers on horseback could track down those murderous Apaches. Sam and the other men of Company A may have been a ragtag bunch—wide-brimmed hats creased ten different ways, worn duck trousers tucked into cracked leather boots, shabby coats of wool or buffalo hide—but they had firepower and *Cinco Peso* badges that gave them the authority to butcher those soulless animals.

It was a reason worth living for, all right.

"Damned cold weather to be in when we ain't got paid in so long."

Sam was unconcerned about the forty dollars a month, and he certainly didn't need a reminder about the weather from Matto, a stocky rider on a leggy bay at his left. A swarthy twenty-eight year old, the square-jawed man had mustered in out of New Mexico Territory during the summer heat, but frost now clung to the drooping black mustache that accentuated his perpetual scowl.

"Sets me to shakin', it's so cold," Matto added.

He had an aggravating habit of making an unpleasant situation worse, and Sam snugged his ratty wool overcoat around his neck. Still, the biting north wind in his face managed to find his marrow.

"Rattles my teeth," Matto grumbled.

Sam flexed his gloved fingers, which abruptly seemed as

numb as they were stiff.

"Toes about gone too." Matto just couldn't keep his gravelly voice quiet.

Sam, suffering now, shivered to an icy gust and hunched over the saddle horn.

But Matto had even more to say. "No part of me but's not froze. I—"

"If only that lingual organ of yours might freeze," interrupted the rider ahead of Sam.

Sam didn't care to engage Matto, but he was glad that Arch Brannon had, even if Sam had no idea what this ranger with the red-checked neckerchief had meant. Arch may have been a onetime hide skinner, but he had a vocabulary better suited to the classroom than the buffalo plains.

"Always tryin' to prove you're smarter than anybody," charged Matto.

"Your tongue," simplified Arch. "A frozen lingual organ would hinder your boundless protestations."

Sam hadn't expected to make friends when he had joined the Rangers at Fort Davis three months after Bass Canyon; he had set out on a mission and nothing else had mattered. But he did have a friend in Arch, a wiry rider of thirty who wore his frayed neckerchief winter and summer. Sam welcomed anyone who could take his mind off things, but Matto was in no mood for foolishness.

"One of these days," Matto growled at Arch, "you're goin' to take a step too far with me."

"Oh, I dare say I'm not much for waltzing," said Arch.

Arch had a caustic wit as sharp as the bone-handled knife at his hip, but Sam wasn't so sure that he should test Matto. There were good-natured men a person could hooraw and expect the same in return, and then there were scowling men like Matto who seemed to carry something dark and sinister inside.

Sam sat upright in his saddle. "Better get our jawin' over before we hit those hills. Looks like a place to be on our guard."

"The foothills of Sierra Diablo, the Mountains of the Devil," said Arch. "Do you suppose His Satanic Majesty has set it aside as a playground in which his Mescalero minions might frolic?"

Sam flinched at the memory of that Mescalero war club falling toward Elizabeth. "Shut up, Arch."

It was the most abrupt Sam had ever been with Arch, and his reaction wasn't lost on his friend.

"Samuel, I'm sorry," said Arch. "What's said in jest can still be insensitive. I know what those Mescaleros took from you."

All Sam could do was look down at the saddle horn.

"If yonder's the Devil's mountains," spoke up a rider from behind, "then a right proper place for chastening, it is."

In memory, Sam was still in Bass Canyon, but he didn't have to pull himself back to the here and now to recognize the drawl. Back at Fort Davis, Boye had introduced himself as "Boye, the preacher boy," and a boy of late teens was what he was. He couldn't muster more than peach fuzz on his freckled face, but judging by his frequent comments, he had man-sized guilt.

"He's had me by the collar, the Lord has, and he's ready to separate the wheat from the chaff," Boye added.

"Why don't you stuff that collar of yours down your throat," snarled Matto. "Or better yet, I'll do it for you."

"An instrument of the Almighty, you'd be. Just more retribution for all I done."

"Sweet Mary, I don't want any chastening," another rider spoke up from behind. "All I want's to get back to New Jersey and be with my Mary Jane."

Mary Jane.

If there was anybody who aggravated Sam more than Matto, it was the fast-talking young Yankee named Jones—Jonesy to the men—who never let anyone forget that he had a sweetheart waiting for him back home. Didn't he ever give a thought to the possibility that not everybody was so lucky?

Suddenly Sam didn't want to be around any of them. Urging his gray ahead, he came abreast of Captain Franks on point. The captain rode the best horse in the company, a muscled black gelding with bright eyes. Sam just wished that Franks was equally as stout. Old enough to be the father of any of the men, the captain had suffered ever since they had struck out on scout from their Musquiz Canyon headquarters four days before.

"Captain—"

Franks broke into a coughing fit that discouraged conversation. Unable to step up into the stirrup at their Eagle Springs bivouac that morning, Franks had brought his horse alongside a rock in order to gain the saddle. For half a week he had wiped his draining nose against his sleeve, but today he had also developed a frightful cough.

Clearly, the captain wasn't up to a chase through a winter storm, but just minutes ago the rangers had stumbled upon this fresh Mescalero trail. For months, the raiders had eluded the Army, and for Company A to pass up this opportunity was out of the question.

"How far ahead you think they are?" Sam asked.

"I expect closer than New Mexico and farther than a Winchester shot," rasped Franks, patting the stock of the carbine angling up butt-first behind the cantle. As they all did, the captain carried a lever-action Winchester '73 in a saddle scabbard.

Sam's .44 carbine, with an effective range of a hundred yards, had cost him twenty-eight dollars, all deducted from his first month's pay. From the moment he had hoisted the weapon, he had dedicated its twelve-round load for that war party. If the rifle didn't finish the job, he would turn to his Bowie knife or the cartridge belt at his waist, where his .45 Colt revolver with the seven-and-a-half-inch barrel rode butt first, ready for an easy cross-draw. One way or another, those filthy Apaches would be his.

"I want us to wipe out ever' one of them," said Sam, noting a canyon that opened up ahead. "Exterminate them like the den of snakes they are."

Franks hacked up phlegm and expectorated into the wind. But not all of it made it to the snow at his horse's forefoot; an unsightly streamer caught on Franks's gray-stubbled chin. Sam was embarrassed for him, for the captain seemed not to notice, as if his senses already focused on survival at the expense of propriety. Just days ago, his shoulders had been square and broad, but now they were bent like those of a man who had seen too many years.

"I know you've got special cause, son," said Franks. "Too many people have shed tears because of what those Indians have done."

When Franks coughed again, Sam thought he could hear a rattle in his chest. It persisted, inducing the captain to wince and bring a hand to his rib cage.

"You hurtin'?" asked Sam.

"Got my horse shot out from under me by Yankees in the war. Tore something loose. Ever since, my ribs ache when I get a chest cold."

Sam wondered if that's all it was, a chest cold. He could remember his father's rattling cough before pneumonia had killed him, and the thought preyed on him as they approached those ominous foothills. After all these months, this was Sam's chance—his *chance,* damn it—and he needed Franks's leadership and experience to lead them straight into a hornets' nest if necessary.

"I'm worried you're not up to this," said Sam.

The captain gave him a hard stare. Remarkably, Franks's

shoulders straightened, and no sooner had he wiped the phlegm off his face than he set his jaw.

"I've got a score to settle too," he said. "Just one bunch of Indians, and the Tenth Cavalry riding every which way can't do a thing about it. We've been fighting Indians on our own since Texas was a republic, and before the war I killed my share and more. It's time I showed those clueless Yankees how it's done."

With the disrespect he put into the word *Yankees*, it almost sounded as if Franks was still fighting a war that had been over for a lot of years.

"Know much about the country ahead?" asked Sam. "The Diablos?"

"Word of mouth and Army maps. Trail's bearing for what the Mexicans call La Nariz, the nose. Can't see it from here. We're too close to the hills. But you remember that unusual landmark in the north you could see from camp this morning?"

Sam remembered that flat-topped summit, all right. Even from almost twenty miles away, La Nariz had loomed up over intervening hills in dramatic fashion—a great fist of rock, dusted white by snow, that guarded those Diablo foothills.

Franks coughed and dabbed at his nose. "That peak stands at the Diablos' southwest edge. Past it, the land rises west to east, the highest desert around and I guess the driest. Hardly a water hole to be found, just rocky gulches climbing up to a summit ridge along the east. Right there at a cliff is where the Diablos end. One step, you're on that ridge, looking out over the salt flats, and the next you're falling half a mile nearly straight down. The Diablos are like that their whole length, twenty-five miles north to south. I suppose that's how they got their name—the Diablos, the Devils."

Franks coughed, and then added something that seemed to say it all.

"I don't know how the Almighty did things, but if He had

16

any brimstone left over after finishing hell, He must've used it to make the Diablos."

As the Mescalero trail brought them to the mouth of a canyon with two-hundred-foot bluffs, Franks ordered a halt and instructed Jonesy and a ruddy-faced private named Red to conduct reconnaissance. It would be risky, and Sam wondered if Jonesy's Yankee heritage played a role in his selection. For that matter, Sam doubted that *any* of the rangers liked the loudmouth northerner, about whom Arch had once remarked, "Perhaps a kindly buzzard will lift Jonesy from the saddle and spirit him back to New Jersey." It was true that Sam was sympathetic about Jonesy's repulsive features—a crooked jaw that froze his face in a grimace—but sympathy couldn't make up for Jonesy's constant talk about the girl back home.

Just as the two rangers started away, something akin to a sob came into Franks's voice. "You boys be careful. The last thing I want is to write bad news to somebody."

"That'd be my Mary Jane," Jonesy said predictably.

As the pair rode on into a howling wind—receding figures framed by the canyon's snowy bluffs—Sam looked at Franks and felt guilty for thinking what he had. After all, he had always found the captain a good and honorable man. If he had a fault as an officer, it was that he was too kindhearted, for he treated each man in the company almost like a son.

As the reconnoiterers entered the gulch, the situation reminded Sam all too much of Bass Canyon. He too had ridden in advance, foolishly confident in his ability to detect trouble. Once inside, he had turned to the three schooners and, with a wave of his arm, had summoned Elizabeth to her grave—*Elizabeth, for God's sake, his entire world.* But she hadn't been alone. Trusting, five fellow strugglers had also followed, negotiating a winding trail past side gulches and sculpted arroyos and jutting rock shoulders.

A hundred yards ahead of the schooners that spring day, Sam had just reached the end of the pass when gunfire from behind had startled his bay. Spurring the animal back, Sam had shouldered his Spencer against figures exploding on foot and horseback out of a left-side gulch and up from an arroyo thick with ocotillo. He had cocked the hammer and fired, and levered in another cartridge and fired again. Both shots had gone wide, and then a third had slumped a painted warrior across his horse.

The way the breast had gushed blood, Sam had realized that he had delivered a killing shot. But a mortal wound hadn't been enough to keep the fiend from riding Elizabeth down, or his war club from descending in a terrible arc. Every mile was to have brought Sam and Elizabeth closer to New Mexico for the birth of their first child, but that moment in Bass Canyon had delivered instead a purgatory that Sam was living even now, here with Company A on the trail of her killers.

"If your stare were a fire, it would sear your saddle horn."

Sam recognized Arch's voice, but he couldn't understand what his friend was doing in Bass Canyon.

"Samuel." This time Arch was straightforward. "We have orders to march."

Sam looked up from his saddle horn to see a sorrel pulling away with Arch, his breath cloud visible. Ahead, the other rangers had already created separation, and inside the gulch one of the reconnoiterers repeatedly signaled "forward!" with his arm.

Sam just hoped the two rangers were better at their job than he had been.

He took his gray after the company and rode abreast of Arch as they entered the canyon. The bluffs were steep and intimidating, particularly on Sam's left where rimrock was a mere ghost through fog. Under the rim, as far up-canyon as Sam could see, the slope consisted of slide chutes with ice-glazed gravel, rocks, and boulders. The boulders, some as large as wagons, were especially troubling, for they hovered over Sam like sinister things ready to swoop.

"I do say, there reside some wicked widow-makers above us," remarked Arch. "That is, were any of us bonded in holy matrimony in order to engineer widows."

With no furloughs permitted during a ranger's term of service, no enlisted man in Company A had a wife. But only Sam had ever buried one, and the lone person he considered a friend had pointed it out once again.

This time, Sam held his tongue. What good would it do, railing against Arch? Better instead for Sam to grit his teeth against memories of that shovel blade glinting in the bright day of Bass Canyon. By the snatch of that Apache fiend's hand—the same hand that had wielded the war club—Sam had been denied even the solace of Elizabeth's locket as the dirt had sprayed her veiled face in a shallow grave. At least he could have worn that silver pendant against the heart that was still hers, that would *always* be hers.

Once more, Arch's voice intruded on that terrible scene.

"Samuel, I can't seem to refrain from saying something inappropriate. If you're willing to accept my apology again, I sincerely tender it."

"Hell," spoke up Matto. "Don't see where DeJarnett deserves an apology. I don't ever get none from you."

For better or worse, Sam was back in the present, rocking to the gait of his gray and shivering to a wind that whistled through the boulders. He didn't want to keep remembering, to keep living in the past. But the past was the only place where Elizabeth still lived—just as the future was the only place where he might avenge her.

Matto, his remark ignored, couldn't resist repeating it. "Said, I don't see where DeJarnett—"

"Forget it, Arch," interrupted Sam, angry at Matto for meddling in a private matter. "Talkin' about it, or not talkin' about it, don't change what is."

With slopes pressing in on either side, the snowy canyon bottom squeezed down to only a few horse-breadths in width. Avoiding the overhanging rocks, Sam fell in behind Arch, who, like the riders ahead, hugged the less-threatening bluff on the right. Boye, the preacher boy, however, rode along directly under those jutting boulders.

"You're braver than me, Boye," said Sam, who was nearest him.

Boye cast wide eyes up at the rocks. "Bring these down on me, O Lord, and if there be any Apache enemies here, let them die with me!"

From two horses ahead, Matto looked back. "Somebody shut him up."

For once, Sam agreed with Matto. Boye damned sure knew how to send a chill down a man's spine.

"Boye—"

Sam couldn't hear his own voice, for the preacher boy persisted in urging the boulders to rain down judgment.

"I dare say, Boye," said Arch. "Three months have elapsed since Chief Victorio departed for the Apache hereafter. But I wager he can still distinguish your words without inclining an ear."

Undeterred, Boye stretched an arm to the rimrock. "Like Samson in the Philistine temple, Lord, bring this mountain down on me if it be Your will!"

As the preacher boy paused for a breath, the subdued words of Captain Franks on point filtered back through the riders. "You men hold it down back there!"

Arch turned around in the saddle. "Samuel, do we muzzle our self-proclaimed chaplain or merely wedge a neckerchief against his warbling tonsils?"

"Hell," said Matto, "just shoot him and be done with it."

Sam knew that Matto wasn't necessarily joking; the man was just that mean, even when it concerned someone with obvious problems. Boye, however, had no issue with responding to Franks's authority, and his voice dropped to little more than a whisper. Nevertheless, he continued to call upon the Almighty to deliver punishment, and evidently his words were loud enough for Matto to hear. When Matto's shoulder twitched as if he wanted to reach for his revolver, Sam didn't know where this would end. For God's sake, if Sam was going to ride down the vermin who had killed Elizabeth, he needed the help of every one of these men.

"Matto," he said, not wanting to take sides, "best wait on Apaches before gettin' so riled." Sam turned to the preacher boy. "Boye, you got me rattled. Please quit it."

Still, Matto's .45 had almost cleared its holster when the rocky heights began to rumble.

CHAPTER 2

Sam could hear it and feel it in almost the same instant.

Thunder rolled down from the left-side rimrock, and a quake surged up from the canyon floor and shook eight hundred pounds of horse under his thighs. The gray shied and Sam whirled to the bluff's highest reaches, where a cloud of snow and dust rose up turbulent and terrifying, showing flashes of churning rock and boulders. An unstoppable force racing hell-bent for him, it grew in size and threat like the monster it was.

"Let's get out of here!" someone cried above the roar.

Sam didn't know which way to go, but the gray bolted up-canyon with Arch's sorrel and Sam gave the animal its head. He had never felt such upheaval. The end of the world seemed upon him, and all Sam could do was cling to the gray and let the inevitable take its course.

He glimpsed shadow riders as a quick dusk descended, suf-focating and shrouding the way. Suddenly a rider was down ahead, a helpless figure on hands and knees, sinking to the crush. But Sam was a victim too, the debris pelting him and beating a cadence on his hat. With no time to reason, he came up alongside the figure and leaned down in search of a hold.

His hand locked on a forearm and the gray leaped forward, carrying Sam and dragging his burden. It was precarious for both men, for any moment the one below could plow into a rock, or impede the gray's legs and drop the animal. Maybe the latter was why the horse stumbled to its knees, but the gray was up and away quickly with Sam still clutching the deadweight that twisted under the stirrup.

The way ahead grew brighter, and just before the gray broke into the clear, the dragged man slipped from Sam's grasp. In the time it took Sam to check the overhanging slope and find it stable, the horse accomplished several more strides. He wheeled the animal back into the haze, where the rumble had given way to a whispering rush of gravel.

Finding an unidentifiable figure rising, Sam yielded the stirrup long enough to let the man step up behind him. Then they were away again, and Sam didn't slow the gray until they negotiated a bend to the right and overtook the company.

He met Arch approaching on horseback with a bay in tow, while a stony-faced Boye looked on from astride his roan. Beyond, strung out along a thirty-yard stretch of canyon, the remaining six riders and horses stirred in the drifted snow.

"I was just starting back to check your welfare, Samuel," said Arch.

"Hell, I'm the one you oughta been worried about."

Matto's grating voice in his ear told Sam who he had risked his neck for, and he didn't know how to feel about it.

Matto dismounted, grinding his jaw. Not only that, but his face was crimson and the bulging veins in his temple seemed ready to burst. Without even a glance at Sam, he stalked away in the direction of his horse. Sam supposed that an expression of gratitude wasn't in his makeup.

Arch extended the bay's reins as Matto approached, but the surly ranger stormed by. Too late, Sam realized that he bore straight for Boye, who, with head down now, didn't seem to know that he was near.

"Matto, don't start somethin'," Sam warned, taking the gray after him.

"Start it, hell!" Matto never slowed. "I'm finishin' it!"

He drew his revolver, and the cock of the hammer brought Boye's gaze up.

"All your doin'!" charged Matto. "You near' got me killed!"

He was in such a rage that the revolver trembled in his hand, but if he merely intended to frighten the young ranger, it didn't work. The preacher boy opened his arms wide like a man crucified and threw out his chest.

"A vessel of a just God, you'll be!"

Sam knew that he had to intercede, but he didn't know how. "It's what he wants, Matto! Is it worth hangin' for, givin' him what he wants?"

"He called them rocks down and near' got me killed!"

Sam's voice dropped; he had to convey calm reason. "Listen to what you're sayin'. He don't have that kind of power. Arch, tell him."

"Indeed, he does not," said Arch. "Three forces could have provided impetus for that slide—nature, man, or the Almighty— and only the Almighty might have done so with mere words."

"I'll kill him!" cried Matto.

Boye only lowered his head in a prayerful pose. "Into thy hands, O Lord," he whispered, "I commend my spirit."

"You heard Arch, Matto," pleaded Sam. "Who you think had reason to roll rocks down on us? We's chasin' Apaches, for God's sake."

"What's happening back here?"

Sam looked up at the sound of Franks's voice and saw the black horse bearing the captain approaching in a lope. Perhaps placing too much trust in Matto's respect for his authority, Franks turned his animal between that wavering .45 and Boye.

"Son," Franks said to Matto as he drew rein, "lower your revolver and tell me what the trouble is."

For a moment, Sam wondered if Matto's rage was so great that he would shoot whoever was before him. Then the ranger holstered his revolver and walked away a few steps, his face as swollen as a threatened horned toad.

Franks turned to Boye, who no longer offered himself up for sacrifice. "Son, you all right? I know the Almighty's got a place for you, but let Him take you in His own good time."

Franks alone carried sway with the preacher boy, but Sam didn't know how the captain could be so patient with him, or with Matto either. He guessed it was because not many men were willing to put their lives on the line for the promise of a silver dollar and change a day.

By now, all the rangers had gathered around Franks, and with a bobbing forefinger, he tolled them off, one through nine.

"I can't tell you men how glad I am you're all accounted for," he said, fighting through a cough. "This would be a lonely place to await Judgment Day."

Franks proceeded to address each man by name and ask about injuries. Once through, he spoke to the entire company.

"Seems our overcoats and luck did their jobs, but we cannot expect such good fortune next time. Those Mescaleros saw us coming, so we need to be vigilant."

Franks paused, suffering another coughing spell. "If they think they've deterred us, they're wrong. They're not dealing with the US Army this time—we're the Frontier Battalion, serving at the pleasure of the State of Texas. And we can take care of our own state better than any damned Yankee. Men, let's get ready to march."

Sam appreciated Franks's encouragement; a leader had to show confidence. But after what they had endured, he wondered if anyone else was concerned that this wasn't going to be easy.

Well, at least there was one. Falling into march formation, Sam came up alongside Jonesy and heard the New Jersey native's shaken whisper.

"Mary Jane . . . sweet Mary Jane . . . I . . . I don't want to die so far from home."

CHAPTER 3

Nejeunee wondered if the pain inside would ever go away.

Three seasons had passed since he-who-cannot-be-mentioned had been laid to rest in a shallow rock cleft. She had watched the *gutaaln,* medicine man, sprinkle pollen and ashes about the grave, and scar-faced Gian-nah-tah close it with stones and dirt. Fearing the dead—even the one who had been her husband— she had hurried down the craggy hill before the owls could come and spirit him away to the Land of Ever Summer.

Before that day had ended, Nejeunee had shorn her black hair close and smeared her face with ashes. Secreting away a single item in her phylactery, she had helped burn his belongings and wailed her grief. Even now, in this snowy winter under the rock-capped mountain La Nariz, which jutted up like a great nose, she still wore her mourning blouse, a striking blue-calico cape that fell past her hips.

But the greatest reminder of her loss was the child who graced the cradleboard of split sotol that hugged Nejeunee's back as she and the three other women went about setting up camp for the twelve warriors in the party. She had knelt and given birth more than a season after the owls had come for her husband, and yet in Little Squint Eyes's face she saw his father every time she peered into the cradleboard or drew him out to nurse at her breast. The ache in her heart was most unbearable whenever she relived the birth ceremony, at which there had been no father to sing the *gutaaln*'s prayers with her, or to sprinkle the herbal waters to the sun above and earth below, and to the spirits that guided the four winds.

Fatherless, Little Squint Eyes was, and fatherless he would always be unless Nejeunee chose to enter a *kuughà,* teepee, alone with Gian-nah-tah or another warrior. But such a union was unthinkable for now, her wounds still too fresh, and she was glad that this band had followed Victorio from the teepees of the New Mexico reservation. There, a male relative of her husband could have claimed her, but here she was free, and neither Gian-nah-tah nor any other man could initiate courtship without some sign from her.

Nevertheless, ever since the flowering of her womanhood, Nejeunee had been taught that a woman's greatest purpose was to serve and bear the children of a good man who would call her "My Wife." It was the way of the *Ndé,* the People, and she knew that someday she would have to consent.

From a travois angling down from a mule's hindquarters, Nejeunee removed the teepee poles that formed the framework and added them to a stack on an elevated flat just below La Nariz's slope. Here between lechuguilla daggers, the other three women brushed away snow so Nejeunee could help erect six eight-pole teepees with canvas covers. The *gutaaln* had chosen this place because of its great power, for in the cliffs and high places of the Sierra Diablo lived the *Gáhé,* mountain spirits who communed with the supreme being *Bik'egu'indáán.* Tonight, perhaps, masked warriors would impersonate the *Gáhé* and seek *Bik'egu'indáán's* help and protection by dancing the spirit dance.

Nejeunee knew that Little Squint Eyes needed all the blessings that *Bik'egu'indáán* could bestow, for it had been a winter of privation, quick strikes at the *Indaa,* and relentless flight from these white people. Ranging throughout a land that had once been the People's alone, the *Indaa* seemed determined to wipe out this last free band of Mescaleros, or at least drive them back to the starvation and sickness of the reservation.

Out of a sense of duty, Nejeunee had always celebrated with the other women when the men had returned with accounts of a successful raid against an enemy. But ever since the *Indaa* had taken from her he-who-cannot-be-mentioned, conviction had replaced obligation. Now she utterly loathed white men and all others who were not of the People. So great was her hatred that it seemed to burn inside her like *Sháa,* the sun, did in the sky.

And yet she could not forget that she herself was not originally of the People.

Nejeunee remembered it almost as a dream now, those ten summers in the adobe village three days' travel across the Rio Grande from the place called El Paso. There had been dusty streets with dirty-faced *hijos* and barking *perros,* and sun-baked fields of corn and beans where her father had toiled alongside other *peones.* Of all the images, that of the kindly *señora* with the *rebosa* drawn over her black hair was strongest, for a mother's love endured like no other. Indeed, Nejeunee had gained from her a nurturing spirit that guided Nejeunee even yet with Little Squint Eyes.

And then had come that final journey with her *familia* to the base of the Guadalupe cliffs where a great saline basin gleamed in the desert sun. As was their custom every autumn, the villagers had embarked by caravan, the drivers popping rawhide whips against ox teams plodding with empty *carretas.* Upon reaching the Guadalupes' shadow, the men had set about loading these wooden-wheeled carts with life-sustaining salt for the return trip.

Of the ensuing events, Nejeunee recalled nothing clearly, except the wind tugging at her mother's *rebosa* as it had rested in a red pool where only pure white should have been. Even today, that image troubled Nejeunee, more so than any other memory of her first life. She was *Ndé* now, and proud to be one of the People. But even in her hatred for the *Indaa* and *Mexicanos,* she knew that a great evil had been done to her mother.

Recently, brief visions of that day had begun flashing through Nejeunee's mind. Sometimes a painted and disfigured face joined the disturbing portrait of a *rebosa* draped across blood-soaked ground crusted with salt. There was a stone-headed war club as well, descending in terrible judgment. Nejeunee realized that in her ten winters with the People, she had only known one man disfigured in such a way, and when she heard muted hoofbeats behind her, she turned and saw him riding up.

Astride a paint pony, Gian-nah-tah was a warrior of thirty winters with a gaudy red headband holding his straight black hair in place. Eagle feathers waved from his war cap, a turban of mountain lion pelt with the tail hanging in back. The remainder of the skin hugged his torso as protection against the cold, while buckskin leggings served a similar purpose.

Bearing a bandolier of cartridges and a quiver of hardwood arrows, Gian-nah-tah presented a picture of ferocity that Nejeunee knew was certain to instill fear in the *Indaa.* He carried a Winchester carbine in his hand and a bow of wild mulberry about his shoulder, a bone-handled knife in his rawhide belt and the loop of that haunting war club about his wrist.

But all these things paled in comparison to a face streaked black on the right. The other side, he left bare, so that an enemy might see the eyeless socket and the long scar that wrenched his upper lip into an animal-like snarl. Nejeunee had heard whispers that he was a witch, manifesting evil through his power, and she could believe it every time she looked at him.

"Listen!" said Gian-nah-tah, halting the paint near Nejeunee. The warriors and other women turned, and he gave them a moment to gather. "Behind come *Indaa,* as many as we. The power to find enemies told me where they were. From the rim I watched them approach in the snow, and I lay in wait where the tilted rocks lie over the canyon. With my hands I rolled down *tsé ntsaa,* big rocks, and made the black wind roar through the canyon. The *Indaa* ran like *ga'i,* the rabbit. They still follow, but we will celebrate as we ride until *neeldá,* the dawn, lights the sky."

Even as Nejeunee rushed about, helping pack onto travois all they had unloaded, she rejoiced with the other women at Gian-nah-tah's victory in the canyon. They retold his exploit repeatedly among themselves, their outward joy a little greater each time. Nejeunee, for her part, recounted it more than anyone, hoping that by doing so she would bury a sudden thought that no *Ndé* should have.

What deeds of bravery had Gian-nah-tah told upon returning ten winters ago from the salt bed with the stained *rebosa*?

Practiced in breaking camp quickly, they were on the move within minutes—Nejeunee, the cradleboard at her back, astride a small roan; Gian-nah-tah, eleven warriors, and three other women on mounts of their own; and the six teepees, sleeping blankets, and meager provisions on three travois pulled by mules. There had been five travois before the hard winter, but the band had been forced to butcher two of the work mules for food. For the last week, Nejeunee had subsisted on jerky and what the women had scrounged from the desert, but now her stomach had a great emptiness. For herself, Nejeunee wouldn't have been concerned, but her milk might diminish, and Little Squint Eyes could gain only so much nourishment from moist sugar wrapped in a teat-like cloth.

They marched as daylight faded into a hard dark that brought bitter cold seeping through the woolen blanket about Nejeunee's shoulders. She had learned to bear discomfort without complaint, but it was too much to expect of Little Squint Eyes. Early in the night, as ice crackled under the horses' hoofs and the dragging frames of the travois sang against snow, he began to cry. Nejeunee didn't know if it was from hunger or cold, but she halted long enough to remove the child from the cradleboard and take him under the blanket. There at her breast, he could find warmth and nourishment.

"A *Ndé* baby doesn't cry."

It was too dark to see who rode beside Nejeunee, but she had no trouble recognizing the complaining voice. He-who-cannot-be-mentioned had taken One Who Frowns as wife before Nejeunee had ever joined the People, and when he later had brought Nejeunee as well into his teepee, One Who Frowns immediately had lived up to her name. She had never borne he-who-cannot-be-mentioned a child, and from the start the older woman had resented Nejeunee's youth and the possibility that Nejeunee might be the one to present their husband with that for which he had yearned.

Then had come the day when Nejeunee had announced that she was with child, and as pleased as their husband had been, One Who Frowns's hostility toward her had risen in equal measure. Of course, he-who-cannot-be-mentioned had never lived to see Nejeunee give birth, but One Who Frowns had been there, midwifing even though Nejeunee had not welcomed her. With his first breath Little Squint Eyes had cried, and his crying had persisted as Nejeunee had allowed One Who Frowns to take him so that Nejeunee could move near the fire and clean herself. Meanwhile, One Who Frowns had squirted Little Squint Eyes with water from her mouth and dried him with bunched grass.

This, Nejeunee had expected of any midwife, and also the cattail pollen that the older woman had blown upon the newborn. But Nejeunee had been unprepared for what One Who Frowns had said in extending the crying baby to Nejeunee.

"You know the ways of the People with wailing babies.

Strangle him!"

But Nejeunee had brought Little Squint Eyes to her breast and his crying had ceased. From then on, however, One Who Frowns had seized every opportunity to remind Nejeunee that her baby was unworthy of being called *Ndé*. Now, in the dark and the piercing cold, One Who Frowns continued to criticize Little Squint Eyes.

"He who was my husband would be ashamed to call him his son."

"We shouldn't speak of *yah-ik-tee,* he who is not present." Nejeunee cast a furtive glance into the night. "*Niishjaa,* the owl that hunts the winter snows, may give voice to the dead."

"The owls will bring evil ghosts because of Little Squint Eyes. The owl was ready to call his name and summon him to the Land of Ever Summer the moment he was born. You should have strangled him and burned the cradleboard you fashioned. The cradleboard is as evil as he."

"I don't want to hear this!" Nejeunee exclaimed quietly.

"May he die tonight. Like an animal so I can say '*yah-tats-an,* now it is dead.' "

"Shut up, old witch spirit!" Nejeunee wrapped her arms even more securely around Little Squint Eyes, but she knew that were the time to come, there would be nothing she could do to keep the owls from taking him.

Until Nejeunee lashed out at One Who Frowns, they had spoken in hushed tones. But Nejeunee's outburst caused the two shadowy riders ahead to drop back alongside. To intrude on an argument was typical of only the band's other two women, sisters by birth who were notorious for idle talk.

"One Who Frowns must be speaking of Gian-nah-tah again, Nejeunee," said one woman, whose voice she recognized as that of Brushing Against. "You should give him a sign that you're interested. He among all the People has the power to find enemies."

Nejeunee was not surprised that Brushing Against was the first of the women to speak, for she was the older of the sisters and had made it her purpose to tell Nejeunee what to do.

"We know he wants you to warm his *kuughà*, teepee," said the younger sister, whose rapid speech had earned her the name Quick Talker. "We've been telling you since first frost."

"Look at One Who Frowns," added Brushing Against, who always viewed matters practically. "She's already taken another husband for the good of the People. Why can't you?"

"*Idzúút'i!* Go away!" Nejeunee told both of them.

"A woman so upset by the mention of a man means she has strong feelings for him," said Quick Talker. Highly excitable, she was more in tune with emotional matters than was her sister. "Next time you walk by, hit him with a stick." She giggled. "Just a tap—don't knock him out. That's how I chose the one who's now my husband. Four mornings later I was cooking for Klosen outside his *kuughà* and bringing his horse up for him."

"Does the cold make your tongue flap like chattering teeth?" asked Nejeunee. "I had no interest in Gian-nah-tah when I was younger and could choose any man on the reservation."

"Who knows when we'll ever return there?" Brushing Against responded. "Here the women are few, just the four of us, and most of the men are alone. Gian-nah-tah has had no one to warm him at night since the sickness on the reservation took his wife."

An image of the bloody *rebosa* surged through Nejeunee's mind, darkening the night even more.

"Evil in a *Ndé* is its own sickness," she said, surprising herself.

"What do you mean?" asked Brushing Against. "Are you now insulting me? Or is it Quick Talker?"

But One Who Frowns was evidently more perceptive—or

perhaps she saw an opportunity to create a problem for Nejeunee. "Maybe it's Gian-nah-tah she speaks of."

"Is that it, Nejeunee?" pressed Quick Talker. "Any available woman should be proud to serve Gian-nah-tah. Weren't you singing his victory over the *Indaa* the same as we were?"

"One Who Frowns just wants to make trouble," said Nejeunee. "All she has to do is chatter like a squirrel and leave the rest to the biggest gossips in all the People."

"Now you are insulting me," said Brushing Against.

"And me," added Quick Talker.

Nejeunee could hear one of them begin to cry, for Mescalero women were more emotional than the *señoras* in the village of her youth.

"I was only wanting to help you," sobbed Quick Talker. Nejeunee should have guessed it was she who wept; Quick Talker was as fast with a tear as she was with her words.

Nejeunee sought out the shadow that was One Who Frowns. "Why is it all right for a *Ndé* woman to cry and not a baby in his cradleboard?"

"Hmph!"

It was One Who Frowns's only response, and Nejeunee supposed it was because she had no answer that wouldn't bring an angry retort from the other women. Not only that, but One Who Frowns had been known to weep as well.

"The tiny ears of a field mouse could hear our women from *Tl'é'na'ái*, the moon."

Nejeunee had been so intent on the conversation and on One Who Frowns's silhouette that she hadn't realized that a trailing rider had come abreast on the opposite side. A snowdrift evidently had muffled the hoofbeats to the level of a soft patter of rain.

Nejeunee shuddered as she turned, for she realized who had spoken.

"If the field mouse could hear," added Gian-nah-tah, "think what the *Indaa* could do."

Nejeunee wished she could crawl into a burrow with *ga'i*, the rabbit, and hide. In the impenetrable night, she had lost Gian-nah-tah's position in the march. How long had he been riding within earshot, and what had he heard?

"Nejeunee's child was wailing," spoke up One Who Frowns. "She must keep it quiet, or the *Indaa* will track us down. From birth it has wailed."

"He was hungry and cold," defended Nejeunee, readjusting the blanket about Little Squint Eyes. "He doesn't know the *Indaa* are behind. Without our children, the People have no tomorrow."

"Then a woman without a husband should warm a man's *kuughà*, teepee," said Gian-nah-tah. "It is her duty as a *Ndé*."

With a cluck of his tongue, Gian-nah-tah took his pony ahead, but his words stayed with Nejeunee.

She didn't have long to ponder, for from one of the nearby horses came subdued giggling. "See, Nejeunee?" Quick Talker pointed out quietly. "One rap on the head and things will be different for you."

But maybe it wasn't always a tap on a would-be suitor that could alter a life. Maybe a crushing blow on a *rebosa*-draped *señora* could do so with far greater consequences to a ten-year-old girl.

CHAPTER 4

Stooping at the flank of his unsaddled horse, Sam lifted its hind leg out of the snow. He was careful to work from the front, protecting himself from being kicked. Slipping a loop of leather over the animal's pastern, he buckled it into place and lowered the hoof. As he stretched the attached sideline toward the gray's foreleg in order to hobble the horse, he looked across the small flat at Franks.

The captain had taken a turn for the worse. He had managed to unsaddle his black and unfurl his tarp and bedroll between lechuguilla daggers, but now he sat slumped, coughing and expectorating phlegm. It was as if he had exhausted all his energy just as dusk had overtaken them, here where Mescaleros had stirred the snow below La Nariz.

Sam hoped a pot of coffee brewing nearby at a just-kindled fire would revive Franks, for a supper of hardtack and jerky wouldn't do much to restore strength to someone of his years. Franks could have used a lot of things they didn't have— nourishment, medicinal powders, shelter from the cold—but what he didn't need was trouble among the men.

Matto obviously hadn't shrugged off his anger at Boye, and Sam had noticed him glaring at the oblivious young man as they had unsaddled their horses. Now, the preacher boy stood warming his hands at the fire while Matto and Arch came up out of the arroyo beyond with dead creosote limbs. The fire, more smoke than flame, was in danger of going out, but Boye

seemed unconcerned, content instead with talking to himself—
something about the tongue being a flame.

Through the drifting gray haze, Sam watched a grinning Arch
approach the fire. Sam could even hear the jingle of his friend's
spurs; for the moment, the currents were just right to carry
sound.

"Words of wisdom for the heathen, Boye?" Arch asked,
depositing his wood beside the ring of flat rocks on edge.

Boye's gaze stayed on the struggling flame. "The tongue of
the heathen defiles the body, I tell you it does. It's set on the
fire of hell."

"Right where somebody's liable to send you, you lazy SOB."
Matto came up abreast of Arch and angrily threw his limbs on
the pile. "Your arm broke or somethin'? We's out gatherin'
wood, and you're standin' here too lazy to fan the fire. Can't
you see the damned thing's goin' out?"

Boye wasn't intimidated. " 'Go out from one fire, and another
fire shall devour.' "

"You even know what in the hell you're sayin'?" challenged
Matto.

"Methinks he quotes Scripture," opined Arch.

Sam, who had been so distracted that he only now buckled
the sideline around his horse's foreleg, watched under the
animal's neck as Matto removed his hat, revealing greasy hair as
black as his thick mustache.

"Yeah, well," said Matto, "they'll be readin' verses over *him*
one of these days." With a few waves of his hat brim, Matto
stirred the smoke enough for flames to ignite.

"Best a heathen like you comes into the Almighty's fold while
you can."

Boye, still in preacher form as he spoke, looked at Matto, and
Matto looked at him. Sam didn't like where this was headed
and started for the fire, which erupted into a blaze that showed

in Matto's scowling face.

Matto stepped toward Boye. "You've smarted off to me for the last time."

Arch casually gestured for Matto. "What say you assist me in procuring more wood?"

But Matto stayed focused on Boye.

" 'Resist the devil, and he will flee from you,' " said Boye, holding his ground.

"You callin' me a devil?"

Sam walked faster now, his duck trousers rasping with every stride.

"I think you misunderstand about His Satanic Majesty," Arch interjected. "Young Boye here proposes that you defy Lucifer's—"

Matto wouldn't listen. With both hands he shoved Boye hard in the chest, sending the young man stumbling back. Desperate to right himself, Boye flailed his arms and inadvertently clipped Matto in the jaw. As the young man fell, an enraged Matto swung a fist that missed and lunged for him with an oath. Suddenly both men were down, a tangle of arms and legs thrashing in the snow.

"That's enough!" yelled Sam, breaking into a run.

Captain Franks said something as well, but it was lost in Boye's cries and Matto's swearing. Boye, for someone who had courted death in the canyon, surprisingly made a fight of it, if only out of instinct. They rolled into the fire, the sparks flying and limbs popping. Knocking over the coffee pot and smothering the flames, they bowled over the upright rocks on the far side and came out in the snow again as Sam and other rangers converged on the scene.

Boye was on top when Sam helped pull him away, and separating the two while the young man held a superior position infuriated Matto even more. He scrambled to his feet and would have lunged at Boye again—if not shot him—had Jonesy and another man not held him back. As it was, Matto swore at his restrainers as viciously as he did at Boye, until Captain Franks's voice behind Sam put an end to things.

Turning, Sam saw Franks stumbling up, his cough still plaguing him.

"Boys," the captain said when he was able, "we cannot have this." His shoulders bent as he suffered another coughing spell. This one didn't seem as if it would end, and when he sagged at the knees, Sam took his arm.

"Let's get you to your bedroll," said Sam. "Trouble's over now."

Sam could feel Franks's weakness as he helped him back to his tarp, where the sick man sank to a sitting position with his back against his saddle. The captain was shivering, too much for even a dusk this chilled, and Sam bundled the bedroll around Franks's shoulders.

"Gonna bring you some coffee soon's it's ready," said Sam. He reached for the captain's war bag and canteen beside the saddle. "Here, get you some hardtack and jerky, make sure you drink plenty."

Franks was coughing unrelentingly when Sam left him and returned to the fire. He thought about helping the captain relocate his bedroll closer to the warmth, but the wind had turned unpredictable and could choke him with smoke. The poor man seemed to have trouble breathing as it was.

At the fire ring, Jonesy hummed something about his "sweet Mary Jane" while Arch stirred the fire and blew on the underlying coals. About the time flames reappeared, Boye and Matto independently wandered away to their saddles.

"Well, that was a most unpleasant episode," said Arch.

"Somethin' the captain sure don't need," said Sam.

"Franks is suffering considerably, all right."

"I tell you, Arch. I'm startin' to worry about him. Don't know how much of it's from sickness, and how much is ridin' all this way in the cold and snow."

"I anticipate the terrain will cooperate even less on the morrow."

"Yeah, and the cold too, way this trail's climbin' up in the Diablos." Refilling the blackened coffee pot from a canteen, Sam twisted it down inside the coals. "Tough as things already are, Captain's right—can't go havin' trouble amongst ourselves."

Jonesy and the other rangers soon dispersed, leaving Sam and Arch alone at the fire.

"Wish I knowed why Boye does like he does," said Sam, studying the young man from afar. "Preachin' one minute, and actin' like he's itchin' to die the next."

Arch stayed silent for a long while, and when he did speak, something—the smoke maybe—muted his voice. "Every man is a product of his past. Aspire to rise above it, he may, but it abides nevertheless."

Bass Canyon, thought Sam.

As their gazes met, the shadows seemed to cast a dark mask over Arch's face, even as the firelight flickered in his eyes. Then Arch's voice dropped even more, until it was little more than a hoarse whisper against the crackling fire.

"What's passed before . . . our life experiences . . . all we've done and all that's been done to us . . . they're always here, ever reminding, doing their utmost to govern us."

Sam had never seen features so tormented, especially in someone who had always seemed so composed and self-confident. It was as if a door to the man's soul had opened, and just as it closed again, Arch readjusted the frayed neckerchief that Sam had never seen him without.

Even in Musquiz Creek as they had scrubbed themselves clean of sweat and trail dust, Arch had always kept that red-checked rag around his neck. Sam had never given it much thought, but the way Arch trifled with it in the context of the moment made Sam wonder about its significance. Sam had a lot of questions for his friend, and then out of the corner of his eye he saw Boye approaching and he knew that this wasn't the time.

But with Matto's escalating feud with Boye—the kind of thing that could demoralize and divide the company—maybe the moment was ripe to pry answers out of the preacher boy.

Boye dragged a large rock close to the blaze and sat. Not until the firelight was in his face did Sam realize the fight had brought a trickle of blood from the young man's nose.

"Coffee will be ready soon," Sam told him. "Got somethin' to drink out of?"

Boye, busy gnawing jerky, held up a battered tin cup.

"I want to ask you somethin'," Sam went on. "You been in the company what now? Week? Ten days? With our butts glued to the saddle, hadn't been much chance to talk. All I know is you're a preacher boy."

"Born to a preacher, so a preacher boy I am, by birth and by calling."

"So you and your father both," said Sam. "He preachin' still?"

"Lord called him to shepherd a flock, He did. Town of Cora on the South Leon, Comanche County. Still pastoring the little church I growed up in."

"Whole different country, these parts. How come you traipsin' off out here, joinin' up?"

"The Lord knows what for, so no reason to hide it. Chastening me like a father with a wayward child, He is."

"You was sayin' that earlier."

"Hard with a rod, and I'm giving Him ever' chance."

Arch joined the discussion. "Sounds as if you've imposed penance on yourself, my young man."

"Nothing I don't deserve. Stand up to His chastening and He'll take you under His wing."

For a moment, Sam watched the fiery sparks trailing on the currents and disappearing. If there was indeed someone in the clouds meting out correction, he couldn't imagine a form any crueler than Bass Canyon.

"You're the youngest one in the company," said Sam. "What could you done that was so bad?"

Boye turned his face to the sky, and for all the pain that Arch's features had shown earlier, the preacher boy's were vexed more. His jaw trembled, and the firelight blazing in his eyes seemed like hellfire.

"Lord, strike me down right here! Sinned against You, I have, like David with Bathsheba. 'Cause of me she's dead and so's our baby. Lord, strike me down!"

Maybe back in the canyon Arch had been right about Boye not having the power to call down judgment, but that didn't keep Sam from looking up with a shudder. Boye, though, wasn't through, as if confessing his sin was part of his penance.

"Seventeen, she was, pure like a bride in white, and I go and seduce her. Lord help me, I seduced her, that sweet innocence, all gone 'cause of me. Me a preacher boy, watching her grow with child, and stay quiet I did, letting her bear the shame. Whore, they called her, whore! I wouldn't stand by her even when her time come, and right there she dies. Our baby too, and my fault it is, 'cause 'whosoever committeth adultery destroyeth his own soul.' A murderer, I am, sure as I stand here. Strike me dead, O Lord, strike me dead and let me go to them both!"

To a howling gust, thick smoke rose up and turned on Sam like a thing bent on retribution. It burned his sinuses and stung his eyes, and he wheeled and retreated half-blind. But no matter which direction he went, how far he lurched through the snow, he couldn't escape the suffocating cloud any better than he could a terrible realization.

If Boye deserved the worst kind of chastening for what he had done, was there a place deep enough under Bass Canyon from which to summon punishment for what Sam had failed to do?

Elizabeth! Elizabeth, I'm sorry!

But Elizabeth couldn't answer, because he had chosen blessed oblivion rather than reach for his revolver to save her.

Still tasting bitter smoke as he shivered in his bedroll, Sam lay awake yearning for the silver locket that a Mescalero hand had snatched away from Elizabeth. If he could only feel its smoothness, cling to it through this and every lonely night, relive the moment under the San Antonio live oak when he had first fastened it around her neck . . .

Sam had never seen the midnight sky so black, but it was no darker than the gloom that crept through his soul. It was like a fog rising up from Elizabeth's grave, an evil force determined to destroy. It searched out his hopes and his aspirations and whisked them away, stripping him bare of everything that made a man alive.

Well, almost. There was still his hatred of Apaches—hatred and a consuming obsession to avenge Elizabeth and their unborn child who would never draw a breath.

"Walter . . . Walter . . ."

Hidden in the night, Franks lay a few feet to Sam's left, and over the rush of the wind Sam kept hearing him mumble as if stricken with fever. Franks was incoherent mostly, except for that one name that occasionally bridged the chasm between delirium and consciousness. Usually he spoke it with affection, but sometimes it was more of a despairing cry, like the summons of a despondent man who knew that it couldn't be answered.

"Walter . . . Walter . . ."

The whisper reached deep into Sam's inner gloom, touching that part of him where Elizabeth once had lived, and he closed his eyes and felt his own forsaken cry tremble silently on his lips.

"Samuel."

Sam rolled over on his shoulder, away from Franks, and saw a looming shadow against the greater shadow of La Nariz. "Already?"

"Indeed," said the voice he recognized as Arch's.

Sighing, Sam threw back his covers and sat up. He had squandered precious sleep to dwell on his hopelessness, and now he faced two hours of standing guard in the piercing cold. Already fully dressed, all he had to do was slip on his boots, but they were like blocks of ice against his feet as he stood and took up his Winchester.

"Walter . . . Walter . . ."

Adjusting his overcoat collar against the wind, Sam looked at Franks, although there was little to see in the dark.

"Feverish, I fear," Arch said quietly.

"Yeah. Callin' and nobody to answer. Least, not who he's askin' for."

"Not unexpectedly, I would say."

Arch started away and Sam followed, dodging hidden lechuguilla the best he could. Considering the conditions, Sam normally would have expected him to head straight for his bedroll. Arch's remark, however, had teased of something perhaps better said out of the captain's earshot, and Sam wasn't surprised when he continued on to the horses.

The sudden *click! click!* of a revolver hammer froze Sam in mid-stride.

"Who goes there?" challenged a frightened voice.

"Easy, Jonesy, my man!" Arch said quickly.

"Sweet Mary, I thought you were an Indian."

"Mere moments ago I cautioned you to expect my replacement."

"Want to ease that thing off full cock?" asked Sam.

Jonesy laughed nervously. "Oh, the stories I'll have when I go back to my Mary Jane." His Yankee accent always seemed more pronounced in the dark, maybe because Sam couldn't be distracted by his deformed jaw. "Pulling down on a couple of wild Indians, I thought."

"Just don't go shootin' none you can't see," said Sam.

"She's never been out of New Jersey, you know. Her father's in the mercantile business there. She's the oldest of three sisters, and you'd agree with me she's the prettiest. I wish I had a picture to show you. Oh, I'll have so much to tell when I go back and marry her, all right."

It was more information than a grieving man wanted to hear, but it was typical of Jonesy, who obviously had no idea how much darker he had just made Sam's night. But Jonesy wasn't through.

"Did I tell you people about the time my Mary Jane—"

"Jonesy, my man, could you secure a headcount on the horses?" interrupted Arch. "Should it be too dark, you could tally their ears and divide by two."

Sam didn't know if Jonesy was insulted, but he heard the squeak of boots growing fainter. When there was again only the whistling wind, Sam turned to Arch's outline. "I think you had more to tell me."

"Indeed. Your earlier concerns for the captain may be more warranted than you realize. There's mounting reason to believe he's compelling himself to actions beyond his ability, and I fear it may endanger the company."

Sam didn't like where this conversation seemed headed. "We can't turn back, Arch. I want him to fight through this."

"Avenging a loss should never come at the price of a person's own life or those of his comrades in arms."

Sam breathed sharply. "If you was walkin' in my boots, you might think different." He had been aggravated at Arch before, but never angry until now.

"I know what overtaking those Mescaleros means to you, but I'm speaking of—"

"Not me that's in charge anyway," Sam interrupted. "I ride where I'm told."

"Samuel, you misunderstand. I—"

"If you don't want to be here, take it up with somebody else."

"Please permit me to complete what I was saying."

"Nobody stoppin' you."

Sam thought he heard Arch draw a long breath. "It's not you I'm speaking of, Samuel. It's Franks who's permitting vengeance to compromise his judgment. You need to help persuade him to yield to his illness and the weather, not to mention the Diablos. The high country's certain to exacerbate matters for everyone."

"Mescaleros took ever'thing I got. If Franks thinks he's up to trackin' them down, not my place to tell him different."

"I'm concerned he may be in a dark place emotionally. Have you heard him speak of settling a score with the Yankees? And now there's 'Walter' for whom he's calling. I'd be bewildered, had I not ridden into Fort Davis for tobacco last week."

"What's tobacco got to do with it?" Sam asked impatiently.

"You know how amicable Franks is—'so kindhearted he treats us like his own sons,' you've said. Your analogy is a perfect characterization, considering what the post sutler related."

Sam remained unconvinced. "Sutler's always got a big bear story."

"This is one that I place credence in, Samuel. Will you hear me out?"

To the sough of the wind and distant *yip-yip* of coyotes, Sam listened. As the sutler had told it, he had shared a bottle with Franks one night. As the alcohol loosened the captain's tongue, Franks opened up about things. When he had last seen his son, the boy had been thirteen, a mere child holding back tears as Franks had ridden away from their East Texas cabin to fight a war in a distant land. By the time Franks returned four years later, that child had grown into young manhood, taken up arms in the conflict, and died a senseless death in a far-off corner of hell. Ever since that moment, Franks had blamed himself for choosing duty over family, for marching off to fight a rich man's war instead of fulfilling his role as a father. If he had just chosen allegiance to his only offspring rather than to the foredoomed cause of the South, his son might still be alive.

"I haven't told you his son's name," added Arch. "It's Walter."

Sam winced. Even after all these years, memories still bedeviled Franks. Would Sam's own torment follow him to his grave?

"I believe the captain still has a vendetta," continued Arch. "His son's death by Yankees compels him to continue a fight that ended sixteen years ago. His only chance at victory is to accomplish what the Army has been unable to—annihilating those Mescaleros."

"Worthy cause, no matter the reason," said Sam.

"The captain will die out here. Perhaps some of us as well."

"Don't expect me to try talkin' him out of it."

"His judgment is clouded by emotion, Samuel. Do you understand what I'm contending?"

"I understand that you didn't lose somebody like I did. Like Franks did too."

"Wisdom needs to prevail. There'll always be another day, another opportunity."

"Not for me. And I guess not for Franks either."

Sam started past to check the horses and bumped Arch solidly in the shoulder in the dark. He hadn't meant to—or had he?—but he continued on without apology. Within a few steps more, he ran squarely into someone else, and for a split second he wondered if an Apache knife would find his ribs.

"Whoa!" said Jonesy. "That you, DeJarnett? Or is it a wild Indian?"

Sam wondered how long the New Jersey native had been within earshot. The company had a bellyful of troubles already, and it sure didn't need friction stemming from a grudge the captain might hold against Yankees. Sam just hoped that the wind had drowned out what Arch had said.

Brushing around Jonesy without comment, Sam trudged on through the snow. And then Jonesy said something that added more concern to Sam's plateful of worries.

"Oh, the stories my Mary Jane's going to hear from this damned Yankee."

The fog wraiths that swirled against La Nariz's rocky heights at daybreak seemed like something out of Sam's disturbing dreams.

Nightmares, they had been, really, dreams in which Elizabeth had cried for him across Bass Canyon. Strangely, his dream-self had experienced no trouble gripping his .45 as the Mescalero had turned his horse after her. How easily Sam had cocked the hammer and swung the barrel with the rider's flight. The trigger's curvature had almost been soothing against his finger as he had begun to squeeze—and then Arch had stepped in, seizing his gun arm, preventing his saving shot.

All night long, it seemed, Sam had struggled with Arch in a dream world. Now, with the company breaking camp, Sam worried that his friend would try to stop him for real.

Maybe it was wishful thinking on Sam's part, but Franks seemed better this morning. He continued to cough, but he had partaken of coffee and jerky and had led his bridled horse to the saddle beside his bedroll. Still, after he hooked the right-side stirrup and cinch strap over the horn, he was unable to hoist the saddle high enough to throw it across the blanket behind the horse's withers.

Even several feet away, where Sam stood shaking snow from his tarp, he could hear the captain wheeze as he lowered the saddle to the ground. Sam was about to offer help when he noticed the jangle of spurs from the direction of the fire.

"Captain, might I possibly take a word with you?"

Sam tensed. The schoolteacher diction told him all he needed to know, but he turned nevertheless and saw him nearing through the snow—a man right out of a nightmare, the ice crackling underfoot with his every step.

"Arch . . ." appealed Sam.

For an instant, their gazes met, but his friend continued to approach Franks from behind. Uncharacteristically, the captain hadn't responded, instead placing a supporting hand on the point of the horse's hip. As Franks rested his forehead against his extended arm, his shoulders began to rise and fall in labored breath.

"Arch."

This time, Sam's voice was sharper, more warning than appeal, but Arch ignored him as he came abreast of Franks, two men and a horse standing over a saddle.

"May I offer assistance?" Arch asked.

Franks never looked up. "The day . . ." He coughed that rattling cough. "The day I cannot saddle my own horse . . ."

Another coughing spell struck him, and as it lingered, Arch bent and took the saddle by the pommel and back housing.

Like the moment when Sam had challenged Franks's fitness on the snowy plain, the captain called upon a hidden reservoir of strength. He seized the saddle out of Arch's hands, lifted the thirty-five pounds seemingly effortlessly, and placed it on the horse.

"I know you mean well," Franks said. "But I'll saddle my own horse till the day I stop riding."

The captain clearly wasn't going to be persuaded that he was unfit to command a chase, and Arch obviously realized it. Just before he walked away, he gave Sam a look that no one should give a friend, a look that said *I cannot do this alone, and you've failed me.*

In response, Sam smiled ever so slightly in satisfaction. He wanted to tell Arch, *Hell, if I can live all these months without Elizabeth, I can damn sure live with your disappointment.*

But as Sam watched Franks stumble around to the horse's far side to lower the cinch strap and stirrup, a troubling question gnawed at him.

Letting Arch down was one thing, but what about failing Franks and the whole company?

CHAPTER 5

Nejeunee awoke with Little Squint Eyes tugging at the phylactery between her breasts.

She had lapsed into sleep nursing him, the two of them bundled under woolen blankets in a teepee with Quick Talker and her husband Klo-sen. Afraid that Little Squint Eyes would slip from her arms, Nejeunee had staved off sleep throughout the night march, even though the gait of the roan had been like the soothing sway of a cradleboard under a limb. Not until the breaking of *neeldá,* the dawn, had she and the other women made camp for the band, unquestioned miles ahead of the hated *Indaa.*

Nejeunee peeled back the blankets so she could smile at Little Squint Eyes. Now four months into his young life, he had already learned to bat at objects and bring one hand to the other, but never before had he grasped. She thought how fitting that he did so first with the phylactery, the cord of which she always kept about her neck. Brimming with power that safeguarded her, the small buckskin pouch was marked by a meandering pair of yellow lines that passed through similarly crooked streaks of red. To Apaches, this cross symbolized the yellow and red snake, but for Nejeunee it had greater significance.

She had never forgotten the faith that the kindly *señora* had taught her in the village of her upbringing. There had been an adobe mission, and a looming figure of Jesucristo on a cross not

52

too dissimilar to the representation on the phylactery. Sometimes in Nejeunee's dreams she again stood below that crucifix and sipped sweet wine and took bread on her tongue—Cristo's blood and body, her mother had explained. Nejeunee hadn't understood it all, and there was no one to instruct her now, but she had often yearned for the warmth and peace that she had always felt in that moment.

Long immersed in the culture of the People, Nejeunee now believed as Mescaleros from birth believed. Power lived in all things, whether of this world or in *Sháa,* the sun, or *Tl'é'na'ái,* the moon. Furthermore, this power yearned for a role in the affairs of the *Ndé,* and it was an individual's responsibility to draw upon it. Supreme over all things was *Bik'egu'indáán,* the Life Giver, who had drawn the People up from the earth's depths and assigned them a homeland. *Bik'egu'indáán* reigned over not only the *Ndé* and the denizens of the deserts and mountains, but also over all the ghosts and supernatural beings.

But Nejeunee knew something that most of the People did not. *Bik'egu'indáán* had a son, and he was the Jesucristo of her childhood. When Little Squint Eyes was older, she would teach him to kneel in prayer not only to *Bik'egu'indáán,* but to the One whose blood and flesh sustained Nejeunee even to this day.

Inside the phylactery were three perforated shells, a bluish-green specimen of *datl'ijee,* or sacred turquoise, and an actual cross carved from a twig of a pine tree struck by lightning. For a *Ndé,* this cross carried the power of the black wind, but to Nejeunee it was also like a tiny crucifix.

There was yet another object in the phylactery, although she dared not reveal it in a culture so fearful of the dead. All belongings of the deceased were always burned, thereby eliminating anything that could be exploited by ghosts bent on harm. Before he-who-cannot-be-mentioned had died, Nejeunee had accepted this practice, even though it was foreign to her upbringing. But when he had fallen on that terrible day, her inconsolable grief had created sudden conflict between her two worlds.

The *Mexicano* had won out, and in secret she had taken from his person a keepsake that was ever at her heart, comforting her just as it now seemed to soothe Little Squint Eyes. Someday, she would take it out and let him hold it while she told him about the father he would never know.

Ever since Nejeunee had awakened, the teepee's canvas walls had rippled and popped. Now the wind abruptly rushed in from behind her, so chilling that she quickly drew the blankets closer around Little Squint Eyes. Sitting up, she found One Who Frowns framed in the open flap, her dour face as disapproving as ever.

"Must I tend the fires alone?" the older woman demanded. "Does Nejeunee think by hiding in blankets that she can keep the owls from her wailing child?"

The old witch!

Not wanting to disturb Quick Talker's sleeping husband, Nejeunee said it only under her breath. But that didn't keep her from turning away in disrespect.

"The fire-place *kunh-gan-hay* can wait till Little Squint Eyes is in his cradleboard," she said, reaching for the frame.

"Don't be angry with us, One Who Frowns," Quick Talker said sleepily from across the teepee.

Nejeunee began bundling Little Squint Eyes in his cradleboard blankets. "She's only happy when she's angry."

"Hmpf!"

With the exclamation, the cold draft ceased, indicating that One Who Frowns had lowered the flap and left. Nejeunee didn't care that the woman was even more upset now, but Quick Talker was always eager to appease and called after her.

"We'll hurry and awaken Brushing Against!"

From outside, One Who Frowns gave another exclamation of

displeasure.

"Brushing Against is lazy!" One Who Frowns added. "Your sister pretends to be sick to stay in her blankets!"

With Little Squint Eyes riding on her back by cradleboard, Nejeunee accompanied Quick Talker to a nearby teepee to check on Brushing Against. They found her stooped outside, vomiting clear fluid on the snow.

"What's wrong, Brushing Against?" asked a worried Quick Talker, placing a hand between her sibling's bent shoulders. The older woman continued to vomit, charging the air with a sickening stench. "Tell me, my sister!"

Even as Brushing Against's heaves relented, she remained doubled over, moaning and clutching her abdomen. "For hours . . ." She paused to moan. "Sick . . . So sick."

Turning away, Quick Talker buried her face in her hands and began to sob uncontrollably. Surrendering to emotion always rendered her useless, leaving it up to Nejeunee to take Brushing Against by the shoulders.

"Let's get you inside," said Nejeunee.

Helping the groaning woman to the teepee flap, Nejeunee saw her features for the first time. Her face was drawn and her eyes sunken, and there was a bluish-gray cast to her skin. Her arms were still folded against the midsection of her spotted-calico overblouse, and Nejeunee was troubled to find her hands wrinkled like a very old woman's.

"When you're warm in your blankets again," said Nejeunee, "I'll bring the *gutaaln* to drive away the evil."

She could only hope that he could do so, for Brushing Against showed signs of the Blue Death that had swept through the reservation three years before. Four children and a woman had died, and the *gutaaln* there had blamed lurking owls for spreading a sickness beyond the cure of anyone except a special *gutaaln*

55

who might draw power from *niishjaa,* the owl, itself.

Stricken with concern for Little Squint Eyes, Nejeunee made Brushing Against as comfortable as possible and then summoned Nah-kay-yen, the band's old *gutaaln.* As Quick Talker stood sobbing and the medicine man sprinkled cattail pollen and chanted to *idói,* the great cat through which he claimed power, Nejeunee hurried away to assist One Who Frowns with the cook fires and more. She had done all she could for the ill woman, and now she must tend the horses and mules. The animals had to have water, or the *Indaa* would track the People down and kill Little Squint Eyes as they had his father.

Against a nearby rock bluff, a deep snowdrift had formed in a basin so large that it could have held a teepee. Along the edge, Nejeunee helped build fires as Little Squint Eyes's cradleboard hugged her back. The crackling flames would provide warmth and permit cooking, but more importantly the heat would melt the snow and allow the animals to drink.

Nejeunee wanted nothing more than to linger by the life-giving blaze and let Little Squint Eyes stay as comfortable as possible. But as soon as the warriors gathered to eat, she yielded to duty. The mules were hardy and could survive on little to drink, but the horses would need the equivalent of two wagon barrels of water. With snow always melting down to a small portion of its original promise, she set out for more to add to the basin.

The rock bluff was part of an icy outcrop springing up thirty feet, and to its right Nejeunee scrambled up a game trail too steep to hold more than a sprinkling of white. Advancing and sliding, she broke out on top in ankle-deep snow that blanketed a small flat set against the higher ridge beyond. The rising smoke danced between a couple of twisted yuccas and a stand of pitaya cactus, but what surprised Nejeunee was that Gian-nah-tah was here, packing snow around a snowball already larger than a man's head.

He didn't look up, and Nejeunee had no interest in engaging him in conversation. Making her way to a drift against a thick yucca stalk, she piled and compressed snow into a sphere too heavy to carry. It picked up grass and additional snow when she rolled it away, a trail forming in its wake. Intent on keeping the snowball in motion, she paid no attention to Gian-nah-tah until she came alongside his lowered shoulder at cliff's edge.

Stooped over an even larger mass of snow, he shouted a warning below and rolled it down into the billowing smoke. Turning to assist Nejeunee, he reached between her arms, his hand pinning one of hers against the icy ball. Revolted by his touch, she flinched and pulled her fingers free. It was instinctive, but as he pushed the snowball over the cliff, she wished that she could have endured the moment. Gian-nah-tah was not someone to anger.

Nejeunee started away, smoothing the mourning cape at her thighs as she focused on the deeper snow around the yuccas. During the brutal night ride, she had used her woolen blanket as an outer wrap; still, upon trying to dismount, she had found herself all but frozen to her horse. Hoping to stay warmer this morning, she now wore the blanket inside the cape. She was only vaguely aware of how arresting the blue calico was against the snow, but apparently it did not go unnoticed by Gian-nah-tah.

"How long will you wear the clothes of mourning?" he asked.

Such a personal question caught Nejeunee off guard, and all she could do was stop and look back at him standing in the smoky haze.

"Three seasons have passed," Gian-nah-tah added. "Soon your hair will reach your shoulders again."

She lowered her gaze to her tracks in the snow. "I'll mourn longer. The pain inside stays strong."

"Nine men have no woman to warm their blankets. Nine men await the end of your mourning. I am one. I alone of all the *Ndé* have the power to find enemies."

Nejeunee looked up at Gian-nah-tah, keying on the jagged scar that ran down his forehead, split his eyeless socket, and twisted his upper lip into a snarl. Abruptly, like lightning flashing behind a veil of clouds, more visions came. She saw a *señora's rebosa* streaming as the woman fled with her across a shining salt bed. She saw a fierce warrior on a muscled black horse riding them down, his stone-head war club framed against the cloudless sky. She saw the gleaming ground fly up and strike her face, and the quick wheeling of the Guadalupe cliffs as she rolled to her shoulder and looked up.

But most powerfully, she saw Gian-nah-tah lower a war club fresh with blood and matted hair, and the wind tug at a *rebosa* in a massing pool.

As Nejeunee stood now in the snowy foothills of the Sierra Diablo, vision and reality merged. If she had harbored doubt about who had killed her mother, it had vanished, replaced by conviction. Suddenly, Gian-nah-tah's face seemed worthy of the whispers that he was a witch.

"Why are you backing away?" he asked. "Why do your eyes grow wide? For what reason do you shake?"

Nejeunee hadn't realized that she had retreated a step, or that her demeanor had betrayed her.

"Tell me!" he demanded.

Startled, she could only stare, her heart pounding.

"Am I like a sickness to you?" Gian-nah-tah asked. "Is that not what you said in the night?"

"I-I did not," she managed.

"Do you also lie now?"

"It was One Who Frowns who spoke. She hates me and calls down evil on me."

"She has taken another husband already. She knows that our warriors' blankets are cold. She is true *Ndé,* and she cares that she is *Ndé.*"

"I'm *Ndé.* I care as much as One Who Frowns."

"Then show it. Remove your mourning clothes and make known your interest in a man. In me."

In a society in which a woman had sole right to initiate a relationship, Gian-nah-tah had crossed a boundary. But Neje-unee was afraid to tell him so, and the only thing she knew to do was turn and continue on for the snowdrift.

"You walk away from me?" he challenged.

A rough hand on her shoulder spun her around so forcefully that her legs twisted. Off-balance, she went down hard, the impact of her hip and forearm against snow and ice jolting the cradleboard. Little Squint Eyes began to cry, and Nejeunee quickly sat up and removed the straps from her shoulders. Placing the cradleboard across her lap, she peered into his unhappy face and tried to calm him. But even her soft words and gentle rocking couldn't soothe.

"One Who Frowns is right."

At Gian-nah-tah's gruff voice, Nejeunee looked up. He towered over her like a mountain spire, a powerful figure in a position of dominance.

"A child that always wails is not fit to be *Ndé,*" he continued. "The owls should come for him."

"No!" She pressed the cradleboard to her breast and cast frightened eyes about for a swooping shadow with claws and hooked beak. "He's *Ndé!* The owls won't come!"

Nejeunee didn't know where she had found the strength to defy Gian-nah-tah, and now she trembled.

"You would bear me a true *Ndé* son," he growled. "You *will* bear me a son."

"You . . . You're not permitted." Out of Nejeunee's throat the quivering words rose up unfamiliar and distant, as if someone else spoke them. "It's not the way of the People."

"You dare tell me what is *Ndé*? With my very hand I seized you by the hair from the *Mexicanos* and lifted you to my horse. Now you dare tell me the ways of the People?"

Nejeunee was terrified, but she had the wherewithal not to blurt what was on her tongue: *Gian-nah-tah, killer of helpless women!*

"I . . . I don't remember that day," she said instead.

"I remember it. I remember you wailing as I held you in front of me and rode away. I remember you striking me with your little fists when I told you, '*Ink-tah*, sit down!' I would have opened your throat with my knife, but you fought with the bravery of a *Ndé*, so I let you live. Do not make me sorry that I did."

Gian-nah-tah's outburst did nothing to pacify Little Squint Eyes, and Nejeunee took her wrapped son from the cradleboard and held him close. Looking past Gian-nah-tah, she scanned the gray skies and foggy bluffs for the owls she hoped would never come.

"For now, I will be content to escape the *Indaa*," Gian-nah-tah added. "When we are safe, you will show interest and join me in my *kuughà*, teepee."

"I . . . I will not," Nejeunee heard herself say.

Gian-nah-tah's single eye narrowed, and he lunged at her as though he were a mountain spirit descending from a sacred summit. Seizing her by the hair, he pulled her to her feet.

"Like this I picked you up and carried you off!" he bellowed. "You were *Mexicano* then, but when the time is right you will come to my blankets like a *Ndé*!"

"I will not!" she cried out through the pain. "First I'll die like—"

My mother! she wanted to say.

Gian-nah-tah tightened his fist in her hair, his grip burning every root.

"You will come, or your wailing child will die."

With a vicious shove to her head, Gian-nah-tah stalked away through the snow. And Nejeunee was left to comfort Little Squint Eyes and shed tears for the husband whom the heartless *Indaa* had taken from her.

She may have ridden with Little Squint Eyes in a party of twelve fierce warriors and three other women—one of them violently ill—but Nejeunee rode alone with her thoughts.

She was adrift in an uncaring world, and she didn't know where to turn. She dwelled on Gian-nah-tah's ultimatum, and the answers seemed as far away as *Sháa,* the sun that lay hidden behind somber, gray clouds.

In this remnant of Victorio's band—these final few *Ndé* who refused the indignity of the reservation—Gian-nah-tah's authority was supreme. No one would dare challenge him, even if Nejeunee had someone in whom to confide his transgression of the ways of the *Ndé.*

To any of the warriors, or even to Quick Talker or her sickly sister, who slumped astride a sorrel, it wouldn't have mattered that Gian-nah-tah had killed Nejeunee's mother. He was *Ndé,* and the *Mexicanos* were their enemy. Indeed, they would consider Nejeunee's first life unimportant in light of what was best for the People. But how could she ever forget, now that the visions had come?

Little Squint Eyes.

From the cradleboard at Nejeunee's back, he began to express himself with gurgles and coos, a milestone she had first noticed that morning. Was there anything she wouldn't do to protect him? Wouldn't she sacrifice everything she was—all that she had ever been—to give him a tomorrow?

As the drum of unshod hoofs played against cacti-strewn bluffs, Nejeunee's eyes blurred and she was again an unmarried *Ndé* of eighteen summers. For days in the cluster of *kuughà* dwellings on the forested reservation, she had played a court-ship game with Too-ah-yah-say. Summoning her courage one morning, she had tapped his arm upon passing, and as he had lifted his gaze after her, she had cast a coy glance over her shoulder. When he hadn't reciprocated immediately, Nejeunee had been embarrassed and crestfallen. But a mere day later as she had stooped over a cookfire, something had brushed her shoulder and she had turned to see Too-ah-yah-say striding away. Thereafter, he had become the aggressor, routinely rap-ping her lovingly with a stick when she had least expected it.

Then had come the day when Nejeunee had struck out for the spring with a woven water basket dangling on her back from a head strap. Much of the way was in open meadow, but as she approached a stand of ponderosas, she noticed a series of rocks lining the trail on either side. Shining in the sun, they stretched for twelve or fifteen feet—more evidence of courtship play. From the trees wafted the strong scent of pine, and as she lifted her gaze toward the timber, she saw a grinning Too-ah-yah-say crouching behind a tender ponderosa too small to conceal him.

For Nejeunee, this was a dream come true. If she skirted the rocks, it would mean that she had rebuffed his advances. But if she continued down-trail between the stones, it would signify that his arms would be welcome about her.

With a silent cry of joy, Nejeunee proceeded straight, the rocks crowding close on left and right. While she was inside this make-believe gauntlet, Too-ah-yah-say raced out in rescue. Seiz-ing her, he took her by feigned force to his teepee, with Neje-unee playfully protesting.

One Who Frowns met them at the canvas flap, but even her scowl couldn't tarnish the occasion. That night, Too-ah-yah-say never touched Nejeunee, nor did he on the second night, or the third or fourth. It was the *Ndé* way, just as it was on the following morning when she slipped outside without awakening him, cooked his breakfast, and led his horse to the teepee.

This was the moment of truth. Would Too-ah-yah-say eat what Nejeunee had prepared and welcome her offer of his horse? Or would he refuse and cast her away?

Never had Nejeunee been so nervous. But when Too-ah-yah-say stepped outside and saw what she had done, he put her at ease with a smile. Moments later, he had partaken of the food and accepted his animal's reins—thereby sealing their marriage as assuredly as any ceremony.

How different from what Gian-nah-tah had done! How gentle and caring Too-ah-yah-say had been by comparison! The latter had wooed her as a *Ndé* should, with love and respect for both her and the traditions of the People. But Gian-nah-tah had dishonored the old ways, and in so doing had dared evil to descend upon him.

Far worse, his actions may have left all of them vulnerable. Appeasing evil was always better than incurring its wrath, and any punishment due a leader might sweep up anyone in his charge. What sorcery was at play for Gian-nah-tah to court evil at such a time? The *Indaa* were in chase! Didn't he realize that vengeful spirits might use these white men as instruments of judgment?

Nejeunee didn't know, but she feared the consequences to Little Squint Eyes and herself and everyone else in this last vestige of a free and proud people. At their next camp, she would pray about it to the Son of *Bik'egu'indáán* before whom she had once sipped sweet wine that was more than wine.

Suddenly, on blood-splattered snow off to the side of the marching horses, Nejeunee saw a mass of fur and entrails that once had been *ga'i,* the rabbit. She cringed, for *niishjaa,* the owl, had killed and fed here—an owl that must still lurk along their very path, serving as an omen of dire things to come.

CHAPTER 6

All through the morning march, it was clear to Sam that Arch avoided him.

Typically, they would ride near one another, two friends talking and sharing the makings for smokes. But whether the company lengthened out single file through a snaking gulch, or marched two abreast along an exposed ridge, Arch stayed near point, keeping his distance. Finally, Arch dropped back one level to surly Matto and struck up a conversation, although Sam knew that Arch couldn't tolerate the troublemaker any better than he could.

None of it should have bothered Sam, but it did. Maybe he had underestimated how much Arch's friendship meant to him. Maybe he had never before understood how alone he was. Maybe only now did he realize that, even if he searched to the ends of the earth, he would still be just as alone.

As the hoofs of the company's mounts churned the icy rubble of a rising drainage, Sam broke formation to the right and took his gray forward through the slapping limbs of a thorny mesquite. Arch and Matto were two levels ahead, and as Sam fell in beside Arch's sorrel, the well-spoken ranger kept his gaze straight ahead.

The two of them continued that way, Sam studying Arch's profile and Arch ignoring him. Under Arch's stubble, the skin was flushed from the cold and the chapping wind, the redness extending below his ear. As always, he wore a ragged, red-checked neckerchief, but today it was a little loose, riding up and down on his neck with the sorrel's gait.

As Sam stared from close up, he noticed a band of discoloration appearing and disappearing with the neckerchief's movement. It seemed to be a scar about his neck, and it gave Sam pause. Was this why Arch always wore a neckerchief, to hide it? And could there be any reason to hide it, except for the blemish being exactly what it looked like? A rope burn?

But Arch's neck was a matter for another time. Right now, Sam needed to resolve their differences.

"Arch, need to talk to you."

Still, Arch remained like a statue as ice crackled to the beat of hoofs.

"Wasn't no changin' Franks's mind," Sam added, quietly enough so that only Arch could hear. "You saw that yourself."

For all of the response Sam generated, he might as well not have existed.

"Put yourself in my boots," Sam persisted. "With what happened to me, I can't let this go. You know I can't. And I don't think you could either."

"Samuel, we've nothing to discuss."

"Damn it, Arch, least give me the courtesy of lookin' me in the eye."

Now, Arch did turn, his face showing the same disappointment it had at camp.

"I wish you wouldn't look at me like that," said Sam. "You and me, we's . . ."

Sam glanced down at his saddle horn. Just what were the two of them? Friends? Acquaintances? Or just a couple of men in the same Ranger outfit?

"You know my position is unimpeachable." Arch's hushed words were obviously meant only for Sam. "Not merely in regard to Franks, but in respect to every man in the company."

"Arch, I just can't see it that way. If I was able to look ahead, know trouble was comin', I'd've never gone anywhere near Bass Canyon. Figurin' out what's to come of Franks or any of us is like tryin' to rope the wind."

"It's a simple equation, Samuel, like two plus two. Even without variables, the outcome is obvious when you posit an ill commander and a winter storm and add Mescaleros and exposed high country."

"I know you're a lot smarter than me," said Sam, "and maybe your book-learnin's reason enough for you to believe all that. But your smarts also oughta tell you that we got just the one captain, and he's the one dishes out powders."

"I've already expressed my thoughts about the effects of emotion on judgment. All I ask is that you approach him with me. He realizes the reason you're here, and he may be inclined to listen to you because of it."

"Arch, just 'cause there's fire in a man's belly don't mean he can't see straight. Maybe it can make him see better."

"How so?"

"You know how when you take aim? How you get that sight dead square on what you're shootin'? Go through what I been through—Franks too, I expect—you can see that target bigger than ever. I don't know; maybe some part of you just focuses better. Whatever it is, you get a lot clearer picture what it is you got to do."

"I'm speaking of decisions, Samuel. You're speaking of identifying a goal and finding motivation."

"I don't see the difference."

"Decisions that stem from the heart are rarely prudent. Emotion can prevent a man from assessing a situation in its wider context. It can also keep him from anticipating consequences."

"Consequences," repeated Sam. "You ever thought what happens if we *don't* chase those Mescaleros down? Look what they done already, the killin' at Paso Viejo and Ojo Caliente. Look what they done couple of weeks ago in Quitman Canyon. And look what they done last May in Bass . . ."

Suddenly Sam's voice didn't want to work. He swallowed hard, his eyes beginning to sting. Lowering his gaze, he found the reins quaking in his grip and a mist blurring the saddle horn. At the same time, a crushing ache built in the base of his skull.

Damn.

He tried to mutter the word, but it just wouldn't come.

"Samuel, I know this is difficult for you."

Sam turned away, wishing for privacy that he didn't have.

"If I were in your place," Arch added compassionately, "perhaps I would feel exactly as you."

It was an admission that Sam didn't expect, and for a long while there were only the sounds of march—the rattle of accouterments, spurs jingling to the gait of the horses, the snap and pop of ice under the hoofs. Finally, Sam heard his friend draw a deep breath.

"I'll grant that you've presented a powerful case for prosecuting the chase," said Arch. "Of all the reasons you've tendered, preemptive action is one I can't dismiss."

Still, Sam wouldn't turn; he needed to brush his eyes, and he didn't want anyone to see.

"If I seemed critical of you, Samuel," Arch continued, "it was another thoughtless act on my part. I know what a burden trauma is. It destroys a part of you that never learns to live again. It shadows your every step, reshaping who you are, influencing everything you do. You flee from it, perhaps as far as the devil's own mountains, but it's always there, crushing your hope."

Now it was Arch's voice that held emotion—so much so that Sam turned with a squeak of leather. He found Arch riding with head down, his hat brim shielding as if he too tried to hide from the world.

"That's the second time you said somethin' like that," Sam managed hoarsely.

Arch went silent, and Sam again keyed on that ragged neckerchief. "You talk like you been there," Sam added.

The ranger turned to him, and for long seconds it was as if Sam stared into a looking glass—the same misting and troubled eyes that bared a lost and hopeless soul.

" 'Long is the way and hard,' " whispered Arch, " 'that out of Hell leads up to light.' "

The two men rode on as Sam looked past his gray's ears and pondered those words. He supposed they were Arch's way of admitting that he too had been in a dark place, and maybe still was.

"Sure no pullin' our way out by our own bootstraps," Sam said in despair.

For a long while the cadence of the hoofs dominated as the futility of life weighed on Sam.

"We mustn't be defeatist," Arch finally said, almost as if to himself. "Our friend also wrote that 'the mind is its own place, and in itself can make a heaven of hell.' "

Now Sam looked at him. "What friend's that?"

"Milton. *Paradise Lost.*"

"Oh."

Sam was still clueless, but at the moment it didn't matter. "So which is it, Arch? Can we ever crawl out by ourselves or not?"

Arch shrugged. "A question for the ages. But believing the struggle useless is certain to make it so."

"What you two whisperin' about over there? Damned sure don't like people talkin' behind my back."

Past Arch's profile, Sam could see Matto's dark face puffed

up like a bloated dead cow as his mount kept pace with theirs.

Arch gave Sam a quick wink that squeezed out a glistening drop. "Methinks him paranoid."

"Hemorrhoid, hell," replied Matto. "Think I can't set a saddle?"

Sam was unable to appreciate the play on words that brought a painful smile to Arch's face. Regardless, it was good to hear him hooraw someone, if only halfheartedly.

Or maybe not.

"I'm damned tired of you smartin' off all time," Matto told Arch. "I'm puttin' a stop to it right here."

As soon as Sam had put out one fire, another one had erupted.

"Better save our energy," he said diplomatically. "We's liable to have bearcat hell with those Indians."

"Don't be tellin' me what to do, DeJarnett," growled Matto. "Ain't let nobody boss me around since I was nine years old and run off to fend for myself."

"Captain Franks has had his say, I expect," said Sam, and then he thought better of it.

"He don't lord it over me nothin' like that Meskin woman done, the bitch. Me just a boy in that Juarez cathouse, my own whore-of-a-mama not even lookin' out for me. Just turned her back anytime that cathouse madam locked me in with some man wantin' a boy to—"

Matto went silent, his face growing ashen as he seemed to realize what he was saying. Sam looked at Arch, and Arch looked back. Had Sam heard right? A secret that dark, that heinous, wasn't the kind of thing a man like Matto would ever reveal. And yet unless Sam had misunderstood, it had slipped out in front of both of them.

Sam wished he could ask Arch what he had heard, and then the only confirmation necessary came from Matto himself.

Hanging his head, he passed a hand across his colorless face and turned away—one more rider apparently set on blocking troubling memories with a low-set hat brim.

But that wasn't the end of it. Matto proceeded to pull his bay out of the march, letting the trailing riders pass two-by-two. Sam, twisting around, watched him fall in on drag, three horse-lengths behind everyone else.

When Sam straightened in the saddle, he saw Arch glancing back.

"You hear what I did?" Sam asked quietly.

"I intended to inquire the same thing of you, Samuel."

"I couldn't believe what he was tellin' us. How's anybody get over somethin' like that?"

Arch shook his head. "No child could."

"Guess we know now why he's the way he is."

"I wonder if his upbringing might explain another facet of his character, a matter he broached in a fit of anger at Musquiz Canyon."

"Matto's always havin' fits around headquarters," said Sam.

"I believe you may have been away at Fort Davis. The men were discussing the relative merits of ladies of fair complexion versus those of darker hue. Jonesy, of course, mentioned his fair Mary Jane and her golden tresses. Then someone referenced the allure of certain *señoritas* and squaws, and it sent Matto into a rage. He apparently has a vendetta against any dark-skinned woman, and now we may have learned why."

Sam glanced back at Matto again. "Still don't like bein' around him, but knowin' what we do now, can't help but feel different about him. Not even nine years old . . . Damn."

CHAPTER 7

Because she knew *niishjaa*, the owl, was about, Nejeunee rode in fear.

They were ascending the Sierra Diablo heights where dwelled the *Gáhé*, the spirits to whom the People cast their fate. These beings could protect, but they could also abandon the *Ndé* to evil that threatened in so many forms: the crippling cold, the biting wind, the gnawing hunger, the *Indaa* from whom they fled.

And the Blue Death.

Before Nejeunee's very eyes, Brushing Against had faded from a tireless, young gossip to a wrinkled old hag too sick to speak. Weakened by vomiting and diarrhea, she had clung to her horse for less than an hour before tumbling to the snow. When Nejeunee had dismounted and rushed to her side, she had found Brushing Against cold to the touch, as though little blood circulated beneath the withered, blue skin that suggested bruising on a person already dead.

With the *Indaa* in chase, all Nejeunee and the others could do was engineer a travois out of teepee poles for Brushing Against's horse and tie the suffering woman on. But as the drag poles carved trails for Nejeunee's roan to follow through the snow, Brushing Against's breathing grew labored. Soon she began to convulse, a violent shaking that persisted for agonizing minutes as Nejeunee looked on helplessly. By the time it was over, the poor woman had lapsed into a coma from which, Nejeunee knew, she would never awaken.

When the band reached the confluence of two rocky gulches, Brushing Against's husband checked her welfare and made a simple pronouncement that set Quick Talker to wailing. "*Yah-ik-tee*," he said, "She is not present."

Nejeunee knew why. Gian-nah-tah had violated the ways of the People, and now they all would pay.

In a shallow overhang only yards away, they quickly buried Brushing Against under rocks as Nah-kay-yen the *gutaaln* sprinkled pollen about. Then Nejeunee and the band rode on, for the dead were to be feared. For days, so Nejeunee had been taught, a person's spirit haunted the place of death and tried to communicate through the medium of an owl that was intent on bringing harm.

But whether meted out by ghost owls or nature or the hated *Indaa*, terrible punishment could still lie in the mountains ahead because of Gian-nah-tah.

Quick Talker was inconsolable as she rode alongside Nejeunee. The moisture that had streamed down her cheeks had frozen in place, but the cold couldn't numb her knife hand. With every rise and fall of her horse's hoofs, the blade chopped away at the straight, black hair that dangled past Quick Talker's shoulders.

Nejeunee grieved with her. In a way, they had all been sisters, even spiteful One Who Frowns, and to lose one was a terrifying reminder that the owls were always waiting to whisk someone away. With Nejeunee's sorrow came added hatred of Gian-nah-tah, and she pictured that knife of Quick Talker's plunging between his shoulder blades.

"Will you weep like a child also?"

Until One Who Frowns spoke, Nejeunee hadn't realized that the ill-humored woman rode directly behind her. A glance back confirmed that One Who Frowns's scored features were as disapproving as her words.

"Look at Quick Talker," continued One Who Frowns. "Are you now as worthless as she is?"

"There's no dishonor in grieving," said Nejeunee.

"The dishonor is when a *Ndé* woman is too lazy to work. That's why the owls came for she-who-is-not-present."

Nejeunee twisted around on the roan. "Witch spirit! There's a reason, but it has nothing to do with she-who-is-not-here!"

"What do you mean, Nejeunee?" interjected a voice so emotional it could have only been Quick Talker's.

Nejeunee turned to her. "Evil is on us because the *Gáhé* spirits are angry. They watch from the sacred heights and see the old ways violated. A witch offends them, and the punishment falls on all of us."

In their haste to probe, the other women spoke over one another.

"Who is it that offends?" asked Quick Talker.

"Does Nejeunee insult me again?" demanded One Who Frowns. "What are you saying about me?"

Dismissive, Nejeunee addressed only Quick Talker. "One Who Frowns always thinks *Sháa,* the sun, rises only to shine on her."

From behind, One Who Frowns grunted in objection.

"So it's not One Who Frowns," said Quick Talker. "Who could it be you speak of? Tell us!"

Perhaps Nejeunee had said too much already, but she was frightened for Little Squint Eyes and anguished by so many things.

"He wields the power of evil," she said. "*Niishjaa,* the owl, has cast its eyes on him and turned him against the ways of the People."

"Nejeunee blows like a tired horse through its nose," criticized One Who Frowns.

Quick Talker, her ragged hair swinging with the motion of her head, checked the riders ahead and behind before leaning closer, her dark eyes welling. "I burn with grief," she whispered to Nejeunee. "Please tell me who's taken she-who-is-not-present away from me. He must be banished!"

To a *Ndé*, to be sent away from the People—never to be allowed to return—was a greater punishment than death itself. But Nejeunee knew it couldn't be done without a trial before a band's leader.

"There's no one here to banish him," Nejeunee muttered.

"Did I hear you, Nejeunee? Who is there that couldn't be sent away?"

Just one, and from the front of the march he was signaling a halt.

Gian-nah-tah was the only warrior with a war cap of mountain lion skin, and the dangling tail twitched against his back as he cast his eyes to the brightening sky. Nejeunee looked up as well, finding *Sháa* a perfect circle through the gray clouds. On Nejeunee's right, a snow-dusted outcrop of sheer rock sprang up twenty feet, and no sooner had Gian-nah-tah dismounted than he began to scale it effortlessly.

Every *Ndé* took pride in honing his climbing skill, knowing it might someday benefit him in escaping an enemy. In seconds Gian-nah-tah squirmed over the summit rim. As he rose to lift his face to the clouds and *Sháa*, his mountain lion pelt suggested that he was more than a man—and Nejeunee knew that in one way he was, because he alone possessed the power to find enemies.

Nejeunee watched in awe as he stretched out his arms with palms up, his cupped hands ready to receive power from the Creator of Life. As he prayed, the lilt of his voice was like a song playing against the bluffs.

*"In this world
Where we live
All power is Bik'egu'indáán's.
To me He granted
The power most coveted,
The power to find the enemy.
Now I search for what
Bik'egu'indáán alone can show me.
I search for our enemy."*

As Gian-nah-tah chanted, he slowly turned, catching the veiled sunlight in his palms. Nejeunee had seen this before, and even though she couldn't discern details from below, she knew that the *Indaa* would be revealed as soon as Gian-nah-tah faced in their direction. He would find them, and the tingle in his hands and flush of his palms would tell him how far away they were.

But there was something different about this time. Even after he finished the prayer and a full revolution, he continued to turn, imploring *Bik'egu'indáán* again and again to show him the enemy. His petitions grew increasingly louder, more fervent, until it almost seemed as if he begged.

Finally, Gian-nah-tah's head sank and his arms dropped to his sides, and as godlike a figure as he had seemed only moments before, he was now but a beaten man standing on an icy rock amid mountains far greater than he. When he began to descend, he seemed unsure of himself, hesitating and groping for holds that had been there so short a time ago. Eight feet from the ground, he slipped and fell, the jarring impact sprawling him across the snowy rubble.

He was slow to regain his feet, and when he did, he reeled and leaned into the cliff that had bested him. As he stood against the ocher lichen staining the rock, Nejeunee saw something in his eyes that had never been there before.

Fear.

Nejeunee glanced at Quick Talker, and then back at One Who Frowns. The *Ndé* had always looked upon Gian-nah-tah with a reverence that no killer of innocent women deserved. Even Nejeunee had been in wonderment at his great power that had allowed them to elude the *Indaa* all these months. But now the confident expectation in the women's faces had given way to dropped jaws and furrowed brows.

Except for a howling wind, there was only silence as Gian-nah-tah stumbled back to his horse. Never once did he make eye contact with anyone, his demeanor completely without the poise that he had always displayed in matters of war. Normally, he swung astride his animal with ease, but this time he struggled. Finally, the paint nodded forward with its slumping burden, and Nejeunee and the other *Ndé* fell in behind.

Just as they did, a gloom spread across the land, and Nejeunee looked up to find that *Sháa* had hidden its face behind a descending gray fog. With it came swirling motes of frost and a creeping chill unlike anything she had experienced. It stung her cheeks and rasped down her throat, a piercing cold so intense that it was as if *Bik'egu'indáán* Himself had stripped away all warmth from the world.

Or maybe He withheld it only from the *Ndé* because a witch led them.

"We're all lost!"

Quick Talker wailed the words too quietly for anyone else to hear, but Nejeunee knew that she spoke the fears of many.

The cold persisted into the dusk, an evil cold that seemed to lurk in the shadows and reach for Nejeunee as she rode by.

Nothing could drive it away, and once more she removed Little Squint Eyes from his cradleboard and held him skin to skin under her clothing, the warmth of her breasts the last line of defense. Even the chanting prayers of Nah-kay-yen the *gutaaln* had no effect on *guu' k'as,* this ghost-cold so intent on harm. Riding a little ahead of Nejeunee, the toothless old man rattled beads of turquoise and waved the feathers of eagles. When he extended a pinch of *tádidíné* in his fingers and blew the yellow powder toward the point in the sky where the sun had vanished, the wind turned on him like a living thing and threw it back in his face.

At sixty summers of age, Nah-kay-yen was the eldest of the men, a stooped-shouldered figure with sparse gray hair and features cracked like old leather. A mountain lion had once mauled him, so Nejeunee had been told, and even though the attack had left him with a limp, he claimed power through the great cat. Too, he drew power from lightning, for on a high crag he had survived a strike that had exploded a nearby rock. Even now sky-fire lived in an arrowhead-shaped amulet about his neck.

As mighty as the panther and lightning were, however, *Sháa,* the sun, was far greater. Of all the *Ndé* Nejeunee had known, the *gutaaln* was one of the few who channeled its power.

Nah-kay-yen's medicine was indeed impressive, and yet Nejeunee had seen a marked difference in him ever since *Sháa* had fled into the fog. The left side of his face had withered, a malady that had also stricken his left arm to some degree, for he kept it folded across his torso. The same affliction must have gripped his hand as well, for his fingers were stiff and awkwardly bent.

For a *gutaaln* to be rendered impotent was distressing, and Nejeunee was in awe of the far-reaching consequences of Giannah-tah's blasphemy against the ways of the *Ndé.* Abruptly, she felt guilty, even though the fault wasn't hers, and she wondered if there was a way to soothe the anger that had turned the *Gáhé* against them.

Nah-kay-yen begin to chant again, mostly in words that only

the *gutaaln* or his spirit agents could understand. But there was one Apache phrase that Nejeunee heard him say repeatedly in the heightening gloom.

> "Be good, O night.
> Twilight, be good."

And then he added something that caused Nejeunee to hold Little Squint Eyes even closer as she searched *yá*, the sky, for an owl bent on stealing him away.

> "Do not let us die.
> Save us from *ént'i*,
> he who is a witch."

No night had ever been so dark, for the evil could not be appeased.

"We'll never see *neeldá*, the dawn!" said a weeping Quick Talker.

As Nejeunee worked blindly alongside the women to unload a travois, she had the same terrible dread. But she refused to speak of it, fearing that to do so would only ensure that the worst would come to pass. Her response to Quick Talker was to place a teepee pole in the woman's hands.

"Why bother with this, Nejeunee?" asked Quick Talker. Like all the *Ndé*, Quick Talker had difficulty speaking clearly in the paralyzing cold. "The dead have no need for shelter!"

"Shhhh!" admonished One Who Frowns, who already had taken up a pole. "Maybe the evil sleeps. Maybe it's gone away into the night. Don't awaken it with your flapping tongue."

"Even Nah-kay-yen the *gutaaln* has no hope!" Quick Talker persisted. "We—"

"Work quickly," interrupted Nejeunee. "Over there—take your pole to the place where we scraped away the snow."

Nejeunee found a third pole and manila rope and followed after the women through a flesh-eating wind. Nothing was easy in the pitch black, but soon they had the tripod poles laid out side-by-side on the ground so that the smaller ends were even.

Kneeling, Nejeunee found the matching notches two or three feet from the ends and set about trying to lash the poles together. But her fingers were numb and she couldn't see, and all the while the ghost-cold gnawed at her marrow. As her misery and frustration grew, her will faded and she began to moan.

One of the women must have recognized her note of surrender, for Nejeunee heard a sob over her shoulder.

"Let's die and be done with it!" whimpered Quick Talker.

"Hush!" scolded One Who Frowns. "Wish for it and the owls will take you first."

But Quick Talker couldn't be deterred, and Nejeunee felt fingers dig into her arm.

"Help me! Please, Nejeunee!" Quick Talker pleaded. "Who's offended the *Gáhé*? Tell us before we die!"

"Hmpf!" exclaimed One Who Frowns. "Nejeunee knows nothing. When she talks, she's like a horse blowing dust from its nostrils."

Abruptly, Little Squint Eyes began to cry from the cradle-board at Nejeunee's back.

"He cries for the dawn he'll never see!" said Quick Talker.

"Maybe the owls will be appeased if they take him," grumbled One Who Frowns.

Nejeunee again felt the bite of fingers.

"The *gutaaln* could do something!" persisted Quick Talker. "If he knows who wronged the *Ndé*, he could do something, Nejeunee!"

Considering all that Nejeunee faced, she almost yearned for the long sleep from which no *Ndé* awakened. But hers was not a life she could give, not when Little Squint Eyes depended on her. Like metal arrow points, his cries pierced her heart. They tugged at the wellsprings of her soul, and she knew that no sacrifice could be too great if it gave him a chance to live.

"Tell me, Nejeunee!" begged Quick Talker. "Please, before it's too late!"

Only now did Nejeunee succeed in lashing together the poles, and she rose and faced Quick Talker in a night ready to kill.

"Bring Nah-kay-yen the *gutaaln*. Bring him, and I'll tell how Gian-nah-tah has brought us evil."

The voice leaped out of the dark like a thing on the attack.

With the teepee's standing tripod pegged down, Nejeunee stood beside One Who Frowns as they positioned the seventh pole in the teepee's skeleton. This pole provided more than structural strength, for it held the bunched canvas that, when unfurled, would wrap around the frame and create a shelter. The wind was more vicious than ever, flapping a loose corner, but suddenly Nejeunee heard only the *gutaaln*.

"Do not let us die!"

Nejeunee spun, not realizing that Nah-kay-yen was behind her.

"You who know the witch and keep it from us!" the *gutaaln* addressed Nejeunee. "Do not let us die!"

"I-I sent Quick Talker to bring you. Are you there in the dark, my sister? You didn't tell Nah-kay-yen who it is?"

Quick Talker was there, all right, for Nejeunee heard her sob.

"Don't be angry, Nejeunee! I was afraid to say his name. Don't be angry with me!"

"Hmpf!" exclaimed One Who Frowns. "It's for Nejeunee to make the accusation—and to pay the consequences."

"Who is it that offends the *Gáhé*?" demanded Nah-kay-yen. "Who is to blame for the mountain spirits taking their favor from us?"

"Gian-nah-tah."

Even the wind seemed to go quiet as Nejeunee said the name, and she stared at the *gutaaln*'s shadow for so long that she could almost see his startled eyes and his forehead's pronounced scoring.

"To lie about such a thing brings *Bik'egu'indáán*'s judgment," warned Nah-kay-yen.

If it was possible for Nejeunee to grow more chilled, the *gutaaln*'s words accomplished it.

"Judgment is already here," she replied. "Gian-nah-tah lost the power to find enemies. The Blue Death takes whoever it wants. *Guu' k'as*, the ghost-cold, calls us to sleep the long sleep. Even you, our *gutaaln*, carry the punishment in your twisted mouth that slurs your speech."

"What is your charge against Gian-nah-tah?"

"He denies me the choice that is every *Ndé* woman's. When we escape the *Indaa*, I must join him in his *kuughà*, teepee, or Little Squint Eyes will die. So Gian-nah-tah has said."

"Gian-nah-tah is a man. There are nine men—ten, now—cold in their blankets. You are without a husband. For three seasons, you have mourned, while our men sleep alone."

"It's my right to mourn," said Nejeunee.

"Among a people so few, mourning must end. You must bear *elchínde*, children, or the *Ndé* will be no more. It is your duty."

"I will not choose Gian-nah-tah. He's violated the ways of courtship. He offended the *Gáhé* spirits and brought punishment on all of us."

A hand seized Nejeunee's arm, but Nah-kay-yen's words startled her more.

"You are to blame! You refuse to choose and forced Gian-nah-tah to defy the traditions. It is because of you that the mountain spirits no longer protect."

Quick Talker began to wail above a wind that had resumed its moan. "Nejeunee! Nejeunee!"

At first, it was Quick Talker's only intelligible word, but through her sobs came more condemnation.

"The Blue Death, Nejeunee! It took she-who-is-not-here! How could you let it happen? Oh, Nejeunee, Nejeunee!"

"Hmpf!" interjected One Who Frowns. "Do I summon Gian-nah-tah so he can banish her into the night with her crying child?"

"The *Gáhé* must be appeased," said the *gutaaln.* "Nejeunee must not rebuff Gian-nah-tah. If she chooses him, there will no longer be a wrong to be righted. The mountain spirits will smile again on the *Ndé.*"

Nejeunee listened in disbelief. She was to blame, not Gian-nah-tah, killer of innocent women and blasphemer of *Ndé* ways! What sorcery was this, when good became evil and evil became good? Or was the *gutaaln* intimidated by this witch, the same as everyone else?

She wanted to ask if disfavor could fall on the victim and spare the offender, but abrupt self-doubt took away her boldness.

"What of Gian-nah-tah?" she managed.

"Maybe he will return to Mother Earth as a bear," replied Nah-kay-yen. "Maybe he must return many times to creep through the forests on all fours. Only *Bik'egu'indáán* knows when a man can ride the ghost pony to the place of happiness."

One Who Frowns couldn't hold her tongue. "Because of this woman, won't the owls call our names before night is finished?"

"What must be done must be done quickly," said the *gutaaln.* "She must go to Gian-nah-tah now and let her choice be known. From the lightning-struck rock at my neck, I will crush a piece and mix it in water. When all of us drink, the lightning will drive away the dark that kills."

"I—"

Nah-kay-yen cut short Nejeunee's protest. "Come with me!" he ordered. "Come now or we die!"

CHAPTER 8

Sam had never known a day so cold.

Even at midday, as the rangers prepared to melt snow for the horses at a basin under a bluff, conditions were brutal. Fortunately, the abandoned fire rings of the Mescaleros still glowed with live embers, simplifying the task of rebuilding the fires. Huddling before a blaze, Sam watched the wicked dance of the flames, but while he might thaw his numb extremities, the cold at his back intensified.

As the company pushed on, the temperature plunged and the wind picked up, the kind of chilling blast that could peel the flesh from a man's face. The only way Sam could endure it was to pull his collar up around his temples and tilt his hat brim down for a shield. Even so, he didn't know if he would still have ears if this ever ended.

But not until the company halted at dusk did Sam realize the full impact of this ruthless day in the snowy canyons of a range named for the devil. As he tried to climb off his horse, he discovered that he was frozen to his saddle.

He wasn't alone. Around him, men labored to dismount, victims of ungodly cold and long hours in fixed positions that impeded circulation. Merely removing a boot from a stirrup was a challenge, and even after Sam extricated his right foot, he thought he would never swing his leg over the cantle.

Finally, he flopped under the far stirrup and lay exhausted in snow that rose fetlock-high on his animal. Panting, his will all but stripped, Sam pulled himself up by means of the stirrup leather. Ahead, through the bunched horses and barely animate men, he could see a statue-like figure still in the saddle, his horse a stark black against the white beyond.

No one could say the captain wasn't game. A lesser man would have asked for help in dismounting, but Franks struggled without a word, his cough the only sound that passed his lips. Maybe it was typical of a man who bore even the memory of a lost son in silence, except for that heartbreaking summons for "Walter" during the previous night's delirium.

Jonesy, who stood watching as he held his roan just ahead of Sam, said something unintelligible. Sam supposed that everyone's lips were numb, but that didn't keep the New Jersey native from working his crooked jaw.

"The old man can't even get off his horse."

This time, Sam understood, even though Jonesy pronounced his words like a man roaring drunk.

"Guess whipping us damned Yankees," the northerner added, "is just as hard now as it was in the war."

Sam had never before wished for Jonesy to limit his topics to Mary Jane.

"Lost someone, did he?" Jonesy went on. "Well, he's not the only one. No, sir. Maybe it was my own father that put his precious Walter in the ground. Or maybe it was Franks himself who killed my father."

Good God, thought Sam. He hadn't known about Jonesy losing his father in the war, but the way the ranger openly mocked the captain was shocking. In an ordeal like this, open disrespect for Franks could drop morale even lower.

Sam decided to ignore the remarks and hope that Jonesy would drop the subject, but Arch unaccountably followed up.

"Perchance, Jonesy," said Arch, straining to enunciate as he stood alongside Sam, "growing up bereft of a father merely spared you misery and abuse."

Jonesy turned. "What's that mean?"

"He might have proven at home in these mountains."

"Huh?"

"If not *diablo* incarnate, he may have been a worthy minion of his."

Jonesy's face may have been too numb to show much expression, but Sam could see plenty of confusion in his eyes.

"What are you talking about?" Jonesy asked. "What little I recall of my father is all good." He slung a hand toward Franks. "He didn't deserve some Yankee hater like that killing him, that's for sure."

Jonesy spun to the captain, who still fought to dismount from the black gelding.

"You hear me?" Jonesy shouted at him. "If not, I'll come over and yell it in your ear!"

Sam quickly looked at Franks. The captain either hadn't understood or didn't realize the comment was meant for him, for he merely continued his pitiful attempts to swing off the horse.

"Let it go, Jonesy." Sam's plea was quiet, measured, but inside he screamed. *For God's sake, let it go!*

Then Jonesy took a step toward Franks, and Sam knew he had to do something quickly.

"So how's Mary Jane like the cold?" Sam asked. "Reckon she's all warm by the fire someplace?"

But Jonesy kept walking, leading his horse as he brushed past the ranger ahead.

Sam, the reins of the gray in hand, stumbled after him. "What's that you was sayin' last night about her? You know, somethin' about—"

Abruptly Boye stepped in Jonesy's path, forcing him to stop.

" 'Lust not after her beauty in thine heart,' " quoted Boye.

" 'A whore is a deep ditch.' "

Even from behind, Sam could see Jonesy tense before the preacher boy.

"You calling my Mary Jane a whore?" Jonesy demanded.

" 'She also lieth in wait as for a prey,' " Boye continued. " 'Come not nigh the door of her house.' "

"What right you got talking about my Mary Jane that way? She's the sweetest, most innocent girl in all of New Jersey."

Jonesy had closed what little space there was between the two, but the preacher boy wasn't deterred.

" 'Neither let her take thee with her eyelids. Her house is the way to hell.' "

Jonesy drew back a fist. "Why, you little bas—"

He tried to throw a punch, but Sam seized his arm. It would have been a powerful blow, judging by the strength Sam needed to prevent it.

Jonesy whirled on Sam with wild eyes. "Let me at him, De-Jarnett! You hear what he said about my Mary Jane?"

Jonesy broke free and tried to lunge at Boye, but the icy footing wouldn't cooperate. He went down hard at Sam's boots, leaving the preacher boy to hover over him.

Boye pointed down at Jonesy, as if singling him out in admonishment. " 'Walk in the Spirit,' " Boye warned, " 'and ye shall not fulfill the lust of the flesh.' "

It was like throwing kerosene on a fire. With an oath, Jonesy tried to kick him, but the preacher boy had taken a step back.

"Y'all quit it!" Sam ordered. "We don't need this—we's freezin' out here!"

Sam reached down to offer Jonesy a helping hand, but the New Jersey native angrily pulled away. As he came to his feet, his puffed face still showed plenty of fight, but Boye had wisely retreated beyond a horse.

"It's all over now," Sam told Jonesy. "Here, hold my horse for me."

Hoping it would distract him, Sam stuffed the reins in Jonesy's hand and went to Franks. The captain had slipped his right boot out of the stirrup but had yet to swing his stiff leg across. Sam knew better than to ask if he needed help, so he stayed silent as he came abreast of the gelding and guided Franks's foot up and across the animal's rump. When the captain stepped down, Arch was there to support the coughing man and make sure his left boot cleared the stirrup.

"Awful cold, Captain," said Sam as he went around the black's hindquarters. "Best you move around some till we get a fire goin'. Arch, let's rustle up some wood."

At this confluence of two gulches, the temperature was falling as fast as the night. With frostbite a growing danger, it was important to gather fuel quickly. As other rangers searched the slopes, Sam and Arch started up the shadowy drainage on the right, their boots spraying snow with every shuffling step. As soon as they were out of earshot of everyone, Sam turned to Arch.

"You want to tell me what that was about?"

"Pardon?"

"Back there. All those things you was sayin' to Jonesy about his father."

"Merely the truth, Samuel. Nothing more, nothing less."

Sam breathed sharply. "You aggravated a situation that didn't need aggravatin'. Jonesy was done poppin' off, and you went and got him riled up even worse."

"That wasn't my intent."

"You near' caused a fight. Even worse, look how he was yellin' at the captain."

Arch went silent as they found a tangle of driftwood and began pulling limbs free, the wood groaning and popping. When

Arch finally spoke, his voice was subdued.

"Samuel, you're right. It was imprudent of me. I confess to allowing my own feelings to exacerbate matters."

The gloom didn't allow Sam to see Arch's eyes, but he studied his friend nevertheless.

"Arch," he said with concern, "is there somethin' you needin' to talk about?"

Arch looked down and stirred the snow with his boot. Twice he glanced up, as if wanting to speak but denying himself. The third time, he managed a single syllable before his gaze fell again. Finally came spiritless words.

"I think not."

Sam could respect that. There were things that lived inside a man that he just had to deal with on his own.

As dusk faded into unyielding dark, all that seemed to matter anymore was survival.

They crowded a blazing fire, exhausted men caught in frigid weather that grew worse by the moment. Sam hoped the firewood held out, for he feared that not even a bedroll could stave off what lurked beyond the flames. He began to think of it as a living presence, something evil and pitiless, a frozen death ready to pounce.

Captain Franks seemed the most vulnerable. All through supper, he had sat hunched over, as if his shoulders had lacked the strength to support him. Now, across from Sam, he lay in a fetal position in his tarpaulin, his back to the fire. Even in a spot cleared of snow, a bedroll and tarp offered little insulation; the ground itself was frozen. As the firelight flickered against the canvas drawn about the captain's shoulders, Sam thought he could see the poor man shivering.

"Bunch of fools we are."

As Matto began to complain, Sam hoped that Franks had

already drifted off to sleep. Someone as sick as the captain didn't need the added burden of knowing that Matto was sowing seeds of discontent.

"Never knowed it so cold," added Matto, who hunkered by the blaze as far from Sam and Arch as possible. "Get away from the fire and it'd peel the hide off. What the hell we doin' here?"

"Dying is what," said the ranger named Red.

"No use in this," agreed someone else.

Jonesy seemed shaken as he stared into the fire. "My Mary Jane, so far away . . . I . . . I don't want to die."

"We's fools to just let it happen," said Matto. "We's fools to traipse off up here in the first place."

Sam had to put a stop to this. He could still hear Elizabeth's screams, and tomorrow, or the next day, or the one after that, they would catch up with those Mescaleros and turn them into good Indians. Dead Indians. But he couldn't do it alone.

"Let's hold it down, let the captain sleep," he said, scanning the firelit faces.

Matto scowled but wouldn't look at Sam. "Nobody tellin' me when I can talk and when I can't. Ain't takin' nobody's orders no more, not his"—he nodded to Franks—"not nobody's. If I want to get up tomorrow and ride out of here, I'll damn sure do it."

"I'd be right behind you," spoke up a previously silent ranger.

"You ain't the only one," said Red.

Sam could only hope that Franks hadn't heard.

Arch, standing quietly over Sam, cleared his throat. As Sam looked up through the curling smoke, he was sure that his friend was about to join the chorus of malcontents. Then Arch made brief eye contact, and his cheek began to twitch as if he grappled with indecision. The spasm persisted until the wind gusted, tossing the yellow flames.

"Perhaps for now," said Arch, "we should concentrate on

enduring the night."

Boye sat closest to Franks, and abruptly the firelight seemed like hellfire in the preacher boy's eyes. "It's the Lord's doing, sending a whirlwind out of the south and cold out of the north. Handing out punishment, He is."

"He can take a horsewhip to you for all I care," growled Matto.

"Yeah, but this freeze don't care who's who," Red added. "It's got ahold of us all."

"The Lord knows what He's about," said Boye. " 'By the breath of God frost is given.' "

Sam leaned toward the popping fire, seeking warmth. He didn't know whose doing this was, whether some uncaring God or nature or the devil himself. He just knew that the frozen death was all around, creeping closer by the minute.

"Never saw a fire give out so little heat," he said, watching the sparks rise from the flames. "Man go to sleep in this, might not ever wake up."

Jonesy pulled a limb from the dwindling pile and started to add it.

"Hold off on that," said Sam. "Wood's got to last us." He looked up at Arch. "Arch, fast as this wood's burnin', we goin' to have enough?"

"I fear we greatly overestimated our supply, Samuel."

Sam stood and adjusted his coat collar. "Yeah, and as fast as this temperature's droppin', we got to do somethin' about it quick." He dug into his trousers pocket. "Won't be easy by match light."

Sam turned to the impenetrable dark, and so did Arch. As they started away, Sam checked over his shoulder. All those able-bodied rangers still hugged the lapping flames, and not a single one had the courage to leave the fire and help.

At Arch's shoulder, Sam cut trail to the crackle of ice, his boots growing heavier by the step. The warm blaze quickly became like a distant memory, but their shadows stayed ahead of them for a while, long and dark and crawling wickedly across the snow.

Sam didn't like what he was feeling—the growing sense that something evil waited in the night ahead.

"The frozen death," he muttered. "Like somethin' ready to jump on us."

"You as well," remarked Arch. "I thought it was only I."

"You feel it too?"

"Ever since night fell, Samuel." He took a quick look around. "It's as if something malevolent is stalking us, manifesting itself in a numbing cold."

Now as Sam searched the mysterious dark, he wasn't just perplexed. He was scared, and he drew his revolver and carried it muzzle down. Still, he didn't feel one whit safer, and he thumbed back the hammer with a click.

"Careful, Samuel," warned Arch. "A .45 slug is of no consequence to a phantom, but potentially lethal to us should you trip."

Arch was right. How could a man shoot something he could only feel?

He eased the hammer back into place but kept the weapon at his thigh as they ventured farther into the night, which seemed to loom up like a black veil that not even the flickering firelight could pierce.

Suddenly the darkness began to moan—a plaintive, lonesome wail that seemed at once both wind and something more.

Sam froze, his hand tightening on the walnut grip of his Colt. "Good God, what is that, Arch?"

Arch stopped with him, and for long seconds Sam heard nothing but that eerie sough that made him want to turn and run.

"Except for nocturnal denizens," said Arch, "the night holds nothing that the day does not."

Arch sounded like a man trying to convince himself, a tack that Sam also tried.

"Just wind, I guess." But even Sam wasn't satisfied with the explanation. "Think there's such thing as ghosts? Or at least Indian spirits?"

" 'There are more things in heaven and earth than are dreamt of.' "

Sam supposed that meant that Arch didn't know any better than he did. Sam was still pondering when a flaring match startled him and he saw Arch shielding the small flame with a cupped hand.

"On your left, Samuel."

Sam brought his Colt up in full cock as he pivoted to a shadowy form a few feet away on a rising bluff.

"Easy, my man!" exclaimed Arch. "It's merely a dead juniper ripe with firewood."

"Damn it, Arch, don't be pointin' things out in the dark thataway."

"Apology tendered. I—"

Another unearthly cry exploded out of the up-canyon gloom—and this time it seemed to rise up from so near that Sam wouldn't have stretched out an arm for all the silver dollars in Texas.

"Arch, let's grab all the juniper wood we can carry and get the hell out of here."

CHAPTER 9

The small fires blazed in the night, but they also seemed to burn through Nejeunee's soul.

There were four in all, each representing one of the four winds. Spaced thirty feet apart, they marked the corners of a square that held not only Nejeunee and Little Squint Eyes, but Gian-nah-tah and Nah-kay-yen. Looking on from outside were the rest of the band, a dozen hunched and shivering men and women crowding the blazes.

Chanting to the spirit winds, the *gutaaln* went from fire to fire and cast *tádidíné* that set the flames leaping. But the ghost-cold remained, growing ever deadlier, and it would never go away unless Nejeunee yielded to the killer of her mother.

Bitter was the smoke that hung in Nejeunee's throat, but not nearly so bitter as what she carried in her heart. For the love of the child who slept in the cradleboard at her back, she would give herself over to a living death from which there could be no escape.

Nah-kay-yen briefly disappeared into the night, and when he returned he bore an empty cast-iron kettle. In the center of the square, he placed it on the snow and removed the lightning-struck amulet from his neck. As he knelt, Nejeunee saw that he still had only limited use of his left arm. Nevertheless, with stiff fingers he held the dark stone over the cookware and began chipping at it with a knife.

The *gutaaln* claimed the amulet held the power of lightning, and Nejeunee had no reason to doubt it. With every strike of the metal blade, fire flew as surely as lightning streaked across a stormy sky.

Soon Nah-kay-yen tilted the cookware in such a way that Nejeunee could see firelight glinting from the fragments. Evidently satisfied, the *gutaaln* produced a stone mano and set about grinding the flakes into a powder. Completing the task, he motioned to a warrior, who responded by bringing a woven basket. At the *gutaaln*'s instructions, the man added water to the kettle and then retreated, leaving Nah-kay-yen to stir the concoction with his knife.

With the powder suspended, if not dissolved, the *gutaaln* stood. Holding the cookware up before a fire, he prayed to the spirit of the wind that it represented, and then slowly revolved until he had done the same with the other fires. At the conclusion, he implored the lightning to fight the ghost-cold. As a dozen voices beyond the flames rose up in supplication, Nah-kay-yen brought the kettle to his lips.

Next, he handed it to Gian-nah-tah. For hours Gian-nah-tah had appeared beaten, a stoop-shouldered shell of a man unworthy of the mountain lion skin he wore. Now as he drank, he seemed to transform into at least a semblance of the fierce warrior who struck fear in Nejeunee.

Nejeunee drank next, tasting the grit. She prayed especially that the power of the lightning would charge her milk, for Little Squint Eyes would be the beneficiary as he nursed at her breast. As for herself, Nejeunee felt no sensation, but what could she expect, considering how violently her stomach churned as she stood beside Gian-nah-tah?

Nah-kay-yen summoned the water bearer again and relinquished the cookware with instructions to pass the mixture from *Ndé* to *Ndé* outside the fires. Then he turned to Nejeunee.

"The *Gáhé* must be appeased. Do what you must before we die."

Nejeunee looked down at the snow. She couldn't face Giannah-tah, not when she was so overcome by the image of a cruel horseman overtaking a helpless *señora*. Strangely, the white salt bed of memory and the snow of this night looked very much alike—except that the snow at her feet was alive with firelight, while the salt bed cried of death through its red pool.

Without looking up, Nejeunee made her way to a fire. There she removed the cradleboard and placed it on the ground. She took a moment to rearrange Little Squint Eyes's blankets and then stood upright and stared into the flames. They reminded her of *infierno*, a place of judgment that she had learned about as a child. In her mother's arms she had felt safe from those terrible fires, but now they would rage throughout her as long as she lived.

For three seasons, her mourning blouse had draped from her shoulders, but she would wear it no more. Removing it, Nejeunee held it in her hands, dwelling on all that it had meant— the loss, the pain, the endless loneliness. The blouse had been a tragic reminder of an enduring love, but even if she searched to the farthest reaches of the winter, she still would never find he-who-cannot-be-mentioned.

Her eyes blurred as she laid the blouse almost gently across the blaze, blue calico briefly holding its color against fiery tongues of red and yellow. Then the calico began to scorch, a black death crawling across it, and when it burst into flames she closed her eyes and felt the moisture squeeze out.

For a moment, she wanted to open her wrists with the knife at her hip, but Little Squint Eyes began to coo, and she knew that she had a noble cause that was worth any sacrifice.

Once more positioning the cradleboard upon her shoulders, Nejeunee went to the woodpile beside the fire and took up a slender stick. Turning, she started back toward Gian-nah-tah, her head hanging lower with every step. The few steps seemed to take almost forever—and she supposed they did, for they stretched from that long-ago day, when a war club had descended, to this moment when she stopped before the one who had wielded it.

Still, she wouldn't look up, focusing instead on the firelight playing against his buckskin leggings. The thought of him clinging to her and grunting was more loathsome than ever, but she blindly lifted the stick and lightly rapped Gian-nah-tah above the elbow—a lover's tap to the arm of a witch to signify that she would accept his advances.

From beyond the fires, Nejeunee heard a girlish squeal of delight, and she knew that Quick Talker had seen.

"Look at me!" shouted Gian-nah-tah.

Nejeunee thought he addressed only her, but as she looked up she found him scanning the bystanders as fire reflected in his single eye. Maybe it was the contrast with the shadowy socket where his other eye had been, or the flicker of the blazes against his disfiguring scar, but never had he appeared so evil.

"Inside the fires we dance to bring the *Gáhé* down from their sacred caves!" he cried. "We dance, and the *Gáhé* will drive away the ghost-cold and the *Indaa!*"

That eye so alive with fire looked down at Nejeunee, and his voice dropped to an arrogant snarl. "And when the *Indaa* turn back, you will come to *kuughà,* my teepee, and never leave."

Somehow the rangers had survived the night and its frozen death.

Sam awoke beside the smoldering fire to the smell of woodsmoke and the realization that he couldn't feel his toes. He sat up in his tarp and saw men stirring in the bedrolls that crowded the ring of blackened rocks, where Arch squatted over a coffee pot in the glowing coals. Someone behind Sam moaned, and he checked over his shoulder and found Franks rising to an elbow.

"Captain, you make the night all right?" Sam asked.

As Franks faced him, his gray eyes had a blank look as if Sam's question hadn't registered.

"Captain?" Sam repeated.

Franks's brow wrinkled and he winced.

"Still feelin' poorly?" persisted Sam.

But Franks only lowered his head and brought quaking fingers to his temple.

Concerned, Sam glanced at the fire. "Let me rustle you some coffee."

Sam turned away to throw back his tarp, only to hear Franks moan again. This time it came with intelligible words.

"Walter? That you, Walter?"

Once more, Sam faced him.

"You're all grown up," said Franks, staring at Sam but not seeming to focus. "Walter . . . Walter . . . Come back . . . Please come back."

Then Franks's eyes began to well—vacant eyes as sad as the emotion in his trembling whisper.

Sam would never know what it was like to love a son, not after Bass Canyon. But the plaintive plea of a father who had lost more than a war stirred something in Sam's heart that he had believed buried with Elizabeth and their unborn child.

Franks lay back again, and when he closed his eyes he seemed to rest easier. For a few moments, Sam watched the rise and fall of his chest, a peaceful rhythm abruptly broken by a coughing fit. When it passed, Sam readjusted Franks's cover and rose. As soon as he turned to the fire, he found Arch extending a steaming tin cup through the drifting smoke.

"Hear all that?" Sam asked quietly as he accepted. "Way he

looked at me, seemed to think I was his boy."

Arch poured a second cup of coffee for himself. "Sometimes a person may be asleep even if his eyes are open. The captain may have looked at you, Samuel, but I doubt he saw you."

Sam sipped, feeling the black coffee's warmth all the way down his throat. "Yeah, his eyes was like a dead man's."

Sam wished he hadn't phrased it that way; it brought a terrible memory of Elizabeth's lifeless eyes staring but never seeing.

"The captain suffers from a lot of unresolved trauma," said Arch, "and he's not alone."

"I wanted to tell him, 'Yeah, it's me, it's Walter,' so he'd rest better."

Arch stoked the fire with a few unburned twigs left over from the night. "It wouldn't have been fair to him, Samuel. No one should attempt to live a lie, even for a moment."

Sam watched him rearrange the red-checked bandana about his neck. "I'm guessin' more of us try to than ever 'fess up."

"A defense mechanism, pure and simple. To ignore something in our past is to pretend it never happened."

Sam had long-since realized that it was useless to pretend. For him, the past and the present had merged into a never-ending hell. As for Arch, Sam wondered if he was aware that he continued to fidget with the bandana knot.

"It'll eat you up, the bad stuff will, Arch. Holdin' it in—tryin' to, anyway—I've done my share of it, and it's just not any good. What little I've told you about my troubles has helped. Can't change things, but it's helped."

Still, Arch fussed with the knot, and Sam wondered if his friend had understood a thing he had said. Or maybe he had.

"I tendered an offer to listen, and you did so voluntarily," said Arch.

Sam wasn't sure if there was a trace of agitation in Arch's

voice, but he got the message. If and when Arch was ready to talk about things, he would do so of his own accord.

Across the fire, someone swore. Looking over, Sam saw Matto sit up in his frost-covered bedroll and survey the heights, ghostly bluffs through a swirling fog.

"Hell of a thing to wake up to, snow all around," Matto grumbled. "How high he expect us to go in these damned mountains?"

No one bothered to respond, but that didn't keep Matto from protesting more. Interspersed with his complaints was profanity, much of it in Spanish, a tongue Sam had become fluent in during his years in the South Texas brush country.

By the time Matto rolled up his bedding, his discontent had spread. As Red and another ranger huddled with him and conversed in hushed tones, Sam was troubled to realize that they were the men who had been so eager to bolt with Matto the night before. Even now, there was nothing to suggest that their topic was anything other than desertion, for Red motioned toward Franks, and the other ranger pointed back down-canyon. When Matto slung an arm toward the sidelined horses, the three seemed to reach an agreement, for they took up their saddles and started for the animals.

"Don't like the looks of this, Arch," said Sam, watching through the rising smoke.

"I'll grant you that it doesn't bode well."

"If they go, we all might as well go."

"Indeed. They represent thirty percent of our force."

"Arch, I know you're still havin' doubts about this, but we got to stop those three."

Sam looked at him and found that same twitch in his cheek that had suggested indecision the night before. Finally, Arch drew a deep breath.

"Samuel, I wish you hadn't convinced me of the innocent

lives we stand to save."

It was all the reassurance Sam needed, and he edged around his friend and started for the horses. "We talk Matto out of leavin', others will stay too. Let's see if we can get him off to himself."

"I fear we are the last two men he wants to see privately."

" 'Cause of what he let slip out?"

"Indeed."

As chance would have it, Matto's sidelined bay was isolated from the other nine horses, thereby promising Sam the two-on-one discussion he wanted. He was dismayed by the bay's condition, and he was equally discouraged by a quick scan of the other horses. Even this quickly, all the animals had deteriorated into sorry, beaten-down nags. Sam supposed it was no wonder; their scant allotments of grain would barely have kept horses serviceable even in ideal conditions.

As Sam approached, Matto had his back turned and was busy trying to fit a bit into the bay's mouth.

"Matto, need to talk to you," said Sam.

The ranger wheeled. Sam couldn't tell what showed in his eyes—dismay or embarrassment or shame—but Matto tried to cover it up with an angry outburst.

"What the hell you want, DeJarnett? Leave me alone. I ain't done nothin'."

"No, but you're about to, I think." Sam nodded to the other two rangers. "Y'all goin' someplace?"

Matto didn't seem anxious to look at him. Turning away, the ranger set the bit against the horse's teeth and tried to place the bridle crown over the ears. But the bay sensed his agitation and slung its head, complicating the task. Matto needed to calm the horse, not an easy matter when he couldn't calm himself, and he resorted to swearing.

Sam stepped forward to Matto's shoulder so that the bay

could see him clearly. "Easy, boy, easy." He showed the gelding his hand and passed it down the angular face. He followed up with more soft words and gentle coaxing, and finally the horse relaxed enough for Matto to secure the bridle.

"Didn't ask nothin' from you," the ranger complained, still avoiding eye contact. Tying the reins to a nearby scrub juniper, he took up a blanket and laid it across the bay's withers.

"You can't do this," Sam pleaded. "The three of y'all can't ride off this way."

"The hell we can't," said Matto, keeping his back to Sam as he hoisted the saddle.

Arch finally spoke up. "Matto, my man, a force split seventy-thirty would be exceedingly vulnerable for the thirty if the Apaches circle back."

"We's goin'," said Matto, throwing the saddle across the horse.

Sam stood by helplessly, watching his hopes of wreaking vengeance on those Mescaleros grow fainter by the second.

Elizabeth!

He could see her yet in Bass Canyon, an innocent and terrified woman fleeing a butcher out of hell.

Elizabeth!

To what lengths would Sam go to avenge her, to avenge a child who would never be born? Was there anything he wouldn't do? Could there be any act too vile? Any words too despicable?

"You climb on that horse and I'm tellin' them."

Sam could hear his own voice, but a cruel and heartless stranger was behind it.

Matto turned, furrows in his brow.

"The other two," Sam added. "They'll spread it through the whole country."

"What are you—"

"That boy in Juarez. I'm tellin' them what all those men did to him."

Matto's jaw dropped and his face blanched, and for a long while the two of them stared, one soulless man at another. Finally, Matto lowered his gaze and walked lifelessly toward the fire.

"You, Samuel, are a royal bastard," said Arch.

Sam couldn't disagree, and he wondered what had happened to the person he used to be.

"Don't go judgin' me, Arch," he said as they faced each other. "Till you've been in my place, don't go judgin' me."

"You prevailed on my sense of decency—we'll save lives, you contended—but you've lost sight of what's decent."

Sam turned and walked away. "I'm not listenin' to this."

But Arch stayed at his shoulder. "No consideration is too great for someone mistreated as a youth."

"When it comes to dealin' with those Apaches, Matto's the last person I'd feel sorry for." Sam was getting angry, and he stopped and whirled on Arch. "Or is it even Matto you're talkin' about?"

Arch flushed and, almost reflexively, adjusted his neckerchief.

"You have no noble cause, do you, Samuel. You're just a pathetic figure reveling in self-pity, seeking retribution no matter the cost to anyone."

Sam didn't respond. What could he say? That he knew it as well as Arch?

As so many emotions raged inside him, Sam pondered what Elizabeth would have thought.

CHAPTER 10

The morning sun had just burned away the fog when Sam and Company A rode upon four smoldering campfires set at the corners of a square.

Through a winding canyon, they had tracked the Mescaleros to this small bowl cradled by mountains. Here the canyon ended, while ahead loomed a steep, narrow gulch that poured down from the heights. Thick with brush, the rocky ravine was impassable for horses, but the Mescalero trail continued on, a zigzag scar in the snow of the sharp slope on its right.

For the first time since the company had embarked on scout, Sam could see his shadow, starkly black against white. After sodden days under depressing clouds, there was something exhilarating about bright sunlight, and for an instant his spirits soared like the slopes ahead.

This might be the day.

Franks ordered a dismount, something the captain managed for himself this time. Sam, once on the ground, stood rubbing the backs of his thighs and watched Franks lead his horse to a fire ring. Although the captain's cough persisted, he had been clearheaded since awakening fully, and warmer conditions today seemed to have restored a little vitality to his step.

Franks took up a stick and stirred the ashes. Flames broke out almost immediately, a sure sign that the fires had not been abandoned long. As smoke rose, he turned and seemed to trace its drift along the ascending Mescalero trail.

Sam had learned for himself how rugged this range was. It was a huge rock, broken by canyons snaking down from the highest reaches. White-frosted juniper, madrone, and piñon pine crowded gulches and north-facing slopes, while dominating elsewhere were agave, ocotillo, cholla, and prickly pear, all growing between exposed areas of sharp-edged limestone. Everything seemed poised to prick or scrape.

But alongside the Apache path, the snow had softened the slope, hiding the threats behind an almost heavenly beauty. Several hundred feet up, the beaten track disappeared over the contour of the mountain. From where Sam stood, the trail seemed to reach the sky, the bluest of blues in contrast to the snow.

For a moment, he wished he could believe as Elizabeth had—that there was a better place waiting beyond that blue veil, a place where they might be together again.

How much easier life would be for him, if he could only live a lie.

"DeJarnett . . . Jones."

Hearing the captain call, Sam walked his horse forward and converged on the fire at the same time as Jonesy. Franks was stooped, trying to scoop snow to smother the flames and keep the increased smoke from alerting the Apaches. Still weak, he would have gone down if Sam hadn't grabbed his arm. Sam knew better than to say anything, so he assumed Franks's task and buried the fire.

"Boys, I need you to reconnoiter on foot." A cough rattled Franks's chest as he motioned to the gulch. "Hold to the cover in the ravine. If you top out on the summit ridge, it's bare and exposed, so stay low. I want to see you back."

"Yes, sir," Sam acknowledged.

He slid his Winchester out of its saddle scabbard and passed the animal's reins to Boye.

"May the heathens save their judgment for me," said the preacher boy.

"DeJarnett," added Franks, "don't shoot unless it's a matter of have-to. We're about to overtake them, son, and we can't afford to give up our position."

With Jonesy following, Sam started up the ravine, a cut that exposed the mountain's underlying rock. The gully was dense with alligator-bark junipers and piñon that kept it in shade, but the undergrowth was worse, a tangle of rabbitbrush, sotol, and needlegrass that hid pincushion cacti. The pitch was steeper than Sam had expected, and as he maneuvered up through the thicket, his boots slipped in the unstable footing. His Winchester was a hindrance, catching in the brush, and the Bowie knife at Sam's waist was a problem too, for the scabbard probed his groin.

"Hell of a thing that Yankee-hating captain did," whispered Jonesy as they paused for a respite. "Sending me off up here, not caring if I come back."

"Where you're from don't have nothin' to do with it," Sam whispered back. "I've lived my whole life in Texas."

"Then why's he keep picking me? First that landslide canyon and now this."

Sam was getting annoyed; there were more important things to worry about. Parting the vegetation at his face, he futilely tried to peer ahead. "Thought you'd be glad to have somethin' new to tell."

"Oh, my Mary Jane's going to be enthralled, all right, hearing all my experiences."

As he voiced his sweetheart's name, Jonesy's voice rose in excitement. But Sam had no sweetheart, and he sank inside before cautioning the New Jersey native to silence and pushing on.

For days, Sam had thought he would never be warm again.

But as he struggled higher for agonizing minutes—his throat burning from furiously inhaling the cold, thin air—exertion succeeded where even a campfire had failed. He paused to unbutton his coat, and as Jonesy stopped alongside, Sam heard shuffling ahead.

Sam alerted Jonesy with a gesture toward the ravine's head. The sound died away, but Sam waited patiently, knowing he hadn't been mistaken. Then it came again, and he quietly separated the slender sotol leaves before him and saw movement through the brush. It was only twenty yards away, a dark form stirring against bright sky, but the intervening growth was too dense to give up its secrets. As Sam craned left and right, however, he finally pieced together his glimpses.

"What is it?" Jonesy whispered.

Not wanting to risk even a quiet exchange, Sam patted his hip as if whipping a horse. Sure enough, in the last clump of piñons at gully's head stood a staked bay.

Sam wormed forward, a scared man who had to learn more. Never had the rasp of brush across his hat seemed so loud, or the grate of forearms and belly against rubble been so jarring to his ear. Considering a horse's sense of smell, he was thankful that he and Jonesy approached from downwind. But just as Sam advanced to within several yards of the bay, the animal raised its nose and curled back its upper lip, a sure sign that it had detected them.

Sam froze. Now that he was closer, he could see the horse framed against a sky so low that the bay had to be just below the crest. The ravine was relatively shallow here, its undergrowth hiding between limestone bluffs three or four feet high. Motioning for Jonesy to check left, Sam crawled to the ice-glazed bank on the right, knowing that the Mescalero trail summited beyond.

Removing his hat, he peered out. He squinted to the sparkle of the sun against snow, but twenty yards away he distinguished a lone figure, squatting just off the bare crest on a rock shelf overlooking the trail below. The Apache lookout adjusted a woolen blanket about his shoulders as a stiff wind set the eagle feathers in his war cap dancing.

Sam quickly dropped behind cover. There had been a single-arc bow and feathered arrows, a war club and a bone-handled knife, a metal-tipped lance and a glinting rifle—implements of death that had taken so much from him.

Sam sat back against the icy limestone and gripped his Winchester so tightly that it quaked. His temples pounded as a great rage surged through him. Here at last was what he had sought for months, and all he needed to do now was slide the barrel of the carbine over the bank and squeeze the trigger. He wanted to watch the filthy animal flop in the snow. He wanted to see the murdering devil jerk to slug after .44 slug.

Then Sam remembered Franks's counsel, and he knew that greater vengeance lay ahead if he and Jonesy could dispatch the lookout without gunfire.

The mountainside on the opposite side of the ravine must have been clear, judging by Jonesy's unchanged demeanor as he withdrew from the far bank. But Sam's bearing must have revealed plenty, for Jonesy's face went white as soon as the northerner turned. In case the ranger had any doubts, Sam held up one finger and motioned over his shoulder.

From here, Sam knew he would have no chance to rush the lookout unawares. But he had a plan, and by gesture and by mouthed words, he conveyed it to Jonesy and then started alone for the ravine's head.

He worried most about the reaction of the horse, which had turned and pointed its ears toward him. But the bay stayed calm even as Sam quietly broke through a final goldeneye bush and came up before its forelegs, which framed the gentle swell of a summit ridge that was bare except for snow. Beyond, only thirty or forty feet distant, the world abruptly fell away—the half-mile cliff Franks had described.

But it was what grew at Sam's right that seized his attention. Here at the head of the ravine, he lay in the shade of one last piñon, its wind-twisted limbs hovering over a smaller piñon with gray-green growths that he knew as old-man's beard. Through it, thirty-five feet down and away, he could make out the Apache.

Sam rose to a crouch and drew his knife. It seemed strangely heavy, and he tilted it one way and then another, watching a ray of sunlight play in the blade. He rasped his thumb across the sharp edge and the weapon shook in his grip. The whetstone in his war bag had done its job, but there had been nothing with which to hone Sam's courage.

Then he remembered why he was here, and he steadied himself. A man already dead had no reason to fear dying.

Picking up a dead limb, Sam snapped it in two. The Apache glanced around but disregarded it; the horse frequently shifted position. But when Sam popped a limb a second time and then a third, the warrior lay aside his woolen blanket and approached through the snow.

With the Mescalero's every step, Sam could see the sun gleaming in the Remington carbine. He could see the gaudy headband of red flannel, and below it a face hideously painted in streaks of white and black. But most of all, he could see the heartless eyes of a butcher who had been party to a murder that had taken away Sam's soul.

He just hoped that Jonesy was vigilant and would do as promised.

The Apache was only strides away when Jonesy's shrieking epithet exploded from down the ravine. The warrior spun away, and Sam broke from his hiding place and lunged for him.

But Sam hadn't counted on a snowdrift slowing his attack.

With a cry he met a rifle barrel swinging in his direction, and then he was at close quarters, falling upon the fiend with eight months of pent-up hatred.

The rifle fell and they went down, rolling across the barrel in the cold snow, the knife catching sunlight as they struggled over it. Sam shed the grip of one hand on his wrist, only to see an Apache blade flash up from the warrior's waist. For a moment, all seemed lost, and then a shadow fell over them and the Indian went limp to the thud of a Winchester butt against his skull.

Gasping for breath, Sam rolled away and looked up, finding Jonesy silhouetted against the sun. He was surprised at the ranger's courage, but he felt less thankful than angry.

"You had no right!" Sam climbed up weak and trembling. "He was mine!"

Jonesy seemed perplexed. "What difference does it make?"

Sam stepped away from the Apache so he could see Jonesy's deformed features without looking into the sun. "All you was after was somethin' to brag to Mary Jane about!"

"I still don't understand why it should matter."

"Damn it, that son of hell was mine!"

For a minute or two, they continued to argue, but while they did, something else was happening, and the New Jersey native was the first to notice.

"There!"

Sam wheeled. The Apache was up and staggering across the narrow crest in a daze, his scalp dripping blood in the snow.

"I have him!" Jonesy yelled, his carbine swinging up abreast of Sam.

"No!"

Sam knocked the barrel aside and gave chase across the snow, his knife poised to kill silently. Some corner of the bewildered Apache's mind still must have functioned, for the warrior hesitated as he reached the snowy rimrock. There, just shy of the terrifying precipice, he sank to his knees, a helpless figure shaking his head pitifully as he tried to regain his senses.

But Sam showed no mercy as he overtook the Indian. With a cry that could be heard across all the months since Bass Canyon, he plunged the knife between the shoulder blades. He drove it deeper and twisted, the most personal of kills. He kept the blade there through all the terrible squirming and gurgling, and as the body collapsed to the snow, he could feel the death throes through the bone handle.

Sam stepped back and looked at the blade. It dripped with another man's blood, and there was much more of it pooling before him. A minute ago, the snow-covered rimrock had been pristine, but now with its stark contrast of red against white, it was as horrid as it was beautiful.

Sam lifted his gaze to the cliff and the shining beds of salt far below, and then up to the bluest of skies staring down at him. Across so many dark days and fitful nights he had anticipated this moment, but now that it was here, he felt nothing.

Nothing!

Elizabeth was just as dead, and even if he wiped every Mescalero off the face of the Earth, she would still be just as dead— and so would he, deep inside.

CHAPTER 11

Nejeunee's sacrifice of her dignity may have spared the People from the ghost-cold, but the spirits were still displeased.

As soon as the *Ndé* band gained the Diablo crest in early morning, Gian-nah-tah stood on the frozen rimrock and again sought the power to find enemies. With arms outstretched, he faced *Sháa,* the sun, and prayed for *Bik'egu'indáán* to show him the *Indaa.* He caught sunlight in his upturned palms and chanted desperately, but no matter how many directions he turned, *Bik'egu'indáán* continued to withhold the power.

Gian-nah-tah rode away as a man twice destroyed, his shoulders slouched and his head hanging. Nah-kay-yen the *gutaaln* and all the other *Ndé* who followed him north along the summit ridge did so in grave concern, their confidence in him no longer merely in doubt, but shattered. Nejeunee could see it in their faces, and in the way they too slumped on their horses.

Gian-nah-tah had brought it on himself, something that Nejeunee understood well as the only marriageable woman. Only after she had set her blouse afire had the four winds warmed the darkness—an indication that she must have grieved the *Gáhé* by persisting in mourning. Now it was clear that the spirits still held Gian-nah-tah culpable for blaspheming the traditions of courtship, if not for committing outright sorcery. If any *Ndé* had used his power for evil rather than good, Nejeunee knew it to be Gian-nah-tah.

Maybe the sins of the long-ago salt basin were just now catching up with him.

Unfortunately, his penance was also judgment against all of them. Without his power to find enemies, no one knew if the *Indaa* still followed, and if they did, how far behind they might be. Gian-nah-tah's only recourse had been to station Quick Talker's husband, Klo-sen, where they had summited, so that he might watch for pursuit and bring warning.

In one way, Nejeunee reveled in Gian-nah-tah's humiliation, for his standing among the *Ndé* was so dependent on his special power. If not for Little Squint Eyes, whose safety was all that mattered, she would have mocked this killer of innocent *señoras*. After all, it was the way of *Ndé* women to motivate the men by upbraiding them when they failed.

But only a woman as spiteful as One Who Frowns could do so and criticize Nejeunee at the same time.

"Your man's weak," One Who Frowns said as they rode abreast. With hoofbeats deadened by snow, her voice must have carried even to Gian-nah-tah. "His power is no more. He's like a pitiful old woman. He turns around on the rock like a blind child. You're even weaker for choosing him."

"*Idzúút'i,*" Nejeunee said quietly. "Go away."

"The power to find enemies—hmph! Any man among the *Ndé* has greater power. He couldn't find *itsá,* the eagle, if it perched on his head."

One Who Frowns was so pleased with her last comment that she repeated it. As the woman broke into derisive laughter, Nejeunee saw Gian-nah-tah sag even more astride his paint pony. Had it been any other warrior, she might have felt sorry for him.

On a sorrel just ahead of Nejeunee, Quick Talker had been too distraught about their plight to do more than wail and brush her eyes. But incited by One Who Frowns, she too joined the criticism.

"How could you do it, Nejeunee?" she asked as she turned. "How could you pick him? His power is gone!"

"She's a fool," said One Who Frowns.

"We'll die like she-we-cannot-speak-of!" cried Quick Talker, whose grief for Brushing Against was still strong.

"Nejeunee's child will be the next one the owls take," One Who Frowns was quick to add.

"The *Indaa*—they're many and Klo-sen my husband is just one!" Quick Talker continued. "The *Gáhé* are upset and won't protect him as he watches from the mountain. Nejeunee! How could you choose someone who must have made them angry?"

Nejeunee knew the consequences of losing the blessings of the spirits, but she could endure no more from Quick Talker.

"Who is it told me to rap him with a stick?" Nejeunee reminded her. " 'Next time you walk by, do it'—isn't that what you said?"

Quick Talker began to weep more, but Nejeunee wasn't finished.

"That's how you got your husband, you told me. Don't you remember?"

"I never!" sobbed Quick Talker.

"Does my sister have the memory of a field mouse? Four mornings later you were cooking for Klo-sen at his *kuughà.*"

"Oh, Nejeunee, how could you be so mean? The owls may have already come for Klo-sen!"

Maybe they had, and maybe they hadn't. But Nejeunee knew what it was like to lose the one who was above all others. Her eyes began to sting, and she wanted to tell Quick Talker she was sorry. But Quick Talker had already fallen across her horse's neck with sobs so loud that she wouldn't have heard.

For a long while, Quick Talker rode that way, letting her sorrel nod along behind Nah-kay-yen's horse. She didn't look up even as the old *gutaaln* rattled beads of turquoise and chanted to his spirit animal, the great cat whose claws he had survived. But Nejeunee saw every detail: a medicine man's face more withered on one side than ever, an arm so crippled that he could no longer wave the feathers of eagles, fingers so stricken that taking a pinch of *tádidíné* between thumb and forefinger was a challenge.

Facing the sun, from whom he claimed his strongest power, Nah-kay-yen blew the yellow powder into the air and sang even more fervently.

> "Do not let us die, o *Sháa.*
> O *Sháa,* do not let us die."

Nah-kay-yen's wavering voice grew weaker the longer he prayed, but finally it awakened something in Quick Talker. Collecting herself, she sat up to watch and listen. Eventually, the weary chant became a whisper and then went silent as the old man's shoulders bent and his chin dropped to his chest.

"Gutaaln," Quick Talker asked, "is there nothing you can do?"

At first, Nah-kay-yen did not answer, as though it was pointless to respond. When his words did come, they were as lifeless as a man whose spirit was broken.

"The *Gáhé* have forsaken us," he said. "They deny me the power of lightning and *ídói,* the great cat. Even *Sháa,* the sun, hides its strength."

"Help us, *gutaaln,*" pleaded Quick Talker, her emotion all but exhausted. "Please help us!"

His head still hanging, he looked over his shoulder at her with wide, wild eyes.

"No one can help a People already dead."

Overcome with fear, Nejeunee scanned the sky, knowing there was nothing she could do to fight away the owls when they came for Little Squint Eyes.

They rode on, a People without hope, stripped of strength and will. Nejeunee had felt this way only once before, on that numbing day when she had walked with warriors as they had carried he-who-cannot-be-mentioned to the cleft in the rock for burial. Now she followed another dark, lonely path that wouldn't end until she and Little Squint Eyes joined him in the afterworld.

Following the meandering Diablo backbone, they trailed alongside the sheer precipice on their right and the snowy descents and brushy canyons on their left. Nejeunee could feel the waning strength of her small roan as it carried her up steep rises of two hundred feet and down again, a course through rock and ice that demanded more than her animal had to give.

In one respect, the summit ridge was like the top of the world, for Nejeunee could look down on clouds that cast shadows across the salt flats. What she couldn't understand was how a hogback so lofty and frozen could make her feel as if she rode through *infierno,* the fiery trenches of judgment.

This was a place fit for witches, and chief among them must have been Gian-nah-tah.

In midday he held his horse and let all the *Ndé* pass, and as Nejeunee's roan topped out on another rock-rimmed prominence, she looked back and saw him. Still in place astride his paint, he seemed a helpless figure against the majesty of the snow-capped ridge and the sprawling flats far below. Desperate to draw power from wherever he might, he had his arms spread wide to *yá,* the sky.

Gian-nah-tah disappeared from sight as Nejeunee descended into the next swale, but One Who Frowns did not let anyone forget him. As the miles dragged on, she kept up her ridicule to the swoosh of travois frames against snow, and no one reproached her for it.

In a hollow between two close-set summits, where chalky

rocks and tufts of bullgrass protruded from the snow, One Who Frowns voiced her favorite insult yet again.

"Your man's a fool," she told Nejeunee. "The droppings of the eagle could run down his cheek, and Gian-nah-tah still couldn't find *itsá* perched on his head."

Unexpectedly, Gian-nah-tah rode up behind the older woman. Nejeunee, facing her, saw him first—the same broken warrior who could no longer sit upright on his horse. But he was still as evil as ever, and Nejeunee didn't like what she saw in his single eye.

"Down his cheek," repeated One Who Frowns in delight. "He couldn't—"

Gian-nah-tah pulled abreast on the far side of the woman's horse. Just as she turned, he leaned toward her. As if wielding a war club, he backhanded her in the face—a blow as brutal as it was surprising.

It would have knocked One Who Frowns from her mount if Nejeunee hadn't reached for her. Even so, Nejeunee's support only delayed the inevitable. As Gian-nah-tah rode on, One Who Frowns fell across the neck of her horse and began to slide, a moaning woman dazed and hurt. Smearing blood down the animal's shoulder, she went down hard between the sets of hoofs ready to crush.

"My sister!" exclaimed Quick Talker.

"Take her horse!" cried Nejeunee, swinging off the roan.

Nejeunee dropped to her knees beside the sprawled woman. Nejeunee had never liked One Who Frowns, but they had been sister wives of he-who-cannot-be-mentioned, and that in itself made her worthy of grudging respect. As Nejeunee slipped a hand under her head, blood rushed from One Who Frowns's misshapen nose and painted the snow red.

"Her nose is broken," said Nejeunee.

"My sister! My sister!" Quick Talker continued to cry from her sorrel.

"Hush!" Nejeunee looked up at her dominating the sky. "Make too big a fuss and he'll come back."

From her own garments, Nejeunee found a blue calico cloth as One Who Frowns came to her hands and knees, blood dripping from her lowered head. Weeping with pain, she was a pitiful sight as she sat up groggily. For the sake of their late husband, Nejeunee ached with her. It was all she could do, except watch blue calico turn red as she pressed it against One Who Frowns's nose.

"Why would Gian-nah-tah do such a thing?" Quick Talker was still emotionally wrought, but at least she had the common sense to ask quietly.

Nejeunee looked up but had no answer. If a *Ndé* man failed at something, he was expected to endure the women's criticism and not even comment, much less retaliate.

"The *Gáhé* will be even angrier!" Quick Talker added with a furtive glance around. "They'll stay in their caves and let all of us die!"

One Who Frowns evidently regained her senses, for she slapped Nejeunee's ministering hand out of her face. "Go away!"

Nejeunee withdrew, still holding the soaked cloth. She wanted to be done with this hateful woman, but the compassion she had learned from the kindly *señora* wouldn't let her. As One Who Frowns's nose continued to bleed, Nejeunee extended the cloth.

"Please," she said. "It will stop the flow."

To Nejeunee's surprise, One Who Frowns not only accepted the square of calico and applied it to her nose, but looked up with a muffled *"Ixéhe,"* a term of gratitude.

Nejeunee acknowledged with a nod. "One Who Frowns, your nose is broken. You must let me set it."

"No."

"Please, my sister."

"No."

"It will hurt, but it will be much worse if you do nothing."

It took more persuading, but finally the injured woman agreed. Tightening her jaw, One Who Frowns steeled herself for the pain to come. It was the Apache way, but as Nejeunee took One Who Frowns's nose in her hand and applied pressure, she admired her courage. Tears were in the woman's eyes before Nejeunee succeeded in setting it, but One Who Frowns endured the moment in silence.

As One Who Frowns turned away to suffer privately, Nejeunee considered the blood in the snow and remembered how caring their husband had been. He would have comforted One Who Frowns, and Nejeunee found herself stretching a hand toward her. Maybe One Who Frowns had always been in an impossible situation: a childless older woman forced to compete with someone of prime childbearing years. In no way did that excuse her vile treatment of Nejeunee, but maybe Nejeunee hadn't been blameless in the matter. How many times had she purposely flaunted her youth before her sister wife?

Edging closer, Nejeunee put her arm around One Who Frowns and began to stroke her long, black hair, and the woman responded by resting her head on Nejeunee's shoulder.

Nejeunee wondered if this would be the last campfire before which she would ever sit with Little Squint Eyes.

It was dusk as he nursed at her breast, and the gloom seemed to rise up out of her soul and settle over this west-lying hollow below the summit ridge. The slope beyond the flames was gentle at first, but grew increasingly steep as it neared the crest, a hundred yards away and seventy-five feet closer to the budding stars. For troubling hours, the *Ndé* had held to the ridge and attained the mountains' highest reaches. Then the long hogback had bent northwest, dramatically yielding its northerly course to sculpted canyons and far-below desert.

Nejeunee and the other women had erected the teepees immediately upon reaching this agave-strewn flat, which backed up to a sharp arroyo that separated it from a moderate rise with cholla and scrub juniper between rock outcrops. In one sense, this was a sheltered place, but Nejeunee felt only misgivings, her doubt and apprehension heightened by the somber mood that hung over camp.

Across the fire, Quick Talker stood weeping for her missing husband. At Nejeunee's left, One Who Frowns sat wincing, her face showing the pain that she wouldn't vocalize. Down the line of crackling fires beyond, men squatted sullenly in bunches—all except for Gian-nah-tah, who sat alone with bowed head at the farthest blaze.

"Klo-sen . . . Klo-sen . . ."

Quick Talker sobbed her husband's name, a lament so mournful that it touched the wellsprings of Nejeunee's heart. He should have caught up with them by now, and the fact that he hadn't done so meant that he probably never would. Nejeunee didn't know what to say to Quick Talker, except that her separation from him might not be long at all.

But Quick Talker already realized it as she lifted her gaze skyward.

"Klo-sen!" she wailed. "You'll never come back to me, but before *Sháa*, the sun, shows its face, I'll go to you!"

Nejeunee looked into the fire, and the flames blurred as though a reflection in stirring water. *I'll go to you.* Quick Talker had given voice to Nejeunee's own abiding hope: that when the time came, Nejeunee would at last pass into the waiting arms of he-who-cannot-be-mentioned.

Little Squint Eyes, his appetite satisfied, began to gurgle and coo as he toyed with the phylactery at her neck. She wondered if *Bik'egu'indáán* would let the two of them remain long enough for her to do as she had planned: remove the forbidden keepsake of he-who-cannot-be-mentioned and let him hold it as she whispered of a father's love.

But maybe Quick Talker's prophecy was also theirs, and before the rising of the sun, she would watch Little Squint Eyes's father tell the child in person.

"*Inádlu,* he laughs," said One Who Frowns.

Indeed, as Little Squint Eyes grasped the small buckskin pouch, he was laughing for the first time ever. But Nejeunee was more surprised by the way One Who Frowns leaned into Nejeunee's shoulder and peered at him with genuine interest. As the moment persisted, something akin to a sense of loss deepened the scoring in the older woman's face, and her welling eyes began to shine in the firelight.

"I have failed two husbands," One Who Frowns whispered with emotion. "A wife should bear *elchínde,* children, and raise them as *Ndé,* and I have failed."

One Who Frowns stretched out a hand and caressed the back of Little Squint Eyes's head. Now her cheek glistened, and Nejeunee felt such compassion that she did what would have been unthinkable a short time ago.

She passed Little Squint Eyes into her arms.

Showing a tenderness that belied everything Nejeunee had thought about her, One Who Frowns cradled him with a bittersweet smile.

"If only . . . ," she sobbed.

With sudden regret, even guilt, Nejeunee wished that she and One Who Frowns had lived together as intimates rather than as bitter competitors.

"You didn't fail, my sister," said Nejeunee. "It was the *Indaa* who denied you. If *yah-ik-tee,* he who is not present, had lived,

Little Squint Eyes would have been yours as much as mine."

They faced one another, two women who had loved—and been loved by—the same man. Then One Who Frowns turned again to their husband's son, and like the sister wives they should have been, she and Nejeunee joined in a quiet lullaby that soothed Nejeunee as much as it did Little Squint Eyes.

CHAPTER 12

The trail in the snow couldn't have been fresher.

Company A had pushed hard ever since Sam had descended far enough down the mountain to summon the rangers waiting in the basin. Once on the crest, he and the others had taken the dead Apache's horse and ridden on, leaving the body stretched out on the bloody rim. Throughout the day, they had persisted in the chase: eight privates following orders, one grieving officer re-fighting a foredoomed war, and one lost and lonely man now burdened by self-doubt.

Franks, who had rallied some in the lower elevations, didn't take well to the thin air. With shoulders bent, he rode wheezing and coughing with almost every pace of a horse that was more scarecrow than the muscled black animal it had been just a few days ago. Yet Franks seemed as determined as ever, even if he was far from clearheaded as Sam took his gray up along the officer's left flank in late afternoon.

"Makin' it all right, Captain?" Sam asked.

"Walter," Franks greeted him.

Sam winced, because this time Franks wasn't asleep.

"It's DeJarnett, Captain. Sam."

"Oh, yes, of course. DeJarnett, those Yankees cannot be far ahead."

"You mean Mescaleros. It's Mescaleros we's after."

"Yes, Mescaleros. Didn't I say . . . ?"

"No, sir, you said—"

"I've got a score to settle," interrupted Franks. "What they took from me . . ."

Sam studied the addled man against a sweeping sky that must have stretched a hundred miles to the eastern horizon. From the sagging posture to the drawn cheeks and weary eyes creased at the corners, Franks was the portrait of privation and illness—a man spent in everything but obsession.

As Sam turned to the trace ahead, watching the beaten snow rise and fall with his horse's gait, he could barely distinguish his own subdued voice from his troubled thoughts.

"Say we do all this," he offered, "take our pound of flesh. It make any difference? You know, in what you and me's been through, what we lost?"

"Maybe my boy's never coming back, but going after his killers this way, I've never been so close to him."

It was the first time Sam had ever heard Franks refer to his son's death. Sam wasn't surprised that the captain continued to confuse Apaches with Yankees, but he hadn't expected a response that spoke so powerfully to his own situation. Franks was right; through every mile of this chase, Elizabeth had lived inside Sam in a way she hadn't since Bass Canyon.

"So what happens when this is done?" Sam pressed. "Is it like losin' who we had all over again?" He stared at a rocky rise that hid the way ahead. "Better we don't ever catch up, if that's how it'll be."

Franks turned to him, and for a moment his distressed eyes must have mirrored Sam's. Then the captain straightened in the saddle, as if from some submerged stock of resolve, and he gigged his horse faster down the vengeance trail.

Left to ride single file, Sam looked into the uncaring sky and dwelled on so many matters he couldn't understand. Everything he had done since failing Elizabeth in that canyon—eight months spent reeling from one memory to another in search of peace—had been futile. Utterly futile. It had taken an enemy's blood on his hands to realize it, and yet here he was, closing in to take revenge on the rest of the Mescaleros, and for what?

Just an emptiness so great that not even the sky could fill it.

You's here for a reason.

They came for the first time in days, his father's long-ago words as the two had sat before a dog-eared book aglow in lamplight. The statement had been so easy to believe in boyhood, and so impossible to accept now. If only there had never been a Bass Canyon . . .

Behind Sam, Boye was preaching aloud to himself, something he had been doing increasingly often. In spite of his youth and unrelenting death wish, Boye seemed to know things that many people didn't, and Sam found himself dropping back abreast of the ranger's jaded roan. Sam's presence didn't seem to affect Boye's concentration, for he kept up his quiet sermon.

"You make me think of my father," interrupted Sam.

Boye turned, his peach fuzz shining in the rays of the low-hanging sun.

"A preacher man, he is?"

"Died when I was thirteen but used to talk about things a lot. You know, the whys of life and all that."

" 'Fear God, and keep His commandments,' " quoted Boye. " 'For this is the whole duty of man.' "

Something about the smugness with which Boye said it touched a nerve in Sam, and he could feel his pulse begin to pound.

"My father wasn't no preacher, but he'd say somethin' like that too, like he had it all figured out." Sam gave a bitter half-laugh. "Thought the world of him, but if he'd ever been in my place, he'd've knowed better."

He rode on in silence, staring ahead into nothingness, the rhythm of the hoofs tolling away a life as meaningless as it was empty. As disquieting thoughts crushed what little promise he might have had left, he whirled on Boye with questions.

"What the hell's today about? Or yesterday? Or tomorrow, if there is one? Soon as I think I have a reason for bein'—chasin' down those Mescaleros, wipin' them out—I start thinkin', what difference it make? Somebody lives or dies, so what?"

Boye went wide-eyed, but Sam wasn't finished.

"What makes livin' any better than dyin'? Best we can do is just get by, one moment to the next, till we don't have to put up with it no more."

Boye started to respond, but his face grew troubled and he looked down. "Sinned like David, I have," he whispered as if in prayer, "and hypocrite I be to think I could shepherd even this flock of one."

Then he lifted his gaze to the sky and closed his eyes, and when he opened them to Sam again, his features seemed different somehow—firmer at the jaw, stronger around the mouth. For the moment, at least, it was as if he shrugged off the guilt and showed a confidence Sam had never seen in him before.

"Serve," Boye said. "That's what we be here for, to serve. If your days be dark, do something for somebody that needs it. Help them out, and it'll be you that it helps too."

Consumed by terrible blackness, Sam didn't think a ray of light would ever find its way again into the hollow where his soul had been. But as he pondered the preacher boy's words, it occurred to him that the only glimmers of hope he had known during this scout had come when he had assisted Captain Franks. Maybe the concept of service wasn't nearly enough to rescue Sam, but it was more than he'd had a moment ago.

"You got a different way of lookin' at things, Boye," said Sam, calming a little. "Guess it was what I was needin' to hear."

Boye looked pleased, for he flashed a smile and straightened in the saddle. Maybe Sam's words were what *he* needed to hear.

"Yes, sir," Boye said with greater vigor, "help somebody else, and ol' sun, it'll shine way down in your heart."

"If that's the case," said Sam, "maybe you oughta not be so hasty offerin' yourself up to get killed. Might be able to dish out some help yourself."

Boye knitted his brow and gave Sam a long stare. "But . . ."

The preacher boy's protest died in the wind, and he looked down toward his saddle horn and went silent. Maybe what Sam had told him was true, and maybe it wasn't, but Sam felt better for having said it.

As the sun sank behind faraway clouds as blue as Elizabeth's eyes, Sam knelt with reins in hand and wondered what life would be like the next time he saw a sun.

In the beaten snow at his knee were horse feces, still faintly warm to his touch.

Sam lifted his gaze down-trail, picturing the passage of those Mescaleros, and then looked around at Franks, who hovered over him from the stirrups of his exhausted horse. Like the men behind him, the captain had stayed in the saddle.

"A hour ago," Sam said quietly. "That's all, just a hour."

Indeed, something was about to happen, and Sam expected it by the time night was done. But would sunrise bring him hope, or just a continuation of the gloom that crept this very moment across the canyons below?

Or maybe he had already seen his last sun.

Franks ordered a dismount, which he accomplished himself only with Sam's discreet help. The captain was even weaker than before, and Sam kept a hand on the stumbling man's arm as he made his way to a large rock and brushed away the snow. Franks sat there coughing and wheezing as the rangers gathered before him.

"Boys," he finally rasped, "they're almost in our sights. I'm guessing they already made camp. That's right where we want them. We'll rest the horses here, and when it's dark I want two of you to reconnoiter."

More breathless than ever, Franks craned to see around Sam, who obliged by stepping aside. Tracing the captain's gaze, Sam studied the bunched men and their animals. There was only one name that Franks mustn't call for reconnaissance duty, only one ranger whose crooked jaw was set tightly in anticipation. Surely Franks wouldn't—

"Jones. Private Jones."

The captain's summons was barely above a whisper, but it seemed to roll across the ridge's every peak and swale.

What the hell's he doing?

Sam only asked it silently, and Jonesy only muttered it, but every word was unmistakable on Jonesy's lips.

"Matto, you as well," Franks added after finding a breath. "Boys, step up here so we can talk."

It was probably fortunate that Franks doubled over with a coughing fit that drowned out Jonesy's protest. Still, as the New Jersey native brushed past, Sam heard it clearly: "Damned if he's sending me again."

Matto, for his part, didn't grumble, but he looked about as surly as Jonesy as the two rangers stopped before the captain.

"It's the dark of the moon," Franks said wearily. "If they've stopped for the night, stay low and you can skyline their teepees against the stars."

Matto pressed a finger against a nostril and blew mucous out his nose. "Devils liable to sneak up on us out there."

"Son, you be careful," said Franks. "The last thing I want is for you to get yourself killed. If anybody's to die, I want it to be a damned Yankee."

Sam flinched. *What the hell, Captain? What in Billy hell?*

For a moment, everything seemed frozen in time. Then Jonesy

whipped out his .45 with a cross-body draw and leveled it between Franks's startled eyes.

"You son of a bitch!" Jonesy cried.

"Hold it!" exclaimed Sam. "He don't mean—"

But the New Jersey native had heard it, and so had everyone in the company except Franks, who looked bewildered as he tried to respond.

"Son—"

Jonesy cut him off. "Anybody dies, it'll be you!"

"Son, I cannot have you speak to me that way."

"Speak to you? I'm putting a bullet in your Yankee-hating brain!" He thumbed back the hammer with an ominous click.

"No!" said Sam. "You got it wrong, Jonesy!"

"Let's you and I discuss this," the captain told Jonesy. "How have I offended you?"

There wasn't a trace of stress in Franks's voice, and Sam didn't see how. For God's sake, he was staring into a muzzle primed to kill.

The longer Jonesy gripped the .45, the more it shook. "Yankee, am I? Damned right I am, and proud of it. My father whipped you once, and I'll do it again. The hell with you and your Walter both!"

Franks's face went dark, exposing a rage so sudden that it must have lurked in his tortured soul. In a split second he had his revolver out at full cock, the muzzle hard against Jonesy's abdomen.

"I'll gutshoot you!" Franks cried. "Talk about my boy and I'll gutshoot you!"

Eternity was a twitch of a finger away for both rangers, one of them a livid madman with bulging eyes and the other a now-sober young man with a face gone white.

Sam had to stop this, but what could he do? If he grabbed either of them, both could die. Good God, what could he do except appeal to their reason?

"It's a mixup!" he said. "Captain don't know what he's sayin'. He meant Indian, not Yankee!"

From behind Sam came Arch's composed voice. "Jonesy, my man, some deeds cannot be undone. Remember thy sweet Mary Jane."

But a .45 in his abdomen had already taken the fight out of Jonesy, who seemed afraid to be the first to back down. "Get his gun out of my belly!"

Sam tried to project calm as he turned his plea to Franks. "Easy, Captain. Please, just listen to me. You said Yankee but meant Mescalero."

Franks looked at Sam but kept his revolver in place.

"Jonesy heard Yankee," explained Sam, "and he thought you was tryin' to kill him. It's Mescaleros we's after, remember? Not Yankees."

Franks's eyes began to relax. "Yes, Mescaleros. That's right, Mescaleros."

He withdrew his weapon and, almost in the same instant, so did Jonesy.

As the captain bent over to labor for air, the New Jersey native stumbled away with a shudder. But Sam was doing some trembling of his own.

As dusk yielded to a troubling blackness, Sam didn't know how Company A could hold together—if it even mattered anymore.

Franks and Jonesy had almost killed one another, but the strife didn't end there. Sam and Arch were still at odds over Matto, and Matto wanted nothing to do with them. Matto's partners in the abandoned plan to desert were at odds with Matto, and to avoid their questions, Matto wanted nothing to do with them either. Matto was also at odds with Boye, while Boye seemed in conflict with himself.

But there was more going on than discord. With a possible fight with Apaches at hand, everyone was on edge, and the need to maintain stealth ruled out lighting a smoke that might calm a man's nerves. All Sam could do was gnaw on jerky and pace in the dark while he waited for Matto and a second ranger to return from reconnaissance. With Jonesy so shaken, a tow-headed ranger had volunteered to go in his place.

"Been thinking about what you told me, I have."

In a night so dark, Sam didn't know that Boye was beside him until he spoke. Now he saw the young man as a silhouette against the stars on the horizon.

"You and me both ought to be restin' up, Boye. Hard to do, I guess, when we might be goin' up against Apaches."

"Was me killed that poor girl, I did, same as pulling a trigger."

Sam had already heard Boye tell it, but he let the preacher boy talk.

"Wouldn't stand beside her, no, sir. Whore, they called her, and my part in it I hid like David with Bathsheba."

Boye paused, and for some reason Sam felt compelled to speak. "My father used to read to me about it."

"Committed adultery and murder both, David and me. Been thinking hard about the way David up and repented. He sure done it, yes, sir, and the Good Lord forgive him and called him a man after His own heart."

Forgiveness. Boye spoke as if he was on the way to finding it. But as the silhouette faded into the night as discreetly as it had come, Sam relived again his failure to act during Elizabeth's final moments and wondered if a man could ever forgive himself.

About midnight, Matto and the tow-headed ranger rode in with a reconnaissance report that Sam listened to with mixed feelings. No more than two miles ahead, up and over yet another crest peak, the Mescaleros were in camp. Just a day ago, Sam's anticipation would have soared, but retribution now seemed less a passion than an obligation that might rob him of Elizabeth a second time. As Franks had made him realize, she had been an increasingly powerful presence throughout the chase, and he never wanted that intimacy to end.

Franks, surprisingly clearheaded for the moment, held a council of war and presented a plan of attack. Sam admired his attention to detail, which included factors such as the lay of the land and the angle of the coming sunrise. More than two decades may have passed since the captain's last Indian fight, but even ill and exhausted, he had a poise that inspired confidence.

The company dispersed to get a few hours of sleep, but it seemed to Sam that he had barely dozed off before it was time to get up. Within minutes, he was astride the gray and marching with the company for a rendezvous with revenge. Now, more than ever, Elizabeth seemed to be present with every nod of the animal's head, but he couldn't tell if she urged him on or pleaded another cause. Was she imploring him to ride with caution? Or was she trying to tell him that she was gone and never coming back, no matter what he did to those Apaches?

He could see her lips move in the dark, but no matter how hard he concentrated, he couldn't make out the words.

Sam didn't realize he was asleep until a sound from alongside woke him. He turned, looking for Elizabeth, and found only the moving shadow of a rider with the hushed voice of Boye. Sam could distinguish only a phrase here and there, but he pieced together enough to realize that Boye prayed for the souls of the heathens they were about to face.

Soon, the rider ahead of Sam whispered an order that had come down the line: Maintain absolute quiet. Franks no doubt had given it, but even from Sam's position in the march, he could hear the captain's muffled coughs. Nevertheless, Sam passed the order on to Boye before focusing on the great shadow that blotted out the stars ahead. This must be the massive rise Matto and the tow-headed ranger had reported, a site where the ridge thrust sharply upward to a rounded summit higher than any other point they had navigated in the Diablos. Considering the amount of horizon it hid, the mountain was broad as well as lofty.

At its base, the company dismounted. Sam, securing the gray to a scrub piñon, slid his Winchester out of the saddle scabbard and stuffed his pockets with cartridges for both the carbine and his revolver. From here on, they would be on foot, and every extra round might be critical.

Sam didn't know how Franks had managed to step out of the stirrup, but his was the whispering voice of the upright silhouette before which everyone gathered.

"Walter," Franks said. "You stay put. This is a man's war."

Sam turned to the shadow beside him, and the shadow seemed to turn to him. He didn't know who it was, but everyone had to be thinking the same thing: Here they were, about to put their lives on the line at the orders of a man who was in another time and place.

Sam knew only one thing to do.

"Captain," he whispered, "better stay with Walter and guard the horses."

Franks stifled a cough. "Yes, the horses."

Sam scanned the dark figures alongside. "Boys, it's up to us."

For a moment all the dark figures stayed in place. Then one separated, followed by a second—Matto and the other reconnoiterer, he supposed—and within moments Sam was climbing a steep slope with eight men he couldn't see.

As his boots dug into snow, however, a light that was only a memory seemed to lead the way. It was a sliver of sunlight, dancing against blue calico. The locket from which it reflected had bounced against Elizabeth's breast as she had fled through Bass Canyon, and then that dying Apache had snatched it from her neck.

No larger than a seated liberty quarter, the silver ornament was as lost as Elizabeth. Still, he could almost feel its polished contours between his quaking fingers again, a weak-kneed cowboy releasing its catch on a long-ago day and opening it for a pretty miss under a big live oak. Too backward to ask her any other way, he had let the engraver choose the formal words inside:

May I
Have your
Hand in marriage?

The locket had cost Sam a month's pay, but the answer he had found in her eyes would have been worth a lifetime of eighteen-hour days in the saddle.

Now, three years later, that's all he had left: memories. No Elizabeth, no locket, no shred of hope for today and even less for tomorrow. Just memories that prodded him on, almost against his will.

After a grueling climb, the ground leveled off, and Sam could see three fires aglow on a lower level ahead. Distance was always difficult to judge at night, but he figured that he and the company had closed to within half a mile. Around Sam, the silhouettes of rangers dropped into a creep, and so did he, knowing that any Apache lookout might skyline them.

From the middle of the company came the sudden *click-click* of a Winchester lever, and every silhouette froze. Sam pivoted with his carbine at his hip and leveled it on a man-like form ten paces to his right. There were other forms as well, peering out of the night, a small army ready to ambush. Almost too late, he recognized the shadows for what they were.

"Spanish daggers!" he whispered.

He heard a murmur pass through the men, but somehow no one squeezed off a shot.

They went on, a shaken company of rangers bearing to the right of the fires as the wind soughed a lament. Little by little, day began to break, although Sam had a limited view of the east. A lot of shadows roamed the intervening night, obscuring the horizon's glow—the work of outcrops and swells in the summit, he figured.

When the company neared a point overlooking the fires, the men in the lead crouched lower and stopped, far too soon to suit Sam. From here, he could see muted streaks of red back in the east, allowing him to gauge the angle of the coming sunrise. Advancing, he came abreast of the ranger in front. *Not here,* Sam wanted to say, but all he could do was tug on the man's arm and proceed in a crawl.

As he slowly led the way along the undulating ridge, the mountain pushed back, its snow numbing his fingers, its spiny cholla and ocotillo clawing his coat. Once, he planted a knee on a pincushion cactus, all but crippling him. But he pushed on, driven by memories that flashed like images through the spokes of a rumbling wagon wheel in a canyon of death.

Finally, Sam wormed his way to the mountain's far slope and found the kind of strategic position for which the captain had hoped. Down and away to his left lay the campfires, flickering in a gloomy flat, while to his right, past a jutting outcrop that he saw only in silhouette, the eastern horizon burned orange in anticipation of the sunrise. Most importantly, the first rays seemed sure to strike the campfires—and Sam now had eight men with Winchesters flattening themselves almost directly between the camp and the imminent sunrise.

Sam, down on his belly, peered through the long, flexible blades of a beargrass clump. A hundred yards away and maybe seventy-five feet below, three figures draped in blankets tended small fires that rippled in the wind. The firelight cast a soft glow against a row of teepees just beyond, while fifteen or twenty horses or mules were staked nearby.

There was something serene about the camp, a charmingly simple quality that was strangely appealing. For a moment, Sam had to remind himself that these were the ruthless Apaches who had upset his entire world. What the hell was the matter with him? Had these animals hesitated for even a moment before swooping down on Bass Canyon?

Searching for bitterness, he found it, and with it came a hatred greater than any he had ever known. They had taken Elizabeth away from him, and they would pay.

Sam shook with rage as he glanced over his shoulder. A pinpoint of light had just broken the flaming horizon. In three or four minutes the full sunburst of January 29, 1881 would flood the camp—and just as Franks had said, the Mescaleros would be blinded as Company A attacked out of the sunrise.

As Sam watched and waited, he consciously slowed his breathing, knowing he must in order to draw a bead on those devils. But the sun seemed suspended, half above the horizon and half below. Would it never rise higher? How long must he be caught up in this purgatory of endless waiting?

Suddenly the sun was there, a swollen fire exploding over faraway crags in full glory, an orb too dazzling to look upon. Whirling to the camp, Sam whispered to the ranger at his left, a whisper passed down the line from one man to another.

Captain's orders!

Sam didn't look to see, but he knew that every ranger did as he did: rose and knelt with one knee to the snow. He threw the rifle butt against his shoulder and supported it with a forearm against his upraised thigh. At this distance, the camp was at the limit of a Winchester's range, but he hadn't been this close to those butchers since he had lain in Bass Canyon and done nothing.

He worked the lever with a double click, and the hammers of eight Winchesters joined his in springing back, the firing pins primed to snap forward against .44 cartridges. He looked down the barrel at a smoke-shrouded teepee and held his aim for a moment, wondering if he would ever again feel this close to Elizabeth—wondering with dread because he already knew the answer.

"Now!" he cried, and he squeezed the trigger.

CHAPTER 13

The roar was like thunder.

Stooped over sotol hearts roasting in the coals, a startled Nejeunee looked up into the brilliance of *Sháa*, the sun, as quick groans came from the teepee behind her. Wheeling to the flap, she heard a second roar and more groans, and then there was bedlam.

"*Indaa!*" came a shout.

Blanket-draped and bleeding warriors burst from the teepee, simultaneous with a chorus of yells from the ridge across the fire. From the cradleboard at Nejeunee's back, Little Squint Eyes began to cry as she spun from the teepee and looked up through the rising smoke. Down the snowy mountainside charged *Indaa*, maintaining a battle cry that echoed across the hollow.

Confused and shaken, Nejeunee turned one way and then another, not knowing what to do. Suddenly Quick Talker and One Who Frowns were with the wounded *Ndé* milling beside Nejeunee. The older woman seemed too stricken with fear to utter a sound, but Quick Talker repeatedly called out for the husband she believed awaited her on the other side of death.

More gunfire erupted, individual shots rather than a volley, and *Ndé* began to fall. Nah-kay-yen the *gutaaln* went down at Nejeunee's feet, the first to validate his own concerns about the fate of a People already dead. Two other men dropped almost as quickly, one of them sprawling lifelessly across the roasting so-

139

Patrick Dearen

tol hearts. A fourth warrior managed to reach the horses and leap astride a paint, only to collapse across the animal's neck and slide headfirst to the hoofs.

For a moment more, stunned *Ndé* huddled about Nejeunee, and then a warrior broke for the arroyo and rising slope behind the teepees. Others fled in his wake, leaving Quick Talker standing in the line of fire, incapable of doing anything but wail. One Who Frowns brushed past Quick Talker and rushed after the men but made only a few steps before an unseen force twisted her half-around. Nejeunee didn't know how One Who Frowns stayed on her feet, but she did, a pitiful figure clutching her side and hobbling on, laying a blood trail in the snow.

One warrior alone stood his ground. From beside the staked horses, Gian-nah-tah shouldered his Winchester and fired three quick shots at the *Indaa*. Evidently out of ammunition, he too fled. He momentarily disappeared in the arroyo behind the teepees before reappearing beyond, enemy gunfire chasing him up the agave-studded rise. Bullets shook cholla stalks and scrub juniper and sprayed snow against his heels, but somehow he eluded even the slugs that ricocheted off outcrops and whizzed back through camp.

To Nejeunee, the sequence of events came rapid-fire, images and sounds playing out almost simultaneously as the smoke from campfires and rifle muzzles hung in her throat. It was too much to process, but Nejeunee acted instinctively.

"Run, my sister!" she shouted, taking Quick Talker's arm.

The two of them bolted after the others to the crying of Little Squint Eyes. Ahead, One Who Frowns sank to the ground and began to squirm, painting the snow a stark red. As Nejeunee neared, the wounded woman made eye contact and stretched out an imploring hand. It was heartbreaking, and so was the pain in her wrenched face. But there was nothing Nejeunee could do as she passed, not even when One Who Frowns

140

moaned Nejeunee's name. The *Indaa* were about to kill Little Squint Eyes, just as they had his father, and Nejeunee would do whatever necessary to save him.

But Quick Talker had no such responsibility to a child, and seeing their sister bleed out was apparently too much for someone so emotional. She pulled free of Nejeunee's grasp, and when Nejeunee glanced back she saw Quick Talker standing over the dying woman and wailing as the bullets splattered the snow all around her.

The arroyo's sharp bank was slippery, and Nejeunee lost her footing as she started down. She plopped to a hip and a hand, the impact lifting the weight of the cradleboard off her shoulders. But her arms were still through the straps, and the willow frame dragged behind as she slid down and spilled off a limestone shelf less than eighteen inches high.

Her shoulder met the rocky bed, a place that shielded her from direct gunfire but not from the screaming ricochets. She started to get up, only to see a black recess under the shelf. Six or seven feet long, it offered the kind of hope that the exposed mountainside ahead did not.

Sitting up quickly, she removed the cradleboard to the rising shouts of the *Indaa*. She tried to soothe Little Squint Eyes with a soft word, but he continued to cry as she squeezed inside the musty overhang and pulled the cradleboard in after her. She was prone, her cheek against underlying rock, the only position possible in a space so confined. Still, there was just enough room to rock the cradleboard as she calmed Little Squint Eyes the way only a mother's voice could.

Quick Talker's wailing persisted as the gunfire grew sporadic, and then both seemed to end at the same time. But now came strange words, neither Apache nor Spanish, and long, frightening shadows began to dance like evil spirits against what little of the snowy far bank that Nejeunee could see.

For minutes that seemed hours, Nejeunee held her position, the cold rock on three sides numbing her. Any moment the *Indaa* would find her. Like the soulless beasts they were, they would drag Little Squint Eyes out first and take him by the heels in preparation for dashing him against the ledge. They would make her witness it from her place in the overhang, and the shadow wraiths on the bank across from her would mimic the heartless act. Before true death could spare her, she would experience in her heart the most terrible of all deaths, and there was nothing she could do but pray to Jesucristo and wait for it to happen.

Then Little Squint Eyes began to gurgle and coo, abruptly silencing the nearest voice that spoke in a strange tongue. In utter terror, Nejeunee did her best to quiet Little Squint Eyes, but it was too late.

Through the rock above came the resonant drum of boots coming down the bank.

Blood against snow.

As Sam had fired, and fired again, he had been back at Bass Canyon. His ears were still ringing, but now it was over—not just the surprise attack, but so many other things that he didn't know how to digest. And yet he had to, for the carnage around him demanded it.

They lay about camp, five lifeless forms in gaudy calico and filthy woolen blankets, and a gutshot sixth Mescalero who writhed in snow no longer white. Eight or nine other Apaches had crossed an arroyo and fled up the far slope, but they had escaped at a terrible cost, judging by the trails stained red. Whether the wounded bled out or not, Sam doubted that any of them would survive after Company A torched their stores and killed their animals. One thing seemed clear: this band of devils would never commit another outrage.

So why was Sam so nauseated by everything he saw? Through dark nights and darker days, he had lived in anticipation of this moment. How could he be even more troubled than on the day before, when he had killed in the most personal of ways?

He lifted his gaze above the defiled snow. Except for the rise ahead and the ridge behind, he had a boundless view. From what he had learned about this country, he could identify the dramatic, sunlit cliffs of the Guadalupes thirty miles to the north, the isolated cones of the Cornudas farther to the west, the dominating ridge of Eagle Mountain to the south, the sprawling Davis Mountains to the southeast. It was as if he looked down from the wings of an eagle, so why couldn't he see inside himself?

"Man's inhumanity to man."

Sam turned, finding Arch at his right shoulder. "What?"

Only after Sam asked the question did he realize that Arch wasn't necessarily addressing him. After all, they hadn't spoken since Sam had used the worst kind of leverage to keep Matto from deserting the previous morning. Even now, Sam was sickened by the thought of the sexual abuse to which the Mexican madam had subjected Matto in his boyhood. What was it Arch had said a couple of days ago? That Matto still hated every woman who wasn't fair-skinned?

Arch, to his credit, didn't leave Sam's question unanswered. Instead, he nodded to the dead and dying. "The beauty of the scenery, marred only by man's inhumanity to man."

As Sam looked things over again, there was no denying it, even though Sam himself had been instrumental in causing it. As his eyes settled on the gutshot Apache, squirming in silent anguish beside another bloody figure whose suffering was over, he was struck by a terrible realization.

"Squaws, Arch," he said in disbelief. "We shot squaws and all."

"Indeed."

"Damn us to hell. Squaws."

"What is it you expected, Samuel? Franks's orders were to fire indiscriminately into the teepees."

"Those two was shot in the open."

"There was no way to distinguish them. One and all were draped in blankets."

Sam tried to tell himself that. He tried to convince himself that killing women along with the men had been justified in the fog of battle. But no matter how much he wanted to believe it, he couldn't dismiss the fact that these women had been just as defenseless as Elizabeth.

"We shouldn't've done it thataway," he said, unable to take his eyes off the writhing woman. "We's no better than they are, killin' women like that."

"This is what you wanted, isn't it? Preemptive action?" Arch's tone was strangely challenging. "Isn't that how you prevailed on my decency? Or was that a mere ruse?"

Nothing else could have pried Sam's focus off the wounded woman, and he turned in surprise.

"If it was vengeance you sought," Arch went on, "you now have it in the extreme, and you're more responsible than anyone. So you can cease and desist with your hypocrisy and false piety."

For a moment, Sam just stared at him. "Arch, get the hell away from me."

Sam started away, but Arch's words followed.

" 'Regret, remorse, and shame—many and sharp the num'rous ills inwoven with our frame.' "

Sam figured it was just as well that he had no idea what any of that meant. In a near daze, he wandered toward the surviving woman, his head down, the crimson stains in the snow a blur. Gun smoke lingered, collecting in his throat, and so did the pungent odor of singed flesh back at a fire; no one had dragged the dead Apache off the coals.

Sam stopped before the wounded woman, his boots almost touching the dark discharge that had soaked her calico blouse and discolored the snow. He could only imagine the pain she endured, and he wondered if he had been the one who had shot her. Even if he hadn't, a few feet away was a younger woman, stretched out dead, and he couldn't forget all the blanketed figures he had seen down the barrel of his Winchester.

What was the matter with him? Every one of these butchers had contributed to what had happened in Bass Canyon, so how the hell could he feel even a twinge of guilt?

But that wasn't the worst of it, and across time and distance and the black divide that no one could span, Sam silently cried out for Elizabeth, and more.

I'm here, right where I promised I'd be! I buried you and told you what I'd do, and now I'm here!

He was here, all right, but there was truth in what Arch had implied the day before. He was just a pathetic little figure driven so long by vengeance that, now that it was over, he had no reason to take another step.

"Well, looky what we got here—a damned squaw and her papoose."

The sharp arroyo wasn't far away, and from where Sam stood, he couldn't see over the rocky rim dusted with white. But Matto's voice from the arroyo bed was unmistakable, and so was a woman's cry in a language Sam couldn't understand.

"Come outa there!" he heard Matto say.

A baby began to wail, and the voice of the woman grew louder, frantic, increasingly desperate.

"Let me have that brat!" ordered Matto. "I'll put a stop to that squallin'!"

Sam didn't know the situation below, but he wasn't about to compound the company's misdeeds.

"If you got a baby there, don't hurt it!" he shouted, starting for the bank. "You hear me, Matto?"

But the commotion continued, and as Sam's field of vision widened with his approach, he found Matto clutching a baby upside down by the foot and fending off a young Apache woman at close quarters. Her straight black hair flew as she flailed away at him, a mother fighting for her child. But Matto was so much larger and stronger, and he seemed to delight in keeping the baby just out of her reach. There was cruelty to his teasing, and no one had to tell Sam that Matto would end this in the most heartless of ways.

"Quit it!" Sam yelled, pausing at the drop-off.

But Matto seemed completely unaware, his attention fixed solely on the Apache woman. Or could it be that it wasn't she he saw at all, but a dark-skinned madam in a long-ago whorehouse?

"Mi niño! Por favor, mi niño!"

Even as the Apache woman pleaded for her child with Spanish words that Sam understood, Matto kept up his ruthless taunt. But maybe the ranger underestimated her, for her hand went inside her clothing and reappeared with a glinting knife.

Sam's warning was still in his throat when the blade flashed against Matto's overcoat. It must have pierced the thick wool, for Matto flinched and drew his left arm close to his ribs.

"What the hell!"

"Look out!" cried Sam.

Just in time, Matto dodged a second thrust and stumbled back. His heel caught on a rock and he began to go down, leaving himself vulnerable as she lunged at him again. But this time her concern was for the dangling baby, and just as it seemed certain that Matto would drag the infant down to the crushing rocks, the woman snatched the child away.

Matto went down with a loud grunt, his boots flying up as he rocked back on his spine. The spill must have taken the wind out of him, and for a moment he wallowed in the icy rocks as if searching for air.

The woman withdrew, displaying a mother's tenderness as she clutched the baby to her breast, and an Apache's ferocity as she brandished the knife. As Sam slid down the bank, her frightened eyes darted from Matto to Sam and back to Matto. Her alarm about Matto was justified, for just as Sam broke between the two, the sprawled ranger reached under his coat for the .45 that Sam knew was in its holster.

"Leave it there!" cried Sam, swinging the barrel of his Winchester around to the woman.

As the morning rays winked in the twisting knife, Sam stared at her, and she stared back. She was no more than twenty, and with her shapely facial features, he would have considered her pretty if she hadn't been a Mescalero. But she looked more Mexican than Indian, for she didn't have the rounded face and drooping nose of the Pueblo scouts back at Fort Davis. Her cheekbones were softer as well, and her skin lacked the rich, coppery complexion common to the scouts.

Still, everything else about her cried "Apache!"—the crimson bow of calico in her hair, the dark-blue tattoo of a new moon on her forehead, the beaded necklace with tiny, dangling mirrors flashing sunlight. Maybe from a hiding place in Bass Canyon, she had celebrated the attack that had robbed Sam of hope. Maybe she had watched and planned for the day when her child would perpetrate his own cowardly act against someone innocent. Maybe breeding-stock such as she was more to blame than anything for all the tears wreaked by her merciless band.

The hell with this dirty squaw and her whelp! Shoot them both and be done with it! They stood for every renegade Mescalero's hopes for a tomorrow, so finish them once and for all!

But the crying of the baby, his bare skin exposed to the frigid morning, touched a place inside Sam that he didn't know existed anymore. His own child would have been about as old now. Elizabeth should have been cradling him, sheltering him from the winter chill in their New Mexico home. Even now, Sam could almost see Elizabeth in the actions of this Apache woman, a mother giving her all in sacrifice for the most innocent and helpless.

"Out of my way! I'm killin' the whore!"

Checking over his shoulder, Sam looked down into the wavering muzzle of Matto's revolver. The ranger lay back on a hip and an elbow, an awkward position from which to cock a .45. But maybe the support of a rock under his elbow was vital to someone who trembled in fury the way Matto did.

"She drawed blood!" Matto exclaimed. "Blood, damn her!"

Sam didn't doubt it, considering how Matto kept his left arm against his rib cage. How easy it would be to step aside and let someone else do the dirty deed. One squaw was already dead and another gravely wounded, so what difference would a third make?

Elizabeth! Elizabeth! What would you have me do?

There was no Elizabeth to tell him, but as he faced the knife again, the baby's crying and the pleading eyes of his mother were answer enough.

Without turning, Sam shouted at Matto. "Put that gun away! We killed enough squaws!"

"But she—"

"Damn it! Do like I say!"

"The hell I will!"

Another look over his shoulder found Matto scrambling to his feet, but Sam was determined. "Two ways you can shut me up about Juarez. And the other one's to kill me!"

Matto lost all color, but his revolver remained a deadly force.

For a moment, Sam wondered if he had pressed the matter too far, if he would hear Matto's gunshot and see the snow fly up in the last instant of life. Then Matto relaxed his grip on the Colt and hung his head—another man crippled by memories too damning to overcome.

Still, as Sam focused on the young woman again, she seemed as terrified as ever—and who could blame her, considering the bloodshed of the last couple of minutes?

"It's all right, nobody's goin' to hurt you."

Sam's softer tone did nothing to diffuse the threat of the blade, and he tried addressing her in Spanish. "The knife. You need to put it down."

He was certain she understood, but she maintained her hold on the weapon as her eyes dropped. Sam traced her gaze to his hip and realized that his Winchester was still leveled on her.

"Mira aquí," he said. Stooping, he found a soft place in the snow for the rifle and then showed her his empty palms, fingers up. "Nobody's takin' your baby. Look, he's turnin' blue, he's so cold."

Still, she hesitated, and Sam turned to the disheveled cradleboard before a black overhang in the bank. Leaving his rifle where it lay, he continued to watch her while he retrieved the small blankets unfurled in the snow. Approaching within striking distance of the knife, he extended them.

"Por favor," he said, studying her dark eyes and hoping that trust would work both ways.

For a moment she hesitated, and then she dropped the weapon and accepted. Her attention now fixed solely on the baby, she snugged the woolen fabric about him and calmed his crying with gentle words.

Sam, leaving the knife but taking up the carbine, made eye contact with her again and indicated by a sweep of his arm that she was to ascend the bank. She asked a question he didn't understand, but when she pointed to the cradleboard, he let her retrieve it and secure the baby inside. As soon as she slipped the straps over her shoulders, he motioned again to the icy slope and she scrambled up.

When she broke out on top, she abruptly stopped, and as Sam came abreast, he found her staring with stunned eyes.

Before her lay the two women—one dead and the other bleeding out on the snow.

In raid after terrible raid, these Mescaleros had proven themselves less than human. Animals, Sam had thought of them. But as he considered the young mother's reaction, he realized that grief wasn't limited to his own kind. For all the grimness and savagery of her people, she displayed the same shock and vulnerability that he would have expected of a white woman.

Slowly she advanced, her jaw quaking and her balance unsteady. At the dead woman, she halted and stretched down a tentative hand. A word—perhaps a name—trembled in her throat, and Sam allowed her a moment before escorting her a few steps more.

At the wounded victim she stopped again, and this time the young mother wouldn't be denied. Kneeling in snow smeared red, she checked the gutshot woman, who remained unresponsive even as the young mother stroked her hair and addressed her in Apache.

Sam, concerned that she might find a knife and secret it away, took her arm and urged her to stand. She resisted, but as soon as she adjusted a blanket about the dying woman's shoulders, Sam pulled her up with a quiet *"Por favor"* and they continued to camp.

He found a flurry of activity. Several men dragged stores out of the teepees and fueled the fires, as Franks had instructed. The material included camp equipage, wagon sheets, buckskins, American-made clothes, and bolts of red and blue calico. Collecting in a pile between the fires were spoils worth keeping: two Winchester carbines and one Remington, a pair of Colt revolvers, and lead, powder, and empty cartridges for reloading. At the far end of camp, other rangers assessed the horses and mules, most of which the company would have to kill to prevent recapture. Boye, meanwhile, prayed over a fallen Apache as his voice carried across the flat.

At the sight of more of her people dead, the *señora* went weak-kneed and might have fallen if Sam hadn't steadied her. He could feel her prolonged shudder, and he let his hand linger compassionately until he realized anew that she had been a party to the killing of Elizabeth. Elizabeth, for God's sake!

"Damned if you didn't find you a squaw."

Sam turned to the flap of the teepee on his right and saw the ruddy-faced ranger named Red step out.

"Pretty one too," Red added, depositing a buckskin on the nearest fire.

Jonesy looked up from the stack of firearms and stroked his crooked jaw. "With a papoose, no less. Oh, my sweet Mary Jane—do I have some things to tell you."

Red grinned, revealing buck teeth. "Captain didn't say nothing about no squaws. What we going to do with her?"

"Haven't got that far yet," said Sam.

"My, my, the ideas she gives me."

As Red pressed near the woman, she seemed set on avoiding eye contact. But she had no choice when the ranger clutched her shoulders and turned her by force.

"Show me that pretty face again," he said, grinning even wider. "Think I'll take you home for myself."

Maybe the woman couldn't speak English, but Red's demeanor needed no translation. Her eyes flashing, she pulled away with an exclamation in Apache.

"That's enough," Sam told the ranger. "We got things to do."

"Yeah, and I'll start right here."

Red tried to seize her again, but Sam met him with a hand to the chest and shoved him away. "Stop it. No place for that."

The lanky redhead flushed as he stumbled back. "Where you come off pushing me? I'm as white as you are."

"Captain give us orders, and manhandlin' a squaw wasn't one of them."

By now, Arch had walked up, dragging a soiled wagon sheet across the snow. He must have witnessed the incident, considering what he had to say.

"You, Samuel, are a study in contradictions."

Sam had heard enough of his snide remarks. "A what?" he asked angrily.

"Suffice it for now to say that you've burdened us with a dilemma."

Sam waited, not caring to discuss anything with him and yet knowing the ranger might have something important to say.

"We cannot humanely leave her and the baby to die," Arch elaborated, "as they most certainly would without stores, shelter, or saddle stock."

"Matto's for killin' them right now."

"From what I overheard, you were not in favor of the prospect. For the record, neither am I."

Studying mother and child again, Sam relived his first kill on the snowy rimrock and the emptiness that nothing seemed to satisfy.

"I guess they's comin' with us."

Maybe it was the only thing a man who had once had a soul could say, but that didn't mean Sam didn't hate himself for it.

Arch seemed to look past Sam's shoulder. "If only a decision about the casualty down by Matto might be solved as easily."

With his back to the scene, Sam had momentarily forgotten the gravely wounded woman. She might die in the next minute, or she might linger until wolves were drawn by the scent of blood. If the latter were the case, so what? Wouldn't there be a measure of justice in leaving one animal to be finished off by another? Who would there be to care?

Then Sam looked at the young mother and knew who would care, for her face was like a window into a guarded part of himself.

"Maybe," he said, "we could—"

He flinched at a sudden gunshot from behind. He turned, his carbine ready at his hip as the report echoed across the hollow.

In the blighted snow down and away, Matto stood over the woman in question, smoke trailing from the muzzle of his revolver.

CHAPTER 14

Even as the Mescalero camp receded behind him to the slog of his boots up the snowy slope, Sam could hear in his mind the repeated gunfire that had felled women and warriors and horses. Pungent smoke from the roaring bonfires drifted up the mountainside with him, and together the real and the remembered seemed to hold Sam in a man-made hell.

There had been death and destruction, but only one scene had burned itself into his memory as vividly as Bass Canyon— Matto's .45 extended downward after an execution.

The image was as much a part of the march back to Franks as the eight rangers around Sam, or the two mules loaded with spoils, or the lone dun horse spared for the purpose of escorting the young mother and child to Fort Davis. Instead of ridding himself of Bass Canyon, Sam had succeeded only in adding to his host of troubling memories.

Upon Matto's return to the fires, an enraged Sam had stepped in front of the ranger. Never had Sam been so determined to tear a person limb from limb, and at first even he couldn't understand. But before he acted, the reason came to him as surely as a descending war club. Two helpless women— one white, one red—had died, and they had died senseless deaths that could never be undone. Never!

Sam knew he needed to dwell more on the role of his misplaced anger, so without comment he had moved aside and let Matto pass. But even as he proceeded now in the man's tracks, a cauldron of invectives churned inside Sam. He had no idea that he was talking out loud until Arch, trudging at Sam's right shoulder, spoke quietly.

"Glad, indeed, am I that Matto marches so far ahead of us. Otherwise, your expressed vehemence might incite even more conflict."

Sam looked at Arch and found only his profile.

"Praise him or damn him," Arch went on, "Matto performed a service."

"Service?" Sam repeated in disbelief. "He out and out executed her."

"For all intents and purposes, she might as well have been dead already. Matto's actions spared prolonged suffering and freed the company from yet another burden."

Sam breathed sharply. "Matto was all heart, all right. Like hell."

"As I said, damn him if you wish. But he ended it quickly and painlessly."

Sam's rage was building, occupying the place where emptiness had been.

"Pin a medal on him then," he snapped. "While you're at it, go back and pin one on a dead Apache for bein' so damned thoughtful how he killed Elizabeth."

Arch wouldn't grant him even a respectful glance. "I—"

Surprising even himself, Sam seized Arch by the shoulder and spun him so that they were face-to-face. "Look at me if that's what you're sayin'! Tell me how that Indian was just tryin' to do right by Elizabeth, like Matto with that squaw. You unfeelin' bastard, that how you see things?"

No sooner had he said it than he regretted looking into Arch's eyes, for they seemed to probe the depths of Sam's unrelenting torment. But Arch's reply touched an even deeper nerve.

"It was not sufficient, was it?" Arch fidgeted with the bandana

155

about his neck. "The yearning and scheming, the way you manipulated Franks and Matto and me in order to pursue revenge—you've accomplished it now, and vengeance was never going to be sufficient, was it?"

Sam went silent. Turning away, he fell off the pace, his head hanging, his boots growing blurry as they moved one after the other through the snow. Maybe he could have defended himself, but what purpose would it have served when everything Arch had said was true?

When the rangers gained the shelf from which they had opened fire at sunrise, Jonesy pointed out something that only the light of day might reveal: an Indian trail. The snow lay more softly in it than elsewhere, and it stretched like a fleecy blanket down into canyon country at Sam's left. The trace disappeared in places, hidden by frosted outcrops and hogbacks, but across a rugged gulch it reemerged as a gentle, snaking thread. At a canyon mouth three thousand feet below and a few miles away, it spilled out into the broad salt flats that separated the Diablos from the Guadalupe cliffs.

"Ain't that a way down from here?" asked Matto.

"The sweetest sight I've seen since my Mary Jane," said Jonesy.

"After our communion with the wintry mountains of His Satanic Majesty," observed Arch, "I think our captain will welcome a quick course to the lowlands."

It meant nothing to Sam. Whether he followed one course or another, or none at all, meant nothing, for at the end Elizabeth would be just as dead and he just as alone. Suddenly he wished that a Mescalero bullet had left him facedown in the snow.

Nevertheless, the discovery of the descending trail seemed to invigorate the other rangers. Veering in the opposite direction from the canyon lands for now, they fell into their predawn tracks that would lead them back to Franks and the horses they would need for the drop into the salt flats.

"Walter . . . Walter . . ."

The raspy voice was weak and broken by a rattling cough, but Sam could hear the passion in it as he slid down the final icy yards in the wake of the other rangers and the captive who had marched in silence with her child. The traverse of the massive rise over now, Sam was back on the Diablos' backbone, Company A's staging grounds of the night before. The rangers who led the seized stock veered for the staked horses, and other men sought out the saddles and stores, but Sam went straight to a scrub piñon under which Franks lay in a latticework of shadows.

Semiconscious at best, the captain had the look of a man already dead. His color was bad, and his bristly cheeks were as sunken as his eyes were hollow. Suspecting dehydration, Sam confirmed it by pinching the back of Franks's hand; the skin had lost its elasticity.

Between coughs and the intermittent summons for Walter, Sam took a canteen and dribbled water between the cracked lips. The ill man half-choked, but instinct led him to swallow, and thereafter Sam was able to support Franks's head and tilt the canteen to his mouth. After a few minutes, the captain seemed to revive a little, but his mind was still somewhere else.

"Walter? That you, Walter?" Franks asked of Sam.

"It's me, Captain—DeJarnett."

"Yes, DeJarnett. The Yankees, what about . . . ?"

Sam hoped that Jonesy wasn't in earshot. "We took care of them for you, just the way you told us."

"The way . . . ?"

"Surprised them at sunup. What we didn't kill, we shot all up when they was runnin'."

"They're crafty, those Yankees." Franks struggled for breath.

"Falling back . . . to regroup."

"No, sir, they was bleedin' ever' step. They disappeared over a mountain and we set about burnin' the camp and killin' the horses. Their raidin' days is over."

For a moment, Franks seemed to meditate over what Sam had said. "Are you certain? Are—"

"I expect ever' one of them's breakfastin' in hell."

Franks began to blink a lot and the corners of his mouth bent upward in a faint, satisfied smile in which Sam wished he could share. But the captain's was a pained smile that also suggested the crippling grief that Sam knew he carried.

Franks's lips trembled. "Avenged," he whispered. "My boy, he's . . ."

Franks abruptly went silent and stared at Sam with wide, wild eyes, and then his hand stole up and seized Sam's arm. "You've come back. Walter, you've come back."

Sam didn't think a dehydrated man could make tears, but Franks's eyes began to glisten. His ashen face blotched, and for a full minute his chin quivered. He seemed overwhelmed at finding the son he had lost so long ago, and there was no way that Sam was going to correct him this time. Then the captain lapsed into unconsciousness with a look of peace, and Sam gently pried a loving father's fingers from his arm and laid it across the man's heart.

Sam wandered away, his chin on his chest as he considered Franks's plight. When he came upon boots in trampled snow, he looked up and found several men resting on their respective saddles and eating. On a rock alongside, the Apache mother sat nursing her baby.

"No way the captain can ride," Sam said quietly.

"Has he deteriorated to that degree?" asked Arch.

Sam still didn't care to have anything to do with Arch, but everyone needed to hear the answer. "Looks of things, he could go any minute."

"Won't catch me mourning any," interjected Jonesy.

Sam glanced around at the horses and thought out loud. "I could try takin' him double, hold him in front of me. Maybe fix up a travois and let a mule do the work."

"Given our mounts' condition, the former is infeasible," said Arch. "As for the latter—"

"I say we leave him and ride out of here," said Jonesy.

Sam gave him a hard look. "Nobody's leavin' nobody."

Matto snorted. "We's done our job. Damned if I'm stayin' up here and freezin' my butt off another minute." Rising, he started past Sam for Franks, and at the same time his hand casually went across his body for the revolver under his coat. "If he's that near gone, just look the other way."

"Stay away from him!" Sam seized Matto's gun arm, pinning his hand against his side.

"What the—"

"Just stay the hell away!"

Startled at first, Matto's dark eyes quickly went cold as the two men faced one another. For the second time that morning, Sam wondered if he had pushed the man too far, for there was something deadly in Matto's features, as if he were a predator sizing up prey. The tension persisted for long seconds, but when Sam let him withdraw his fingers from his coat, his hand was empty.

And tinged with blood, thanks to the prick of the young woman's knife.

Sam looked at the other men, none of whom had risen.

"What the hell's the matter with everybody? He kills that squaw and nobody says a thing, and all of you sittin' on your hands when he's fixin' to do worse!"

Only Arch responded. "Samuel—"

"That's Franks he's talkin' about, not some Apache!"

159

"He's a Yankee hater, is what he is," said Jonesy. "Should've taken care of him myself yesterday."

"You'd've hung for it!" said Sam. He took a sweeping look at the others. "I'll see any man among you hung!"

Arch again tried to speak. "Samuel—"

"Stay away from him!"

"Samuel, I would've prevented Matto had you not. You were just positioned to intervene sooner."

"Didn't bother you none, him killin' that squaw!"

Now Arch stood. "Your hypocrisy knows no bounds. It's you who's spoken repeatedly of exterminating the entire Mescalero race."

"That's different. We's in a war with them!"

But some part of him must have realized that Arch had a point, for Sam began to calm. As everyone fell silent, he looked down and stirred the snow with his boot. Maybe he had overreacted. Maybe he had made a fool out of himself. All he knew was that there were rangers in the outfit who would rather help a good person die than be burdened.

Sam lifted his gaze. His outburst had drawn every able man in the company, and they were bunched before him, eight weary figures who had been through hell and looked it. How could he blame them for wanting to get out of these mountains?

"All right," he said quietly, "nobody's got to stay but me. I'll watch after him till he's able to ride—either that or he's . . ." Sam couldn't bring himself to say it; there had been too much death already.

"Sinners we be, all of us," said Boye, who stood closest to Matto. "There be a righteous man among us to pray over him? Book says the 'prayer of a righteous man availeth much.' "

A couple of rangers glanced at each other, but only Matto responded.

"Not a mother's son here *I'd* waste a breath over." He hacked up phlegm and expectorated within inches of Boye's boot.

Prayer wasn't something in which Sam would squander a breath either—not since Bass Canyon—but he didn't like Matto's disrespect. At least Boye was well-meaning, and what was Matto?

"Boye," said Sam with a glance at the other ranger, "some people's not worth a bucket of warm spit, but Captain's not one of them. Better take it on yourself to do the prayin'."

Boye looked toward the twisted piñon under which a good man lay in need. "Chief among sinners, I am," he confessed. But he already had a fervent prayer on his lips as Sam watched him stride away toward the piñon.

"Let's get our horses saddled," urged Jonesy, drawing Sam's attention. "My Mary Jane's waiting on a letter from me."

"I'm all for it," agreed Red, taking his saddle by the back housing and pommel. "Can't wait for a warm night's sleep."

Judging by the enthusiasm with which Matto and another ranger followed suit, it seemed a foregone conclusion to Sam that a march was imminent. But then an objection came from someone he didn't expect.

"Gentlemen," said Arch, "we must consider what our noble captain stressed more than once: Company A does not abandon a ranger. To do so now, even if one of our own were to stay, would be irresponsible."

"Toes on my left foot's been numb for two days," said Red.

"Hell, mine too," interjected Matto.

Red continued. " 'Irresponsible' is somebody tellin' me to hang around till all my toes is froze off."

Sam didn't disagree. These men had lives to live, people to return to, hope for tomorrow. He had nothing, and a man with nothing had nothing to lose.

"You men mount up and go," he said impatiently. "Just go."

But Arch continued to object, and the discussion persisted

until tempers flared. This time, Sam stayed out of it, but he couldn't help but admire Arch's unflagging stance.

Then Boye's pronouncement from where he hovered over Franks settled the matter.

"The Almighty be praised! His angels have carried away our brother's spirit."

CHAPTER 15

Nejeunee may have rocked to the gait of a horse descending a steep trail alongside a gaping canyon, but she was still back at the red snow.

Through no fault of her own, she had left Quick Talker and One Who Frowns lying in disrespect, the final gunshot ringing in her ears. And now that the owls had spirited Nejeunee's sisters away to the Land of Ever Summer, she must never speak of them again.

Hours had passed since the rising sun had cast a great darkness over Nejeunee's life for the third time. Even yet, she experienced things distantly. There was little room between the beargrass-studded mountainside at her left shoulder and the sheer precipice on the opposite side of her pony, but she saw the *Indaa* rider ahead as if through a fog that shrouded every danger, and she heard the hoofbeats of the other horses and mules as if with someone else's ears. Even the slippage of her dun's hoofs came to her like a trifling rumble underfoot when thunder sounded.

Nevertheless, Nejeunee was aware that the *Indaa* with red hair rode directly behind her, and to his rear, the scowling killer of One Who Frowns: Mat-to, she had heard others call him. The uncertainty of the next moment was terrifying, for back in the arroyo Mat-to would have killed her and dashed Little Squint Eyes against the rocks if not for the rider several horse-lengths ahead of Nejeunee.

Another man had called this rider Sam-el, and twice he had intervened in her defense. But he was an enemy like all the rest, an animal without decency who was probably saving her for his own pleasure. Nejeunee hated him. Wolves of his kind had taken he-who-cannot-be-mentioned away from her, and now they had unmercifully killed her sisters. If it were in her power, she would draw a knife across his white throat.

From behind, Red Hair began to speak in a language she didn't understand. She suspected that he addressed her, but not until a pebble struck her thigh did she reflexively look back. Red Hair was grinning, showing his tobacco-stained teeth, and Nejeunee didn't need to speak his language to know what was in his eyes. With a look of contempt, she turned away, but now Mat-to spoke up in the trade language familiar to every *Ndé* and especially to Nejeunee.

"Meskin, ain't ya," he said in Spanish. "One 'fore you turned A-pach', anyways. A damned whore draw blood on me again, I'll finish what I started when I dragged you out of that hole."

Nejeunee rode on as if she hadn't understood. She had her back to this killer of women and it gave her a sense of refuge.

"Breed just like cockroaches, you Meskins do," Mat-to continued. "No tellin' how many whores that half-breed *muchacho* of yours will be papa to. You hearin' what I say?"

Nejeunee heard, all right, but she didn't dare acknowledge.

"Turn around here to me," Mat-to demanded. "Show me that spiteful look I seen all them times in that cathouse."

The rising anger in his voice must have alarmed Little Squint Eyes, for he began to cry.

"You waitin' for me to shoot that squallin' *muchacho*? Turn around to me!"

Nejeunee heard a revolver hammer spring back to full cock, and she looked back in utter fear. Caught in the line of fire, a dodging Red Hair leaned so far off his horse that the mountainside's beargrass scraped his hat. Over his shoulder he was shouting at Mat-to, but so was Nejeunee as she saw the scowling man's six-shooter trained on her.

"Por favor, no! Mi niño! Mi niño!"

"Your *niño*, hell!" mocked Mat-to. "Since when's a Meskin whore care about a boy?"

"I am *Ndé*, Apache! *Mi niño* is *Ndé*! *Por favor!*"

Mat-to spat between his teeth and smiled cruelly. "That's it, beg. Go on, louder! Like a boy not wantin' a man draggin' him to a room no more. Beg, you bitch!"

Nejeunee heard a shout from down-trail and saw Mat-to's eyes shift. He was looking past her, even as his revolver stayed fixed. More shouts came, shrill and dire in the *Indaa* tongue, and Mat-to yelled back.

Facing down-trail again, Nejeunee understood as soon as she squared herself astride the dun. Ahead and below, framed by her horse's ears, Sam-el was twisted around on his mount in confrontation, his glinting carbine upright in his hand.

More shouts ensued, from below and behind, before the voices calmed and Sam-el slid the rifle back in its saddle scabbard. When Nejeunee glanced over her shoulder, she found Red Hair upright in his saddle and a crimson-faced Mat-to without a visible weapon.

The dun carried Nejeunee and Little Squint Eyes on down to Sam-el, who waited beside a chalky boulder at a momentary widening of the trail.

"Lo siento, señora," he said as she reached him.

Sam-el's words of regret were unexpected—but he was still an enemy, and she would not dignify an enemy with a response.

"Por favor," he added, motioning for her to bring her horse alongside his.

They waited there, letting the others go by, and at first Nejeunee didn't know the purpose. But as the last rider passed with a pack mule, and Sam-el had Nejeunee fall in behind, she realized that he had placed her in a position of greater safety.

But maybe this *Indaa* who now followed was just biding his time for his own cruelties.

As troubling as the clashes with Matto had been, something else dominated Sam's thoughts as his gray picked its way down the treacherous trail.

Captain Franks was dead, and so was he.

Haunted, focused, determined, obsessed. Traits born of tragic circumstances that Franks had never escaped, the terms also described Sam, who still lived every moment in Bass Canyon. For Franks, everything had ended with a look of peace on his face, although a peace based on delusion. But Sam couldn't muster even the suggestion of a smile, although he had done exactly what he had promised over Elizabeth's grave.

It made him wonder which of them, he or Franks, was the more dead.

At least Franks's troubled journey was over, buried with his remains under rocks high on a summit ridge. He was safe there from all the crippling memories, at rest from the consuming passions, while Sam rode on relentlessly through Bass Canyon.

That tormenting ride persisted as the hours wore on and the sun burned away the snow. In late afternoon the company spilled out into the desert at the Diablos' northeast point, where the range bent sharply left and right. Turning in the latter direction, south, the men followed the range's base for three miles and made camp at dusk at a marsh in the shadow of the dramatic summit ridge.

The day had been trying for the sleep-starved rangers, who had dismounted and led their spent horses the final ninety minutes. Sam hadn't thought a man could walk and sleep at the same time, but momentary dream figures had flashed through his mind as he had watched his boots trudge one after the other past lechuguilla and spiny cholla.

Throughout, the woman ahead of him had endured without complaint, even with the cradleboard at her back. But now, as she sat nursing her baby while the thirsty stock watered among the common reeds behind her, he could see the tiredness in her face. For a moment he felt compassion for her, this mother whose entire world had turned upside down, and then he reminded himself that she was of the pack of butchers from Bass Canyon.

As his hate surged, Sam wandered away into the skeletons of dormant mesquites that surrounded the marsh. Soon he broke through to the thicket's west side, where a big yucca angled up over his head. He stopped there, a hand on the thick trunk as his hat brushed the daggered crown, and looked up at the Diablos.

Suddenly he realized that the company had worked its way back along the escarpment's base to a location that had to be almost directly below where Captain Franks had died. Three thousand feet up on that sawtooth rim, at a spot barely three crow-flight miles away, a meaningless pile of rocks was all that remained of a man's life. Soon, Franks would be as forgotten as Elizabeth and all the other emigrants who had died in Bass Canyon.

Sam heard a crackling of brush, and he checked over his shoulder to see Arch emerge from the mesquites, a lot of brutal days showing in his bristly face.

Sam nodded to the rim. "Sure left him in a lonely place. The least we could've done was scratch his name on a rock. We was halfway down before I thought about it."

When Arch stayed silent, Sam continued to study the heights. "I know we've had our differences, Arch, but I appreciate you takin' a stand the way you did. You know, against goin' off and leavin' him."

"Spoken like someone as egocentric as you've proven your-self."

Sam had no idea what Arch had said, but he knew it wasn't a compliment. His anger rising, Sam faced him with a request.

"Say it straight out where I can understand it."

"I didn't take a stance because of you," simplified Arch. "I did it for an admirable officer and man who deserved better."

Fair enough, thought Sam. Thinking that was the end of it, he looked back at the ridge, but Arch had more to say.

"It's on your hands. His suffering, his death, it's all on you."

Facing him again, Sam only stared.

"You know it as well as I," Arch continued. "Franks's judgment was clouded by physical and emotional distress, and all I asked was that you join me in persuading him to turn back. You refused, and the fruits of your decision lie atop that mountain."

Sam gave a half-laugh of disbelief. "So you had to follow me over here just to say that? You even *look* at his face when we was buryin' him? He died happy."

"Any epitaph might as well have said *Killed by DeJarnett.*"

Arch immediately started away, but Sam grabbed his shoulder.

"Don't you go makin' it my fault!" said Sam. "Wasn't a thing about his dyin' the captain would've changed. He finished what he set out to do and got his boy back, least in his mind, and he went peaceful. That's a damned sight better than I ever will."

"So I was correct. Vengeance was never going to be sufficient for you, was it."

This time when Arch turned to leave, Sam didn't stop him. Sam hadn't intended to confirm Arch's earlier accusation and see the smug look on his face, but the truth had slipped out.

Peace was just as far away as ever, and Sam had no hope of finding it.

When Sam followed the smell of coffee back to a fire at camp, exhausted rangers sat leaned back against their saddles and ate hardtack and jerky. Headed for his own stores, Sam passed the baby in his cradleboard as the mother knelt at the marsh and drank with a cupped hand. Sam had sampled the water earlier and found it gyppy, so he was looking forward to disguising its taste in black coffee.

Digging a cup out of his saddlebag, he poured a steaming portion from the smutty pot and turned to seek out his supper. As he did, he saw the woman pull a reed out of the shallows. Curious, he watched her wash away the mud and begin gnawing at the rootstock.

Sam was anything but an Apache lover, but he questioned how much nourishment the rootstock could give the young woman. After all, she was eating for two, and he doubted that the Diablos had been any kinder to the Apaches than they had to Company A. As he studied her face, he realized for the first time how drawn it was.

"Anybody offer her some food?" he asked with a scan of the rangers.

Several men looked up, and two or three exchanged glances.

"She's half-starved," Sam added. "Least somebody could've done was give her somethin' to eat."

"Missed the mark again, I have," spoke up Boye, turning and rummaging in his saddlebag. "Running short, but provide, He will."

Matto caught Sam's attention. "We's all short of food. It's your damned fault she's here. If you want her fed, nobody stoppin' you."

Arch never looked up, and Boye continued to rummage without producing anything. Sam supposed he couldn't blame any of them, not after subsisting on half-rations in the Diablos where the shooting of game would have given away their position. Sam's supply, as well, was all but exhausted, but he figured he could sleep just as well hungry as not. Anyway, the company would likely come upon rabbits or a deer tomorrow.

From his saddlebag, he retrieved his last hardtack biscuit and final strip of jerky and approached the woman, who gently rocked the cradleboard as she chewed on the rootstock.

"Toma," he said, extending the food.

Looking up, she accepted without comment. But as her eyes lingered on him, they triggered something inside Sam. Boye had touted the benefits of service, and for a moment, Sam's spirits were strangely lifted. But then it dawned on him again just who and what this woman was, and he stalked away confused and angry at himself.

CHAPTER 16

They rode under the warming sun of a new day, and Jonesy's deformed jaw was fast at work.

Mary Jane this, and Mary Jane that.

Maybe it was because he and the rest of Company A were bound for home camp in Musquiz Canyon near Fort Davis. Or maybe Jonesy just wanted to twist a knife a little deeper into Sam's heart.

Damn it, Sam didn't need a reminder of what Jonesy had that he didn't, but the Yankee seemed determined never to let him forget. He rambled on about his girl as they bore south and watered at a boulder marked "Rattlesnake Spring" under the Diablo rim. The escarpment's passing folds, steep and red-hued under a band of cliffs, listened in silence as Jonesy kept up his blather on into midmorning. Even as the company veered a little west through a three-mile-wide passage between the Diablos on the right and lesser mountains on the left, the New Jersey native never tired of bragging about his sweet Mary Jane.

But Sam began to wonder how long it might be before Jonesy could post a letter to her at Fort Davis. Sam hadn't realized how dependent the company had been on Captain Franks until he and the others faced the prospect of returning on their own. Indeed, the country turned broken, carrying the riders down into gulches and up demanding rises in a pattern that taxed their jaded horses. With distant landmarks obscured, they tried to navigate by compass, but the lay of the land usually dictated their course. And across every brutal mile by hoof or foot, vegetation such as creosote or yucca, sotol or pitaya, reminded Sam that this was a desert—as if the bone-dry arroyos weren't evidence enough.

It was the kind of place a man might ride into and never find his way out.

Along a hidden arroyo lined with catclaw and scrub mesquite, the company came upon javelinas feeding on prickly pear, and Sam felled one with a Winchester shot. It was only mid-afternoon, and this section of maze looked as if it had never seen water, but here was a flat suitable for camp and a cookfire. There was no one to order a halt for the day, but the other rangers must have suffered from hunger almost as much as Sam did, for everyone dismounted and pitched in to butcher the animal. The hide reeked, but meaty strips soon were roasting over a fire and giving off an agreeable-enough smell.

When fully cooked, the meat tasted all right as well, at least according to the first men to sample the fare. Necessity forced Sam to be patient, for he was last in line and even after he stabbed a charred steak with his knife and stepped back, it continued to sizzle on the blade. Looking up through the smoke as it cooled, he saw the Mescalero woman sitting forgotten as she nursed her child. Once more, Sam couldn't bring himself to take a bite when someone as vulnerable as Elizabeth bore her hunger in silence.

Damn it, didn't he loathe himself enough already?

The next thing he knew he was standing over her, their gazes locked. There was something peaceful about a mother with a nursing baby, and for now, at least, the butchers of Bass Canyon seemed far away.

"There's more after this," Sam said, sliding the skewered steak free.

Just as she had the evening before, she received the food in silence, but this time she looked at him more intently. What was in those dark eyes of hers? Questions?

If so, she wasn't alone, for Sam had plenty to ask of himself.

Returning to the fire for his own portion, he carried it by knife to his saddle in front of a mesquite near her. Removing his holster belt, he sat and did more thinking than eating, despite the distraction of Jonesy wearying everyone with another Mary Jane story. Sam hadn't even begun to resolve anything when the Apache woman motioned to herself and then to the brush, a modest way of informing him that she needed to take care of bodily functions.

Securing the baby in the cradleboard, she stood and shouldered the frame. Sam rose with her and followed her through squawbush and other spiny shrubs. Still carrying meat skewered on his knife, he stayed close as they dodged prickly pear scarred by foraging javelinas. When they reached a gnarled guayacan, a shrub taller than Sam and dense with tiny green leaves, the woman motioned for him to stay.

She disappeared behind the foliage, but the hood of the cradleboard soon edged out as she placed it on the ground. Turning away to give her added privacy, Sam stood eating the last of the meat and dwelled on things. His future was a dark haze and his present nothing but confusion, and both were built on a past where the good things of his twenty-seven years had been crushed in a moment.

From behind, Sam heard a rustle and a startled shriek, and he pivoted to glimpse tawny hide as the cradleboard slid out of sight behind creosote. What the—

"*Ídóí!*"

He broke for the cradleboard to the woman's cry and collided with her. An instant later he saw a mountain lion straddling the frame and dragging the baby away, cradleboard and all. Barehanded or not, the woman would have chased after the panther, but Sam was between the two and already bolting for it through creosote and sotol.

Everything was a blur, his actions instinctive. The cradleboard was at an angle, with the powerful jaws locked on the hood's rim only inches from the baby's face. With a yell, Sam overtook the burdened cat just before it gained a thicket of mesquites. He lunged between the panther's striding legs and tried to wrench the cradleboard free, and when that failed he slashed at the predator's rib cage and hindquarter with his knife.

The hide was thick, a challenge for even a sharp blade, but Sam inflicted enough damage for the cat to drop the cradleboard and turn on him. One moment he was staring into a set of cold, yellow eyes, and the next he was fending off fangs and claws that shredded his coat and threatened to take him down.

They might have done so, but suddenly a mesquite club rained down, pummeling the tawny hide, and the cougar sprang away and ran into the brush.

Frantic, the woman dropped the club and swept the cradleboard up in her arms to the infant's crying. Again and again she voiced an Apache word that must have been his name, but Sam shouted as well.

"Good God! He all right? He hurt any?"

She was busy unstrapping the child and removing him from the cradleboard, but she couldn't have answered anyway, not when Sam had posed the excited question in English. He saw no blood as the woman peeled away the blankets, and he took the baby's loud wails for a good sign as he watched a loving mother comfort her child against her breast.

Only now did Sam look up at the mesquites where the cougar had disappeared and consider what had happened. He could still smell the cat's strong, musky scent, and the image of those deadly eyes remained a powerful presence in his mind. Maybe he hadn't had time before to be afraid, but he did now, and it swept over him like a windstorm and left him with a terrible weakness. Only then did he realize that his arm and chest didn't feel right, and he quickly checked and found the front of his coat missing buttons and his sleeve in tatters.

He looked up again. The woman had inclined her head toward her baby, but her glistening eyes peered only at Sam. A word seemed to be on her lips, but before she could voice it the other rangers were upon them, brandishing firearms and firing questions.

Sam's arm and chest felt as if he had twice been branded.

Standing by his saddle at camp in the chill of early evening, he winced as he slipped out of the upper half of his one-piece long johns. He left the woolen garment draped over his belt as he inspected the scratches. Most were superficial, but two bled openly, a four-inch gash over his heart and another of similar length down his left forearm. He had never before been mauled by a wild animal, much less by a mountain lion, and the realization made his wounds hurt that much worse.

"Got you bad, he did."

Sam looked up to see Boye extending a soaked rag.

"Better clean up good," the preacher boy added. "Ol' tomcat, he scratched me once and mighty sick I got."

Sam hadn't considered that kind of aftereffect, and it didn't make him feel any better. After thanking Boye and seeing him withdraw, he began dabbing the gashes and painting the rag with his blood. He sensed that he was being watched, and he turned to see the Mescalero woman looking at him from where she sat only yards away. Was that concern in her features?

As she studied him, she rocked the cradleboard on the ground beside her. After her baby's terrible scare, he was sleeping peacefully, his thumb in his mouth.

"El cuchillo," the woman said to Sam. She pointed to the hilt of the Bowie knife showing in its scabbard beside his saddle.

What could she want with a knife?

"Por favor," she added, motioning to the clearing's edge where prickly pear grew below squaw-bushes and buckthorns.

Sam's face must have shown his confusion. Did she really expect him to give her a knife? She was a prisoner, for God's sake, from a people who would as soon slit a person's throat as not.

Standing, the woman took up her baby in his cradleboard and approached Sam. When she came within arm's reach, she placed the cradleboard at Sam's feet and pointed to his knife again.

"Por favor," she repeated.

Sam still didn't know her purpose. But the message of trust was clear, and he felt strangely uplifted in a way that he hadn't in all the dark months. With no more hesitation he accepted the pledge of her baby for his knife, and she started away across the small clearing.

"What the hell? Squaw's got a knife!" exclaimed Matto from beyond the fire ring.

"Liable to pig-stick somebody!" added Red. "How'd she get a knife?"

"I'm the one let her have it," said Sam.

Matto jumped to his feet. "She runnin' off? Might be bucks out there to bring back. Hey, you! Get over here!"

"Just hold on," said Sam. "She's not goin' anywhere with her baby still here."

The two men continued to question the woman's intent, and Sam was no less clueless until she stopped at the stand of prickly pear. Hacking off a pad larger than Sam's hand, she let it fall to the ground, which was hard-packed with rubble. The cactus didn't earn its name without a reason, for its needles and fine prickles discouraged handling. Using the knife blade, the woman flipped the pad repeatedly, sometimes reaching a height of several feet. With the impacts breaking the larger spines, she left the pad where it had last fallen and set about scraping away the fine prickles with a rock.

During the course of her task, the baby began to coo, drawing Sam's attention. He checked, finding the tiny arms flailing, and for a moment Sam forgot that this was the offspring of an Apache. It could have been Elizabeth's child that he looked upon. It should have been Elizabeth's child, gracing the New Mexico home that they would never have.

Impulsively, Sam knelt and let the infant take his finger. He was surprised at the grip, and even more surprised to hear himself talking to the little one. Apache or not, the baby was exactly that—a baby—and a baby could touch even the hardened heart of a man whose recent life had been about vengeance.

When Sam raised his head, he saw the woman look at him from across the clearing. Was that a trace of a smile on her lips?

Regardless, she continued the scraping process until evidently satisfied. Taking the pad in hand, she split it open into palm-shaped halves and then returned to Sam.

As soon as the woman pressed one of the poultices against the wound at his heart, he could feel the moist pulp already soothing.

"*Su cinturón,* your belt," she said.

Sam held the poultice in place with one hand and removed his leather belt with the other. Working it up to his chest and across the half-pad, he fastened the buckle before allowing the woman to apply the second poultice to his arm.

Until she secured it with the rag, Sam hadn't considered the fact that the knife had been in her hand all this time. As distracted as he had been, she could have parted his ribs. But now she passed the knife to him hilt-first, a moment before gathering up her baby and returning to her resting place.

Sam needed to dress against the growing chill, but for a moment something else was more important. As the woman sat and withdrew her baby from the cradleboard, he approached and drew her attention.

"Gracias, señora," he said.

An hour earlier, Sam would never have believed that he would extend thanks to an Apache, but the words came without regret. Her eyes welled, but the greater surprise came when she embraced her baby as only a mother could and smiled at Sam.

"Mi niño, mi niño," she said through all her emotion. *"Gracias, señor. Gracias."*

Sam slept better that night than he had in months, but his buoyed spirits didn't last long enough for him to hoist his saddle at sunup.

"Taken up with that squaw, have you?"

Bent over with a grip on the pommel and back housing, Sam didn't know who had come up behind him. But the accusation was reason enough to leave the saddle on the ground and turn.

Before him stood Red, the sunlight accenting his rust-colored bristle.

"Know now why you pushed me away from her," Red added.

"Don't be startin' somethin'. We got ridin' to do."

Sam turned again to the saddle, but Red wouldn't let the matter go.

"Been hearin' you mumble for months about that dead wife of yours," Red added. "So much for her, I guess."

Sam spun, the old rage flaring. "You son of a—"

He didn't know that anyone else was near until a pair of arms separated them.

"Cease!" shouted Arch.

In the heat of the moment, Sam didn't like Arch's arm against his chest any better than Red's remark. For one thing, the pressure against Sam's wounds was painful, but what irritated him more was Arch butting in where Elizabeth was concerned.

"Stay out of this!" he yelled at Arch. "It's between him and me!"

But Arch held his ground as he addressed Red. "Some boundaries aren't to be crossed. Preying on a man's loss is one of them."

Red, his face flushing, said something under his breath and walked away. But that didn't dull Sam's anger, and he whirled on Arch.

"Don't do that no more. If somebody says somethin' about Elizabeth, just stay out of my way!"

All that morning, as Sam's gray traced winding arroyos and crossed ridge after ridge, Elizabeth rode with him. She was there as the south Diablo cliffs retreated behind, and the Eagle Mountains began to show themselves ahead to the southwest. Her presence grew more powerful with every rise and fall of the Eagles' distant, blue face as his horse struggled up inclines and plunged into drainages. If not for that unmistakable landmark, Sam would have thought Company A lost, but just because a man could pinpoint his location on a map didn't mean he knew where he was.

Sam studied the young Apache woman, riding just ahead with her child strapped to her back. Why had Red made such an accusation? Had acts of common decency come to mean more than what they were?

Sam didn't know, but he hoped he would never again do anything to cast a shadow over his love for Elizabeth. To that end, he summoned up his deep racial hatred for Apaches, in the hope that every squaw and whelp would be included. But somehow this mother and child refused to be a party to it. For these two, Sam could muster only a pretense of hatred, without passion or reason.

And he didn't understand why, considering where the hoofs of his horse were taking him.

In midday, Company A dropped off the final hills and pushed south into the desert plain that five days before had been a sea of snow. On Sam's immediate left rose the barren Carrizos, and for the next four or five miles he would ride under their looming crags before veering southeast with the range. A few miles farther, Company A would intersect the beaten road from El Paso to Fort Davis, and now that the weather had warmed and Mescaleros no longer were a concern, the company's desperate ride finally seemed over.

But Sam knew that his was just beginning, for as soon as he struck the road, he must pass through Bass Canyon.

CHAPTER 17

So it had come to this for Nejeunee.

All of Sam-el's attention—the food and protection and rescue of Little Squint Eyes—had been a lie acted out with evil intent. His kindness had been deception, his strife with Mat-to and Red Hair an invention, and he had even accepted the wounds of *Ídóí*, the great cat, in order to preserve this chance to inflict the cruelest of torture on her.

Yawning ahead was the canyon where *Indaa* had died at the hands of the *Ndé* the previous spring, and she knew now that Sam-el had brought her back so he could kill her here, and Little Squint Eyes as well.

Teasing kindness and then denying, Sam-el had perpetrated torment worthy of Gian-nah-tah. But even Sam-el couldn't re-alize the depth of Nejeunee's pain, for before she died she would relive the greatest loss of her tragic life: he-who-cannot-be-mentioned.

Inside this broad pass eight moons ago, he and other *Ndé* had fallen, even as she had waited with his unborn son in the boulders of a side gulch echoing with gunfire. There had been no line of sight by which to watch the attack, but she had heard it all—the rumble of wagons and the thunder of horses, the war cries of the warriors and the screams of the *Indaa*.

And then the terrible silence that had taken he-who-cannot-be-mentioned away forever.

This pass was a place of awful memories, a rugged cut

181

between bare mountains either gray like ashes or dark with rocks created in fire. Had it been she alone who the *Indaa* escorted between its wide jaws, she would have accepted it and joined her sisters in the Land of Ever Summer. But Little Squint Eyes deserved to grow into boyhood and beyond, to find his place under *Sháa*, the sun, and Nejeunee would seize the only chance he had.

As she came abreast of a crooked Spanish dagger, only Sam-el rode behind her.

"*Ayeee!*"

With a cry borrowed from the warriors of the People, Nejeunee wheeled her horse around the yucca and fled back for the open desert. Rubble flew from the furious hoofs as a blur of lechuguilla and pitaya surged by. She heard shouts in a strange language as ocotillo clawed at the ruffle of her dress, but she raced on, asking *Bik'egu'indáán's* Son, Jesucristo, to give the dun more than it had left.

A rifle boomed and a ricochet whizzed through the creosote, and then came more shouts and growing hoofbeats from behind like the pounding of an earthen drum. Out on the desert plain, her horse broke through scrub mesquites and stumbled in a hidden arroyo. She fell against the dun's neck and barely held on, and no sooner had the animal regained its stride across the narrow ditch than a rider came up on Nejeunee's right and cut her horse off, forcing a halt.

It was Sam-el, and she knew that the end was at hand.

With a silent prayer she reached inside her blouse for her phylactery. If *Bik'egu'indáán* would just spare her long enough to remove it from her neck . . . If Jesucristo would allow her to part the buckskin and withdraw that special item . . . Only then could she find comfort in facing the journey to the afterworld exactly as had he-who-cannot-be-mentioned.

It was all that Nejeunee asked as she waited for death before this heartless *Indaa.*

But for a moment, Sam-el paid her no mind. His attention was focused on someone behind her, and their shouts back and forth were loud and angry. Then the yelling stopped, and Sam-el looked at her.

"Matto near' killed you," he said. "How come you runnin' off this way?"

Little Squint Eyes began to cry, and Sam-el took notice. "Your *niño's* all scared. You need to see about him?"

Nejeunee understood the words, but not the man. Was this just more of his cruel game?

Maybe, but he had granted her a chance to hold her baby one last time, and she left her phylactery in place and removed the cradleboard. Soon, Little Squint Eyes was at her breast and as secure as her arms could ever make him. Soothing him with soft words, she thought about his father as she closed her eyes against the afternoon sun and waited for what was to come.

All her emotion must have been obvious, for Sam-el prolonged the moment with words she didn't expect.

"How come you shakin' so? You look scared to death."

Nejeunee opened her eyes, anticipating a muzzle before her. But against the backdrop of a blue sky, there was only Sam-el with a look of concern.

"Nobody's fixin' to hurt you, *señora.*" He glanced past her. "Matto's already rode on."

Nejeunee only stared at him, weighing his words against what she might find in his features.

"I ever tell you what's goin' to happen to you?" Sam-el asked. "We's carryin' you and your baby back to the Army post at Davis. I figure they'll take you back up to the reservation in New Mexico. We got to keep ridin' for that to happen, though."

As Sam-el motioned to the pass and Nejeunee turned her horse and started back, she wanted to believe him. Despite the conclusion to which she had jumped, he had given her no reason not to trust, except that he was an *Indaa,* and the *Indaa* had been an enemy for too long to think of them as anything other than animals.

Until now.

Where the road cut through a grove of big Spanish daggers not far inside the pass, Nejeunee dismounted with her captors to rest the horses. The gap was a few hundred yards wide here, and while the other men stretched their legs or massaged cramps, Sam-el seemed preoccupied with something past the left-side arroyo that bordered the road. After turning briefly to the other men—he seemed to take special interest in Matto sitting back against a dagger trunk—Sam-el motioned to Nejeunee.

"Best you stay with me," he said.

Was that emotion she heard in his voice?

She did as Sam-el and secured her horse to a yucca, and then followed him across the bone-white rocks of the arroyo. She had no idea where he was going, but she traced his steps in silence through lechuguilla and pitaya and over ground too sterile for even cacti. Occasionally he looked back, but he seemed less concerned with her than with the receding distance. Checking for herself, Nejeunee saw Mat-to still resting against the Spanish dagger.

At a place where nothing grew, near the base of a sharply rising slope equally bare, Sam-el hesitated, and Nejeunee did so as well. A rising wind tugged at the back of his shirt and drew her attention to his shoulders, which strangely drooped as if stripped of life. Something was wrong, and she stayed back while he continued on alone.

Up until now Nejeunee had followed too closely to see around him, but as Sam-el pulled away she saw swirls of dust crawling across an *Indaa* grave only yards ahead. Unlike the crevices which her people preferred, this grave consisted of an eroded mound stretching left to right and stacked with rocks.

Nejeunee cringed, for her ingrained fear of the dead was strong.

At the head of the grave, Sam-el stopped and stifled a sob, and Nejeunee was surprised. Animals didn't mourn their dead, unless it was a lone, mournful howl of a dog that had caught the death scent of its master. But maybe Nejeunee was coming to realize things she had never considered before.

In an act that stirred memories of the adobe mission of her youth, Sam-el fashioned a cross out of dead sotol stalks bound with rawhide from his pocket. His lips trembling, the dust whipping about his legs, he set it at grave's head and stood staring down until a shout came from the *Indaa* among the Spanish daggers. Without looking up, Sam-el raised an arm in acknowledgment, and then when a second summons came he started back and Nejeunee followed.

All the way, his shoulders stayed bent, and Nejeunee wondered who lay buried in this place of tears.

Sam wished he had never returned to Bass Canyon.

The pass was behind him now, ten miles and an entire craggy range away to the northwest, but he might as well have still been standing over that mound of dirt and rock. He had never realized how much his wounds had healed until the canyon had reopened them. The hopes necessary to sustain every man bled out as if the events of the previous May had just happened.

At least at Elizabeth's grave Sam had accomplished one thing, not because it meant anything to him, but because it would have to her.

Setting a cross.

Bitterness had kept him from doing so when her grave had been fresh, but he had come to regret his decision. Now that it was in place, the strange thought that she might rest more comfortably because of it was the only thing that buoyed him as Company A stopped for the day, just outside the adobe ruins of a Butterfield mail station at Van Horn's Wells.

Here among scattered creosote bushes under a mile-high desert crag, Sam and Elizabeth had spent their last night together, before falling in with the other wagoners at daybreak for a march that had taken his measure as a man and found him wanting. Now, Sam was alone, even though eight other rangers and an Apache woman set about making camp.

While Red and Boye gathered firewood, and Matto and another ranger skinned jackrabbits to roast beside a mud-brick wall, Sam hung the straps of the empty canteens over his saddle horn and led his horse toward the well. Self-absorbed, he didn't even give a thought to leaving the Apache woman in camp with Matto. For that matter, he was barely aware that Jonesy walked beside him, although the ranger talked a mile a minute in that New Jersey accent.

Pushing through a row of slapping mesquites, they dropped into a gravelly arroyo and worked their way up it as the canteens bounced and banged. Not until Sam dodged a big yucca in the wash did Jonesy's words pull him out of his private thoughts.

"Oh, she's a fine little girl, my Mary Jane. I expect by this time next year we'll be married. Her father wants her to come of age first, you know."

Sam didn't know, and he didn't care.

"I think I'll bring her to Texas after the wedding," Jonesy went on. "I can barely wait. We'll settle down and I'll raise some cows and when I come in every evening, she'll be smiling that sweet smile. I'll wager you've never seen anything like it."

But Sam had already seen the only smile he cared to see, even though it would always be a memory now.

"Did I ever tell you about her dimples?" Jonesy persisted.

"They're something to see when she smiles. And when she and I dance—oh, my! The things she—"

"I've heard enough," said Sam.

"Speaking of dancing, she took lessons, you know. There was an instructor from Europe, and he taught her how to—"

"The well's about a hundred and fifty yards up here," Sam interrupted, hoping to spur a change in subjects.

But Jonesy couldn't be thrown off stride. "The way she sails across the dance floor, she's just like an angel. I'm sure she—"

Sam managed to ignore him again until they reached the arroyo's brushy head under a sotol ridge that angled up to the heights. From out of a muddy seep covered in animal tracks, the cone of a well rose waist-high from a base constructed of the same native rock. Over the well stood a crude H frame of cured mesquite with a rope and pulley system in place.

Sam had just secured the horse to one of the support posts when, little by little, Jonesy dredged up the worst moment of Sam's life.

"You can't imagine what it means to have a girl like Mary Jane," said the ranger, turning to retrieve a canteen from the saddle horn. "But I suppose you can't miss what you never had."

The hell I can't, thought Sam.

"Let me tell you," Jonesy went on, "there's nothing like the talks and sharing all the little things that make you special to each other."

You don't know the half of it, Sam said silently.

"She's the sweetest thing in this whole world," Jonesy added. "I just don't know what I'd do without—"

Sam clutched Jonesy's shoulder and spun him around.

"No more!" Sam ordered, seizing his collar. "You hear me? Not another word more!"

He shoved the ranger back into the horse with a bang of

187

canteens. Turning away, Sam wanted it to end there, but Jonesy didn't know when to leave well enough alone.

"Why the hell you grabbing me?" Jonesy demanded. "All I was saying was what she means to me. Why, before I'd let anything happen to her, I'd crawl across this desert and take on the whole Apache nation."

Sam wheeled, his fist already cocked. With a cry of self-hatred that had festered for eight dark months, he drove a punch so hard into Jonesy's crooked jaw that the man fell back against the rock cone.

Jonesy lay there in an obvious daze, shaking his head, rubbing a hand across his jaw as blood trickled from the corner of his mouth. Then his glassy eyes seemed to clear and his hand moved toward his revolver.

But Sam's .45 had already cleared its holster, and he watched over the cocked hammer as Jonesy froze.

"The hell with Mary Jane!" Sam yelled. "I pull this trigger and it'll be the hell with the both of you!"

Jonesy turned his head away and held up his palms in a defensive gesture. "God Almighty, don't do this, DeJarnett!"

Jonesy was trembling, but so was Sam's gun hand. "I will, so help me. Tell me why I shouldn't!"

"God Almighty! There's not any Mary Jane. Don't do this!"

"What?"

"I-I made her up, all of it. Everything about her. For God's sake, listen to me!"

Stunned into silence, Sam only stared as the man spoke quietly through a sob.

"All the wanting . . . the never having . . . Jesus, who'd have somebody like me, a face caved in by a horse? I-I was just getting by, day to day, dreaming what I won't ever have."

Only now did Sam realize how much his knuckles hurt from the punch, but the guilt inside was a hundred times worse. Holstering his .45, he stretched out his hand as the ranger looked up at him.

"We fought Indians together, Jonesy. You deserve better from me."

But the ranger's eyes held a lot of concern as Sam helped him up.

"You . . . You telling everybody about this?" Jonesy asked.

"Not if you don't tell them what an SOB I am for hittin' you."

A blowfly maggot, that's all Sam was.

On into nightfall, long after Jonesy started back with full canteens draped across the horse, Sam sat on the well's rock platform. He regretted and grieved and wept, and when he looked up at the sky, Elizabeth was still as far away and the stars just as indifferent. He didn't want to go back to camp. He didn't want to look Jonesy in the face. The incident had been just one more example of how Sam had used and abused every man in the company to atone for something for which none of them had been responsible.

To the howl of a lobo wolf, he finally dragged himself up and trudged down the arroyo. He was exhausted and so were the horses, but he wondered if it would be best if he rode on alone tonight. Fort Davis was sixty-five miles away down a beaten trail, and Musquiz Canyon was only a few miles farther. Who the hell would care if he proceeded toward company headquarters on his own?

But then for the first time since he had set the cross in Bass Canyon, Sam considered the Apache woman. He was dismayed to realize that, upon going for water, he had left her subject to mistreatment, or worse. Couldn't he ever think of somebody besides himself?

Sam saw the still-distant campfire flickering in the night, and he picked up his pace.

As he climbed out of the arroyo, he could smell the roasted jackrabbit and see exaggerated shadows move against the adobe wall as rangers helped themselves at the cookfire. He could hear the baby crying, and a raised voice as well, but not until he broke through the low creosote bushes did he distinguish the voice as Matto's. The Apache woman sat apart from everyone as she cradled her child in her arms, and Matto approached her and continued to rail.

"That squallin' brat. I'd've dashed its brains out when I found it if DeJarnett hadn't stuck his nose in. Maybe I'll—"

Sam entered camp, and for a moment Matto's silhouette froze against the fire. Then his shadow melted away into the night, and Sam went directly to the woman. There was concern in her face as she tended the infant, and when she looked up at Sam, he could see her troubled eyes glisten in the firelight.

"*Qué sucede, señora?*" he asked. "What's wrong?"

She glanced at the baby. "*Mi niño,*" she said through a half-sob.

Sam's anger flared, and he quickly scanned camp. "Somebody hurt him?"

She shook her head. "*Él ésta enfermo.* A fever."

Sam stooped and felt the baby's forehead. Hot, he confirmed. Like a coal from the fire.

He went to his nearby saddle and dug a rag out of his war bag. From beside the fire ring, he retrieved a canteen, obviously the only one left unclaimed after Jonesy's return from the well. Soaking the cloth on his way back to the woman, Sam found that she had removed the infant's blankets in anticipation and placed him in the cradleboard.

Sam squeezed the excess water from the rag and extended it. She accepted with a quiet "*Gracias*" and began sponging the ill child, but his cry persisted.

Sam turned and stared at the fire. He didn't like this. His

infant brother had taken a fever on a Sunday night and begun to cry, and by the following Tuesday he had been silenced forever. Sam had been only five at the time, but he could still remember the baby in a little coffin.

Even worse, Sam couldn't forget how the loss had affected their mother. Inconsolable with grief, she had lapsed into a bedridden world of denial from which she had never recovered. A year to the day after her child had died, a second coffin had rescued her from the pain, and Sam never wanted to see that kind of anguish from a mother again.

Even if she was Apache.

If Sam was looking for an excuse to ride on, this was it. Fort Davis had a post surgeon, the only doctor for a week's journey in any direction. If Sam could coax a night of steady riding out of the horses, he might have the woman and her baby within striking distance of the fort by sometime the next night.

Sam turned to her. "You and me's leavin'. I'll get your baby some help at the Army post."

As they prepared to ride, Sam didn't say a word to anyone, not even in response to an inquiry from the ranger who guarded the horses outside of camp. But once the woman and her child were on the dun, and Sam began cinching up his gray, he heard Arch's voice from behind.

"Matto and Red have entered into a wager. The former holds that you're deserting, while the latter attributes your actions to carnal desires to be acted on in private."

Sam had nothing to say. Satisfied with the cinch, he untied the reins from a scrub mesquite and swung up into the saddle.

"Samuel?" pressed Arch.

Sam reined the horse about so that he faced Arch's shadowy form against the fire flaring in the background.

"I'll see you in Davis," said Sam.

With the dun carrying his wards keeping pace, Sam rode

away into the hard dark, a troubled captive himself in one respect. Because there was nothing he could do for Elizabeth and her baby, he felt strangely compelled to help this mother and child—even if they were from the very band that had killed them.

CHAPTER 18

The call in the night followed Nejeunee away from the *Indaa* camp.

She heard the hooting only once, but she turned to it immediately. Open country dominated by cacti and chaparral wasn't favored by owls, which preferred adequate timber. Not only that, but this owl hooted with an unmistakable Apache accent.

Nejeunee knew what it meant.

Be ready.

By foot, one of the People had pursued all the way from the devastated camp high in the mountains, for a warrior could trot for days with little rest. Pushing on through each night as the *Indaa* had slept, he had overtaken them and let her know. Now that she and Sam-el were horseback again, the pursuer would fall behind, but that would change once they stopped.

Nejeunee was the captive of a hated enemy, but she was strangely conflicted. The People no longer had a *gutaaln* to cast *tádidíné* and drive away her baby's evil sickness, for she had seen Nah-kay-yen fall at her feet to gunfire. Sam-el, meanwhile, had begun to earn her trust, and he had assured her that there would be help ahead for Little Squint Eyes.

Nothing mattered more than her baby's welfare, but there was something else with which Nejeunee also struggled. When the *Indaa* had attacked the camp, warriors had fled up the snowy slope, but she remembered only one who had not dripped a bloody trail. Only he would have been in any condition—and had a reason—to pursue for so great a distance, and Nejeunee didn't dare say his name even to herself.

She dwelled on these things as she and Sam-el took the horses in a slow trot down the beaten road. Sponging Little Squint Eyes had been effective, or maybe it was just the soothing sway of the horse's gait, but his crying soon diminished.

As the stars crept across the sky, however, the baby's crying returned in force, prompting Nejeunee and Sam-el to stop and sponge him again. They did so twice more to the howl of wolves, and on each occasion Nejeunee looked back into the brooding dark and wondered who might be there, biding his time. She was aware that an Apache seldom attacked at night, believing that to die under such circumstances would set him adrift in blackness forever. But the dawn would come, and with it Neje- unee would face yet another moment that could alter the course of her life.

The lilt of the hoofs persisted far into the dark of the morn- ing before she and Sam-el halted to rest the horses and nap. He stretched out on his back, and even as she reclined near him, her protective hand on the cradleboard between them, Neje- unee couldn't sleep. But it wasn't so with Sam-el, whose breath- ing fell into the peaceful rhythm of a man who had no idea that danger was about.

Nejeunee experienced it all with heightened senses—the hard desert floor under her shoulders, the shifting hoofs of the horses staked at Sam-el's head, the chilled air seeping through her blankets. She peered into the night, searching for what she couldn't see, and repeatedly checked the east sky past Sam-el for signs of daybreak. And throughout, she remembered and deliberated and grappled, her *Ndé* self at war with the part of her that had been *Mexicano,* and even more so with her maternal instinct to protect her baby.

Never was a hint of red against dark horizon so unsettling, but suddenly it was there, showing through the notch between Sam-el's chin and chest. As the glow grew brighter, some sixth sense led her to roll away from Sam-el and watch the desert emerge from the shadows. Two horse-lengths distant, a willowy ocotillo rose out of lechuguilla and pitaya. The ocotillo stalk bent in a slight wind that was cold but not frigid, its currents rich with the scent of creosote that was still too deep in gloom to see.

Peaceful yet menacing, it was a morning that begged for the favor of *Sháa*, the sun. For such a request, Nejeunee needed to blow *tádidíné* to the antlers of the dawn, the orange streaks shooting from the daybreak horizon. But now, as discreet as a field mouse, something was rattling a dead sotol stalk.

Nejeunee froze in anticipation, and from the brush suddenly crept a terrible figure she had hoped never to see again.

Gian-nah-tah!

Cautioning her to silence with an open palm, he approached with his knife out and ready to kill. Here was the *Ndé* to whom she was pledged, the *Ndé* who had butchered her mother and threatened Little Squint Eyes. And now he was at the *Indaa's* feet, ready to drive the blade into the heart of one who had befriended her and had risked his life to save her baby.

"Sam-el!"

Nejeunee's cry came at the last moment, but it was enough to alert Sam-el. He threw out an arm and Gian-nah-tah fell on him with a shriek. She lost sight of the blade as their bodies closed, and then she was busy dragging Little Squint Eyes out of harm's way.

Spinning back around on her hip, she saw the blade flash as the two men rolled in the dirt, their legs flailing. Sam-el's hand appeared to be on Gian-nah-tah's wrist, trying to prevent the blade from plunging, but there was no way to follow it in the

195

struggle. Regardless, this battle of grunts and endurance could end only one way, for she knew Gian-nah-tah for the fierce warrior he was. Any moment he would cast Sam-el aside and leave his lifeless body in a dark pool like the one that had claimed her mother's *rebosa*.

Then a gun roared, startling Nejeunee and Little Squint Eyes and scaring the horses, and Gian-nah-tah rolled away with a moan. Scrambling up, the warrior fled doubled-over, clutching his side as a second shot cut an ocotillo stalk in half at his shoulder.

Smoke trailed from Sam-el's revolver as he jumped to his feet. With an *Indaa* battle yell, he pursued to the edge of the brush but held his fire. When he glanced over his shoulder, Nejeunee was rising with her crying baby at her breast.

The dawn grew brighter as Sam-el held his position, his revolver cocked as he turned toward all four winds. Finally, he lowered the weapon and came up before Nejeunee.

"You saved my life," he said. "Didn't even realize you knowed my name."

For a moment his gray eyes were like a parted flap that let her see him for who he was.

"Maybe," he added with a smile, "you could tell me yours sometime."

Even after a sponging, the baby was too feverish to suckle for more than a couple of minutes. All Sam could do was get mother and child mounted and strike out into the sunrise for still-distant Fort Davis.

He rode with vigilance and a Winchester across his thighs, for the cry of a captive had been all that had spared him. He watched her hair bounce as her horse trotted beside his, and he wondered if he would ever sleep well again.

"How come you to do what you did? Warn me and all."

"You help Little Squint Eyes." She said the name first in Apache, and then in Spanish.

"That what you call him?" Sam dropped his gray off the pace enough to see the baby in the cradleboard at her back. "He does kind of look like he's squintin'. Wish the poor little thing felt better."

Sam brought his pony abreast of her again. "So who was it jumped me?"

The young woman didn't answer.

"He didn't just happen on us out here," Sam observed. "He one of your band?"

Still she rode in silence, her focus straight ahead.

"Diablos to here is a long way to chase," he continued. "Since he nearly finished me off, I expect I got a right to know. He somebody to you?"

"I have no one."

"What about your baby's father?"

"*Yah-ik-tee*, he is not present since before Little Squint Eyes was born."

"That mean he's dead?"

"We mustn't speak of it. Ghosts may be about."

For himself as well, thought Sam with a look back. The ghosts of past regrets.

When he straightened in the saddle, he took a moment to study the woman. So many things about her identified her as Apache, but her features were not among them.

"You was born Mexican, wasn't you," he said. "That somethin' you can talk about?"

"I'm *Ndé*. Apache. It's been so for ten summers since a warrior lifted me up on his horse at the *salado grande*, the big salt."

"Had to be hard gettin' stole that way. Treated you awful bad, I guess."

She turned, her eyes flashing anger.

197

"I'm *Ndé*," she repeated. "I'm proud to be *Ndé*. It's white people I hate."

Sam briefly looked down at his saddle horn. He had never considered that Apaches could hate just as he could. Animals didn't hate; they just killed.

"My people don't do the things yours do," he said.

"Hmpf! They kill the fathers of our babies. Little Squint Eyes has no father because of them."

Sam breathed sharply. "I'm sorry he don't have a father. But it was your people took ever'thing from *me*. My wife and baby both."

She stared at him and the anger in her eyes seemed to fade. Was it understanding that replaced it? Or even compassion?

Sam's voice began to crack as he went on. "You stood right there beside me at her grave. Now I find out you was hatin' me the whole time, after all I did fightin' that cat off."

Sam began to blink a lot and he turned away, finding the desert growing fuzzy. He wished he had never seen this squaw. She was a terrible reminder of so many things, of so many black nights and blacker days. Why the hell didn't he just ride off and leave her?

"Little Squint Eyes, *mi niño. Gracias.*"

Abruptly Sam felt ashamed. He hadn't intended to beg more thanks from the woman, especially gratitude expressed with a sob. When that cougar had dragged her baby away, Sam had only done what any honorable man would have.

He brushed his eyes, and when he looked back at her, she gave him much more to think about.

"You're an enemy," she said, "an *Indaa*. But I can't hate you."

Surprised, Sam didn't know how to respond. But words came out nonetheless.

"Well, *señora*, can't say as I hate you neither. Even with you keepin' it a secret who jumped me."

Sam hoped the horses held out.

Twice during the morning, he and the Apache woman walked and led their mounts for a mile or two. But the animals were still jaded even after Sam let them roll in the dirt and graze while he and his wards nooned at El Muerto water hole under El Muerto Peak. With Little Squint Eyes's fever persisting, Sam didn't dare tell the *señora* that the place had been named for the dead.

After cooling the infant in a spring-fed pool, they pressed on for the Davis range, its far-flung skyline a dark blue as it rose out of a rolling grassland. The four beats of each horse's walking gait—each hoof striking the road separately—soon sang Sam to sleep, but he didn't realize it until the woman spoke from the dun alongside.

"Gian-nah-tah."

Sam looked up, squinting as he found her in the glare. "What?"

"Gian-nah-tah. I'm glad he didn't kill you."

"So that's who jumped me." Sam laughed quietly at her delay in answering. "Only been about six hours since I asked you."

When the woman seemed not to grasp the humor, Sam added, "Sure come a long ways after you."

"I'm pledged to him. But I would kill him myself if I could."

Sam knew she was from a different culture, but he was as bemused as he was startled.

"That how courtin' is with your people?" he asked. "One wantin' to kill the other?"

"Gian-nah-tah is a great warrior, but he has no respect for the ways of the *Ndé*. He's why the spirits turned away and let you white men overrun us."

It was an interesting perspective, thought Sam, but not one

that gave credit to Captain Franks's planning and determination. Or to his own.

"It was somethin' had to be done, the way you Mescaleros been killin'."

Now her face showed the anger Sam had seen before.

"You white men killed women as they cooked," she charged. "Like cowards, you killed them and left the snow to cry tears of blood."

Sam flinched. "I wasn't a bit proud of it. Ever'body looked alike with those blankets. But don't be tellin' me about killin' women, not after what one of your bucks did to my Elizabeth. You think that'll make me want to help your baby? You damned squaw, not another word!"

The woman's chin began to quiver, whether from fear or anger or grief, Sam didn't know. Hell, he didn't even know all the reasons why he suddenly couldn't hold his own emotions in check. But whatever the cause, he trembled and ached as he hadn't in a long time.

The two of them rode on that way as the hoofs drummed and Little Squint Eyes began to cry again. It seemed a weaker cry than before, and Sam watched with concern as the *señora* removed the cradleboard and laid it across her thighs. It rocked to the horse's gait as she peeled away the infant's covers, and Sam took his gray closer.

The woman looked up with unvoiced questions. Sam could just imagine how worried Elizabeth would have been, a captive fearing for her baby's life and terrified that the promised help might be withheld now. As guilt flooded him, Sam stayed silent, and so did the *señora*, but when he unscrewed his canteen, she extended a cloth and he drenched it.

The cradleboard seemed well-balanced across the dun's withers, but Sam stretched out a reassuring hand and supported it as she sponged the infant. Some things were better said with a gesture.

Soon Little Squint Eyes quietened and began to nurse as the hoofbeats kept up their relentless rhythm. Maybe now was the time for words.

"We been at war, your people and mine," said Sam. "There's nothin' we can do to change that. But that don't mean you and me's got to be at war too. I lost somebody, and so did you. They're gone, and they're not comin' back. All we got is what's down the road, the next sunrise. Your baby's sick, and what matters right now is workin' together to get him some help."

Considering the ferocity of Apache warriors, Sam had no idea that their women could be so emotional. But the *señora's* eyes and cheek began to glisten—in relief, he supposed—and when she spoke there was a gentleness in her voice that was like the soothing song of a trickling stream.

"*Que Dios te bendiga.*

"*Y que Su Hijo te bendiga.*"

It was a prayer, and it made Sam wonder how anyone captured by heathens half her life ago could have faith in something that he had shunned since the Bass Canyon attack. As he stared between his horse's ears at the advancing road, her words almost seemed to speak with his father's voice from so many years ago.

"May God bless you.

"And may His Son bless you."

CHAPTER 19

"You're in pain?"

Sam wasn't aware that he groaned until the Apache woman spoke from the horse that shadowed his gray. They were riding past Point of Rocks, a sheer face of stone shorn from a small Davis Mountains peak that was isolated from the magnificent main range immediately to the north. Burned red by the sunset at their back, the Point's three-hundred-foot cliff was a landmark that told Sam that they were only a dozen miles from Fort Davis.

Sam was indeed in pain, which was why he kept his left forearm against his chest as he rode.

"The claws of the great cat cut deep," she added. "I should prepare another cactus."

"The poultice you fixed sure helped. But I'll heal up on my own when this ridin's over, providin' I don't have to fight anybody else off. Hard for scratches to scab over if you don't give them a chance."

The woman went quiet as they rode past green live oaks growing between boulders at the Point's base, one of the grassy plain's few locations with trees.

"You're braver than Gian-nah-tah," she finally said.

Sam looked at her. He had always considered Mescaleros a strange contradiction. In one sense, they were skulking cowards who preyed upon the unwary only when the odds were in their favor—the story of Bass Canyon. And yet from what Captain

Franks had said, in the face of certain death, these same warriors would fight gamely to the end like cornered badgers.

Sam weighed his words before responding; he didn't want to stir up trouble again.

"How's your people measure bravery?" he asked.

"A brave man doesn't threaten Little Squint Eyes."

"That what he did?"

"A brave man stands up to Mat-to to save Little Squint Eyes," she continued. "A brave man fights *idói*, the great cat, to save Little Squint Eyes. A brave man rides through a night and a day and into another night to save Little Squint Eyes. You're braver than the warrior who left a kindly *señora's rebosa* lying in her blood while he pulled me up across his horse."

Involuntarily, Sam pulled rein and turned to her.

"God Almighty, you sayin' this Gian-nah-tah killed one of your family and he's the one stole you? And now you're pledged to him?"

The woman hung her head, and a deep sadness entered her voice.

"Gian-nah-tah will take what's his. The horse soldiers will carry me to the reservation, and Gian-nah-tah will be waiting."

"Don't you have a say?"

She looked up. "I'll go to *kuughà*, his teepee, or he'll kill Little Squint Eyes. He has said so."

"The son of a bitch!"

Sam's outburst was in English; he didn't know a Spanish term strong enough to convey his anger. Indeed, his rage grew until his voice quaked.

"That's wrong. It's just *wrong*. You was Mexican startin' out—why don't you go back to your first people?"

Her dark eyes told him before she answered, for they were those of a person as lost as he. But, somehow, she managed to lift her chin a little higher.

"I have no people but *Ndé*. But I wish your bullet had killed Gian-nah-tah."

"If I'd knowed how it was, I'd've chased him down and finished him." Sam ran his hand across his bristly face. "Maybe he bled out anyway. I can't get over him sayin' he'd hurt your baby."

He rode on, and the woman kept pace on the dun alongside.

"You're more than brave," she said. "For an *Indaa*, you're kind like he-who-cannot-be-mentioned."

"Who?"

"We mustn't speak of *yah-ik-tee*, he who is not present."

"Your man, I guess. Little Squint Eyes's father." Sam leaned around to see the cradleboard at her back. The infant was flushed, but at least he was sleeping. "Speakin' of bein' kind, I guess we was both lucky that way. Don't think anybody was as tenderhearted as Elizabeth. She'd've carried on about Little Squint Eyes the same as she would our own baby. Just be glad you get to hold yours, 'cause she never did."

"She didn't?"

Sam shook his head, and grief muffled his words. "All we wanted was to be left alone. All we wanted was to get to New Mexico so she could have her baby and we could be a family. I might as well be buried in that pass too, 'cause they're not any deader than me."

Sam turned away; he was overcome by the memories, and he didn't want her to see.

"*Lo . . . Lo siento*, I . . . I'm sorry, Sam-el."

There was his name again, spoken with compassion by someone he had tried hard to hate but couldn't. He enjoyed hearing her say it, even though he had every reason not to.

Facing her, Sam forced a smile. "You're awful kind yourself, *señora.* Sure like the lilt in my name when you say it. Now if I just knowed yours."

Sam made sure they rode abreast, but he knew that the woman still had to be frightened.

Somber night squeezed in on all sides as they passed through the settlement of Fort Davis under a black mountain that hid the starlight. Already faced with an uncertain future, she was now about to enter her enemy's stronghold, and Little Squint Eyes was sick. He was very sick, and she probably worried whether an Army surgeon would actually treat him. She had only Sam's word—something he didn't give frivolously—but he knew that in dealing with the Army, there was only so much that even a Texas Ranger could do.

Where the point of the mountain angled down on the left, they reached the military reservation, which had no boundary walls. From out of the shadows stepped four dark forms, blocking their course and raising a challenge.

"Who goes there?"

"DeJarnett," said Sam. "Ranger Company A."

As a silhouette approached and struck a match, Sam opened his coat to let the light flicker in his *Cinco Peso* badge.

"Got a Mescalero woman we captured," he explained. "She's got a sick baby. We need the surgeon."

With two escorts walking ahead, Sam and the woman urged their horses inside the grounds. It was too dark to make out details of the post, but Sam had been here often. Fort Davis lay at the mouth of a three-hundred-yard-wide canyon between mountains with countless vertical columns of rock standing side by side. He and the woman passed between the sutler's store and cavalry barracks, skirted the broad parade ground, and went around the south end of officers' row, a line of a dozen or more houses spanning the canyon mouth.

Two hundred yards ahead in mid-canyon, Sam distinguished the hospital's long outline. On its left, hazy in the night, stood a bungalow with windows as black as the looming cliffs.

The escorts, both Negro enlisted men, abruptly stopped.

"Surgeon done in bed," said one. "I knows we s'posed to take you there, but he don't like bein' bothered thataway."

Sam and his gray brushed past with the woman following. "Let me worry about it."

The escorts had to run to catch up, but thereafter the men proceeded to the surgeon's quarters without comment. After Sam secured the horses, he followed the soldiers up the creaking steps of a covered porch while the woman stayed behind to check Little Squint Eyes. When the soldiers hesitated at the door, Sam took the initiative and rapped on the jamb. There was no immediate response, but he persisted until the glow of a lamp appeared through a window.

"Identify yourself," a slurred voice said through the door.

"Need help," said Sam. "I'm with the Rangers, Company A."

Sam could smell liquor on the surgeon's breath the moment the door swung open. An officer of mid-forties with bushy sideburns and a goatee, he had the flushed face, swollen nose, and bloodshot eyes of someone consumed by the bottle. He sure as hell didn't inspire confidence, but Sam didn't waste time dwelling on it.

"We got a sick baby." Sam turned and motioned for the woman to bring Little Squint Eyes to the door.

"That a squaw?" the surgeon asked.

"Captured her and her baby a few days ago. He's bad with fever."

Sam could hear the steps complain under the woman's weight, but the surgeon waved her away.

"Have her bring him to the hospital tomorrow."

The surgeon tried to close the door, but Sam prevented it

with a boot.

"You need to look at him," Sam insisted. "He might not make it till tomorrow."

The surgeon's eyes narrowed. "Sir, I will thank you to remove your foot."

Sam glanced back at the *señora* holding Little Squint Eyes in the lamplight. The concern in her face was greater than ever.

"Listen," Sam told the officer, "her baby's burnin' up and you've got to do somethin'."

"Must I direct these soldiers to remove you? I will see the child in the morning."

"That's not good enough. We come sixty-five miles, ridin' day and night from Van Horn's Wells. I'll be damned if I let him die on your doorstep."

"This is not a matter worthy of attention so late."

" 'Cause he's Mescalero?"

"Mescaleros, sir, are why this post is garrisoned."

Sam let out a weary breath. "I don't think I'm bein' unreasonable in what I'm askin'."

"In the morning, sir. Now if you will please remove your—"

"Enough of this!" Sam drew back his coat, his downward glance directing the surgeon's attention to the revolver in his holster. "One way or another, you're doin' somethin' for that baby."

The surgeon looked up, and for a sobering moment he stared at Sam.

"Very well," said the officer.

Stepping outside, he spoke quietly to one of the escorts and then led Sam and the *señora* to the nearby hospital in the shadows. Accompanied by the soldiers, the latter two mounted a wrap-around covered porch and followed the wobbling surgeon around the right corner and midway down the long veranda. Beside a window with lamplight, the officer pushed open a door and called for someone. Moments later, a Negro enlisted man in uniform appeared.

"Bring in the child," the surgeon instructed him.

The Negro was evidently a medical corpsman, and as he approached the *señora* and reached for Little Squint Eyes, she hesitated and looked at Sam.

"It's all right," Sam assured her. "We got him help now."

With a kiss to her baby's forehead, the woman passed the infant into the man's care.

The surgeon had already gone inside, and as the corpsman carried Little Squint Eyes across the threshold, Sam motioned for the *señora* to enter next. He hadn't noticed that the soldiers had assumed positions beside the door, but now they moved quickly to block access.

"We's to take you off of the post," said one.

Over the soldier's shoulder, Sam could see the surgeon looking at him.

"What's this about?" Sam asked.

"I will treat this child with the same care I would a white baby," said the surgeon. "But I will not tolerate a threat."

"You can't send his mother off. He's still nursin'."

"She will tent nearby until she's removed to the Mescalero reservation. But you, sir, are no longer welcome."

All Sam could do was stare as a soldier closed the door.

"Sam-el? Sam-el?"

He turned to the *señora*, but a soldier was already tugging on his arm.

"Give me a minute, will you?" Sam requested.

"He say git you off of the post."

"I'll go. Just let me tell her." Finding the woman's frightened face in the light from the window, Sam addressed her in Spanish. "They'll take good care of him. I have to go, but you'll have a tent outside so you're close by when he's hungry."

Even as he spoke, it struck Sam that he wouldn't ever see this Apache woman again. More startling, he realized that in turning her over to the Army, he was giving up more than a mere captive. He wasn't prepared for the suddenness of it all, or the permanence, and he stood there on the porch and searched her eyes.

"We got to git," the soldier ordered, taking Sam's arm.

Sam eased out of the man's hold. "Damn it, let me walk on my own."

As Sam turned to start for the horses, he heard the *señora* sob. Facing her for the last time, he found her cheek glistening in the lamplight and couldn't understand what was inside him. All he knew was that he felt a powerful sense of loss, as if he was once again sprawled in Bass Canyon and letting an outside force take something away from him.

"Hate goin' off this way," Sam told her quietly. "Been through a lot, you and me."

He forced a bittersweet smile and the soldier ushered him away. They were already ten steps down the veranda when Sam heard his name, spoken with an emotional lilt that carried across this strangely dark moment. Looking over his shoulder, he listened as the young woman—a proud member of the very people who had sentenced him to hell—told him at last what he had wanted to know.

"I am called Nejeunee."

CHAPTER 20

The *Indaa* with crooked eyes looked at Nejeunee in a manner in which no one but a woman's husband had a right.

It was morning, and she sat discreetly nursing her baby in the hospital anteroom to which she had been denied entry the night before. Across from her at an angle, the scruffy civilian freighter with the dirty gray beard and foul odor lingered in an interior doorway, his attention divided between Nejeunee and the surgeon who was out of view inside. She could hear the surgeon's voice as he stocked the apothecary's new deliveries.

The moment the wagon had rumbled up as the corpsman had escorted Nejeunee from her tent, she had thought of the tobacco-chewing freighter with the filthy beard as Crooked Eyes. He seemed to look in two directions at once, his eyes unable to work together, and it made her all the more distrustful of him.

Nejeunee didn't need anything else to trouble her. Little Squint Eyes's face was hot against her breast, and he cried as much as he suckled. Throughout the night and morning, no one had communicated with her except by gesture, leaving her to fear the worst for her baby and herself.

But something else also wore on Nejeunee. There was a new hollow in her heart, alongside the breach that an *Indaa* bullet had placed there when it had taken he-who-cannot-be-mentioned from her. Sam-el had earned her trust in a way that she had never expected of an *Indaa*. Repeatedly, he had come to her defense, and that of Little Squint Eyes, and not once had he leered at her as Crooked Eyes did.

But for all the times Sam-el had befriended her, he was gone now, whisked away as suddenly as the mother and husband and *Ndé* sisters of whom she must never speak again.

Crooked Eyes, however, was very much present, and he displayed another characteristic that set him apart from Sam-el. He spoke the *Indaa* language with an accent, and as he moved away from the apothecary doorway and addressed Nejeunee, he did so mostly in Spanish that carried the same unusual pitch.

"*Sacré bleu!* Where hell they get you?"

He directed a question back toward the apothecary, and the concealed surgeon answered in a language that Nejeunee couldn't understand. Whatever the exchange, it failed to discourage Crooked Eyes from approaching her.

"So," he said, "squaw show up and Army got no place for." He looked her up and down, and Nejeunee shrank. "The price you would bring!"

The surgeon's voice sounded again, and Crooked Eyes glanced over his shoulder before continuing.

"What hell he want us do? Stop the talk? *Au contraire,* we got more to say. Soldiers need *señoritas,* and posts need hog ranches to give soldiers *señoritas.* Simple, eh? *Oui,* the price hog ranch here would pay me! Or at Camp Peña Colorado or Stockton!"

Nejeunee had never heard of a hog ranch, but his meaning was clear. He pressed closer and hovered over her, his holstered revolver probing her arm as he stared down at her half-veiled charms. She looked left and right, but there was no place to go. All she could do was cry for the only *Indaa* who had been kind to her—a silent, futile cry that Sam-el would never hear.

But the surgeon, to his credit, apparently sensed a problem, for he appeared in the apothecary doorway and raised his voice at the freighter. Turning, Crooked Eyes threw his hands out at his sides as if in protest. After more words passed between the two, the surgeon went back inside and Crooked Eyes faced Nejeunee again.

"He say your baby sick. Maybe by time I get back from Peña Colorado, he be better, huh? Maybe I set you up at hog ranch so he have good place to live and *mucho* to eat."

Ogling her even more, he tried to stroke her hair and cheek.

Nejeunee recoiled. *"Idzúút'i!"* she yelled, reverting to the language of the *Ndé*.

Her outburst did nothing to deter Crooked Eyes, but it brought the surgeon rushing into the room. Crooked Eyes pivoted to him, and there ensued a heated exchange that ended with the freighter leaving. But just as he went out the door, he looked back at Nejeunee and gave her a smile as crooked as his eyes.

Nejeunee.

Alone at the Ranger camp in Musquiz Canyon, Sam woke up wondering what the name meant. He said it out loud, noting its rare and mysterious sound. The musical way the word played on his tongue, it seemed the ideal complement to the trickle of the creek outside the beaded inner wall of his tent. He didn't think he had ever heard a name so appealing, and he closed his eyes and listened again as she stood in the lamplight and said it.

For eight months, it had been Elizabeth's voice that had lived in his thoughts, and he couldn't understand why it should be different now. He felt strangely guilty, as if somehow he were being unfaithful. But there was no denying that he ached inside in a new way, and there was just as little to soothe this pain as the anguish of a blood sun descending on Bass Canyon.

On this winter day at the camp of Company A, the sun rose bright, finding its way through the folds of Musquiz Canyon and the bare cottonwoods. It melted away the white frost on the canvas tents and the glaze of ice in the creek's shallows. The warmth of the rays was a balm for so much, and Sam should have been thankful for a comfortable place to recuperate. But it was all he could do to drag himself out of his tent and build a fire for coffee.

He was lost.

For eight months, he had lived to track down Elizabeth's killers. For brief days afterward, he had pursued a new purpose as ironic as it was unexpected: aiding a mother and child from that very band. But now his missions were over. Damn it, his *life* was over, just as surely as if he had slipped the muzzle of his .45 under his hat brim and squeezed the trigger.

Sam didn't think any day could be as black as that morning in May, but this one came close. He had never felt so lonely. In every breath of wind was despair. In every murmur of the creek was hopelessness. Together they reminded him not only of the yesterdays he could never reclaim, but all the tomorrows he would see alone. He wished he could talk it over with Elizabeth, but he didn't even have the silver locket that might have helped focus his thoughts. Maybe if that Mescalero rider hadn't snatched it from her neck—even after the warrior had slumped to Sam's surely mortal rifle shot—Sam might have read in the pendant's shining surface what her heart had to say about so many things, or perhaps only one.

Nejeunee.

There was no denying that Sam wanted to see this young woman. He worried about her, and even more so about her baby. Was Nejeunee being treated with the respect due her? How could she be, when the Army considered her nothing but an enemy squaw? And Little Squint Eyes—was he even alive anymore, and how would Sam ever know?

Under the midday sun at the adjacent ford in the Davis-Peña Colorado road, Sam sat flipping pebbles into the water and asked himself these questions and more. But answers were as fleeting as the quick splashes in the currents, even as Nejeunee's name kept bouncing around in his head.

In all the months since he had laid Elizabeth to rest, Sam had learned what it was to want, and never have. Why dwell on Nejeunee and Little Squint Eyes, when he might never be allowed on the post again?

Approaching hoofbeats and the screech of a wheel drew Sam back into the here and now, and he looked across at the Fort Davis road dropping into the creek. Standing, he watched the ears of two lead mules appear over the gentle far bank, followed by four more sets of ears and a wagon stacked high with freight. On the left wheeler—a harnessed mule nearest the wagon box— rode the teamster, evidently a civilian contract freighter for the Army, judging by the three-man cavalry escort alongside.

The freighter was so disheveled that Sam wondered if the long scout to the Diablos had rendered his own appearance similarly offensive. Sam's clothes were probably just as soiled, but at least he didn't have tobacco stains in a gray rat's nest of a beard, as did the stranger. But the man's most striking features were his eyes, for the left looked at Sam while the right seemed to chase imaginary butterflies.

Working the long jerk line, or single rein, the freighter stopped his team in mid-creek to water and spat off the side of his mule. Despite his best effort, just as much tobacco juice ended up on his revolver holster as reached the current. Brandishing his coiled blacksnake at the team, he cursed the animals in Spanish with a vocabulary that could have made Matto blush. He swore with a French accent that became more noticeable as he turned and addressed Sam in English.

"Ranger camp, eh? Quartermaster tell me, 'Dubois, don't let no rangers take flour. Sacks all requisitioned for Peña

Colorado.' " He glanced toward the tents. "Where hell everybody?"

"On scout. Been chasin' Indians."

"*Sacre bleu!* What a pretty squaw I seen at post. They make best whores, do squaws. This one—*mon Dieu!* If I had her tonight, I'd sure hell—"

In terms not meant for polite company, Dubois described intimate details that Sam didn't care to hear. But what did interest him was whether it was Nejeunee of whom Dubois spoke.

"Where'd you see her?" interrupted Sam. "The hospital? She got a baby?"

"Hanging on teat, damn sure. *Sapristi!* I wanted to—"

"That this mornin'? Baby seem all right?"

"Squalling, sucking same time, and squaw she spitting at old Dubois like mama cat. Spitfire she was!"

When the freighter resumed his vivid description of what he would do to Nejeunee, Sam set his jaw in anger. He waded into the stream, his rage growing with the Frenchman's every word. The crooked-eyed bastard! He'd drag him off that mule and teach him what respect was!

But then Dubois popped his long blacksnake against the team, and the mules lunged forward in their harnesses and carried the Frenchman on across with the wagon in tow.

Watching from the shallows as the outfit rumbled away with its escort, Sam tried to understand why he had become so enraged.

Respect.

For an Apache.

A few short days ago, Sam wouldn't have believed he could ever have associated respect with the people who had killed Elizabeth. But that had been before a young Apache woman and her child had touched something inside and given him purpose again—even if for a moment that had passed as quickly as it had come.

CHAPTER 21

Sam-el lived in Nejeunee's thoughts the way *Sháa* ruled the sky.

During her first day at the post, he was especially on her mind whenever a black soldier escorted her from the tent to the nearby hospital so that Little Squint Eyes could nurse. Upon mounting the steps, she would look down the long veranda and expect to see Sam-el return just as he had left: with his boots clicking against the planks.

But when two days had passed, and then three, Nejeunee's expectation and hope gave way to loneliness and fear. By day four, self-preservation forced her to adopt a *Ndé's* stoic acceptance of what had to be.

Sam-el was never coming back.

Just as he-who-cannot-be-mentioned, and her *Ndé* sisters of yesterday and the kindly *señora* of her childhood, Sam-el was now in the lake-of-the-gone-forever, relegated to dreams that would only sadden her upon awakening.

And yet he had taught Nejeunee so much about the *Indaa*, a people she had considered inferior. Maybe the *Indaa* were not so much different from the *Ndé*, or the *Mexicanos* of her upbringing. Maybe every people had their good men, like Sam-el and he-who-cannot-be-mentioned, and their bad as well, like Mat-to and Gian-nah-tah. Maybe *Bik'egu'indáán* and his Son Jesucristo blessed and punished without regard to a person's race.

Jesucristo.

Ever since Nejeunee had awakened that last morning to roast sotol hearts before the teepees of the *Ndé*, she had endured so much. There had been sudden violence and crushing change, followed by threats to Little Squint Eyes that still persisted. Throughout it all, the Beloved Son had seemed to do more than merely walk with Nejeunee. It was as if He had carried her. Even in her captivity, Jesucristo seemed to shelter Nejeunee under His wings as if she again held a chalice and sipped sweet wine, and more.

Maybe she felt His presence so powerfully here because of what stood against the sky at the summit of the adjacent mountain.

On the final night of their hard ride, Nejeunee and Sam-el had passed through the shadow of that mighty ridge and reached the post boundary at the hogback's sloping point. Now, sitting in the open flap of her tent and staring up, she closed her eyes against the afternoon glare and experienced a moment as real as if her steps had just now carried her to that very location in the road.

Before her in vision, the mountain's point loomed up in two stages: a sharp initial rise of perhaps a hundred feet, capped by two hundred feet of rock stacked upon rock. Nejeunee's dream-self struck out for the heights, dodging lechuguilla and prickly pear as she weaved up through scattered boulders. At the base of the towering palisade, the maraca-like warning of a black-tailed rattler stopped her in her tracks.

Just outside a dark recess, she saw it coiled, its deadly fangs poised to attack.

From the *Ndé*, Nejeunee had learned to revere *góbitseeghálególiní*, the rattlesnake, for its power over life and death. Indeed, no Apache would kill one, but that didn't mean that the creature wasn't evil—and this one was as sinister as a serpent striking at the heel of *Bik'egu'indáán's* Son.

"Back in your den, *góbitseeghálególíní,* you evil thing!" she cried, a typical *Ndé* curse on a snake. "Take the world's evil with you!"

Considering Nejeunee's mission, she wasn't surprised that a creature out of *infierno* would try to turn her away. But she wouldn't be denied. Skirting the rattler, she worked her way up a chimney between massive stone columns splotched ocher with lichen. She clawed at the rock, her fingernails searching out holds, her toes digging into crevices. Apaches prided themselves on their climbing ability, and Nejeunee did the *Ndé* justice as she scaled the palisade with intelligence and skill, along with strength that belied her slender frame.

The uppermost section consisted of loose rubble, and as she squirmed over the summit rim and looked up, the sky held a large cross, shining brilliantly under *Sháa.*

Buffeted by wind, Nejeunee crawled onward, the underlying rock digging into her knees. She reached the foot of the cross and stopped, a young woman wrenched out of one world into a second, and now into a third. Adrift, she stretched out a trembling hand, seeking the wood and more, and found the only constant in a life that had spanned the gulf between *Mexicano* and *Ndé,* and between *Ndé* and *Indaa.*

"*Señora.*"

A voice outside her tent shook Nejeunee back into reality. Peering around the dangling flap, she saw two figures approaching from the hospital. One was the uniformed guard, who never ventured far, and the second was a Pueblo scout in *Indaa* shirt, trousers, and boots. The scout, his long black hair secured by a flat-brimmed hat, again addressed her in Spanish.

"*Ven afuera,* come out."

As soon as Nejeunee emerged and faced the men, she also found the post surgeon weaving toward her, his face and eyes inflamed by *Indaa* liquor. In his arms was Little Squint Eyes, his little fists flailing.

"*Mi niño,*" she said, extending her hands.

Speaking in the *Indaa* language, the surgeon passed Little Squint Eyes into her care. Her baby smelled like the white man's breath—strong with liquor—but his color was better than in days, and his temperature seemed normal as she pulled him close.

"The fever is gone," the scout told her. "You are to keep him now."

Through all the stunning events, Nejeunee had held her emotions largely in check, even as they had strained for release. But now, leaning her cheek into Little Squint Eyes and kissing his head, she could suppress her feelings no longer. She looked up at the surgeon through a mist and said two words again and again.

"*Gracias, señor . . . gracias, señor . . .*"

The surgeon acknowledged with a nod before responding in the *Indaa* language, which the scout translated for her.

"*El cirujano,* the surgeon, did not like the ranger showing him a *pistola,* but he says the ranger was right in one way. More hours of high fever and the *niño* would have died."

Now Nejeunee's emotions were a flood, but the surgeon had more to tell her.

"He says you will leave for the Mescalero Reservation soon," related the Pueblo. "Upon his return from Peña Colorado, you are to go with Dubois, the freighter with the crooked look."

Even in her joy at Little Squint Eyes's recovery, Nejeunee flinched. The surgeon must have noticed, for he addressed the Pueblo again and motioned to her.

"Dubois is a *bastardo,*" the scout related to Nejeunee. "*El cirujano* may be a *borracho,* a drunk, but he knows this. He wants you to know that an escort will ride with you."

★ ★ ★ ★ ★

As Sam stooped to gather firewood in a thicket alongside the road on its northward approach to the Musquiz Creek crossing, he heard rising hoofbeats from both left and right.

At his face, a winter-bared mountain sage grew up through a low-hanging buckeye tree, and through the interlaced limbs he distinguished a freight wagon and cavalry escort coming from down-canyon, the way to Camp Peña Colorado. Meanwhile, across the ford on Sam's right, riders were approaching from the direction of Fort Davis and points west, including Van Horn's Wells where he had left Company A five days before.

Sam identified the teamster astride the left wheeler mule first—the vulgar freighter Dubois—and the mere sight of the repulsive Frenchman working the jerk line to halt the team thirty yards shy of the crossing was enough to set Sam's temples pounding. Dubois was only a few paces away on the team's far side as he climbed off to stretch alongside the three dismounting cavalrymen in his escort. Concealed in the brush, Sam knew that no good would come out of showing himself, but that didn't keep him from seething as he replayed the disrespectful things Dubois had said about Nejeunee.

The coiled blacksnake in hand, the Frenchman went about stiff-legged and checked the left-side mules and harnesses. All the while, tobacco juice dripped from his stained, gray beard. He seemed particularly displeased with the flop-eared lead animal, for he swore at it in three languages, and his profanity persisted as he worked his way back up the right-side mules to the wheeler. Now he was so close that Sam almost could have touched him, but who the hell would have wanted to, considering the Frenchman's body odor?

His inspection of the team done, Dubois stood in place against the backdrop of the wheeler mules and the tangle of brush across the road. Chewing and spitting and cursing, this cur of a man with crooked eyes had crossed a line three days before, and Sam was ready to step out and teach him a lesson.

But then Sam heard horses splashing across the ford, and he looked to see the men of Company A riding up, a dusty and weary bunch astride mounts with more flesh than Sam had expected. A measured ride could do wonders for even jaded animals, but he and Nejeunee hadn't had the luxury.

Arch rode at the head of the company, his drawn face and slouched shoulders showing the privation of the brutal scout. Tired-eyed, he seemed worn down to sheer gristle, a shell of the man he had been a week and a half ago.

But maybe the rigors of the Diablos had changed the ranger in another way too. Whatever his unspoken issues, Arch had once been a pleasure to be around, a man Sam had considered a friend. Now it wouldn't have mattered to Sam if he had never seen him again, or his damned red-checked neckerchief either. If Arch couldn't understand the impact of Elizabeth's death, why should Sam care about Arch's ghosts, and whatever role that hidden scar from throat to ear might play?

But maybe a friendship wasn't easily cast aside, for Sam was concerned by Arch's odd reaction as Dubois turned to the glint of sunlight in the ranger's *Cinco Peso* badge. Between the mule team and the shallows, Arch pulled rein hard, his face blanching as he stared at the Frenchman. Arch's fingers went to the knot of his neckerchief, and the longer he studied Dubois the more he fidgeted with it.

"No damn flour for rangers," Dubois told him.

In response, Arch only stared—stared with narrowed eyes and persisted in trifling with his neckerchief. Meanwhile, Jonesy had brought his horse abreast of the lead mules.

"Have you any tobacco?" Jonesy asked Dubois.

"Hell, got nothing for rangers," said the freighter. "They tell me, 'Dubois, you come straight back. Don't let rangers take nothing, damn sure.' "

As the quarrelsome Frenchman turned away and bent over to inspect the front wagon wheel, Arch squeezed his horse past Jonesy and approached. He began to shake, his breathing labored. More striking, from temples to jaw his face seemed to swell until he was all but unrecognizable. He was no longer the composed ranger with a professor's vocabulary, but an animal-like thing with cold, calculating eyes.

Crowding Dubois, his fingers moved to the coiled rope that dangled against his saddle. As Arch took it in hand, Sam couldn't imagine what he was doing; every ranger carried a lariat, but only to stake his horse or beat a rattler to death. But maybe rattlers sometime came in a two-legged variety.

Swinging a sudden loop, Arch dropped it over Dubois's head, and Sam couldn't believe what he was seeing.

The Frenchman's hat tumbled. "What hell—"

Arch yanked the rope taut around Dubois's neck, and the man's outcry became a gurgle.

" 'If you prick us, do we not bleed?' "

It was the kind of thing Arch would quote, but the growling tone was foreign to the voice Sam knew so well.

Dubois dropped the blacksnake and clawed at the noose, his fingers digging into his throat. At the same time, he stumbled toward Arch's mount, but the ranger denied him slack with a choking twist of the rope around the saddle horn.

" 'If you poison us, do we not die?' " Arch continued to cite.

The butt of a revolver showed in Dubois's holster, but instinct must have taken charge, for all he seemed able to do was thrash at Arch's saddle and spook the sorrel. When the animal shied, Dubois lost his footing, but the rope at his neck wouldn't let him fall. Arch was suffocating the life from him, but not without another odd quotation.

" 'If you wrong us, shall we not revenge?' "

Maybe the Frenchman was powerless to act, but no one else had watched idly. With shouts and drawn revolvers the three black troopers rushed on foot around the team, only to have Jonesy's roan block the way. Sam broke through the brush as the troopers yelled at Jonesy and Jonesy yelled back, and just as an Army-issue revolver at full cock leveled on Arch, Sam lunged for the man who had been his friend and dragged him from his horse.

The Army revolver boomed, missing Arch by an instant as he fell under his scared animal's flailing hoofs. When Sam seized the horse's bridle, the unscathed ranger rolled clear, and then the troopers were upon them with drawn weapons.

"On yo' feet!" someone ordered.

No one wanted answers more than Sam as Arch gripped the dangling stirrup leather and sat up.

"What the hell's this about, Arch?" Sam demanded.

But the ranger seemed dazed as he came to his feet alongside the sorrel. Glassy-eyed and still drained of color, he seemed unaware of the significance of the Army revolver trained on him, or of the questions barked by the soldier behind it.

Sam, knowing that instinct might lead Arch into a foolish act, quickly disarmed him. Meanwhile, past the upside-down V of the horse's neck and jaw, Dubois writhed on the ground even after the other soldiers freed him from the rope.

The nearer trooper waved his revolver at Arch. "You's goin' with *us*!"

But Sam stepped between the two. "This is a Ranger matter! I'm the one disarmed him and he's in my custody. Army don't have any say in this."

"He try killin' that man," the trooper contended.

"Yeah, I'm the one stopped him. This is a Ranger camp you're in, so you can get that man on his mule and all of you can ride out of here."

"Lieutenant ain't gonna like this."

"He want to make a fuss, he can take it up with me."

It was mostly bravado, but to underscore his authority, Sam took Arch by the arm and led him back to the brush. For the first few steps, Sam expected a challenge from behind, but he never looked back as the two of them broke through the latticework of buckeye and mountain sage.

Reaching bright sunshine, Sam checked over his shoulder and confirmed that no one followed. He could have taken Arch to camp, forty yards to his left, but he veered down-canyon instead and escorted the ranger through bear grass clumps, scrub oak, and hackberry shrubs. In a small clearing surrounded by alligator juniper and mountain mahogany, Sam stopped and turned to Arch, whose color had returned. Even more encouraging, his eyes no longer had the look of a man somewhere else.

"All right, I'm listenin'," said Sam.

With a long sigh, Arch glanced down and shook his head. "I was aware throughout, but I was helpless to do other than observe."

"So what's that mean? You know how close you come to gettin' killed?"

"I do. And I acknowledge my indebtedness to you."

"I don't give a damn who owes who what. You got some explainin' to do."

Arch looked away—far away, it seemed—and when he turned back, his eyes were wet. He began to tremble as he had in the road, and he brought his fingers to his temple as though it pounded to some terrible memory. Sam knew what it was to suffer inside with a pain that couldn't be deadened, but he never realized what it looked like on a man's face until now.

With compassion that surprised himself, Sam put a hand on Arch's shoulder.

"What was it the Frenchman done to you? I don't like the

SOB either."

"His eyes. The misalignment. That great a deviation from the norm. One other. That's all, just one other person."

"You sayin' he reminds you of somebody?"

For a moment, Arch couldn't speak, and when he did, his voice was hoarse with emotion.

"Trauma and intellect. Daggers of intellect. No matter how many daggers I throw, the unresolved trauma remains too strong."

Arch was talking in riddles more than ever, but Sam didn't interrupt.

"Intellect assured me the freighter wasn't my stepfather," Arch continued, "but the young boy inside refused to listen."

"Your stepfather? That what this was about? You gettin' back at him for somethin'?"

Wringing his hands, Arch glanced down and stirred the dirt with his boot. "Trauma unresolved . . . The power it wields . . ."

Looking up, he faced Sam for a moment, and then he untied the knot in the soiled neckerchief that Sam had never seen him without. In moments Arch's neck was bared to the winter sun, and it was as troubling as Sam's glimpse in the Diablos had suggested. A scar, faint except across the bulging Adam's apple, stretched in a band from ear to ear. Sam had little doubt that his earlier suspicions were correct, but he had to ask.

"A rope do that? Looks it."

"Even as it fades with every year," Arch quietly managed.

"You'd think somebody hung you."

Arch grimaced and his cheek developed a tic. "More times than I can remember."

Sam only stared, but he was trying to piece everything together: a boy, a stepfather, a hanging. No, *many* hangings.

"Never was a man so cruel to a boy or his mother," Arch continued. "Without provocation, he descended into manic fits of violence and assaulted her. For the most minor of offenses, he dragged me to the barn, positioned a rope over a rafter, and hanged me to the point of unconsciousness. In all but body, I died again and again, but it was never enough for him."

"Good God," Sam whispered. "Good God Almighty."

"When I was eight he doused us with lamp oil. He went in search of a match, and she took me and fled into the night. Six months later, we were ensconced with her family in London. I received the best of educations, but no one taught me how to forget a pair of eyes so malevolent, so misaligned—eyes identical to the freighter's."

"So *that's* it." Sam found a deep breath. "When it comes down to it, I guess you and me's not so different after all."

"I suppose you refer to vengeance."

Sam knew that neither of them had to say more, but Arch, to his credit, did so anyway.

"I . . . I may owe you an apology, Samuel. All that's happened between us, the Diablos, the aftermath . . . Perhaps I saw myself in you. Perhaps my criticisms were a way of suppressing my own latent desire for retribution."

"It can take hold of a person, Arch. Vengeance can damned sure do it."

For a moment, Arch stared down.

"I never realized I had the need to avenge," he acknowledged quietly. "Now that it almost demanded my life, I understand why a man on a journey of revenge needs to dig not one grave, but two."

They started back to camp, two men caught up in foredoomed journeys, and at least one of them deep in thought. An extra grave had been dug as soon as a Mescalero had seized Elizabeth's silver locket and killed her, an act perpetrated despite Sam's dead-center rifle shot moments before. Sam knew he might as well crawl inside that three-by-six now and be done with it—except for one faint hope that lingered in the face of all the impossibilities.

And her name was Nejeunee.

Never had Nejeunee been so happy, and never had Nejeunee been so sad.

Little Squint Eyes was well, thanks to Jesucristo and the helper He had sent, Sam-el. But Sam-el, for all his kindness and aid, was only a memory now, destined to fade farther and farther into the past. And soon she would start for the Mescalero reservation where Gian-nah-tah, if he lived, might be waiting to claim what was his.

The extremes of her emotions warred like *Ndé* and *Indaa,* and in her search for peace she focused on Little Squint Eyes. Still, in every detail of his face, she saw the father who would never know him.

She and Little Squint Eyes were alone in the tent, and the infant had just satisfied his appetite at her breast. Cooing and gurgling, he now delighted in batting the buckskin phylactery hanging from her neck.

Maybe the time had come to let him hold the keepsake hidden within and tell him of his father's love.

Securing the tent flap, as if mere canvas might discourage ghosts, Nejeunee parted the pouch and withdrew the very object that he-who-cannot-be-mentioned had clutched on the first stage of his journey to the afterworld. Even in the muted light, the forbidden keepsake was striking, and a smitten Little Squint Eyes reached for it. Whispering of a *Ndé* warrior as tender as he had been skilled, Nejeunee guided it into the tiny hands, and as the infant explored its polished contours, he managed to release the catch.

The keepsake, no larger than a coin, had passed from the

fingers of father to son, and now it sprang open: a silver locket baring everything except the secret of the *Indaa* engraving inside.

CHAPTER 22

The moment Sam awoke in his tent at daybreak, he knew what he had to do.

All through the long winter night, as wind had popped the canvas wall, and the rangers beside him had snored and snorted, a young Mescalero woman and her child had lived in his dreams. Nejeunee seemed with him even now, so vividly had she walked the hours with him. He could see her dark eyes and darker hair, but most of all he could see the smile that was for him alone.

On what must have been a trail of tears for her, Nejeunee had found reason to smile only once, shortly after he had rescued Little Squint Eyes from the cougar. But the impact on Sam had been so great that he yearned to see again the uplift of the corners of her mouth, a smile that had engaged her eyes.

And it would never happen unless he stepped back from his grave and tried to live again.

Still, as he squatted at the fire later in the morning and stared into his coffee, Sam began to doubt. What good would it do to try to see Nejeunee, when soldiers had escorted him from the post and left in question whether he could return? Regardless, with Little Squint Eyes so sick, had Nejeunee paid him even a passing thought since that last moment together?

Then someone spoke Sam's name, and he looked up through the drifting smoke to see Arch standing over him.

"It's imperative I post a letter for the capital through Army channels today," Arch said. "Ranger headquarters must be apprised of Captain Franks and our engagement with Mescaleros. A courtesy report to Davis's commander is also warranted. Should the incident yesterday have been relayed up the chain of command, I may need to maintain the appearance of being in your charge."

Just like that, the decision was made for Sam. He would ride into Fort Davis, and while he was there, he would do everything in his power to see the one person who might spare him from a waiting grave.

"It's time I showed those clueless Yankees how it's done."

A passionate Franks had said it upon setting out on the trail of the Mescaleros. Now that Sam and Arch stood across a cluttered desk from the seated commanding officer in a musty, dimly lighted office at Fort Davis, Sam only wished that Franks were here to relate the Rangers' success where the Army had failed. There was a lot about the sunrise fight that bothered Sam—he had unknowingly helped kill women—but the attack had been justified and vital.

With unexpected ease, Sam and Arch had gained entry to the post, but there was nothing surprising about the images that dominated Sam's thoughts as Arch began to narrate the events of the battle to the major with gray-flecked muttonchops. As the adobe interior wall beyond the officer's balding pate went hazy, Sam saw in memory an overwhelmed young woman, alone and desperate in a snowy arroyo as she fought for her baby. He saw her crush the child to her breast and face him, a man and woman at critical moments in their lives. And he saw her eyes, soft and pleading as they reached across different cultures to touch something inside him that he didn't know existed anymore.

With Nejeunee so powerful in his mind, Sam didn't realize

that the briefing had concluded until the commanding officer bade them good day. Arch turned to the anteroom, but Sam continued to face the major.

"A Mescalero woman and her baby was brought in last week," he said, fearing the worst for Little Squint Eyes. "They still here?"

The officer leaned to his left, evidently to see around Sam. "Lieutenant?" he called.

Looking back, Sam saw the doorway frame a rawboned young man in uniform with a second lieutenant's shoulder boards.

"Sir?" responded the junior officer.

"What was the disposition of the Indian woman and child?" asked the major.

"They departed this morning for the reservation in New Mexico by way of Fort Stockton."

Sam took heart. *They,* he had said. Not just *she,* but *they.* Still, Sam had to make sure.

"The baby too?" he asked the lieutenant. "He all right?"

"Both are accompanying a civilian freighter."

Sam flinched. "That Frenchman?"

"I believe his name is Dubois, sir."

Dubois! Sam's pulse began to hammer. *That disrespectful bastard!*

From behind the desk, the major spoke up. "Was Dubois by your decision, Lieutenant?"

"Does it pose a problem, sir?"

"You've been here but a short time. Dubois is an intemperate man prone to quarreling."

"They by themselves?" Sam pressed the major. "Just them two and the freighter?"

With eyebrows raised, the major looked past Sam again, evidently an unspoken inquiry of the junior officer.

"They travel with a three-man escort from the Tenth

Cavalry," said the lieutenant.

Maybe Sam thanked the major and lieutenant for the information. Maybe he simply brushed past the junior officer and rushed outside where the parade ground unfurled before him in bright sunshine. Whichever, Sam was angry and troubled as he untied his horse from the hitching post and dug his boot into the stirrup.

"You have the look of a man on a mission, Samuel," said Arch from the bottom of the steps.

Sam swung up into the saddle. "He said things about her, Arch. That damned Frenchman said things, and now they give him a chance to act on them."

"It represents an Army matter now."

"It's more than that to me."

Sam could have wheeled his mount and put spurs to it, but there was something in Arch's look that made him hold the animal. Could it be that he *wanted* Arch to pose the question that he had been afraid to ask himself?

"Samuel, have you developed feelings for this woman?"

But Sam stayed silent as the flapping of the parade ground flag tolled off the seconds. If he did need to examine what was inside him, he wasn't ready yet to face what he found.

"She and her child are being returned to their kind," Arch finally said. "You should surrender the responsibility for their welfare."

"I'm goin', Arch. Call it Ranger business or whatever you want to, but I'm goin'."

Reining his gray toward the east-lying guard house and the Fort Stockton road beyond, Sam dodged a waiting grave with the animal's every pace.

Astride a big roan with a US Army brand and bedroll, Neje-unee rode in the dust of Crooked Eyes's freight wagon as it rumbled north through the canyon of the Limpia.

She could see stacked crates bang against one another above the high endgate, and a grease bucket swing with a screech from the undercarriage. Against the groan of a wobbly wheel came the pop of a blacksnake against mule hide. The hoofbeats of the escorts' horses were constant, one set rising up from behind Nejeunee and the other two from alongside the wagon.

But as the canyon walls closed in, left and right—most dramatically across the shining creek where a three-hundred-foot palisade of red rock sprang up—one echo alone made Nejeunee want to unshoulder the cradleboard and shelter Little Squint Eyes.

The freighter's broken Spanish.

He had to twist around on the wheeler mule for her to see his face down the left sideboard, but with a bent smile that matched his eyes, he persisted in shouting intimate things that no *Ndé* ever discussed. He peppered his remarks with cursing that was without equivalent in *Ndé*, which had no profanity. But Spanish had enough swear words for both languages, and Nejeunee wished she could close her ears.

The best she could do was slide her horse to the right so that the wagon blocked her from his view. But Crooked Eyes only grew more vulgar, and when one of the Negro troopers evidently challenged him, the freighter silenced the soldier with a loud outcry.

Where a large, bare cottonwood stood on the left of the road, the wagon creaked to a halt in front of Nejeunee. Checking down the sideboard, she found Crooked Eyes summoning the troopers with a gesture and unfamiliar words. As the riders gathered about him, he swung off the wheeler mule and climbed up against the sideboard. Sunlight flashed in the butt of his holstered revolver as he rummaged inside, and when he faced the soldiers again he tossed one a bottle.

Stepping down, Crooked Eyes called the riders' attention to Nejeunee, for they all looked at her. Whatever he had in mind, they seemed unconvinced, but after he passed out a few silver dollars, the riders exchanged glances and nodded. When one of them dismounted and approached Nejeunee, she didn't know what to expect.

"Git down off'n yo' horse," he told her in passable Spanish.

She did so, and the soldier tied the roan to the rear wheel and led her to the cottonwood, where Crooked Eyes waited with the other men. Again, the freighter spoke to the soldier on foot, and he in turn addressed Nejeunee.

"You's can take off yo' load and rest a spell."

Nejeunee welcomed the chance, for Little Squint Eyes had seemed in discomfort and she needed to check him. Retreating to the cottonwood's trunk, she brushed the furrowed bark as she shed the cradleboard. Placing it on the ground, she knelt on both knees before it with her back to the road.

The day before, she had suspected that Little Squint Eyes was teething, although she had found no sign. Now, though, as she gently pulled down his lower lip, she saw a small, white cap against the pink of his bottom gum. It was yet another milestone of which his father would never be aware.

Moistening her finger in her mouth, Nejeunee set about massaging the tender area as she sang a *Ndé* lullaby in the hope that it might also soothe.

"*Sapristi!* Now we alone, damn sure."

Focusing on her baby's needs and dwelling on two men she had lost in different ways, Nejeunee had no idea that trouble brewed until Crooked Eyes spoke from behind. Turning, she found him hovering, his dirty face a vile blaze in the sky. He smirked through tobacco-stained whiskers as he eyed her, and even though acts of outrage were all but unknown among the *Ndé*, Nejeunee recognized the look for what it was.

Alarmed, she scanned the wagon for the horse soldiers, for they had been kind to her. But not until she noticed a plume of dust at a bend up-canyon did she realize that they had ridden away.

"No damn use you fight," the freighter growled.

Nejeunee tried to get her feet under her, but Crooked Eyes seized her shoulders and prevented it.

"*Idzúut'i!*" she cried.

Twisting out of his hold, she scrambled away a few feet before rough hands clutched her from behind.

"Wildcat, huh? Dubois tame you!"

With fists and elbows and knees, Nejeunee fought, but Crooked Eyes had a dominating position as he fell upon her and attempted to pin her shoulders. She could smell his reek, taste his foul breath, see the decay in his tobacco-stained teeth. His holstered revolver dug into the soft tissue below her ribs, and it must have been equally painful to him, for he cursed the *pistola* and wrenched it free.

"Now we have fun under cottonwood!" he said, tossing the weapon away from the trunk.

In the clash, they bumped the cradleboard, and Little Squint Eyes began to cry. He must have sensed that something was wrong, for his wailing grew louder until it was a heartbreaking shriek in Nejeunee's ears. But Crooked Eyes had a callous disregard for the infant's distress.

"*Sacre bleu!* He holler like panther!" He turned to Little Squint Eyes. "Dubois shut you up!"

Taking his hands from Nejeunee, Crooked Eyes reached for the cradleboard. At the same instant, she squirmed out from under him, and just as the *Indaa* gripped the willow frame, she lunged for the nearby revolver and found it.

"Damn whelp!"

Facing away from the cottonwood's base, Nejeunee only

heard Crooked Eyes's shout and the crash of wood against wood, but she whirled in terror and watched the splintered cradleboard slide down the trunk's unforgiving bark.

"Mi niño!"

With a cry, Nejeunee cocked the revolver and fired, but the roar was muffled as Crooked Eyes fell upon her again.

CHAPTER 23

Sam was troubled and riding hard.

He didn't know how much of a lead the wagon had, but as he pushed his horse through the winding canyon of the Limpia, he was thankful for the store of grain at camp. With the Ranger company a rider down, he had allowed his animal a greater share, and with nourishment and rest the gray had put on flesh almost before his eyes. Now, its hoofs covered ground in a jog-trot that, under ideal conditions, could carry a rider seven miles every hour.

But the lay of the sparsely wooded canyon was an impediment. Repeatedly, the road crossed the Limpia, its banks and gravelly bed slowing the gray's progress even though the creek was dry except for water holes. Still, the frequent crossings would delay a wagon even more, and Sam knew it was only a matter of time before he overtook the party.

Not ten miles out of Fort Davis, he came upon someone sooner than he had expected. In a sunlit stretch of canyon marked by towering, red-rock palisades, he drew rein before three Negro soldiers who sat back against a great, hewn boulder at a water hole on the left of the road. They seemed in high spirits, laughing and poking one another in the ribs, and the glinting whiskey bottle they passed around may have explained why.

Sam didn't waste time with greetings. "Seen a freight wagon come by?"

A soldier with bloodshot eyes rose with bottle in hand. "Jus' de one we's with," he said with slurred speech.

Sam looked left and right, finding only three US Army horses secured to a leafless hackberry tree. "Where is it?"

"Up road a ways." The soldier motioned. " 'Round dat bend yonder."

Sam checked, but saw nothing over his gray's ears except empty road disappearing to the left of palisades that angled up from its bed.

"How come you not with it?" Sam pressed.

"Freighter say give him a hour."

"Hour? What for?" Sam's pulse began to race. "The Indian woman up there?"

Holding the bottle out to the side, the soldier cocked his head and studied it with a frown. "Baby too."

A terrible rage rose up from the dark place where Sam's soul had been.

"You're supposed to be with them! Why the hell aren't you with them?"

"Dat white man have 'portant business with de Army. We do what he say."

The soldier tried to take a swig, but the whiskey flew as Sam lunged and knocked the bottle from his lips.

"I'm reportin' this!" Sam cried, his hand stinging. "You can damn sure bet on it!"

Gigging his horse for the road, Sam left in his wake a startled soldier and a shattered bottle, but the rage went with him as he galloped the animal around the next bend in the canyon. Facing a straightaway, he heard the faint crying of a baby almost as soon as he saw the wagon beside a cottonwood ahead. His ever-present bedroll flopped against the cantle as the gray's forelegs reached out again and again, and when Sam arrived at the tree and shouted for Nejeunee, he pulled rein so hard that his horse virtually sat back on its haunches.

The baby's cries came from the concealed side of the trunk, but there were also outstretched legs with boot heels up, and Sam dismounted with a full spin and bolted for a sudden display of black hair and calico edging into view at waist level alongside the cottonwood's coppery bark.

Nejeunee, her eyes wide and glistening, sprang up with Little Squint Eyes at her breast.

"Tell me if you're all right!" Sam shouted, assessing in a glance the still form beyond her.

Nejeunee seemed too startled to respond, but she rushed to him with a sob and looked up into his eyes as if she needed and expected more. Sam didn't know the conventions of Apache culture, but when he opened his arms, mother and child came inside. Distracted by the unmoving boot heels he saw over Nejeunee's shoulder, Sam couldn't digest all that he felt as he held them tentatively at first, and then closer. Still, for a moment he almost seemed at home.

Little Squint Eyes must have sensed Sam's protective arms, for his crying stopped. At first, Nejeunee had trembled in Sam's embrace, but with the passing seconds, she too grew more composed, although she seemed in no hurry to take her head from his shoulder.

"Mi niño," she sobbed. "Crooked Eyes hurt *mi niño."*

Sam kept his hands on her shoulders as he withdrew far enough to look at Little Squint Eyes.

"What did he do to him? What did the bastard do?"

It wasn't all that Sam wanted to ask. He wanted to ask if the Frenchman had violated her, but he didn't know how. Instead, he listened as Nejeunee told him all that she evidently wanted him to know, limiting her account to what Dubois had done to Little Squint Eyes. As Sam listened, he checked the bruising around her eye and the scratches on Little Squint Eyes's face, and when she finished he eased away and went to the French-man stretched out facedown past the cottonwood trunk.

Taking Dubois by the shoulder, Sam rolled him over to see dilated eyes fixed in a blank death stare. The freighter's last moments hadn't been easy, judging by the thrashed ground at his boots and the dark pool beside his torso. An 1860 Colt Army revolver lay nearby, and when Sam picked it up and smelled the barrel, he could distinguish the fresh powder residue. At the base of the cottonwood lay the cradleboard, its hoop frame broken, and he pieced together the desperate moments of which Nejeunee hadn't spoken. She had experienced a terrible episode, and the only thing he could take heart in was the fact that the Frenchman's body was still fully clothed.

Sam thought quickly. Those drunken soldiers would return soon, and they would find an Army contractor killed by a member of an enemy band. To their superiors, it might not matter that she was a woman and that the killing may have been justified; a white man was dead, and a Mescalero Apache was responsible. In the fight against her band, soldiers had died at Paso Viejo and Ojo Caliente, so her guilt almost certainly would be a given. Whether the escorts shot her on sight, or the Army hanged her or locked her away, the consequences would be severe for both Nejeunee and Little Squint Eyes.

Any way that Sam added it up, he couldn't afford to trust Nejeunee's fate to an Army that believed as he once had: that every Mescalero must be exterminated.

"Listen," he said, turning to her, "we've got to get out of here. Take Little Squint Eyes and anything you need and get on the horse."

As Nejeunee rushed toward the broken cradleboard, Sam looked back at the Frenchman's dead eyes and realized he had something to do. Hurrying to the wagon, Sam climbed up against the sideboard and rummaged inside the cargo bed.

Within arm's reach he found what he expected: the freighter's business ledger, wrapped in a slicker. Marking the page of the last entry was a pencil, and Sam took it and wrote a hasty letter to Fort Davis's commander:

Sir:
Under my authority as a Texas Ranger, I have took the Indian woman and child. I will bring the horse back the first chance I get. The freighter hurt the baby and tried to outrage the woman and was shot in self defense. Please report this to the Rangers at Musquiz Canyon.

Sam DeJarnett
Company A, Texas Rangers

Tearing out the letter, Sam folded it in two places and wrote "Major, commanding Ft. Davis" on the outside. Not bothering to rewrap the ledger, he left the book where he had found it. Spying airtights and jerky, he filled a burlap sack and then carried it with him as he hastened to the Frenchman's body. On the breast just below the filthy beard, a spot free of blood, Sam left the note with a rock holding it in place.

Maybe his words wouldn't do any good, but at least he had tried. There was a chance the escorts wouldn't even deliver the letter, for they had reason to suspect that it related their irresponsible actions. Sam only hoped that one of the soldiers could read, for he purposely had left out any mention of them.

With a glance at the still-empty Fort Davis road past Nejeunee, who waited on horseback with Little Squint Eyes in her arms and the damaged cradleboard at her back, Sam swung astride his gray and faced her.

"*Vámonos!* Let's go!"

Side by side, they fled down the road toward the next shielding bend.

CHAPTER 24

It was a place Sam wished he could stay forever.

Four miles up a narrow, twisting canyon, he sat in warm sunshine before a sparkling stream whose waters quietly sang as they wound through rocks and clumps of cattails. Across from him, a mountain laurel added greenery where dormant mimosa and desert willow hugged the bank. On the sharp rise just beyond, sparrows flitted in the bare limbs of walnuts and gray oaks, while from somewhere above came the throaty gobble of a turkey. After stressful hours, this was a place of peace.

Where the road turned east for Fort Stockton, Sam and Neje-unee had veered northwest into a high-desert valley with yucca and mesquite chaparral. With only naked hills on their right, they had pushed hard for canyon-rent crags standing dark against the west sky. Navigating broken country for hours, Sam had often checked over his shoulder. But not until he had reconnoitered from a high ridge at the mouth of this canyon had he breathed a sigh of relief.

He had been able to look back a dozen demanding miles, almost as far as the Fort Stockton road, and there had been no sign of pursuit. That didn't mean that the Army had forgotten about Dubois. But for now, at least, as Sam watched a floating twig meander downstream between rocks and cattails, he was content and even elated.

He knew why.

It wasn't the setting, or the absence of immediate threat. It was because he was with Nejeunee.

Twenty feet upstream under a small maple, she sat mending the cradleboard with leather tie strings from the saddles. Sam looked at her often, noting her smooth profile and the shapely swell of her calico blouse. He especially liked the brush of her black hair against her cheek as she checked Little Squint Eyes on the ground beside her. Nejeunee had a grace about her that Sam had never let himself appreciate, and when she looked up at him and smiled, he did so in return without embarrassment.

Ever since they had dismounted here, there had been something unspoken between them. Sam could feel it, and he could see it in her glances. Her eyes danced as they did when she played with Little Squint Eyes, but there was more. They seemed alive in a fresh new way, and Sam wondered what his own would show if he could see them.

He kept thinking about how he had held her at the cottonwood. She had turned her face aside, and yet her head had found the hollow of his neck. He had felt the touch of her hair against his jaw, and her warmth as the tremble of her body had faded. There had been something special about that moment, and he longed to take her in his arms again.

Rising, Sam went to her, and she greeted him with another smile as he sat so that Little Squint Eyes was between them. Whatever the immediate effects of the Frenchman's assault, the child seemed all right now, for he lay gurgling and cooing as he batted at imaginary objects. Sam placed an index finger before the tiny hands, just as he had done on the day of the cougar attack, and Little Squint Eyes gripped it with delight in his face.

"*Inádlu*," said Nejeunee, smiling down at the infant.

"That Apache?" Sam asked.

"It means 'he laughs.' He likes you, so he laughs." She lifted her gaze. "You give me reason to laugh also, Sam-el."

Sam read a lot into her statement, but no more than what he

thought was in her expression.

"I'd almost forgot how to laugh myself," he said.

He felt Little Squint Eyes tug his finger. *"Inádlu,"* Sam repeated. "Kind of pretty, the way you say it. Your name too— *Nejeunee.* Mean anything?"

"Kind, or friendly. If I say, '*nejeunee* Sam-el,' it's to say, 'good friend Sam-el.' "

For a moment, he explored her eyes, and she did nothing to discourage him.

"I *am* your friend, Nejeunee. And I hope I can say '*nejeunee* Nejeunee'—'my good friend Nejeunee.' "

Little Squint Eyes had released Sam's hand, and Sam impulsively stretched it toward Nejeunee. He was blind to Apache custom, and when she didn't take it, he realized he must have offended her. But no sooner had he withdrawn his hand than her fingers stole out across the infant and accepted it. As their clasp lingered, things yet unspoken swelled inside him and showed in her eyes. Then Little Squint Eyes batted their joined fingers, and Nejeunee and Sam both laughed and the spell was broken.

"Feelin' left out, are you?" he asked the infant. Working his little finger free of Nejeunee's hold, Sam let the tiny hands take it.

Nejeunee gave a girlish giggle and let the baby take her finger as well. "See, Little Squint Eyes? Now you have *shimá*, mother, and Sam-el both."

Nothing could have relaxed Sam more, and he no longer felt a need to hold some of the unspoken words in reserve.

"I was afraid I wouldn't ever see you again," he said.

Nejeunee only looked at him.

"I wanted to," Sam added, "but I didn't think they'd let me. Then I woke up this morning and decided I wouldn't let anything keep me from it."

Still, she only stared, and Sam began to wish he had remained quiet.

He glanced at Little Squint Eyes. "I know you been worried sick about your baby."

For a moment, Sam looked away, but the squeeze of Nejeunee's hand brought his head around again.

"A hollow was in my heart," she said. "Not even Jesucristo could take it away. It grew greater with every day. I was happy knowing Little Squint Eyes was well. But greater happiness had fled to the lake-of-the-gone-forever.

"And then you appeared around the tree, Sam-el."

Brush suddenly popped from behind, and Sam drew his revolver by instinct and whirled. He jumped to his feet, his every sense fixed on movement in the scrub oaks down-canyon. He counted three gray-brown figures—no, four—and they continued to break twigs as they advanced from right to left through the tangled limbs and shrubby undergrowth. He glimpsed a strange white flag, and another and another, and then Nejeunee was standing beside him and pointing.

"*Tseenaagaai*," she said calmly.

Now Sam saw them for himself: deer flashing their white tails as they grazed the canyon bottom.

Sam turned to Nejeunee. "Want to tell me again how brave I am?" he said with a chuckle.

But at least the two of them were no longer discussing personal things. The truth was, Sam was scared by what Nejeunee had said, and by what he was feeling. It was all too much, too soon, and he needed time away from the influence of her eyes and touch so he could think.

But as the sun crawled across a tangle of limbs above, and matters of the heart stayed safely in the list of things unsaid, Sam couldn't pull himself away from her. He didn't *want* to be out of her presence, not even for a little while, and when she sat at stream's edge and placed her bare feet in the shallows, Sam eased down beside her.

As he listened to the creak of the cradleboard while it swung with Little Squint Eyes from a nearby hackberry limb, Sam smoothed his palm across the stream's surface. Soon, however, he and Nejeunee looked at one another, and for hours that went by much too fast, they engaged in good-natured small-talk. Then without warning, she splashed him in the face with her foot, and he splashed her in return with his hand. She laughed and he laughed, and they kept up their banter and teasing play until she left Little Squint Eyes in his care and went into the brush downstream to bathe.

Alone now except for the sleeping infant, Sam had nothing to distract his thoughts. But he decided he didn't really care to figure things out. There was a connection between Nejeunee and him, and he was sure that she felt it too, and it was better to live in the moment than break it apart trying to understand it.

Nejeunee soon returned, wrapped in a woolen Army blanket and carrying her freshly washed clothes. Her shoulders were beaded with water and her wet hair was glossy, and Sam couldn't take his eyes off her as she stood before the limbs of an oak and hung the garments in the sunlight. Whenever she nursed Little Squint Eyes, she did so discreetly under her blouse, and she was not immodestly clad even now. But for the first time, Sam saw a small, buckskin pouch dangling from her neck.

From a distance, it seemed to be marked by an artistic cross— two meandering yellow lines passing through similarly crooked streaks of red. More than once, she had said things that had suggested a Christian faith, and the colorful design made him wonder even more.

Sam stood as she approached. "I'm next up for a bath, I

guess," he said. Then he motioned. "So what's the little leather bag?"

Nejeunee paused and glanced at it. "Power is in all things. Special power is inside for me alone to claim."

"What you got painted on it?"

With her slim fingers, she brought the artwork to her lips.

"To *Ndé*, it's the red and yellow snake, but I see more. I see the cross of Jesucristo in the long-ago village of the kindly *señora*. The Blessed Son is a power greater than any. When Little Squint Eyes is older, I'll teach him to pray for His help."

Sam looked down and found a weary breath. "Wish it was all that easy."

He knew that Nejeunee came up before him, but he was back at Bass Canyon for a moment.

"Your heart has its own hollow," she said quietly.

"Friend of mine told me it's a long, hard climb up out of hell. I'm thinkin' that once we ever sink that far, it's not much use even tryin' to crawl out."

"Your loss was great, Sam-el."

He looked at her. "So was yours from what you told me. But you seem to get by better than me. I suppose havin' a baby to look after helps."

At his words, Nejeunee went to the nearby hackberry, where Little Squint Eyes still swung in his cradleboard. Removing the infant, she pressed him to her breast with a loving kiss and looked at Sam.

"I hold Little Squint Eyes in my arms," she said, "but it's Jesucristo who holds me in His."

Sam stared at her, wondering if that kind of assurance could ever be his.

"I might've felt the same way too, once upon a time," he whispered. "But I guess I kind of gave up after—"

No. He wouldn't talk about it. He wouldn't relive Bass

Canyon aloud, even if he couldn't control the memories. With a long, troubling sigh, he turned away, and the sunlit stream before him began to blur.

"*Ndé* or *Indaa,* a warrior doesn't give up; he fights," Nejeunee told him from behind.

Sam turned, strangely unafraid for Nejeunee to see the emotion in his face.

"You're a warrior, Sam-el," she added. "And brave."

Through all the yearning, Sam found a bittersweet smile that he could have mustered for no one else.

"Except when it comes to deer?" he managed to joke.

In his bedroll within arm's reach of Nejeunee that night, Sam lay awake, staring up through bare limbs at the jeweled sky and hearing again her words.

His father had believed, and so had Elizabeth, strongly enough for Sam to have regretted not setting a cross when he had buried her. Now he had confirmed that Nejeunee—this young woman thrust into Apache culture against her will—still clung to her faith despite everything that had happened to her.

Once, Sam too might have acknowledged some level of belief, but he figured that the difference between acknowledging and committing was like the contrast of a pebble to a mountain. Even if he *did* yearn for the caring arms of someone greater, was it possible for a man who had shown through his actions that he had lost his soul?

But maybe a spark of it still existed, waiting to flare if he would only answer the summons.

Shortly before daybreak Sam awoke, not even aware that he had gone to sleep. But he felt refreshed, and strangely overjoyed, for just beyond the cradleboard and Little Squint Eyes, Nejeunee lay resting peacefully. She had graced his dreams, and now he wanted to reach for her and relive the glorious moments of the afternoon before.

But bliss could become hell in a moment if the Army seized Nejeunee for a killing that had been justified.

Sam realized he had been remiss in not being more vigilant, and in alarm he rose and saddled his gray in a light frost. As was common in winter, the animal humped its back to the cold leather, and Sam was adjusting a cinch when he heard the pleasing lilt of a voice behind him.

"Sam-el?"

Looking back, Sam found Nejeunee standing a few yards away, a blanket around her shoulders as she held Little Squint Eyes.

"I'll be back quick as I can, so be ready," he said. "If you hear me shoot, head up the canyon and don't never come back."

He straightened the stirrup and started to step up, only to hesitate.

Never.

Sam didn't like the sound of that. Turning, he led the horse up before Nejeunee and, before he would let himself anticipate her reaction, hugged her lightly. Neither of them spoke, but when he rode away, he could still feel her warmth as she had accepted his arms.

He bore downstream, the tightness in the gray's back relaxing as the animal warmed. But as horse and rider navigated the twists of the canyon, Sam's tension only grew, for he knew the consequences to Nejeunee if he met pursuers and she couldn't hear his warning shot.

He made it to the canyon mouth without incident before sunrise and again reconnoitered from a high ridge. If soldiers from Fort Davis were to give chase, they would probably do so no later than today, for the elements could wipe out a trail quickly. From behind an angling yucca, he watched the sun burst over the jagged skyline of faraway mountains. The blaze was as swollen as the orb that had precipitated the attack on the Mescalero camp, and Sam began to tremble.

How close the rangers had come to killing Nejeunee. How close *Sam* had come to killing her. He had fired repeatedly, taking a bead on one blanketed form after another. Damn him to hell, he had taken friends from her, her world from her.

Just as her people had taken his.

He dwelled on that, and more, as the long shadows receded in the broken country below and the distance remained empty. How very wide the gulf was between Nejeunee and him. They had so many things going against them, and he knew he had no right to expect even a friendship.

And yet *something* was happening, and he felt it growing stronger by the moment whether they were together or apart.

On into midmorning, Sam's thoughts were on Nejeunee alone, and then a corner of his mind alerted him to a plume of dust in the ocher reaches of the lowlands. Stepping out from the yucca to orient himself, he was troubled to find that the blight lay on a line to the Fort Stockton road. So distant that it didn't seem to move, the plume could have been a dust devil, but when it didn't dissipate after several minutes, Sam rushed for his horse with a wag of his head.

A cavalry patrol had picked up their tracks, and he and Nejeunee had no choice but to run.

Sam's ride back up the tangled canyon seemed to take longer than before, and when he broke upon the small clearing where he had left Nejeunee, she was nowhere to be seen. But she was of the people who had long eluded the Army's best, and she knew how to hide. When Sam called her name, he heard brush crackle across the creek, and he looked twenty yards up the sharp rise to find her leading the roan out from behind a brushy juniper. With Little Squint Eyes at her back, she agilely descended to the stream, and by the time she waded across,

Sam had stepped off his horse and was waiting.

"Nejeunee, there's nothin' I'd like better than to stay here," he said. "I want to take hold of your hand and us walk up the stream and listen to it singin' with the sparrows. I want to hear what color you like the best and little things like that, what it is you dream about when you're wide awake. But we got Army comin', and we got to save all of that for when we have time. Right now we got to ride."

CHAPTER 25

Nejeunee was a woman on two journeys, and she didn't know where either would lead.

Forging up the snaking canyon, they broke trail through a tangle of gray oak and maple, mahogany and madrone. They crisscrossed the gurgling creek as the bordering slopes squeezed in on first one bank and then the other. They skirted a rock spire that towered from the stony streambed, and passed a deep pool where the gulch momentarily narrowed to only yards wide. And always more canyon waited ahead, hidden behind one bend after another, and they had no choice but to push on because she had killed an *Indaa*.

As challenging as her flight was, and as uncertain its end, Nejeunee's greater journey lay inside. Sam-el was there, bridging the impossible divide and making her more alive by the moment. She knew what he was surrendering for her. She was in trouble, and now he would be as well, and his sacrifice only added to her confusion about what was unfolding between them.

She had no doubt that *something* was developing, even though *Sháa* had made only a few courses across the sky since they had met in the stained snows. They had been through so much together, and the intensity of those shared experiences made the time seem far longer. Indeed, she had never felt so powerful a bond with anyone except he-who-cannot-be-mentioned, and yet Sam-el was an *Indaa,* a hated enemy.

No. He was her friend and more, and she wouldn't fight what

was inside her.

"Blue."

"What?" asked Sam-el.

She rode at his flank through a stretch of piñons under beetling cliffs, and he turned in the saddle with a creak of leather.

"My color is blue, like *yá*, the sky."

"I swear, Nejeunee," he said with a laugh, "if you don't have a way with conversation."

"I want to make that walk with you," she added. "I want to hear the waters sing. I want to see the birds fly and watch the leaves dance in the four winds. I want to feel your hand in mine, Sam-el."

They were in flight, but Sam-el reined his gray about and the two of them held their horses side-by-side so that they faced one another. For a moment they just stared, and then his arm stole out as it had the day before. This time he gently stroked her hair where it fell across her cheek, but it was a tentative caress at best.

"I don't know your ways," he said softly, "so you got to tell me when I do wrong."

In response, she inclined her face to his fingers and prolonged his touch by placing her hand over his.

They rode on, but now the roan carried a different Nejeunee. It was true that Sam-el was unversed in Apache culture, or else he would never have initiated so intimate an act. But Nejeunee knew well the ways of *Ndé* courtship, and she had just signaled to both of them that she welcomed his attention.

They spent that night in the canyon again, and the next three as the bends continued to lure them higher into the mountains. Throughout, they talked of happy things and of each other, even as she kept to herself the feelings that she had yet to process. Sam-el too seemed to leave a lot unstated, but she read much in his respectful glances.

By their sixth day in a country too rugged for night travel, Sam-el's horse developed a sore foot, limiting their miles, and he openly worried that they would no longer be able to outdistance the cavalry. But with day nearing an end, the danger from behind was suspended for a while, and they unsaddled and staked their horses in a small meadow bordered on the right by a half-dozen slender ponderosas on the stream bank.

After so many hours in the saddle, Nejeunee was glad to stay on her feet while they ate airtights of beans and tomatoes. But after Sam-el sat on a ponderosa log and patted the bark alongside, she joined him and let Little Squint Eyes nurse. She and Sam-el talked as dusk came with a creeping chill, and he must have noticed her tremble, for he helped draw a blanket around her.

Still Nejeunee's quake persisted—only now it was because Sam-el's arm remained about her shoulders.

She went silent, and so did he, but they had much to say in other ways. She looked at Sam-el and found him looking back, and she snuggled against this *Indaa* while the stream trickled from behind and roosting birds flitted in the limbs above.

Nejeunee didn't want the moment to end, but Little Squint Eyes soon appeased his appetite and began to flail his small fists.

Sam-el bent his face toward him. "Always gettin' left out, aren't you, nubbin," he said with a little laugh.

Nejeunee didn't understand the last word, since it wasn't in Spanish, but there was no mistaking his tenderness.

"You'll make a good father someday," she said.

"If I get a chance, maybe. But it's sure good Little Squint Eyes has got somebody like you takin' care of him."

Straightening, Nejeunee held the infant up before her and danced him on her knee.

"*Shilth nzhu*, Little Squint Eyes," she told him happily. "*Shilth nzhu, shilth nzhu, shilth nzhu!*"

"The way you say it, ever'thing's pretty," said Sam-el. "*Shilth nzhu*—I say that right?"

He had, and Nejeunee was so caught up in hearing him voice it that she ceased her play and turned to him. Sam-el was an innocent child in the ways of the People, but he was also a man, and no man but he-who-cannot-be-mentioned had ever said such words in her presence.

"So what's it mean?" Sam-el asked.

Embarrassed, Nejeunee dropped her gaze, and when she looked up she had a teasing smile instead of a reply.

Sam-el gave a little laugh. "Well?"

Nejeunee felt mischievous. " '*Shilth nzhu*, Nejeunee.' "

She knew he would repeat it, and he did so, although haltingly.

"Stringin' words together's a little harder," he said. "I know *nejeunee* means friendly, so what is it I said?"

Nejeunee flashed another coquettish smile. "You just told me I'm dear to your heart."

Night may have been falling, but it couldn't disguise the deep flush that swept across Sam-el's face. Nevertheless, he managed a nervous laugh.

"Well, at least I wasn't goin' on about how brave I am with deer."

For a moment, Sam-el's humor defused the situation. But as their mutual gazes lingered, he seemed to explore Nejeunee's eyes, as she did his. Once, his lips parted as if he was about to speak, but his voice stayed quiet. Still, when he pulled her closer and Nejeunee laid her head against his chest, the things unsaid were more powerful than words.

"It's all right, Sam."

Sam awoke with a start, and the soft voice seemed to follow him out of a dream that had lasted the night.

"Sam," Elizabeth repeated. "It's all right."

The words seemed so real that Sam sat up, searching the dark for someone who couldn't be there.

"Sam . . . Sam . . ."

The voice faded and went silent. Lying back and closing his eyes, Sam yearned to hear more, so that he might understand and accept.

The images came again.

He stood with Elizabeth in Bass Canyon, and before them, strangely, was the windswept mound that was her grave. At its head knelt Nejeunee, her raven hair falling across her face as she fashioned a cross out of sotol stalks.

"Go to her, Sam," Elizabeth said. "Sam, it's all right."

He turned to Elizabeth and placed a tender hand on the bulge in her abdomen. "But—"

Elizabeth was pointing. Sam looked, and now he saw tiny hands flailing in the cradleboard at Nejeunee's side.

"Go to them, Sam. Sam, it's all right . . . all right . . . all right . . ."

When Sam opened his eyes again, dawn had broken, and there was a whole new world to greet him. The air was fresh and exhilarating and the trickle of the stream joyous. Through the ponderosa limbs above, the sky glowed with a golden hue that he had never seen before, and he had to hold back a cry of exaltation that would have rolled from slope to slope and shaken the piñons and gray oaks, the junipers and maples.

Turning, he saw Nejeunee facing him in peaceful sleep from beyond the cradleboard and Little Squint Eyes. Had Sam dreamed what he had because he wished it to be true? His feelings seemed so clear now, his conscience so clean, and suddenly all he wanted to do was smile, and smile some more. He was alive, truly alive, in a way he hadn't been for three seasons, and there was hope where there had been despair.

Sam sat up, quietly calling Nejeunee's name, and she awoke with a smile for him.

"*Nil daaguut'é,*" she greeted him, stretching with obvious pleasure. "*Mexicanos* say '*Buenos días.*' "

"It *is* a good mornin', Nejeunee." He reached for her, and she sat up and took his hand across Little Squint Eyes. "It's a good mornin' 'cause you're here with me and 'cause I want it to stay that way. You and me's so different, and ever'thing's happened so quick, but that don't matter. I don't care if I say it in Apache or English or Mex, *shilth nzhu* or *te amo* or ten other ways, I love you. You and Little Squint Eyes both, Nejeunee. I want to take care of you and the three of us to be together."

Nejeunee's eyes began to glisten, and Sam feared that he had crossed a boundary that he should have respected. An uncomfortable silence followed, but her fingers stayed inside his hand as her chin quivered and emotion flooded her cheeks. When she finally withdrew from his clasp, Sam sank inside, and then she flashed him a reassuring smile and rose.

Confused, Sam stood with her.

"*Por favor,* watch Little Squint Eyes," Nejeunee said. "I must saddle your horse and prepare your meal."

She must have caught the quizzical look on Sam's face. "It's the Apache way," she added.

"Way?"

"If you accept the horse and eat, you declare us joined."

With a chuckle of relief, Sam put his hands on her shoulders. "All right, but first things first."

He managed only a quick kiss before she slipped out of his arms with a laugh of her own and went to the horses.

CHAPTER 26

From the sunrise came a horse's nicker, sudden and unmistakable.

By instinct Sam pivoted down-canyon, but he didn't waste time debating what to do.

"They're on us!"

Scooping up Little Squint Eyes in his cradleboard, he ran for the horses staked to ponderosas across the small meadow. Nejeunee had already saddled his gray and had the burlap bag spread open at the log, but she met him and took the cradleboard.

"I'm sorry, Nejeunee, but we got to wait to make it official," he said. "You grab ever'thing while I throw a saddle on the roan."

She obviously was experienced in breaking camp quickly, for when Sam tightened the cinch and turned, the bedrolls and supplies were affixed to the horses and she was extending the gray's reins.

Nejeunee's face may not have shown disappointment, but Sam felt plenty of regret.

"I'll make this up to you," he said, taking the reins. "For the rest of our lives. I promise."

Moments later the three of them were bearing up-canyon as quickly as the brush and terrain and Sam's sore-footed animal would allow.

All that morning, they pushed on without pause, twisting and turning with the canyon's course. They scared up cottontails and a bobcat, mule deer and a gray fox, and once when the horses shied in a piñon brake, Sam glimpsed a large, brown form with white-tipped fur at its back and a hump at its shoulders. The stream grew intermittent and then went dry, and soon the horses weaved through wagon-sized boulders that stood among dense mahoganies, gray oaks, and mountain laurels, along with madrones with their sleek, red limbs.

With the bordering slopes hidden by the timber, Sam didn't realize until it was too late that he and Nejeunee were being funneled into a box canyon.

They broke into bright sunlight to face fifty yards of open gorge ending at a dramatic pour-off between impossibly steep bluffs left and right. From the high notch, stark against the sky, fell a thin stream that struck the cliff halfway to bottom. Splitting in two, the water clung to the rock in a diamond pattern as it rushed down almost vertically to a small pool. There at canyon's head the water apparently sank into the ground, for there was nothing but gravel all the way back to Sam.

It was a beautiful place, but so too had been the Diablo snows before blood had profaned it.

Sam wheeled his horse to Nejeunee. "Can't go back! I don't know what to do!"

He expected to find her paling, but he had forgotten that her people had lived by escape during all the months that the Tenth Cavalry had hunted them.

"*Anee!* Over there!" she exclaimed, pointing over his shoulder.

Sam turned. The bare bluffs on either side were too rubbly for handholds, and the sun-splashed cliff with its shining diamond seemed mostly worn smooth. But a few yards to the right of the pool the rock face was less burnished, and he could see a dark, jagged line springing up from the bottom.

He gigged his horse for it and Nejeunee followed, and the hoofbeats still echoed when they swung off their animals before a crack perhaps eighteen inches wide. But the cliff was undercut by four feet, a daunting first step, and when Sam looked up, the wall of rock seemed to rise into the sky itself. They couldn't do this, neither of them, not with Little Squint Eyes and the certainty of death if they slipped.

But death was exactly what Nejeunee faced if they stayed here and waited for those Army rifles to flash fire.

Already, Nejeunee was reaching for a handhold, and Sam boosted her up and brought his horse alongside the rock and stepped up from the saddle. He gained the crack and dug a boot into it, and then there were just the three of them, fighting their way up a place never meant to be climbed. His doubts only grew as he clawed at her heels and the canyon floor receded, and he could only imagine what it would be like if the soldiers caught them with their faces to the rock and opened up with their rifles.

Sam never should have glanced back, but he did, and in the woods down and away he saw light gleaming, the kind of effect expected when sunlight catches a firearm.

"We's in a bad way," he said, looking up at Nejeunee's legs and the cradleboard blazed in the sky. "If you got any of that special power to call on, now's the time."

"I'll pray to Jesucristo."

In this most desperate of situations, Sam was struck as never before by the Christian faith of this young Mescalero woman who, twice uprooted from her people, had every reason to call upon only Apache gods, if any at all. She was nothing less than inspiring, and he thought back to his boyhood when his father would take his hand and tell him that the Almighty had a purpose for him, if Sam would only walk in His ways. For almost nine months, Sam hadn't understood why he had been spared at Bass Canyon, but he wondered now if an agent of vengeance had ever been his intended role. Maybe his real mission had been to watch over Nejeunee and Little Squint Eyes, for where would the two of them be if Sam hadn't intervened in the Diablo snows and ever since?

Service.

Maybe Boye had been right.

As Sam listened to Nejeunee quietly call upon Jesucristo, he found himself doing something that had been unthinkable from the moment the Apache fiend had seized Elizabeth's locket and killed her: He prayed as his father had taught him.

They had climbed far past the diamond, and now the zigzagging crack bore left until Sam could feel a spray from the free-falling water. Abruptly Sam's hands were wet, every handhold and foothold slick, and when Nejeunee's moccasin slipped and momentarily struck his shoulder, the three of them came perilously close to plummeting. It had become an impossible climb, and all he could do was cry out for Nejeunee to hold on.

His lungs heaving and his strength waning, Sam clung there, knowing it was the end but refusing to accept it. Then Nejeunee shouted "There!" or "Where!" or an Apache word he didn't know, and she inched higher and inward across the cliff face. Sam couldn't understand why she would seek out the falling stream and even slicker rock, but where he no longer had confidence or strength, he found both courage and will and followed. The water's full force was in his face before it was over, but after another harrowing minute, Sam crawled after Nejeunee onto a recessed ledge directly behind the falls.

The sunlit hollow was just high enough to allow a person to sit, and deep enough to escape the spray. But the cold water had already soaked Little Squint Eyes, and his wails were alarmingly loud as Sam came abreast of Nejeunee and helped her shed the cradleboard.

"Got to keep him quiet!" Sam warned as he turned and looked out. "If they can't see us, they'll hear us!"

He had only his .45, and the distance and height would render a revolver shot useless, but he nevertheless drew it. Through the falling water, sparkling in the sunlight, he saw blurry images: the white gravel of the canyon floor, the gray and green of the woods, the swells of bordering mountains stretching into the horizon.

Sam knew when Nejeunee took Little Squint Eyes in her arms and tried to soothe him with soft words and gentle rocking, but the chilled and frightened infant continued to cry.

"There's nothin' you can do?" Sam pleaded.

Concentrating on reconnoitering, he was only vaguely aware as Nejeunee withdrew her phylactery from her blouse and spread the drawstring. But almost immediately Little Squint Eyes grew quiet, not a moment too soon considering the abrupt flashes of sunlight in the last line of brush.

"They're right there!" he said quietly, pointing as he turned to Nejeunee. "See the trees where—"

Suddenly the trees and flashes didn't matter anymore, for in Little Squint Eyes's hand glinted a silver locket.

In an instant Sam was back in Bass Canyon—back in deepest hell. He snatched the locket away from the infant and sprang the catch, and the engraving seemed to seize him by the throat and choke the life from him.

May I
Have your
Hand in marriage?

He clutched Nejeunee by the shoulder, his fingernails sinking into her flesh. "Where did you get this?" he demanded. "Where the hell did you get this!"

He had never addressed her so harshly or treated her so roughly, and her dark eyes were startled and confused. She didn't answer, and his nails dug deeper.

"Tell me!"

"He held it. On his journey to the afterworld, he held it."

"Who held it?"

"*Yah-ik-tee.* He who is not present."

"His father? Little Squint Eyes's father?"

Ashen and trembling, her eyes now insecure, Nejeunee could only nod.

"You sayin' he died with it?" pressed Sam. "He had it in his hand and died with it?"

Her fingers stole out as if to caress his face. "Sam-el, what's wrong? What's—"

Sam shook the locket in front of her. "Elizabeth's! It was my Elizabeth's! I shot him before he got to her, but he grabbed it and killed her! The son of a bitch killed her!"

"You, Sam-el? You killed my . . . ? No! No! No!"

Now there was something new in Nejeunee's face—realization, shock, panic, revulsion—and she shrank from Sam.

"*Idzúút'i!*" she cried. "Get away, filthy white man! *Idzúút'i! Idzúút'i!*"

For a moment that seemed forever to Sam, they stared at one another, two people who had lost so much and found so much.

And lost so much again.

CHAPTER 27

"Samuel! Samuel!"

The voice echoed loudly, but it had to probe the depths of Sam's perdition to find him. Through the falling water, he peered down at the canyon bottom and saw two figures standing beside horses and looking up at him.

"May I inquire why you're perched there, Samuel?" the voice added.

Even if Sam hadn't recognized the face at a distance, he would have known who it was by the diction.

"What are you doin' here, Arch?" he shouted back.

"Seeking Ranger DeJarnett. It seems I have located him."

"How many soldiers with you?"

"I know the reason you ask, and that's why my good man Boye and I have developed admirable saddle sores to overtake you. The major at Davis accepted your account without question, but I feared that you would flee an imagined patrol and never cease to run. From the looks of your perch, it seems my concerns were warranted. Come down and let us have coffee."

Several minutes later, after a descent as treacherous as the climb up, Sam followed Nejeunee down the final few feet and joined the two men on the canyon floor. As Nejeunee wandered away with her head hanging, Sam let his clasp on Arch's hand linger as they shook. There was something different about the ranger, but Sam couldn't identify it.

"How come you to do this, Arch? That's a hell of a ride up

this canyon."

"I decided I owed it to you, Samuel. For all the obtrusive remarks and resistance and general obstinacy I showed you on our scout, I owed it to you."

Not until Sam released Arch's hand did he realize what had changed in his appearance.

"You're not wearin' your bandana no more."

"And I'm all the better for discarding the malodorous burden," said Arch. "I'm a work in progress, but no longer am I in hiding from the troubles of my youth. Our talk in Musquiz Canyon convinced me it was time to confront the past and move on."

Beyond his friend's shoulder, Nejeunee was removing Little Squint Eyes from the cradleboard. Sam's eyes began to sting as he watched this young woman, who would have been his wife, take into her arms the child who would have been his son.

"Arch, my gray's got a sore foot. Can I trade with you for a spell? It's a long ride till I can leave them at the reservation."

"Indeed."

Sam started away, only to hesitate.

"Wish I'd knowed it was you followin' us, Arch," he said as the loss overwhelmed him. "I'd've made a walk up a stream while it still mattered."

They were half a moon in reaching the New Mexico reservation on the Tularosa, half a moon in which Nejeunee had lived with the realization of what she had learned high on the cliff. In all that time, she and Sam-el had spoken only out of necessity, and even that had been painful. But now she faced a day as gray and grim as any she had known, for they rode up to the Mescalero Agency in the snowy meadows of a valley cradled by forested mountains sacred to the *Ndé*.

It was issue day at the Agency, a frame structure built of pine

strips with the bark exposed, and a long line of families waited
to file past a window for rations. Alongside the *Ndé* were small
fires, many of them, for the waiting always required hours of
cold and hunger. Nejeunee knew it was this way every issue
day, a time when a once-proud people held out their hands for
Indaa rations like dogs begging for scraps.

In the crowd stirred a pair of shoulders draped with the pelt
of a mountain lion, and as the figure approached through the
curling smoke, Nejeunee flinched to see a cruel warrior with an
eyeless socket and a face frozen in an animal-like snarl.

Gian-nah-tah!

Sam-el must have recognized him too, for he wheeled his
horse and faced him. Gian-nah-tah only glanced at Sam-el,
perhaps not remembering, but Sam-el did more. He slipped a
hand across his waist and rested it under his coat where Nejeunee knew his revolver butt rested.

"I was hopin' I killed you," Sam-el told him in Spanish.

But Gian-nah-tah ignored him and addressed Nejeunee in
Apache. "You have followed me back, Nejeunee. Now I claim
what is mine."

Grieving for all she had lost, Nejeunee glanced at Sam-el.
"I'm no one's."

Gian-nah-tah's face went crimson. "You are mine! Or the
child will die!"

He continued to yell threats, and Sam-el turned to her.
"What's he sayin'? Tell me what he's sayin'!"

Nejeunee did so—and now it was Sam-el who was in a rage
as he spun to Gian-nah-tah. But she knew that Sam-el's role in
her life was over, and that any fight would be hers alone.

"A brave man doesn't threaten Little Squint Eyes," she told
Gian-nah-tah. "He fights *idóí*, the great cat, and rides two nights
and a day, and stands against his own people, all to save Little
Squint Eyes. That kind of man is brave, and worthy, but Gian-

nah-tah is a coward."

No one had ever dared to call Gian-nah-tah such a thing, and Nejeunee saw dozens of heads turn. But that wasn't the only development, for breaking through the crowd was a yellow-haired *Indaa* she recognized as the Indian agent.

"What's the trouble here?" he demanded in Apache.

But Gian-nah-tah had already lunged and seized the bridle of Nejeunee's horse, and now he was trying to drag Little Squint Eyes from her shoulders as she fought back. Then a knife flashed, striking the frame of the cradleboard, slashing the blanket across Nejeunee's arm, and just as she tried to kick Gian-nah-tah away, a revolver roared.

Gian-nah-tah fell against Nejeunee. For a moment he hung there, more dead than alive. Then she shed him with a cry and he slid down the horse's shoulder and collapsed under the animal's neck. He lay unmoving and bleeding out in the snow—a stark reminder of a kindly *señora's rebosa* against a salt bed profaned by Gian-nah-tah's hand.

Nejeunee looked up and saw Sam-el, smoke still trailing from his revolver, but there were also the Indian agent and *Ndé* police rushing toward them.

"I saw it all," said the agent. "That's one warmonger who won't be jumping the reservation again."

There were conversations to be had with the agent, but finally Nejeunee and Sam-el stood alone with their horses in the gray, bitter cold of a road that would separate them forever. For troubling moments, there seemed nothing to say, not even when Sam-el gripped the saddle horn to climb on his horse. But just as he started to step up, he hesitated and turned again.

"I can't ride off without sayin' this. I just can't."

Waiting, Nejeunee stared at him.

"I'm glad it took so long to get here," he added, " 'cause it give me time to think."

"Yes. Fifteen times *neeldá,* the dawn, rescued me after staring all night at *Tl'é'na'áí,* the moon."

Sam-el glanced back at the Agency. The *Ndé* who had waited for rations had all dispersed now.

"When he tried claimin' you was his, that settled it for me. What happened in war's not your fault, and I don't guess it's mine neither. People we loved are gone, and if we can't let that be the end of it, there won't be just two people that died, but you and me too, in a way."

His eyes glistened, and as he stretched out a hand his voice began to quake. "I miss what we had, Nejeunee. I miss it so bad."

For a long while, she held her stare—remembering, longing, praying. Then she went into his arms, and his touch was a balm to wounds that only time might heal.

"Take me to our canyon, Sam-el," she whispered. "Hold my hand and walk with me by the waters that sing only for us."

AUTHOR'S NOTE

This novel is based on the 1881 pursuit of a Mescalero Apache band into the Sierra Diablo of Texas by Texas Rangers, the ensuing battle of January 29 that proved to be the last engagement with Indians in the state, and the aftermath. Although all characters are fictitious, I have largely held to historic fact and authentic Apache culture and Mescalero language. My most important sources were:

RANGER-MESCALERO ENGAGEMENT AND AFTERMATH

W. H. (Bill) Roberts, SoundScriber interviews by J. Evetts Haley, Big Spring, Texas, 29 March and 21 December 1946, J. Evetts Haley Collection, N. S. Haley Memorial Library, Midland, Texas. Roberts was one of the rangers who participated in the events, and these recently recovered recordings provide much information not previously available to historians.

Captain George W. Baylor, Company A, Frontier Battalion, Texas Rangers, report of scout to J. B. Jones, adjutant general, Frontier Battalion, Austin, Texas, 9 February 1881, Texas State Library and Archives, Austin. Baylor was the ranking officer during the events.

Lieutenant C. L. Nevill, Company E, Frontier Battalion, Texas Rangers, report of scout to J. B. Jones, Austin, 6 February 1881, typescript in El Paso Public Library, El Paso, Texas. Nevill commanded one of the companies involved in the events.

Lieutenant C. L. Nevill, Company E, Frontier Battalion, Texas Rangers, to J. B. Jones, Austin, 7 and 8 February 1881, typescripts in El Paso Public Library.

Lieutenant C. L. Nevill, Company E, Frontier Battalion, Texas Rangers, to Captain Neal Coldwell, Quartermaster, Frontier Battalion, Austin, 9 February 1881, typescript in El Paso Public Library.

Monthly Return for February 1881, Company E, Frontier Battalion, Texas Rangers, Texas State Library and Archives.

Major N. B. McLaughlen, Tenth Cavalry, commanding Fort Davis, to assistant adjutant general, Department of the Pecos, San Antonio, Texas, 5 February 1881, in telegrams received, District of the Pecos, National Archives, Washington, D.C.

Medical Return for Fort Davis, entry for 8 January 1882 by post surgeon Paul R. Brown, Fort Davis Archives, Fort Davis, Texas.

Balmos, Dick, "Trail's End," *The Cattleman* (August 1952), 148, 150, 154, 158, 160, 162, 164. This article comprises the recollections of former ranger Sam Graham, another participant.

Baylor, George Wythe, *El Paso Daily Herald* series on 10, 11, 13, 14, and 15 August 1900. Relating his recollections of the events, the series comprises articles respectively titled "The Last Fight in El Paso County," "Colonel George Wythe Baylor," "A Lively Running Fight," "When the Camp Was Entered," and "Civilization vs. Barbarism."

Baylor, George Wythe, *Into the Far, Wild Country: True Tales of the Old Southwest,* Jerry D. Thompson, editor (El Paso: Texas Western Press, 1996), 213, 304–22. This memoir includes Baylor's account of the events.

APACHE CULTURE AND HISTORY

Ball, Eve, *In the Days of Victorio* (Tucson: University of Arizona Press, 1970).

Ball, Eve, with Nora Henn and Lynda A. Sanchez, *Indeh: An Apache Odyssey* (Norman: University of Oklahoma Press, reprint, 1988).

Bourke, John Gregory, *The Medicine-Men of the Apache, Extract from the Ninth Annual Report of the Bureau of Ethnology* (Washington: Government Printing Office, 1892).

Cremony, John C., *Life Among the Apaches* (New York: A. Roman & Co., Publishers, 1868).

Mails, Thomas E., *The People Called Apache* (New York: BDD Illustrated Books, reprint, 1993).

Sweeney, Edwin R., *Cochise: Chiricahua Apache Chief* (Norman: University of Oklahoma Press, 1991).

Thrapp, Dan L., *The Conquest of Apacheria* (Norman: University of Oklahoma Press, 1967).

Worcester, Donald E., *The Apaches: Eagles of the Southwest* (Norman: University of Oklahoma Press, 1979).

ABOUT THE AUTHOR

The author of twenty-four books, **Patrick Dearen** is a former award-winning reporter for two West Texas daily newspapers. As a nonfiction writer, Dearen has produced books such as *A Cowboy of the Pecos, Saddling Up Anyway: The Dangerous Lives of Old-Time Cowboys,* and *Castle Gap and the Pecos Frontier, Revisited.* His research has led to fourteen novels, including *The Big Drift,* winner of the Spur Award of Western Writers of America. His other western-themed novels include *When Cowboys Die, The Illegal Man, To Hell or the Pecos, Perseverance,* and *Dead Man's Boot,* which received the Elmer Kelton Award from the Academy of Western Artists, the Will Rogers Bronze Medallion, and finalist recognition in the Peacemaker Awards of Western Fictioneers.

A ragtime pianist and wilderness enthusiast, Dearen lives with his wife in Midland, Texas.

The employees of Five Star Publishing hope you have enjoyed this book.

Our Five Star novels explore little-known chapters from America's history, stories told from unique perspectives that will entertain a broad range of readers.

Other Five Star books are available at your local library, bookstore, all major book distributors, and directly from Five Star/Gale.

Connect with Five Star Publishing

Visit us on Facebook:
https://www.facebook.com/FiveStarCengage

Email:
FiveStar@cengage.com

For information about titles and placing orders:
(800) 223-1244
gale.orders@cengage.com

To share your comments, write to us:
Five Star Publishing
Attn: Publisher
10 Water St., Suite 310
Waterville, ME 04901

Diane von Furstenberg's
BOOK OF BEAUTY

HOW TO BECOME A MORE ATTRACTIVE,
CONFIDENT AND SENSUAL WOMAN
BY *DIANE VON FURSTENBERG*
WITH *EVELYN PORTRAIT*

Exercise drawings by Wendy Frost

Simon and Schuster · New York

Designed by Eve Metz
Manufactured in the United States of America

   2   3   4   5   6   7   8   9   10

Library of Congress Cataloging in Publication Data

Von Furstenberg, Diane.
   Diane von Furstenberg's Book of beauty.
    1. Beauty, Personal.   2. Women—Health and hygiene.
I. Portrait, Evelyn, joint author.   II. Title.
III. Title: Book of beauty.
RA778.V68   646.7'2'024042   76-19060
ISBN 0-671-21904-9

Children are all beautiful because they're not aware of it. Look at them watching television, studying something, eating candy, even crying. Their mouths are wide open and they're completely unaware of what they look like . . . and they're beautiful, really beautiful.

To Tatiana and Alexandre—for whom I became a woman.

I would like to acknowledge the assistance of Dr. Robert A. Berger, Dr. Andrew Franks, Nicholas Guercio, Georgette Williams and Sylvie Chantecaille for their help in the preparation of this book, and to thank Katia Perret-Aubry for the use of her exercise regime.

I would also like to thank Evelyn Portrait and Jerry Bowles for helping me put it all together. And a very special thanks to Dick Snyder, whose early enthusiasm got me started; and to Jonathan Dolger, Dee Ratterree, Joni Evans, and Frank and Eve Metz, whose patience made it all work.

Diane Von Furstenberg

CONTENTS

Contents

Diane von Furstenberg's
BOOK OF BEAUTY

CHAPTER ONE

The Woman Across the Room

YOU SEE HER ACROSS THE ROOM. She is an elegant creature with every hair in place, her clothes just perfect. She seems confident and relaxed, cool and unflappable. There, you think, is a woman who feels secure.

It isn't so. She is as scared and insecure as you are.

What the Woman Across the Room has learned is how to handle her insecurities and fears, how to feel relaxed in spite of the pressures of life, how to feel in control of herself.

The greatest natural enemy of women is insecurity. We all feel it and we all think we are the only ones who feel that way. How we deal with these fears determines to a great extent how effective we are in running our lives. Most women present a facade to the world and keep the insecurity locked inside.

The toughest job in the world is to be a complete, happy woman. The reason this is so is that women are expected to play so many different roles in life. We are wives, mothers, maids, lovers, soft shoulders to cry on. If we have careers, that is simply one more role to tack onto the others.

Being a woman today is more difficult and confusing than it has ever been before. There are more options now than

13

have existed in the past. We're confused by the choices because our history has been largely one of servitude—generations of being simply an extension of men.

I don't mean to sound like a strident women's liberationist. I like and respect men. But to be a complete, happy woman, you have to be independent.

Nothing makes a woman feel more insecure than being trapped, doing something because she has no other alternative. I believe that to be happy with a man you have to know that you could leave him and take care of yourself. To stay with him because he pays the bills and supports you financially and because you don't feel that you could take care of yourself is a form of slow death. It leaves you insecure, frustrated and ultimately unfulfilled.

Let me hasten to add that I believe strongly in love, and that one's life should be shared with another person. But every woman should have an identity of her own that is separate from the man in her life. It doesn't necessarily have to come from a career outside the home. When you are a complete person and have a sense of yourself, then staying home to cook or clean doesn't breed resentment. You do it because it is your choice.

There are no easy solutions to the complex problems of self-discovery, but I believe we can all become that Woman Across the Room.

When I was asked to write this book three years ago, I must confess I agreed to do so with one major reservation. While I was confident that I could—with the help of experts and from my experiences in traveling and meeting women—answer questions about beauty in an intelligent manner, I wondered whether I could write something that would be not merely useful but also meaningful in a larger sense to other women.

As I began organizing my thoughts and started writing, it occurred to me that I really did have something important to say, not just about the practicalities of dress and makeup and health care—all of which are useful—but also about that wonderful and terribly frightening journey of self-discovery. That process of growth, of being an independent person, of learning who you are and what you want from life, is the real secret of life, happiness, and beauty.

And I was going through it at the time. I was an emerging woman. My experiences, I felt, could be of value to other women.

Let's start at the beginning. I was born Diane Halfin in Brussels and grew up in a comfortable middle-class family. I grew up without many problems, without really being aware of the process. When I was thirteen, my parents separated, an event that was to have great import in my life. I was sent away to different boarding schools all over Europe, and I've been on my own ever since. It was not really a tragedy. On the contrary, I didn't much like being a child anyway and always wanted to be grown up. So, after having had a simple childhood, I spent my teen-age years infiltrating into more sophisticated groups. Always the youngest, the most awkward, the least experienced and definitely the least glamorous, I kept looking around, wanting to learn how to become one of those secure and glamorous women across the room.

At the age of eighteen I was in Geneva; part time university, part time working . . . and I met Egon! A wonderful, beautiful, cheerful, knowing-everything, having-been-everywhere, nineteen-year-old authentic prince. We became close, closer, the closest. We had the best time playing grownups, going around the world with little money but plenty of enthusiasm and lots of introduction letters to the best places and people. After two years of perfectly ''without responsibility'' romance, Egon left for America. He was too young to get married and we decided to split. I went to Paris, took many different jobs, stayed up very late every night—lived a single girl's life for a year. But Egon and I missed each other, and in the summer of 1969 we were married. In October I sailed in with all my trunks, carrying a child as well as my hopes and expectations for a successful future in New York.

But, I forgot to say, the minute I knew I was about to become Egon's wife, I decided to have a career. I needed to prove something more than ever—I had to be someone of my own and not just a plain little girl who got married beyond her deserts.

Egon was very helpful and as a matter of fact pushed me a lot into my career. Besides working like a dog and having two children, I was going out a lot with Egon.

Everything was new and exciting. There was hardly a party or opening that we didn't go to. Appearing at four or five cocktail parties, a gallery preview, two dinner parties and a discotheque in one evening was routine rather than unusual.

It was a lot of fun in the beginning and I must confess that I enjoyed the attention we were getting. Still, I wondered was this really all I wanted from life—to be a princess and attend parties?

My values were changing and the parties and openings, with their air of sustained superficial cheerfulness, began to depress me and leave me with a feeling of existential emptiness. I was racked with insecurity. I had no identity of my own. No one really knew who I was, not even me. The person who went to parties was Princess von Furstenberg, a character who had stepped out of a fairy tale. It was just as much a fairy tale to me.

My marriage was falling apart but we were still smiling and gay.

The only thing I knew for sure was that I had to strike out on my own. It was a deliberate act of will and I know that my behavior in those days must have been very tough and aggressive. Perhaps, like so many women who are feeling their way into the larger world, I overcompensated. I was tougher than I needed to be.

The thing that really made me stop and reevaluate my life's goals was a cover story about Egon and me in *New York* magazine. The story upset our friends a great deal but—aside from its leering tone—it seemed to me to be painfully accurate. I said some silly things that were really a way of making myself invulnerable to the hurt I was feeling. The quote that seemed to scandalize people most was "We are each other's family. He (Egon) is my best friend and I am his. There is nothing of him I don't know. And besides, we don't take anything very seriously. The only way for a relationship to survive, I think, is to have no sex at all. After all, you marry for friendship, for companionship—and passion after a while . . . pffft. I mean, does it excite you when your left hand touches your right?"

We separated soon after that article and I began the painful process of rebuilding my life. I became more involved with my children and with my work. I started taking the first tentative steps toward discovering myself as a human being and as a woman.

This, I came to realize, was really what I wanted to write about in this book. Women. Emerging women. Women who have learned, or who are in the process of learning, how to live to their fullest potential.

Many of my teen-age friends grew up to be the most talked-about, glamorous young women of the late sixties and early seventies and it amazes me how different we are today from the way we were then.

I recall one summer on Sardinia when Marisa Berenson and Lulu de la Falaise came to stay with me. We were already past twenty but we were still like schoolgirls. We spent hours putting on makeup and changing our clothes and grooming our hair. We were different people every day, sometimes every few hours. We were silly and spoiled and we spent the entire summer giggling and dancing and lying naked on the decks of yachts.

Recently Marisa and Lulu came to my house in the country. Everything had changed. It was May and still cold in Connecticut and we wore jeans and bulky sweaters to keep warm. We walked for hours in the rain and dried our hair in front of the fireplace and just tied it back. No one wore makeup. It occurred to me that we were all more attractive people now than we had been years ago and the reason was that each of us had learned to accept ourselves as we were. We had learned, finally, that simple things are often the most glamorous.

It is not a lesson that one learns without some tears.

A fulfilled woman is a beautiful woman. This is fact. Today, I feel more beautiful and happy than I have ever felt in my life. This book is my way of sharing with you some of what I have learned.

A little Belgian girl out for a walk on the streets of Brussels with her mother and father.

At a costume party, dressed as a Greek peasant.

Age 15, in Spain with my brother, Philippe.

19

July 16, 1969—a beautiful wedding in Montfort L'Amaury, outside Paris.

20

First glamor! Posing for Vogue during my honeymoon in Sardinia.

As a pregnant bride, strolling in Rome with Egon.

On January 25th, 1970, Alexandre is born. Marisa Berenson is the godmother at the baptism on February 16th.

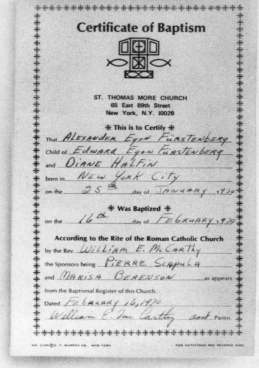

Certificate of Baptism

ST. THOMAS MORE CHURCH
65 East 89th Street
New York, N.Y. 10028

✳ This is to Certify ✳

That *Alexander Egon Furstenberg*
Child of *Edward Egon Furstenberg*
and *Diane Halfin*
born in *New York City*
on the *25th* day of *January, 1970*

✳ Was Baptized ✳

on the *16th* day of *February, 1970*

According to the Rite of the Roman Catholic Church
by the Rev. *William E. McCarthy*
the Sponsors being *Pierre Scapula*
and *Marisa Berenson* as appears
from the Baptismal Register of this Church.

Dated *February 16, 1970*

William E. McCarthy asst. Pastor.

— *figure recovered finally!!*

VIVE LA FRANCE: They should have
had the Tricouleur flying Wednesday at
Restaurant X. Dior director Jacques Rouet
and Cardin's André Oliver were both in
from Paris. Aaslée lunched with Françoise
de la Renta. Rouet was with Bonwit Teller
president William Fine, Danny Zarem of
BT and an attractive blonde lady called
Mrs. Kelly who helps Dior on its New York
PR. Mile . . .
Mary Lane the very trim Princess Furstem
(in a Longuette) Providence radio . . .
Jim Aicara and S.A.'s Charles
. . . also made the Front Room.

A year later, Tatiana is born! Egon wanted a girl so much that we gave her a second name—Désirée.

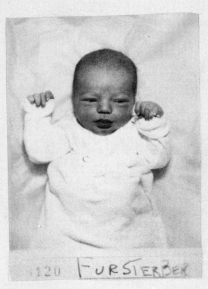

TUESDAY
16
FEBRUARY

BABY FURSTENBERG
Baby TATIANA DIANE
Girl 2.16 7 AM 533
7 lbs 4 1/2 33006ms
Dr J.J. SQUIRE

Date of MacGARE Injection 2-17-71
Hospital Mount Sinai, N.Y.C.
Attending Physician J Squire

FURSTENBERG DIANE
#846083

This is to certify that

Tatiana Furstenberg

has been elected to membership in the

Babies Alumni of The Mount Sinai Hospital

in recognition of generosity and good will to others

Patricia S. Levinson
CHAIRWOMAN

New York Oct 16 1971
BIRTH DATE

50 CENTS

FEBRUARY 5, 1973

NEW YORK

The Couple That Has Everything. Is Everything Enough?

Egon: "You just live once and I am getting the most out of it."

Diane: "I'm afraid that one night I'm just going to stop living. I feel a great urge to hurry to do everything."

The famous cover that was a big turning point in my life! Everyone I knew hated the story, but I didn't; it taught me a lesson and showed me what my life looked like from the outside.

24

The last of the big glamorous balls!

FERRIERES 1971

François   Alexandra   Egon   Diane

Gaby

Odile
Elsa

Alexandra   Marisa   Florka

Meryl   Denise

Maria

Odile

Jacqueline

Grace

Guy   Marie Hélène

Christina

Betty

Flo-flo   Odile

Alexis   Margot

First office! A lot of work. With Marion Stein, second employee and now head of the bookkeeping department.

First invoice book.

Concentrating.

A staff session: Sue Feinberg, my assistant right-hand person, Carol, and Fran Boyer, the "mascotte" and house model.

First tries.

On the phone.

27

Alexandre is two. In Cortina at Egon's family home. Two days of re-laxation before going back to the factories in Florence.

CHAPTER TWO

Discovering You

I'M LEARNING EVERY DAY that it is very hard to achieve perfect equilibrium and that we can't afford the luxury of pretending to ourselves. The older we get, the more we achieve, the more honest we have to try to be.

Whether we like it or not, most people form their first impressions from what they see. When you meet someone for the first time you probably have an overall impression of "She's beautiful" or "She has a great body"—or you may have a negative reaction. After you get to know someone you may feel that even if she isn't great looking, even if she's plain, she may still be dynamic or charming or a warm and kind person. Later on you become aware of her sense of humor or generosity, or intelligence, or talent. But your first impression is usually of the outward appearance.

Begin with an honest evaluation. Look in the mirror and really examine yourself. Think "This is nice. That's nice. This is not so nice." Then think "What am I going to do about it?" That's the first step—to decide what you want to do about something unattractive. You have a choice. You can do nothing and accept yourself as you are. Or, you can choose to reshape your body, color your hair, even have plastic surgery. Know what you want and find out what can be done.

My own feeling is that it is important to be as close to natural as possible; generally, being natural is really a great part of being beautiful.

All the things you do to become better looking should be as easy as possible; very simple, so that you do them quickly. Like all worthwhile things, it cannot be achieved without discipline.

People tell me that I'm very determined, and I've always been that way. I think I just have to prove things to myself so that I'll feel good. That's how I built my business, just proving to myself a little at a time that I could do what I challenged myself to do. And once I proved one small thing for myself I felt more confident to go on and prove the next and the next.

Don't put things off. We'd all like to wait until tomorrow for a lot of things, but it really doesn't work. A woman I see frequently in business is always telling me that she has to start exercising. She spends an awful lot of time asking other women if they think a bicycle is really good. She's always clipping exercise programs from magazines and is never sure whether they're right for her. She's never going to start, never. The only way to begin is to begin. The sooner you begin the sooner you'll see the results. How can you find out if anything in life is right for you if you haven't tried?

I often think that if a genie came along and offered me three wishes, I wouldn't take them. I'd only take one. The only thing that's really important to me is that my children and I are in good health. I sometimes think that because so many unexpected things have happened in my life that I couldn't handle at the time perhaps I now over-prepare myself for the possibility of things going wrong. Now I try to be well prepared for everything. That's why I'd only take one wish from the genie. I just haven't had time to think through what else might happen if I took the other two wishes and they came true.

Being prepared keeps me from getting nervous when something does go wrong, because chances are I've already anticipated all the things that might go wrong in any situation.

But don't be too hard on yourself. You have to start someplace and work steadily toward what you're trying to accomplish. Being too tough on yourself is self-defeating. You'll make mistakes. You'll skip a few exercise sessions. You'll eat too much one day. Don't punish yourself. Start again. When you prove to yourself that you can accomplish a part of what you want to accomplish it will give you satisfaction and the desire to go on.

Concentrate on whatever you're doing. If you're doing nothing, concentrate on doing nothing. If you're taking a bath and you only have five minutes, instead of thinking you have only five minutes, just enjoy those relaxing few minutes.

Finally, I think that somehow you always do things for one person or for people you love. And therefore, it's also for those people that you should be beautiful. I think living is serious. Living well, accepting yourself, using your talents to the fullest, enjoying yourself, that's all serious and important. I care about beauty and I think certain parts of a beauty regimen are very important for good health, a good body, and cleanliness. But I think makeup and fashion should not be taken that seriously. I've tried to make them fun. You should have fun making up for a party. You should have fun wearing a sexy dress. When you're beautiful it should give you pleasure.

You can be the Woman Across the Room but you should do it for yourself and for the person you love. You should always be as beautiful as you can be so you will be desired. And isn't being desired a part of being fulfilled?

CHAPTER THREE

What Should I Wear?

W HAT SHOULD I WEAR?'' It is a question I hear everywhere I go. I always feel like answering ''Whatever you want.
It really doesn't matter all that much as long as you use
taste and common sense.'' But, I don't always say that because, after all, I am a fashion designer and fashion designers are supposed to have authoritarian views.

To be blunt, I think women are often bullied and exploited
by the fashion industry through constant change, new looks,
new lengths, new ''attitudes.'' I've never believed in drastic
fashion changes because they don't last. There are always
trends but they shouldn't be taken all that seriously.

The problem of dressing can be very confusing because of
Fashion (that's with a capital ''F''). We speak of Fashion
when we really mean fashionable. The fashionable woman is
one who conforms to the latest styles. But I'm not much of a
believer in following or conforming. That goes against the
whole idea of being yourself, accepting yourself as you are instead of imitating someone else.

It is more important to be pretty as a woman than to be
fashionable. A nice way around the changing style problem is

to adapt things you see to your own personality. What you wear to be more attractive, what makes you look good, is what clothes are really about.

I believe in dresses. When I first went into business hardly anyone was selling them. Everyone was making sportswear—separates and pants. I never wear pants, except in the country, skiing, or on vacation. Sometimes in the evening I like pajamas, but they have to have flare and flow and movement.

You should wear a dress that moves with your body, clings a little, and makes you feel sensual. It's fun to see a woman in a shirtdress with the buttons opened low, or a wrap dress that's loosely tied and somewhat décolleté. I like to see women who show their bodies because they're pleased with them. I don't mean exhibitionism or bad taste, but I've noticed that women seem to sit a different way to show off their legs when they wear skirts instead of pants. You feel more like a woman. You look like a woman.

Dressing is very personal. I know that people do want change. Some women like a great many changes. For myself, I look for only a few things each season. I need to find something I love and then I wear it all the time and it becomes part of me. That's very much the way I am. I think you add fresh things to your wardrobe and keep the ones you really love. You keep the good things for years and years. But when you add new clothes, you shouldn't get carried away with the latest trend.

One of the easiest ways to change—without sacrificing the style that you wear best—is with color and prints. I love prints. I look for new ideas everywhere, in a man's tie, an old oriental rug, an art deco vase, and then adapt the design idea for my fabrics. You can change your entire mood with a different print even though the shape or the silhouette of the dress is the same. For example, you have to feel different in a leopard print than you do in a garden print. I did my first snakeskin print in black and in brown because those colors seemed natural and they were the big sellers. So I decided to do them again, but in bright green and orange and women liked them, too, and felt sexy in them. I think the shape of the dress was changed slightly, but the mood of the snakeskin was the same. That's important. To wear clothes that go with your mood, or even to establish a bit of a mood by what you wear.

One of my favorite experiences happened in Phoenix, Arizona, when I first began. I had a silk jersey dress at the time with a leopard and a practically naked woman in the print. It was an adaptation of an Erté drawing and it was highly suggestive. A lady with white hair came in who must have been seventy years old. She was with her husband who was also very old and shaking a little, and she asked me if I had that dress in size 14. And I said, "Yes, but . . ." But there were no buts. She tried the dress on and she loved it and bought it and wore it home. She left as if she were going to have a roaring affair with her husband. She really felt like another person. She was absolutely thrilled that she could still wear that kind of dress.

I like clothes to be really effortless and classic, a kind you can wear all day and then wear on into the evening when you don't have time to go home and change. When I was in California to introduce my cosmetic and fragrance collection in Beverly Hills, I wore my black and white popcorn-print dress nearly all the time. During the day at the store I wore the little short-sleeved jacket over it, and at night, for all the parties, I wore just the dress, which had a halter back and was very low cut and bare.

One of the most important things about fashion is to dress as well as you can, look as attractive as you can, and at the same time be comfortable with yourself. Be easy about your clothes; forget about them. You don't necessarily want everyone to notice what you're wearing. It's you they should notice. There are some special evenings, some special moments in your life when you want to be very dramatic, make a grand entrance, something like that, of course, but most of the time people should not be very aware of what you wear. They shouldn't remember that you wore an outstanding couture gown or the latest from a famous designer. They should remember that *you* were beautiful.

It's often very confusing to know what to wear for particular occasions. So many of the rules that previously existed have broken down and women don't have to wear hats anymore if they don't want to, or white gloves, or high heels or low heels. If you're not sure what to wear, if you don't know how everyone else is going to be, then just be at your most beautiful. Then it doesn't matter. Women often think there are big rules about how to dress, but there really are no rules. No matter what questions a woman asks me in the dressing room, I think what she really wants to know is how to put herself together. She might ask me what shoes to wear with a certain dress and I'll say, "Just wear your own." Once a woman with a very big bosom asked me if I thought she could wear a wrap dress. I suggested she try it on to see if she felt good in it. She came back to tell me that she felt sexy and she liked it.

That's very important, how you feel in the clothes. You have to feel comfortable. You have to feel that you look pretty or sexy. You shouldn't have to work at your clothes. If you're wearing something stiff and starched and you're worried about getting wrinkled and looking wrinkled, then you're going to be self-conscious.

I remember once in Philadelphia that a woman asked me to find something sexy for her daughter. She whispered to me that the daughter's husband was having an affair. Although the daughter was forty, she was never going to choose something sexy with her mother there.

Sometimes in dressing rooms I have met happy women, completely and totally fulfilled, and it's marvelous. Or I've seen the most extraordinary figures. But most women have some special problems and there's nothing wrong with camouflaging a fault you simply cannot correct. There are a few common-sense ways to look better and to conceal figure faults.

Most rules of fashion are easily broken and often clothes become much more interesting when these rules are not

35

strictly adhered to. However, if there is one rule for dressing, for fashion, it's pretty much the same rule as for everything else in life: Don't go against yourself, don't go against your own nature. It's only going to show. You can alter or adjust things to your own nature but you can't really go against it. If you're short, don't wear extremely high heels. After a certain age you shouldn't wear little girls' clothes. That's going against your nature.

Spend a lot of time studying yourself in the mirror when you try on clothes and when you wear them so you'll learn what's best and most attractive for you.

Train your eye to see proportion. Proportion and fit are really the two most important things for everyone. Proportion may have to do with scale, the size of a print or a stripe. If you're tall, you're lucky because you can wear almost anything, you can really carry clothes. You can wear large prints, bold patterns, and all the lengths. A smaller woman usually looks better in a scaled-down print. But a small woman doesn't have to be dainty and feminine. I guess I just don't like the word "feminine" because it always sounds like ruffles and lace to me, and that's not necessarily the way you want to look today. It's too fussy. Anyway, proportion is also length and that's very important to you. Not trendy lengths but the length of a skirt that makes your legs look good. And other lengths are important, too, the length of jackets and tops, and sleeves. Women with heavy arms can wear a short sleeve, women with thin arms can wear a shorter sleeve, but you have to make certain that it covers an unattractive bulge or a bony elbow. The same holds true with tops. Longer tunics, cardigans and smock tops are great to cover hippiness.

Balance is also very important. If you're wearing a loose, bigger top to cover a very full bosom during the day, for instance, you can't wear a pencil-slim, narrow skirt. You want to wear a bit of fullness or flare in the bottom. That way people won't notice your attempts to camouflage too much.

Good proportion starts with fit. These days most of the work is done for you by designers and patternmakers. I don't believe in buying a designer's clothes because they're "statusy," but I think when you find a designer whose clothes are scaled to your body, you should stay with them.

Another important thing is to avoid fussiness and too much —too much of anything, too much of one color, too many different colors, too much jewelry. They're all going to get the attention, taking the attention away from you. Anything that calls too much attention to what you're wearing or how you're wearing it is wrong. You can't let your clothes take over or overpower you. I don't think people should comment on a beautiful violet-color dress. They should notice that the color looks wonderful on you.

The same is true for figure faults. If your legs are bad and you wear your skirts too long in order to hide your legs, you're just calling attention to them. The best thing to do is say, okay, my legs aren't so hot, but my bust and my throat are good. Then wear something that attracts the eye to the top, to your good features. Keep your skirt length just a little bit longer perhaps and in proportion to everything else, and concentrate on your best features.

Accessories are fun. If you own a stunning ring or pin, you want to wear it, but all jewelry and belts and scarves and bags should be fun and not self-conscious. They shouldn't be too studied. As a matter of fact, these days it's better and more interesting if they're a bit unexpected. I remember a time when I would go to the beach and wear a tiny bikini and dozens of chains and necklaces. I felt completely covered with them and that was fun until I felt that I had to do it, I had to put them on, and it was no longer fun. Accessories should add something like a breath of fresh air and create a good mood.

What's important is to find a style for yourself. Find clothes that are appealing and attractive and that you feel good in. Then stick with them. When you don't know what to buy, you should always have in mind whom you dress for. And then you should always dress for that person . . . you might be surprised to discover that person is really you.

CHAPTER FOUR

You Are What You Eat

W<small>HETHER IT WAS IN FITTING ROOMS</small>, at the hairdresser's or at the most sophisticated dinner parties, I have always heard women complaining how much they love to eat, especially "forbidden" food. Well, that's the way we all are. After all, isn't "forbidden" always terribly tempting? It certainly is for me. Resisting a beautiful chocolate cake or a wonderful foie gras is as difficult as (the thought of) saying no to Paul Newman. I used to hate the idea of thinking about good nutrition until I realized how much nutrition and health were related, and then I started to think.

The most important asset in life, to me, is good health. Without good health you cannot have energy to do the things you want to do, you cannot be emotionally sound, you cannot have a good body or a good shape, you cannot be beautiful. Nutrition is one of the most important, perhaps the single most important contribution you make to good health. What you eat is everything. What you eat is what you are.

If you are fortunate, you developed a strong healthy body when you were young. As a child I was very normal and I ate well. I had breakfast, lunch, tea and dinner, and I never,

never ate between meals. Then when I was a teenager at boarding school I began to eat badly, like everybody else at that age. To eat badly to me means not to eat well at meals or to skip meals, and then to eat rubbish in between.

I thought that a healthy diet was boring. When I was at the university I sometimes went days and days eating only chocolate and desserts. I also loved elaborate dishes with heavy sauces and spices. A simple meal—a steak, cooked vegetables, a salad—bored and depressed me and I'd skip that meal. If I didn't eat properly at meals or if I skipped meals, all of a sudden I would be hungry in the middle of the day and I'd start eating rubbish. Pretzels, chocolate cake—rubbish. Sometimes I would go to the cheese shop in town in the middle of the day and get a huge chunk of cheese and eat nothing but cheese. That's not too bad, except when that's absolutely all you eat.

Unfortunately, in spite of my early conditioning, those bad habits stayed with me for a quite a while after school. Of course you know what happened. My body began to get a little soft. Sometimes my hair wasn't as shiny as it should be or my skin looked dull and lifeless. My weight fluctuated erratically. Occasionally I'd find myself depressed or nervous, for no apparent reason.

When I was pregnant with Alexandre, I really disciplined myself to eat well again. I was very much afraid to gain too much weight. I stopped eating between meals. I tried to have liver, lots of spinach, lots of vegetables for lunch every day. I thought that a steak, the cooked vegetables, some fish, some milk was all that I needed to get back into shape and to get my energy back. I didn't drink or smoke at all.

But I learned that good nutrition is not quite as simple as that. Once I realized that, I decided to learn about nutrition, about balancing what I ate, what my body needed to work well, to be at top form. I learned that nutrition is a habit and it should be a daily, weekly, lifetime habit. Fortunately I had not done serious damage to myself and I was able to quickly reinstate the good eating habits of my childhood.

* * *

It's important to eat both the right kinds and the right amounts of the foods that contain the vitamins, proteins, fats and carbohydrates your body needs to maintain itself in a healthy and an attractive condition.

It seems to me that many women treat nutrition from extreme positions. One woman is so into health and makes such a fetish of it that her family ends up sneaking away from the protein charts to munch candy bars at the first available opportunity. Another woman knows nothing about food values and just thinks "if it is packaged and sold it must be all right."

Basically there really is no such thing as "bad" food. Yes, there are certain foods we eat which are so artificial in content that they have no nutritional value at all. But except for medical diet controls (for diabetes or high cholesterol, for example), there just is no such thing as food that is bad for you. There are foods that are harmful in excess. Excessive amounts of sugar or fats, for example, can cause imbalances in the system. Overeating any food or groups of food at the sacrifice of others is harmful. Our bodies are best balanced by a variety of animal and vegetable foods. I think you should learn a little about what nutrients are found naturally in foods. Then just try to see to it that you have a certain amount of all the things your body needs to grow on every day. If you eat a variety, not too much and develop the habit of eating regularly you'll be O.K. That's all good nutrition is.

There are many diet fads that proclaim we can all live on certain cereal grains, to the exclusion of all else. There are strict vegetarian diets that shun meat, some even forgo fish and chicken. I don't believe in that.

I don't believe in the health food craze either. I think if your doctor suggests a vitamin booster or a vitamin supplement for a deficiency, O.K. But if you eat properly you'll get all the vitamins you need in their fresh, natural form.

Why do you eat? That's a simple enough question on the surface but not so easily answered by some. I think you should always keep in mind that you eat to be healthy. You eat primarily to keep the wonderful machine that is your body in the best possible working order. You eat for the energy you need to live. Of course you eat certain things because you like the taste, but you really learn that. Taste is acquired. You may have to unlearn a taste for chocolate or ice cream.

One of the problems with weight control, one of the problems with dieting is that everyone is motivated differently. Many women eat or overeat when they're depressed or nervous, or to compensate for insecurity. Of course if they become unattractively overweight they're just increasing the insecurity.

I think the second thing you have to keep in mind always is that you cannot go against the nature of your body and you shouldn't try to. We all have different body types. We all have different metabolisms that control the way our food is turned into energy or into excess fat, waste. You are different from everyone else—you burn up calories at a different rate than anyone else, perhaps faster, perhaps more slowly. Even if you consider all the charts and the so-called "ideal" weight for your height and your frame you have to make your own personal adjustment to an ideal weight. Trying to be excessively thin if it's not your type will only leave you without vitality, without the glow of good health that makes you beautiful.

There are three body types and you're born one type or another. You really can't change that.

The endomorph is round, soft, bosomy and slightly hippy, with lots of curves. Sophia Loren and Raquel Welch are endomorphs.

The mesomorph has broad shoulders, a well-proportioned bustline, and is somewhat straighter, somewhat more square. If there's an "average" figure, it's the mesomorph.

The ectomorph is slim, with long, thin arms and legs, small hips, small bust.

41

I'm an ectomorph and though I'd love to be fuller on top, with all those curves in the right places like an endomorph, there's no way I can change my basic body shape. The best any of us can do is keep our bodies in good tone with exercise and control our weight to keep off unattractive excess body fat.

But notice I specifically said "excess" body fat, and I meant to. If there's one thing I've learned through my experience in fashion and cosmetics it's that being very, very thin makes a mature woman look older, not younger as many women seem to think. If you're too thin, then you just end up wrinkles and bones. A little bit of plumpness rounds out the body, fills out the face, fills out the wrinkles and keeps you younger looking and prettier as you grow older.

I think too thin is also unattractive for any woman, even a young woman. I had a friend whom I considered very attractive. So did an awful lot of people, including many men. Last year she went to work for a high-fashion designer and got carried away with the idea of wearing his clothes. She became involved with her new "image" and got very, very thin. When I saw her again after a few months I was shocked. She was so thin, all bony. Her face was gaunt, just hollows. She was very fashionable—but she was no longer an attractive, desirable woman.

It's more important to be healthy and of good spirit than it is to be thin, just as it's more important to be an attractive woman than a fashionable one.

Here are some general rules for maintenance of a healthy body with good nutrition.

Common Sense Weight Control

Know your type and don't go against it. Eat enough of the right foods to maintain your energy, your body shape, a feeling of well-being. If you're clear about how you should look and what you need for control it will be much easier to lose or gain a few pounds when you have to—you'll have a realistic goal.

Exercise. Keep in mind that you need exercise for the maintenance of good health and proper weight as well as for energy and a firm body. A normal day's walking, working, housekeeping is usually not enough for anybody, but you may at least be able to avoid dieting by playing a few sets of tennis, walking another few city blocks, doing an extra ten minutes of body movements daily.

Don't abuse your body. All the good nutrition in the world won't hold up if you are excessive in your smoking habits, alcohol consumption, if you don't get enough sleep, if you allow stress to take over your mind and body.

Develop good habits. Try to eat three meals, don't eat between meals. When you're eating out you can always find something healthy on the menu. I know when I'm at the office on Seventh Avenue I can always order in a good simple roast beef sandwich or a salad and that's what I try to do—I'm always trying (except when I just cannot resist a triple pastrami on rye).

Don't go on fad diets. Not to lose weight, not because you think it will increase your energy. There is always a new diet, a new theory for dieting—all whole grains, all vegetables, three grapefruits a day, no protein, no carbohydrates, etcetera, etcetera. And then a few years after the diet is published the doctors' and the dentists' offices are SRO with women suffering from unforeseen side effects. Anemia, gum and bone deterioration, fingernail diseases—serious medical problems. In just my own seven years in America I've watched the very magazines and newspapers that introduced some of those famous diets publish feature articles later on why they are dangerous. By the time the dangers are discovered, it may be too late. See your doctor before you undertake any restrictions in your diet.

Don't let any of your good habits get boring. Vary your menu, vary your foods. There is so much to choose from. If food gets boring to you you're sure to start ignoring it, to start cheating.

Prepare your food attractively and serve it nicely. I think food should be attractive. And I think you should try to eat in a pleasant, relaxed atmosphere. It's so much nicer when you can sit down with your family or other people you enjoy. Of course that's not always possible, but it's nice when you can. Bolting down a hamburger at a counter or at your desk is terrible. If you're alone I think you should sit at a table or prepare a pretty tray for yourself. Even when I'm alone at home I sometimes prepare my tea on a tray with pretty china and a lovely porcelain honey pot.

Make everything as simple as possible. The more simply you cook, the more simply you eat, the better off you are. I think there's a false pretension around. People think they should make complicated things. Of course, I guess that's part of my whole philosophy about simplifying. I think far more important than complicated recipes and sauces is to have good quality, the best quality you can find. The freshest vegetables, the freshest eggs, the best grade of meat. Every Sunday night in the summer I come back from the country looking like a market. We grow our own vegetables and buy fresh eggs from a neighboring farmer. Try to buy vegetables when they're in season in your area because they're freshest then. You can buy flash-frozen vegetables, which retain more vitamins because they were just blanched. I think steaming vegetables helps to keep more of the vitamins, and cooking the way the Chinese do is wonderful. They just quick-fry in a little bit of light oil, such as peanut oil, and all of the flavor and food values are sealed in.

Uncooked fresh fruits and vegetables are more nutritious than cooked fruits and vegetables. There is so much nutritional value in the skins and peels that it's a shame to scrape

or stew or boil away that goodness. Eat your fruits and vegetables just scrubbed clean as often as you can. If you're one
of the many women who have trouble digesting certain raw
fruits and vegetables, drink fruit juices. You can probably
drink more orange juice than eat the number of oranges that
make up a glass. Drink fresh vegetable juices, too. If you
can't digest the celery or carrots, all the wonderful leafy
greens, you may be able to drink them from the blender.

Learn to like the foods that are good for you. It's not that
difficult really. I learned to like spinach when I was pregnant
with Alexandre because it was good for me and now I really
love it.

If you think about yourself, you actually know what's good
for you, but you allow bad habits to override your own good
sense. Perhaps your bad habits started with your parents—
they're usually the ones who encourage children to eat things.
Because the parents like chocolate or peanuts, whatever, they
share it with their children and children get used to it.

I feel so strongly about our responsibility for the eating
habits of our children. As parents it's up to us to see to it that
our children don't eat junk foods, that they don't eat between
meals. If we don't keep sodas and all those things to nibble
on in the house, they won't be tempted.

Tatiana and Alexandre are really very wise. I say, "Would
you like some cake?" and they say, "No, we've had enough."
Sometimes I find I'm learning from them. It's true when you
think about it—we all know very well what's good for us and
when we have to stop.

Drink milk if you like it . . . but. I've always been allergic
to milk, but when I began to bone up on nutrition I just
thought the more milk one drank, the healthier. Well, I learned
that nutritionists and doctors are now warning us about the
high fat content of natural milk. I'm not suggesting that you
give up milk entirely, if you enjoy it, but you can drink low-
fat or skim milk, perhaps even with fortified powdered milk

added. Then you have all the values, the proteins, without the fats.

Drink water—six to eight glasses a day. Water is one of the most important parts of the nutrition team. About 92 percent of your blood and 80 percent of your muscles are made up of water. It's the water in your blood that helps to carry vital nutrients to your skin and scalp and throughout your body. Water flushes the impurities out of our bodies. You cannot have a healthy body without drinking a great deal of fluid. You cannot have a glowing skin, shining hair without liquid. But remember, you can't just drink a glass of water and tell a glass of water to please go straight to your skin and moisturize your complexion. Water has to be there all the time, doing what it does naturally in a healthy body.

There are impurities in water and personally I have always preferred bottled water to tap water. I have delicious, pure artesian well water in the country and sometimes I just bring it back to the city in gallon jugs. I admit that I'm not nearly as faithful about drinking six or eight glasses a day as I know I should be. I forget—but I compensate somewhat by eating a great deal of fruit and drinking fruit juices, and I know there's water in many other foods as well.

Your own body is a very fine barometer of how much water you need. When you feel thirsty, dehydrated, drink more water. The only problem anyone can have with water is water retention, a big problem for some women. Certain hormones encourage water retention in the body, as does salt. Discuss it with your doctor if you're dieting and not losing weight or inches.

Learning About Nutrition

Here are simple descriptions of all the nutrients. If you use common sense, if you watch how your own body responds, you'll find that you have many different choices to enjoy for the maintenance of your good weight, your good health, your good moods, and your natural beauty.

THE PROTEINS

Proteins are builders—they build, repair and replenish cell tissues. Most of your hair is protein, as are your skin and nails. The beauty and the life of your skin and your hair, the growth of your nails are determined by protein. Your muscles have the heaviest concentration of protein and the difference between firm, well-toned muscles and weak, soft ones may bear some relation to the amount of protein your body has. If you are not getting enough proteins naturally in your daily diet to serve all your body needs, your body will take proteins from the muscles to keep the important organs—the heart, the liver—in good working order, and you will end up with flabby muscles.

THE AMINO ACIDS IN PROTEINS

For good health and longer life your body requires twenty or so amino acids which are found in protein. Your body can manufacture twelve of these, but you have to bring in the other eight through proteins you eat or the body-manufactured ones don't work. If that sounds complex it's because your body is complex. One nutrient promotes the function of another; sometimes one absorbs another. That's exactly why you can never put yourself on an "all" or an "only" diet of any kind. Fortunately, in this instance, all first-rate high protein foods also contain the essential amino acids and you don't have to think about it too much if you're eating well.

The proteins, and therefore the essential amino acids, are abundant in milk, in lean meat, chicken, turkey, cottage and cream cheese, canned salmon and tuna, and eggs; the dry legumes—peas, lentils, soybeans—also rank high in protein content.

THE FATS

Here are some friends you want to treat like just casual acquaintances, ones you don't see very often. The fats are invaluable for beauty because they help to lubricate the skin and the scalp. They generate heat in the body and produce essential fatty acids which then help to absorb the fat-soluble vitamins: A, D, E, and K. But you must eat the fats with care because they contribute mightily to overweight and are enemies to anyone with cholesterol problems. You cannot do without some fats in your diet, but remember that a little bit goes a long way.

Animal foods are particularly high in fat—for example, fat meats, butter and cream, whole milk. But don't forget natural vegetable oils, peanut butter and avocados also have high fat contents.

THE CARBOHYDRATES

The carbohydrates provide your body with energy. Too many unused carbohydrates will stay in your body, stored in cells or turned to fat. Carbohydrates are worth counting if you're trying to lose weight. Sugar, candy, pastries, the pastas, potatoes are high in carbohydrates. So are the grain foods: rice, oats, corn, wheat, obviously the breads. Alcohol is loaded with carbohydrates. You do need carbohydrates, so try to take them from unrefined and natural sources: fresh fruits, fresh vegetables and honey.

THE VITAMINS

The vitamins and minerals are absolutely essential to good health. I'm not a big believer in health food stores. I don't think stores should have to sell "healthy" foods; *food* is healthy. I'm also not a big believer in popping vitamin and mineral pills—it's much better to feed the nutrients into our bodies in their natural form, in good food. I've seen some serious illness and weaknesses result when people took high doses of vitamin pills and restricted proper food balance. I think you should only take vitamin or mineral pills on a regular program if your doctor prescribes them. Most of the doctors I've known or talked to will let you take a multiple vitamin daily "if you think it helps." Their attitude is that it can't hurt you. Certainly if you're on a weight-reducing diet you want to check with your doctor about supplementary vitamins and minerals. Although we don't yet know everything we should about vitamins and their importance to our diets, I still think we should take them naturally, through fresh, high-quality food.

Vitamin A helps to keep your skin soft and smooth by helping your skin to slough off dry cells. It aids in preventing dryness and roughness of the skin, and helps to keep your hair shiny and not dry. Vitamin A also helps your eyes—keeps them bright, helps you to see at night—and helps your body resist infections and disease. Vitamin A is found in cantaloupe, carrots, apricots, yellow foods, and in leafy, green foods like spinach, turnip and beet tops, parsley—all the yellow and green vegetables that contain carotene, an element that helps your body convert the foods to helpful Vitamin A. Incidentally, A is one of those vitamins that you cannot have too much of because it is never wasted but stored by your body for use when needed.

There is no single Vitamin B but rather a complex, a family of B vitamins, at least twenty in number, including some you're familiar with like B_1, thiamine, B_2, riboflavin, niacin. You need to take them every day because your body does not store the water-soluble B complex. They are important to the texture of your skin and can help to prevent skin discolorations. They help you to sleep well and prevent fatigue; they are also anti-stress—they help to keep your spirits high, help to keep you bright and happy. Many people who take one vitamin pill a day take some compound of the B complex because it seems to increase their energy.

I was amazed to discover that the B's are used up more quickly by alcoholic beverages taken into the body, and by excessive sunbathing. If you take to the sun or take a drink, take an extra helping of B that day as well. Find it in milk, in liver and other organ meats, the whole grains and wheat germ, and beans.

Just how much Vitamin C aids in the prevention of colds and whether massive doses of Vitamin C help in curing the common cold may be in dispute for many years to come, but this vitamin has a reputation as a resister, a fighter against infection through its detoxifying abilities. It also helps to form and to maintain collagen in your body. Collagen is the glue, the natural body cement that helps to hold all of our cells together. (When you get to the section on aging skin you'll see the important part collagen plays in keeping the skin firm and elastic.) Vitamin C is another of the water-soluble vitamins and does not store itself in your body, so you need a daily ration, but that's easy because Vitamin C is found in citrus fruits, in the oranges and grapefruits and the juices we all try to drink daily. You'll also get plenty of Vitamin C with just small amounts of broccoli or kale, red and green peppers. Beef and calf's liver, spinach, cantaloupe and fresh strawberries are all excellent sources of C.

Vitamin D is a lovely vitamin because it helps you to relax, eases nerves, and helps you to sleep better. It also helps bone structure and therefore makes good teeth for a pretty smile. You can take your Vitamin D in servings of fish and fish oils, and from Vitamin D–enriched milk, which may well be why we're often told to take a glass of milk before retiring. If you're a sunlover as I am, you'll be happy to learn that a few hours of sun every day will take care of all your Vitamin D requirements.

You Are What You Eat

THE VITAMINS

VITAMIN	FOOD SOURCE	FUNCTION
A *retinal*	Leafy green and yellow vegetables, yellow food (apricots, cantaloupe, etc.)	Promotes resistance to infection; keeps skin and hair healthy; critical to night vision
B COMPLEX B$_1$ *thiamine*	Meat, fish, poultry, eggs, whole grains, cereals	Enables body to use carbohydrates; aids functioning of nervous system
B$_2$ *riboflavin*	Same as B$_1$ and milk and cheese	Aids metabolism
B$_3$ *niacin*	Same as B$_1$ and B$_2$ and nut butters	Aids metabolism, especially of proteins and carbohydrates
B$_5$ *pantothenic acid*	Whole-grain cereals, animal tissues, legumes	Fights stress and aids adrenal gland function
B$_6$ *pyridoxine*	Ham, liver, lima beans, corn	Aids in protein, fat, and sugar metabolism; necessary for proper functioning of the central nervous system
Other B Complex: *Biotin, choline, folic acid, inositol, PABA*	Liver, yeast, fruits, cereals, eggs	Protects against heart disease, stress
C *ascorbic acid*	Citrus fruit, tomatoes, strawberries, raw greens, calf's liver	Necessary to formation and renewal of intercellular cement that holds the cells of all tissues together
D *calciferol*	Fish, fish oils, fortified milk, sunshine	Aids in calcium metabolism and is therefore good for bone and tooth structure; aids in relaxation
E *alphatocopherol*	Corn oil, wheat germ, avocados	Helps to prevent cholesterol build-up; helps Vitamin A to function; may speed healing; may increase sexual desire and potency

Vitamin E is another of those vitamins that have provoked a great deal of controversy. There are those who maintain that E increases sexual desire and sexual potency, that a capsule broken open and applied directly to the skin will soften the skin and will also heal a cut faster and prevent scarring. Regardless, I think it has been established that Vitamin E contributes to a healthy heart because it helps to prevent a buildup of blood cholesterol. It's a good friend to Vitamin A as well because E prevents certain fatty acids and fat-like substances, which protect Vitamin A and permit it to function, from being destroyed.

Corn oil, wheat germ, leafy green lettuces and avocados are excellent sources of Vitamin E.

There are other vitamins and new ones being discovered all the time. These are the ones we know most about and if you're a little aware of how they work for your body and how they can help you to maintain good health, I think it will be easier to keep a balanced, nutritious diet.

THE MINERALS

Calcium, phosphorus, sodium, iodine, iron, chlorine are just some of the sixteen-plus minerals our bodies need to work. They come from the earth and from the sea and are important to the development of a sound, strong body, and to your nerves. I didn't know, for example, when I started boning up on nutrition, that calcium and magnesium are two of the minerals your body needs to keep you feeling relaxed, to keep you from becoming irritable. Calcium is also a bone builder and is important for stronger teeth. Calcium and magnesium are well represented in milk, in salmon and sardines, and in dark green leafy vegetables.

Iron helps to keep the blood strong and helps it carry oxygen to all the cells of your body. If you're lacking in iron you may find yourself short of breath, tiring easily, even anemic.

SOME IMPORTANT MINERALS

MINERAL	FOOD SOURCE	FUNCTION
Calcium	Milk, salmon, dark green vegetables	Bone builder; relaxer
Magnesium	Same as calcium	Body relaxer
Iron	Organ foods, shellfish, dark green vegetables	Oxygenates body, giving it energy
Iodine	Seafood, iodized salt	Regulates thyroid, which in turn regulates all body functions
Potassium	Kelp	Aids nervous system; regulates body fluids; attracts nutrients into bloodstream
Chlorine	Kelp	Aids digestion; regulates body fluids; attracts nutrients into bloodstream
Sodium	Salt	Regulates body fluids; attracts nutrients into bloodstream

The animal organs such as liver, kidneys, hearts, are high in iron, as are shellfish and, again, the dark green vegetables. Lean meats contain iron, so they're better for you all around, supplying iron while cutting back on your fats.

Seafood and iodized salt are the strongest sources of iodine. Your thyroid glands need iodine to supply the thyroid hormones which regulate all of your body functions, and incidentally help to keep you slim. Too little iodine can leave you listless, depressed, and can effect a weight gain. An imbalance of your thyroid is, of course, a problem for your doctor.

Potassium, sodium and chlorine are three minerals which regulate body fluids, determine the amount of water in your body tissues, and attract nutrients into the bloodstream through osmosis. Potassium also helps your nervous system,

53

and chlorine is used to make hydrochloric acid, which aids in the digesting of food.

There are other minerals which you need traces of—cobalt, copper, zinc, and chromium are a few—but they seem to find their way into our bodies without much help.

Before I go on to diets and dieting I just have to say more definitely how I feel about certain things I think you should eliminate or limit if you want to be healthy. I'm really very opposed to alcohol, certainly excessive amounts of alcohol. First of all, it destroys your appetite by sending too much sugar into your bloodstream, so you just don't enjoy eating. It uses up your supply of Vitamin B, which you need to form proper proteins. It contributes greatly to broken capillaries on the skin and can ruin an otherwise radiant complexion. Last, but hardly least, alcohol is high in calories with none of the other nutritional benefits your body needs.

Some people feel that alcohol relaxes them after a long day. O.K., but don't abuse yourself with excesses. I think more and more Americans are enjoying a glass or two of wine before and with dinner. That's good. The grape is so much healthier for you than the grain.

Smoking cuts down your appetite, your breath, and your life expectancy. It uses up your supply of Vitamin C and that may mean lowered resistance and premature aging. Smoking definitely affects your skin tone, robbing your complexion of its lustre and color.

Each time I see someone puffing away on a cigarette I mentally say "thank you" to my mother. When I first went away to school it seemed that everyone around me smoked cigarettes, and I was at an age where I was very impressionable and thought smoking was terribly sophisticated. When my mother first saw me smoking she was so smart, really smart. Instead of telling me all the things about how bad it was for my health, she said, "Wouldn't it be more interesting to be the only one who didn't smoke?" That did it. I was so anxious to be individual that I just quit. Oh, occasionally I light a ciga-rette but I'm afraid that I've really turned into an anti-smoking crusader.

One other thing I think we should limit is coffee. The caffein in coffee is a stimulant. If you have too much it can really make you nervous, jumpy, irritable. As a stimulant, excesses of caffein can contribute to the broken capillaries just as much as alcohol. I try to limit myself to one or two cups a day. If you can get used to it, try drinking decaffeinated coffees. They're not all that bad, especially iced in the summer.

On Diets and Dieting

Actually, if we could all start life with the right habits and the right attitudes about ourselves, probably very few people would ever have to diet at all. The vast majority of women go through life controlling their food habits, regulating and watching and maintaining a healthy weight. I'm like that. If I let myself gain or lose a few pounds—for example, sometimes I lose a few pounds through stress—then I have to adjust my normal eating habits for a few days or a week. I try not to make too much of it, but I also try to be aware all the time so that I never go too far one way or the other.

But many women are in a constant battle with the pounds. All the rules for good nutrition and good eating habits also apply to the dieter. However, if you're trying to lose weight, you just have to eat less. I mean that. You cannot be healthy with a fad diet. If you're trying to gain weight you can't drink only malteds and milk shakes and eat cakes with whipped cream. You must maintain the balance of nutrients that your body requires. Really, nothing works in you unless everything works together. So you should eat almost everything and just eat less—or more—to adjust your body weight.

The key to understanding diet is in understanding your basal metabolism. The metabolism is at work all the time helping your body to grow, storing energy in the body and burning up calories to supply you with energy. If you have a high basal metabolism you burn up calories quickly; you probably never have enough left for storage in fat cells. You're lucky because you probably won't ever have to diet. You may have to put more effort into regulating that energy flow or even into gaining weight.

If you have a low basal metabolism you burn calories more slowly. Your body started storing fat cells in your body when you were very young. Those fat cells do not disappear once formed. Also, your body is slower to draw on those fat cells to use them up. You must be on a constant vigil. However, when you don't eat your body draws its nourishment from the fat you've already stored up. Even though you get to that storage slowly with a low metabolism, you do get there. You can skip a meal, skip a breakfast, skip a lunch perhaps, and still have the energy to get through the day.

I think reducing diets that are based on drugs are dangerous, and usually self-defeating. The amphetamines that may help to turn off your appetite can turn off your pleasures in life. Amphetamines affect your hormone balance and you end up jittery, irritable and tense. You may also become addicted and unless you keep taking the pills you cannot control your appetite.

Try to understand what motivates your eating habits. It is very important and very helpful to understand both your motivation for overeating and your motivation for dieting. Many women overeat, or eat rich sugar and starch foods, when they are unhappy, worried, nervous. Others don't eat at all when they're under stress. Think about why you eat if you don't eat normally. Don't cheat yourself. Don't fake yourself. Be honest.

If your motivation for losing weight is for other people, that just won't help enough. You should do it for yourself first—for your own energy, your own good looks. Then when others compliment you, if others admire you, good, all the better.

Let me say now, before I go on, that if you have permitted yourself to become seriously overweight or underweight, you should see your doctor first. Before you attempt any change in your eating habits you should have your basal metabolism checked. You should be aware if you have problems with cholesterol or diabetes, or hormonal or glandular imbalances.

Common Sense Weight Loss

1. O.K. No fad diets. No fast diets either. Don't go too fast once you've decided to lose weight. If you take off pounds too quickly, your skin cannot accommodate the loss. The elasticity of your skin needs time to reshape itself over your body. If you lose too quickly you'll end up with those awful "stretch" marks and they can scar your body for life. In addition, at the end of the fast diet you're equally fast at putting the weight back on. You haven't adjusted your total system to less intake, you haven't developed important new eating habits. If the diet included exercise, certainly you've just begun to achieve the discipline you'll need to keep your body firm.

However, I don't disapprove of a little bit of *fasting* when you first start. Although I think a balanced, sensible breakfast, lunch and dinner are most important, I also think that if you can go maybe half a day without eating and lose even a little weight, a little bloat, you just feel better about yourself.

When you are watching your weight, you must do exactly that. Watch it by weighing yourself every day. Record the figure on a chart if you enjoy keeping track of how your weight loss program is working. It is important that you always check at the same time of day. I think the morning is best, because then you can forget about the scale until tomorrow. Also you weigh less early in the morning than later in the day, and that's encouraging. Weigh every day but only once a day. Never step onto another scale (readings vary) or the same scale again until tomorrow. The daily check will tell you all you need to know about the fluctuation in your weight. (Remember that the menstrual cycle, among other factors, causes an up-and-down daily pattern in your weight chart even when the overall direction is toward weight loss.)

2. Pay attention to what you eat. For at least three days keep track of the kinds and amounts of food you eat. Too many overweight people say, "But you saw me, I didn't eat anything for dinner but a small piece of meat and a salad." And then they eat when no one is watching. They feel guilty about eating and guilty about telling those stories. That doesn't help at all.

3. Learn to make substitutions if you eat "emotionally." If you reach for sweets, if you start thinking about a bowl of spaghetti, substitute raw vegetables, a glass of calorie-free water.

Incidentally, nutritionists and physicians have become aware of the fact that starches are even more vicious than we ever thought. In addition to putting on weight, starches seem to create a need in your body for more starches. The more of them you eat, the more you crave. And, to the best of my knowledge, in all the literature I read, I could not find that any of the true nutrient values we need are supplied only in starches. No amino acids, no vitamins, no minerals.

Try to cut down generally on your intake of starches. You can't do without them completely, of course, nor do you want to. But if you feel you have to eat bread, have a thin slice—and eat whole grain breads so at least you receive some nourishment.

4. Vary your diet menu. Change it. When you know what foods you're taking in excess and what foods are putting the weight on, cut down on them; you needn't cut them out entirely. Change often. Keep the same variety in your half portions that you would in any healthy nutritional plan. Try all the greens, experiment with vegetable juice mixes. Just

You Are What You Eat

A brief acquaintance with calorie basics will prove in an instant that a raw vegetable is far less fattening than a cold piece of fried chicken:

FOOD	CALORIES
Apple, 1	70
Asparagus, 1 cup	45
Bacon, 2 slices	90
Beans: green, 1 cup	30
kidney, 1 cup	230
lima, 1 cup	190
Beef: ground, 3 oz.	185
sirloin, 3 oz.	330
Bread (1 slice) : cracked wheat	65
French	81
pumpernickel	79
rye	79
white	62
Butter: ½ cup	810
1 pat	35
Cantaloupe, ½	115
Carrot, 1	20
Cauliflower, 1 cup	25
Celery, 1 stalk	5
Cheese: Cheddar, 1 oz.	115
Swiss, 1 oz.	105
Chicken, ½ breast, fried	155
Clams, 3 oz.	65
Coffee, black	0
Crab, 3 oz.	85
Grapefruit, ½	45
Lamb chops, broiled, 4 oz.	400
Lettuce, Boston, 1 head	30
Macaroni, 1 cup	190
Milk: nonfat, 1 cup	90
whole, 1 cup	160
Noodles, 1 cup	200
Orange, 1	65
Peach, 1	35
Peanuts, 1 cup roasted	840
Peas, green, 1 cup cooked	115
Potato, 1, baked	90
Radishes, 4	5
Strawberries, 1 cup, raw	55

FOOD	CALORIES
Sugar: brown, 1 cup	820
white, 1 cup	770
1 tablespoon	40
Swordfish, broiled, 3 oz.	150
Tea, unsweetened and straight	0
Tomato, 1	40
Yoghurt, 1 cup	125

keep a little bit of starch and some sugars in your diet so you won't build up a terrible craving.

And if you do cheat, enjoy it. I mean, if you finally decide to have a piece of cake, have it, and tell yourself that you're having it because you want to—and *enjoy it*.

5. If you're hungry in the middle of the afternoon or at night try to remember that your body is still taking nourishment from those stored-up fat cells. If that fails, eat a piece of apple, a bit of cheese, a few slim sticks of a raw vegetable.

6. Cut down on salt. If you're used to salting your food heavily it will be hard at first. Substitute fresh lemon, herbs for flavoring.

7. Pay attention to everything and anything that makes fattening foods less attractive and the "diet" foods that you eat more attractive. The general, overall rules which I discussed earlier for healthy nutrition are especially important to you. Serve your food in an attractive way, try to eat slowly in a relaxed and pleasant atmosphere. Eat with friends whom you enjoy. If you're alone, put on some music. Relax with your "cocktail hour" if that's your habit. Pour yourself a small glass of wine, or if your diet prohibits even that, fill a pretty wine glass with soda and a twist of lemon. It will slow you down, relax you. Since I rarely drink alcoholic beverages, except red wine, when I have guests at cocktail time I often

join them with a glass of tomato juice or soda to which I've added a strip of celery or cucumber, and no one knows.

And, as you can see for yourself from the chart below, wine and wine-based drinks are far less caloric, glass for glass, than hard liquor:

DRINK	CALORIES
Wine	60–70 per glass
Champagne	90 per glass
Kir	90 per ounce
Spritzer	70 per ounce
Brandy	75 per ounce
Scotch, bourbon, rye	125 per ounce
Martini	135 per ounce
Whiskey Sour	140 per ounce
Stinger	145 per ounce
Bloody Mary	140 per ounce
Bullshot	110 per ounce
Sidecar	160 per ounce
Rum	155 per ounce
Rum Punch	300 per ounce
Brandy Alexander	225 per ounce
Irish Coffee	335 per ounce
Eggnog	335 per ounce

8. Increase your physical activity. Exercise, walk to lunch if you're going out, take up a new sport. Keep your body in tone as you lose weight. I think my body movements are really helpful to someone trying to lose weight. When you really begin to feel your body it increases your desire to have a nicer body.

Below is a chart which indicates approximately how many calories are used in various activities:

ACTIVITY	CALORIES PER MINUTE
Sitting relaxed	1.0
Washing dishes	2.8

ACTIVITY	CALORIES
Making beds	5.5
Walking, normal pace	2.8
Walking, rapidly	4.8
Biking, normal pace	3.2
Biking, rapidly	6.9
Jogging	11.0
Swimming, crawl	26.7
Swimming, breaststroke	30.8
Swimming, backstroke	33.3
Golf	5.0
Tennis	7.0
Dancing	5.2

9. Have a good night's sleep. The most important way you can help yourself with a diet is to stay healthy and as close to a normal routine as possible. That way you can maintain yourself better later on because you've adjusted the new eating habits into a regular life.

10. As you begin to lose weight, especially if you have to lose a lot of weight, think about how you're going to look when you've accomplished your goal. You may change your hair style or the color of your hair a little bit. Certainly as you lose weight and your size scales down you'll be able to wear different clothes. You may start wearing a more colorful makeup, more dramatic jewelry, different things that make you aware of being prettier.

11. Don't talk about your diet. It's just boring, and the last thing you need now is to be considered boring. You need admiration, affection, help. If you have a friend who can really help, someone who loves you, recognizes your achievements as they come, someone who doesn't make you feel guilty, great. But otherwise, keep it to yourself. If you're invited out to lunch or dinner you can always find something to eat, a small piece of meat, a salad. I think it's awful when I'm with someone at a really fine restaurant and they don't eat

anything, just a glass of water. If you're that obvious, if you talk about it too much, everyone is watching you.

It's so much nicer to meet a friend one day and have her say "You look wonderful. What's different?"

12. When you've accomplished the weight-loss goal you set out for, don't go out and splurge, don't go on a food binge. If you've been going slowly you've learned new habits. Your body has really learned to get along on less. Let it.

Be proud of yourself. I think you should always take time to be pleased with any accomplishment. Being pleased that you've succeeded will help you to maintain the body and the shape and the good health that you worked so hard for.

Try to eat well . . . and when you cheat, enjoy it!

CHAPTER FIVE

I Hate to Exercise!

I USED TO HATE TO EXERCISE. I *really* hated to exercise—
I resented the routine, I even disliked the word "exercise." I
preferred to think that with proper nutrition and enough
rest no one would have to exercise, least of all me. I preferred
to think that a few sets of tennis or an hour's walk or some
swimming would keep me in shape.

I never paid any attention at all to exercising. In fact, if I
had exercised I'd have felt almost silly telling anyone. About
a year ago, after I finished designing and showing my fall collection, I was exhausted. I managed to get away for a few
days in Antigua. It was a marvelous change. I love the sun and
I love to swim. What I didn't love one bit was another change,
the change I suddenly noticed in my body. I honestly couldn't
believe the figure I saw in that bikini was mine. I looked soft—
I *was* soft—and I felt ashamed. Clothes can hide you from
yourself but a bikini sure can't. I also found myself wondering
why I tired so quickly, why I was so exhausted.

When I got back to New York I decided that I just had to
exercise. I tried everything. I subscribed to classes and joined
clubs and hardly ever managed to get to them. The few times I

did manage to go I was bored—bored with the classes, bored with the routines. I resented the time it took to get to the class, the changing into a leotard and then changing back again. I was even angry with all the other ladies around me who seemed to have nothing else to do all day when I had to rush and push myself because I had so many other important things to do. The more I told myself that I ought to go the more I resisted going. I was annoyed with myself. Actually, I was ignoring myself.

I tried doing exercises at home, but after a few mornings I found some excuse or other to forget them. I kept thinking about that, why exercise couldn't be pleasant. I really like to work, you know. I like the challenges, the decisions, the differences of opinion, even the tough problems. I'm very disciplined and I even like the discipline. Why couldn't I discipline myself to exercise? Why couldn't I like exercising?

Finally I decided that since discipline was the only answer, I'd just have to find someone else to discipline me. I asked a friend if she knew of a teacher who would come to my apartment. That's how I met Katia Perret-Aubry, a dancer and a professional teacher, who introduced me to a whole new attitude about exercising.

The first morning we started, all the movements were so slow, so relaxed that I was impatient, and I know I was a bit mean to Katia when she left. I said, "Are *those little things* going to do anything for me?" I wanted to get going, to feel that I'd worked hard and that I was accomplishing something. Katia just smiled and set my impatience aside. We'd started immediately on proper breathing and she suggested I think about inhaling and exhaling and left me, with an appointment for the next morning. The next morning was the same, just more stretching and more simple, easy movements.

When I wake up in the morning I'm awake. I sleep very well and I'm always anxious to start a new day. So, when Katia started my day with lazy, voluptuous stretching I felt frustrated. We talked a lot. She asked me if I could feel the stretch in my leg. She asked me if a movement felt good, if it felt nice. I began to concentrate on what I was feeling.

I can't say that the first week was fun, but I was beginning to pay attention. My mind was watching the way my arms and legs moved and I was intrigued. I began to be involved. It was a little bit like with sex sometimes—you know how sometimes you're kind of disinterested, kind of uninvolved, and slowly you begin to become interested?

One night, maybe ten days after I'd first met Katia, I came home from a party with my all time confidant and true good friend, Olivier. I was feeling relaxed and happy and I turned on some music and began to stretch. Without realizing it I just kept going for a few hours. I was enjoying myself. The room was darkened, the music was relaxing, a bit seductive to me, and I was *enjoying* myself. I felt more in touch with myself than I ever had before.

Olivier, who is not exactly an athlete himself but who knows all about them, was delighted and maybe a bit amused about my "discovery." He could have told me all the time. He explained to me how athletes are really aware of their bodies. It's not all just the game or the competition for them. They enjoy the working out. He told me that "muscle builders," the men who show their muscles, get real physical pleasure when they're working to develop their bodies.

From that evening on I realized that I was thinking about how my body moved, and I began to use the words "body movement." I looked forward to my morning meetings with Katia. I was really meeting myself.

I honestly believe that the time I'm going to suggest you take for body movements is one of the most important things you can give to yourself. Your whole body becomes relaxed for the entire day and everything is a little easier. It's like learning to fall properly. If you can manage not to tighten up you won't hurt yourself as much. The same theory applies to your day, physically and emotionally. The tensions simply can't take hold.

The time you're going to give yourself is also the most sensual. Although learning about good nutrition, skin care, and makeup techniques is important, none of the other programs in the book can help you to discover the honest sensuality you have. Instead of saying "I hate to exercise!", you'll be looking forward to spending time with your body.

Your body is so wonderful. If you keep it healthy and well nourished and don't abuse it with fatigue or excesses of alcohol and smoking, it will perform beautifully. But somehow equally wonderful is the fact that even if you have been neglectful, if you've let the miraculous machinery get sluggish, if you've allowed weight to accumulate or muscles to go soft, your body will respond to correction. At any age. Body muscles can be brought back to tone. After all, *you* control your muscles. Your mind tells your muscles what to do. And the marvelous thing about your muscles is that once you start to strengthen them the effects are cumulative. How long it will take you to have complete control of your body once you start depends on your age and condition, of course. But you can develop better breathing and better circulation, coordination and flexibility quite quickly. You can tighten and firm and reshape your body with patience. You'll *see*—and *feel*— the results.

The rewards are many: a new attitude about your body; a body that feels good to be in and that responds with more energy and vitality to the many pressures you put on it all day; a more attractive body. There's a great deal to be said for the thought that if you look more attractive, you feel more attractive. The corollary is also true. If you feel more attractive, more at ease with yourself, you're more attractive to others. Isn't that also true in sex? A woman who's ashamed of or uncomfortable with her body takes that feeling to bed with her and is inhibited from enjoying her partner, and herself.

Throughout the entire book you'll notice that I keep repeating how important it is to appraise yourself and accept yourself. Look how important it is here. If you're very tall, you're not going to get shorter. You can control your muscles, but you can't change bones. Tall is nice. Accept it. If you're a little hippy and full-bosomed, don't try to remake yourself in the image of a skinny fashion model. It won't work. You can trim down your hips. You should always concentrate on special movements to keep your breasts firm and lifted and young. Hippy and bosomy can be very nice, very desirable. Accept it.

I love the body movements in this chapter because they're almost all designed to keep the whole body fit and firm and flexible. They're not faddish, nor are they the very latest, fast-acting miracle workers. They're a combination of time-tested, proven movements incorporating the best mix of yoga, isometrics, and ballet techniques.

Be very straight with yourself. Concentrate your effort on something you know you can improve. I know I can't kid myself. I did let my thighs go soft, so I take an extra five or ten minutes when I can and I concentrate on the movements that particularly stretch and firm my legs.

Of course there's an initial discipline you need to help you get started when you have so many other things to do in a day. I'm a busy woman and there's no doubt about that, but even if I have to wake up earlier to take that time for myself, I do. At night before going to bed I always prepare my list of all the things I'm going to have to do the next day so my mind will be absolutely clear to sleep. No matter what happens I've learned to stick to that. When I wake up in the morning I have breakfast, I do my exercises and only afterwards do I start to function. My list is on my table. I take it and start the day. Sometimes I remember something in the middle of an exercise. I immediately write it down so I can concentrate on me only.

So be a little bit strict with yourself and be serious about your preparation. But weigh the balance of discipline and creativity. Too much method destroys creativity. Don't let the discipline overcome the natural instinct of what's good for you. Do what is possible, what's manageable for you.

Don't strain, ever. Don't force till you get a cramp. If you hurt yourself, if you end up with stiff and sore muscles, the discomfort will show in your carriage and in your face, and that's the exact opposite of what you want. And anyway, very few subjects of conversation are more boring than aches and pains.

If you're starting a diet, trying for a sizable weight loss, start your body movements simultaneously. You'll stimulate your desire for a nicer body even more.

I don't believe in props. There are no bars, weights, dumbbells, slant boards, or even mats required—they're just more things to go and buy that might well keep you from getting started. Anyway, they don't do the movements, you do. When you're lying down place a clean sheet on any fairly thick rug or carpet you have, just so you don't breathe in dust from the floor. A few bath towels will also cushion you. I use a lovely old quilt I found a long time ago. It has a stain, so I can't use it on my bed but it's beautiful to stretch out on. Wear something comfortable, unconfining, or wear nothing.

How long will it take your body to get into shape? I think you have to give yourself at least six months, maybe even a year. If you've exercised before and just went lazy for a while, you'll get your tone and control much more quickly than if you've never exercised. After six months you can probably maintain your body with every-other-day sessions. After the foundation is solidly established, you could go away on vacation and skip it all for two weeks, though I think you ought to try to do something, the Windmill a hundred times, for instance. Once you've started, I think you'll find that you really *want* to do some of the movements all the time for the wonderful vitality they give you.

Preparation for the Body Movements

Set aside a minimum of twenty minutes of your day for just being with yourself and your body movements. Empty your mind of all thoughts except that you're giving yourself something special, something nice.

Concentrate. Prepare yourself for what you're going to do. Concentrate only on the body movements throughout. You're going to stretch, relax, move and feel all the parts of your body.

Be creative. The point is to get acquainted with yourself, with parts of your body you haven't paid much attention to. You really can't help but want to flex a foot or swing a little when your leg is high in the air. Look what you can do. Stretch. It's nice. Enjoy it. Go slowly. What's your hurry? Close the door behind you, darken the room, turn on some music you like. Maybe you want to bring some fresh flowers into the room, or spray the room with perfume. You've given yourself this time to be free with yourself. Don't rush. Don't strain. *Be patient with yourself.* You're not on a schedule, you're using your time sensually, pleasurably.

All of the body movements which follow are worked out in a continuous pattern. There are no arbitrary ups and downs. You're not sitting to "exercise" the thighs, then lying down to "work out" the legs. One movement flows into the next like a dance so that, once learned, the continuity itself helps to make you aware of the rhythm of your body. Take the time to be aware of your breathing between movements and to concentrate your mind and body for the next movement.

The full cycle of twelve body movements will take you fifteen minutes with the recommended number of times to start. But I always start my day with slow yawning stretches and some bendovers to relax and I know that you'll find adding these few minutes a simple habit to form. As there are no rigid rules, if you have an hour once a week, take it, give it to yourself. Your understanding and your rewards will be further enhanced.

Even though your attitude is simply to enjoy your time with

yourself, I have included notations on the specific areas of the body which are being toned and firmed. It's all really a perfect marriage of movements to get acquainted with and improve every part of your body.

Give yourself a few days to learn all of the movements. Then, forget the counting and start enjoying yourself. Do each posture and movement as recommended at first; then, as you improve your coordination and control, do them as often as you can, or as often as you like. Forget mirrors; they can be depressing. It's not what you see now but what you feel.

Before you start, maybe while you're still in bed in the morning, inhale and exhale consciously a few times. Even though breathing is the most natural activity of our bodies, most of us don't breathe properly. All body movements start with inhaling and end when you're exhaling. All body movement radiates from the center of your body, so the natural flow of air through the diaphragm, the lower part of the chest, the center of your body, helps to ease you through all body movement.

I've included some specific body movements that have really helped me to become aware of correct breathing. It's a good idea to practice your breathing in the beginning. Inhale—and hold for a few seconds. Exhale—holding for a few extra seconds.

Practice inhaling—count 1-2-3-4. Exhale—count 1-2-3-4-5-6. Always inhale through the nose and exhale through the mouth. Most people tend to stress the inhaling for breathing, but Katia has shown me how to concentrate on my exhaling to really flush the air out of the lungs. If you haven't let all the air out, how can you bring a full breath back into your lungs?

As you inhale your diaphragm expands, opening up, filling up like a balloon. As you exhale your diaphragm closes in, lets go, deflates. Now think, inhale-expand-stretch, exhale-deflate-relax. Inhale-expand, exhale-relax. Once you're in touch with your breathing you're truly in touch with yourself.

THE STRETCH AND THE BEND

Say "Good Morning" to yourself. Relax. Breathe in and out a few times. Think about what you're going to do. Start thinking lazy, luxurious thoughts about your body.

In a standing position, set your feet slightly apart, the weight evenly distributed. Let your arms hang loosely at your sides.

Shift your weight to your right foot, keeping it flat on the floor. Start inhaling as you slowly begin to raise your right arm.

Stretch slowly upwards to a count of four, stretching your arm, stretching your fingers to the ceiling. Your left side is totally relaxed. Feel the stretch as it moves up through the entire side of your body. Feel it through your leg and thigh, through your abdomen and waist, in your arm and hand.

Start exhaling to a count of four. Let go through your wrist, your elbow, your shoulder until the arm hangs freely at your side. Feel the complete "collapse" of your diaphragm as the air pushes all the way out. Balance weight on both feet.

Shift weight to your left foot and repeat, now raising the left arm, stretching the entire left side of your body. Make sure that the opposite side of your body and the opposite leg are completely relaxed.

Alternate five times each side for a total of ten times.

Take a moment to relax and to think about the next posture, the bendover.

I Hate to Exercise!

In a standing position, set your feet apart. Your knees should be loose and slightly bent, your shoulders relaxed, arms hanging at your sides.

To a slow count of ten, letting your head lead the movement, let your head roll down to your chest and fold your chest downward. Let your shoulders fall, your arms fall, until you're entirely folded over in a U position. As you're folding over, feel that your hands and your head are heavy, as if they were pulling you downward.

Breathe easily. Inhale and exhale naturally and stay in the U position for as long as you feel comfortable. Don't close your eyes. Don't think about whether you can touch the floor.

Now, unfold slowly upward to a count of ten, letting the lower part of your back lead the way. Unfurl yourself until your spine is straight, your shoulders back in position, arms at your side, and head erect last.

Start by doing this just twice. As you become more co-ordinated you'll build to ten times.

The bendover is one of the most tension-releasing movements I know. I often alternate it with another I've included at the end of this chapter to clear my mind and relax my body after a busy business day.

And now, slowly lower yourself to the floor, stretch out on your back, breathe a few times. The movement that follows begins the fifteen-minute cycle; it will start you thinking specifically about your breathing and help you to breathe properly.

BODY MOVEMENT #1

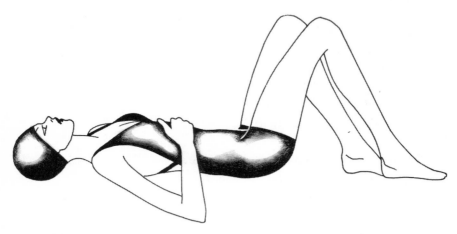

Lie on your back on the floor, your knees bent, your feet apart, flat on the floor. Place both hands, palms down, on your diaphragm (the lower part of your rib cage).

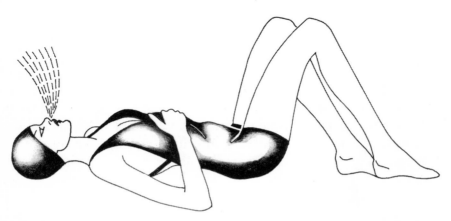

Inhale to a slow count of four. Feel the rib cage expand. Your spine will be slightly raised or curved off the floor.

74

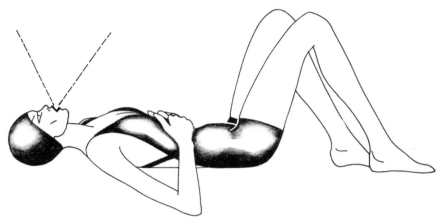

Exhale to a count of four, pressing the flat of your hands on the lower rib cage, depressurizing the diaphragm completely. As you do this also press the small of your back to the floor. Empty your lungs of all breath, exhaling through your mouth. Hear the breath escape your mouth.

Repeat slowly six times, concentrating on your breathing. You're also developing control of your stomach muscles and helping to flatten the stomach.

75

BODY MOVEMENT #2

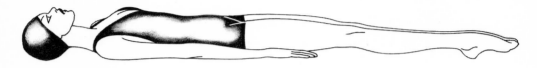

Lie on the floor with your legs extended, your shoulders flat on the floor, your head straight back. Feel your body weight against the floor.

Clasp your hands over your right knee and bring the knee up to your chest. Press the knee slowly to your chest, holding the knee while pressed for a count of four.

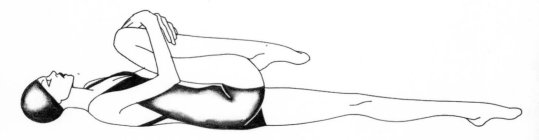

Lower right leg to the floor.

Alternate. Clasp hands over left knee, raise left knee to chest. Press. Hold for a count of four. Return leg to floor.

Alternate legs five times each to start for a total of ten times. This movement tones and improves the entire body. And here's an example of improvising later on. In the same position, bring both knees up to your chest with your hands clasped around the knees. Press knees gently toward your chest ten times. You're cradling yourself really, so move your lower body in a rocking motion. Be aware of your breathing throughout. The cradle is often recommended by doctors for women with weak back tendencies.

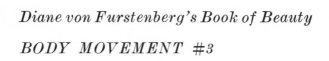

BODY MOVEMENT #3

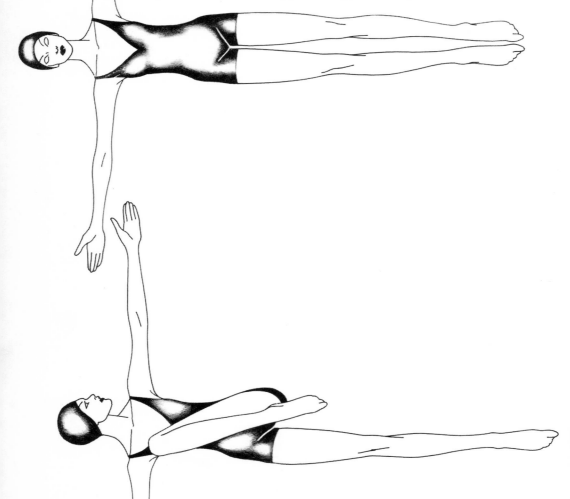

Lie on the floor, legs straight ahead of you, your arms straight out to the sides, palms up, so that you make a T.

Bring your right knee up towards your chest; then cross the knee over to the left side of your body, turning your head to the right as you do so.

78

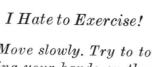

I Hate to Exercise!

Move slowly. Try to touch your knee to the floor, keeping your hands on the floor. (If you can't touch, don't strain—wait until your body is more coordinated. Just go as close to the floor as you can.)

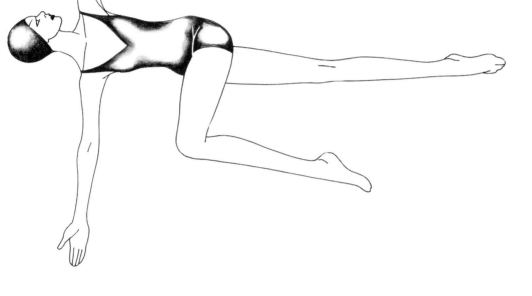

As soon as you touch the floor, return knee to chest position, then lower the leg to the floor, returning your head to center position.

Raise left knee to chest and repeat, rolling it toward the right side of your body with your head turned to the left.

Alternate action five times each side for a total of ten times. As you become aware of this movement you'll also be aware that it's stretching your spine, tightening your thighs, upper arms and throat, and firming your middle body and waist.

79

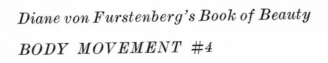

BODY MOVEMENT #4

Lie on the floor, back flat, arms outstretched to a T, palms facing up.

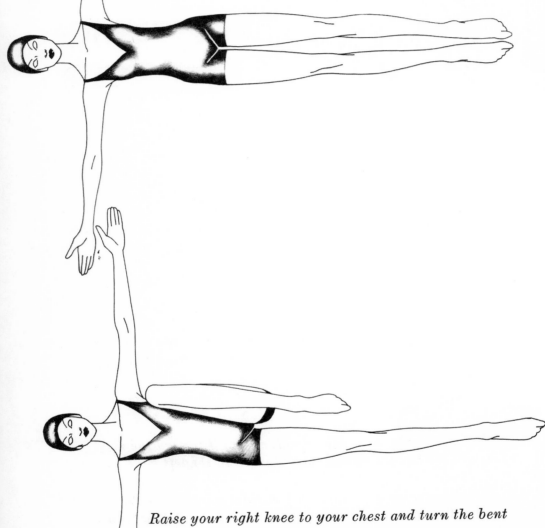

Raise your right knee to your chest and turn the bent knee out to your right.

80

I Hate to Exercise!

Try to place the knee flat against the floor. When you touch the floor—or come as close as you can without straining—return knee to chest. Lower leg to the floor.

Raise left leg, touching left knee to chest and to the floor on the left side of your body.

Alternate five times each leg for a total of ten times. Feel the muscles in your inner thigh as they elongate. Eventually you might combine Movements 3 and 4. Bring your right knee up to your chest, touch the floor on the right, return knee to chest, cross the leg over to the left, touch floor, return knee to chest and lower leg to the floor. Or reverse the movement, starting with your right leg crossing over to the left and then touching the floor on the right. I always add one of these combinations when I have time.

BODY MOVEMENT #5

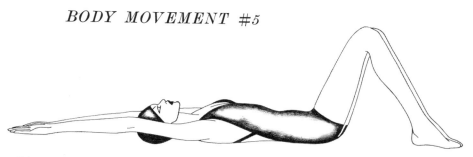

Lie on the floor with your back flat, your knees bent, feet flat on the floor. Stretch your arms straight back over your head, elbows relaxed.

Bring your right knee up to your chest; as you bend the knee flex your foot so the sole of your foot is facing the ceiling.

Straighten your leg, raising it straight up, straightening your foot so your toe is pointed to the ceiling.

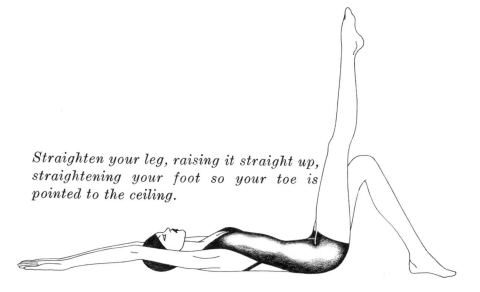

Concentrate on your body. Pull your stomach flat to the floor under you. Lower the leg straight down, toe pointed, until you almost touch the floor.

Do not touch the floor but repeat the movement, lifting the same leg, ten times.

Repeat movement with left leg ten times.

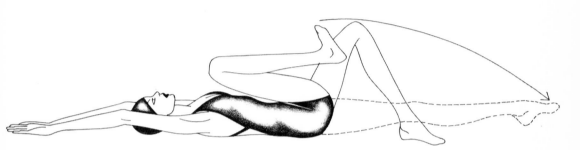

You'll start doing this for a total of twenty times. And here's an easy one to add as your legs get stronger: Lift your right leg straight up from the floor toward the ceiling, your toe pointed. Now, flex your foot, bend knee to chest, and lower leg straight out, a few inches off the floor, with your toe pointed again. Don't touch the floor but repeat ten times and alternate. Both movements are particularly good for strengthening the stomach and back muscles and help firm and tone the entire leg.

BODY MOVEMENT #6

If I had to choose my favorite movement, I'd choose one I call The Windmill. I do this on occasions when I just cannot fit twenty minutes into a hectic traveling schedule and sometimes I just do it a hundred times because it's so graceful and it makes me feel so good.

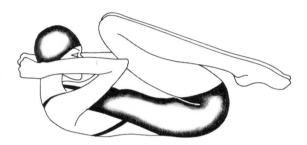

Lie on your back on the floor. Raise both knees to your chest. Now, clasp your hands behind your head and lift your head and shoulders off the floor using your arms.

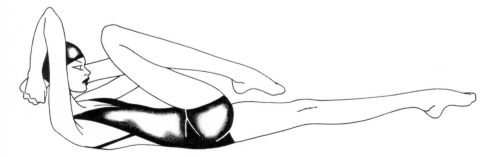

Extend your left leg straight out, toe pointed, keeping the leg raised off the floor, while touching your right knee to your left elbow.

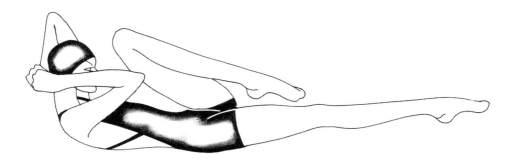

Change over. Return your left leg to the bent position, stretch your right leg straight out and touch left knee to right elbow. Don't pause. Keep the movement continuous.

Alternate ten times to start, building to a total of at least twenty times.

The most important part of the Windmill movements is the fluid, rhythmic way you stretch and draw in, open and close in a slow, flowing pattern. The Windmill is just marvelous for coordination, for toning the entire body, and it's particularly helpful for the abdomen.

Here's an excellent point to pause and relax. Bring your knees up and do the cradle movement a few times. Breathe. Rest. Renew your energy.

BODY MOVEMENT #7

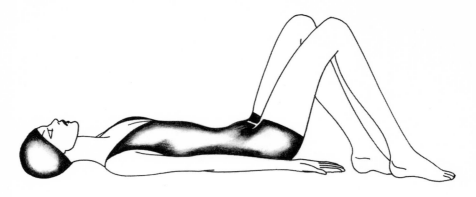

*Still lying on the floor, bend your knees with your feet apart,
flat on the floor, your arms parallel to your body, palms up.
Press the small of your back down, tipping the pelvis up.*

*Slowly raise your hips off the floor. As you tilt up, place your
hands under your buttocks for support.*

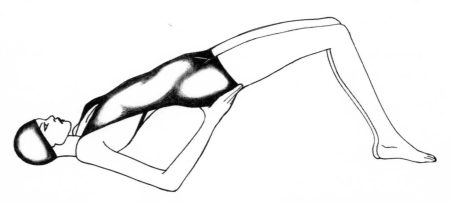

*Straighten your spine and lift yourself until your weight is
resting on your shoulders and feet.*

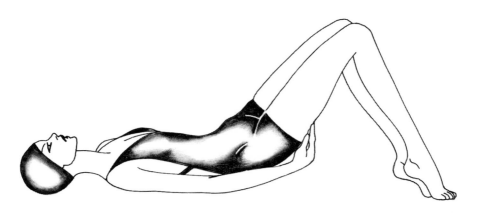

Now lower yourself. Lower the top of your spine first, then "roll" your spine down until the small of your back touches the floor; your buttocks and the heels of your feet should come down last.

Do this four times slowly, in a steady rhythm. This is a marvelous movement for legs, stomach, and for lifting the buttocks.

When you do this movement you become aware of nature's way of countering all movement with opposite movement. When your back arches it wants to come back to a straight position. You're also countering the curled-up posture of the cradle with these elongating, stretching motions.

BODY MOVEMENT #8

Stretch out fully on your right side. Bend your right knee with your right foot on the floor. Place your right arm above your head, pillowing your head on your extended right arm. Place your left hand comfortably on the floor in front of you. Extend your left leg a few inches off the floor.

Raise your left leg straight up and down, parallel to your body, without touching the floor or your other leg. Do this ten times.

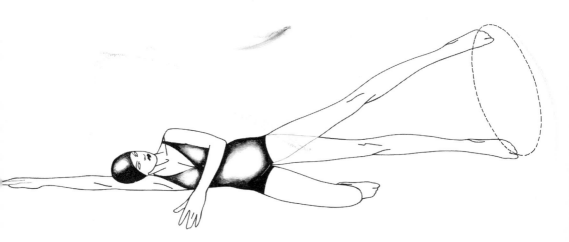

Roll over. Repeat movement resting on left side, left knee bent, left foot on the floor, raising your right leg up and down ten times without touching the floor.

I love to sneak that one in almost anytime. When I'm home talking on the telephone or watching television, I stretch out on the floor, prop myself on my elbow and just start moving. I usually start with the basic up-and-down movement and keep improvising, adding on. Sometimes I swing the leg from my hip making large even circles, or I'll start with a small circle, build to a big one, and then pare it down to the small circle again. Sometimes I kick my leg into the air and bend and unbend the knee. It all depends on what I feel like, how I feel like moving my body.

Sit cross-legged with your back straight, head erect.

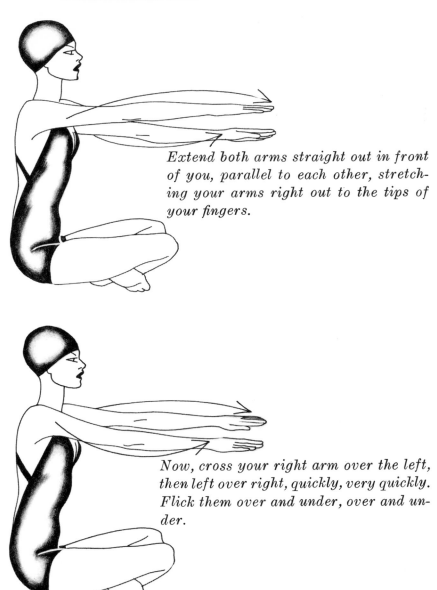

*Extend both arms straight out in front
of you, parallel to each other, stretching your arms right out to the tips of
your fingers.*

*Now, cross your right arm over the left,
then left over right, quickly, very quickly.
Flick them over and under, over and under.*

You can do this fifty or one hundred times for toning the
whole arm, the upper arm, and the breasts.

In the cross-legged sitting position, bend your elbows in front of your body, level with your shoulders, and cross your arms. Clasp your left forearm, just above the wrist, in your right hand and your right forearm, just above the wrist, in your left hand, palms facing in opposite directions.

Push out. Hold for count of ten. Release. Relax. Repeat.

Do this a total of five times. It's another excellent movement for firming the pectoral muscles.

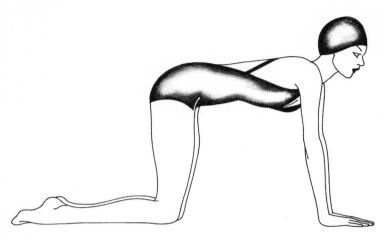

Place yourself "on all fours," balancing your weight between your hands and knees. Your back should be straight, your head up.

Lift your right leg straight out behind you, toe pointed. Bend your right knee, keeping it as high as possible. Then stretch out, straightening the leg. Bend, straighten, bend, straighten. Repeat ten times.

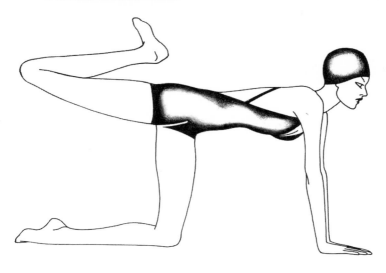

Alternate with left leg, bending left knee. Repeat ten times.

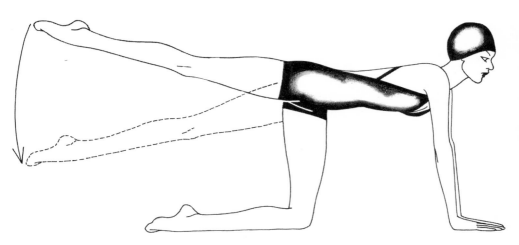

This is a simple but most effective movement for tightening falling buttocks. Equally simple is another variation you might add on later. In the same position, extend the right leg straight out and, without bending the knee, lower and raise the leg ten times without touching the floor. Repeat with left leg.

BODY MOVEMENT #12

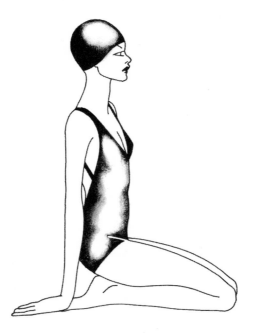

From "all fours" posture, sit back on your heels. Your arms are at your sides, the backs of your hands on the floor alongside your feet in a relaxed position.

Exhale as you slowly lower your head. Let your chin fall onto your chest, relax and lower your shoulders. Curl down until your forehead touches the floor, and your chest rests on your thighs. Inhale.

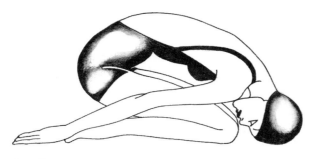

This is the Sphinx position. Breathe naturally. Hold the position for as long as you feel comfortable.

Slowly roll yourself up again. As you come up keep your chin on your chest and uncurl through the lower part of your body, bringing your neck and your head erect last.

You're completely relaxed. You're really in touch with your body, with yourself. What a wonderful way to start the day!

POSTSCRIPT

Here's an extra body movement that's wonderful for total relaxation at the end of the day, plus an add-on to relieve the tension in your face. Try this before you take a bath and get ready to go out or before you start making dinner. You'll be amazed at how just ten minutes in a darkened room dispels the tensions. If you have trouble falling asleep, do a few minutes before you get into bed. It really unties you. The contrary of being all tied up, yes?

Lie on your back on the floor and place your legs comfortably on a chair, an ottoman, or a stool, knees bent and resting on the edge of the seat. Place your arms at your sides, palms up.

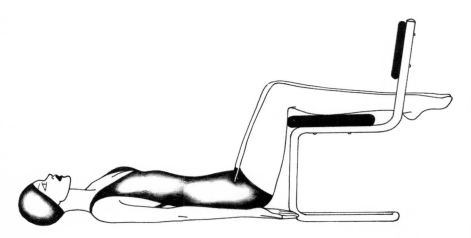

Concentrate. Concentrate on your spine resting on the floor for support.

I Hate to Exercise!

Place your right hand palm down on the lower part of your abdomen and breathe "through your hand." Breathe in, breathe all the way down, slowly, concentrating on the lower part of your spine.

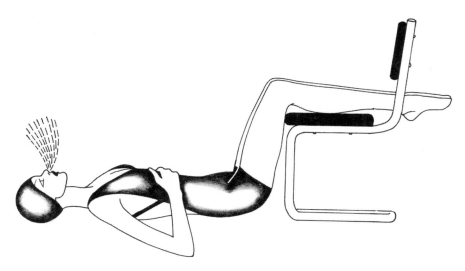

Exhale slowly, concentrating. Repeat as desired.

To release all the tension in your face, the tension that builds up around your eyes and brows, stay in the same position but cup your hands over your open eyes. Empty your mind of all thoughts and just concentrate on letting the dark penetrate.

As you go through the day, think about breathing properly. Just thinking about it will help your posture to be straighter, your carriage nicer, because you're aware of the center of your body.

Is there anyone who doesn't associate the word "posture" with childhood reprimands, reminders to sit up straight? The word is boring, but the results of correcting your carriage are fascinating. I have seen dumpy women become taller, almost willowy, when they stopped sagging and slumping. A beautiful way of standing has a lot to do with improving your circulation, too. So it makes you more beautiful inside and out. But good posture is not rigid. Instead of stiffening into a wooden soldier, relax your body into the long, fluid lines of an attractive woman. It takes only a minute. Stand so that you are in profile before a full-length mirror. Do the Stretch and the Bend, the first of the body movements on page 72. Now look carefully at your body. Knees should be bent very slightly forward, not "locked back." The pelvis should be tucked in, tilted up in front to provide support for the lower organs (and make the rear end look smaller). Your spine should be straight; but that word "straight" is the probable cause of all the unattractive tenseness most women take for good posture. Rather than a straight line, think of a long line and you will have it. Draw yourself up from the waist, rib cage up and away from the waist, roll your shoulders up into a shrug and then relax. Look into the mirror, and you will see a very attractive difference.

And stretch whenever you can. Those first stretches you take in bed as you wake up in the morning are the best, aren't they? You don't have to become an exhibitionist and you don't have to stop and say, "Oh, here I am stopping to exercise." There just are so many times in every day when you can relax a bit, get in touch with your body again.

Make yourself aware of your movements. Then make those movements just a little bit longer. A longer movement is so much more graceful, anyway. Stretch your legs in a taxi cab. Take a deep yawn and stretch your arms way out to the sides. Cab drivers are so busy driving they hardly notice. Relax your hands when you're talking on the phone at your desk. Start from a closed fist, then open your fingers out like a fan and stretch the fingers so you feel every one of them, and then close them up again. Around the house just remember to stretch a little longer whenever you reach for something or when you push a piece of furniture away from you. Think about your legs and your feet when you climb stairs at home.

I Hate to Exercise!

Tiptoe up and back down sometimes, leaving the heel of your foot off the tread. Another time go up and down flat-footed. That really stretches muscles. At business, don't take elevators all the time—climb a few flights of stairs every day.

Walk. Don't take a taxi, a bus or the car if you can walk. Walking is my favorite, I guess, because it does so much for me at one time. It gives me time to think and usually it gives me fresh air—which we never really get enough of.

Swim when you can. It's a wonderful way to develop coordination and to tone muscles. Your muscles have to work a little bit harder against the resistance water creates but water is also soothing, which helps compensate for the additional exertion.

But the most important thing is to stretch all the time. Stretch lazily. Stretch sensuously. It feels so good!

How Can You Fight Cellulite?

Certainly you have heard of cellulite. If you are a bit of a fatalist, you may even have decided that your figure problems cannot be helped by exercise, that you are a helpless victim of cellulite. That is ridiculous. In Europe, almost everybody subscribes to the idea of a mysterious and special form of fat which clings in distorting bulges to the tops of a woman's thighs, and which is practically impossible to remove. Bulges in these areas below the waist can be unsightly and hard to get rid of. Even the cellulite "experts" agree that poor circulation and elimination, improper diet and inadequate exercise are major factors in the formation of cellulite. Eliminate them by getting more exercise in the fresh air, by substituting lots of fresh fruits and vegetables (raw if possible) and other high-fiber foods for the rich and overprocessed foods. It is especially important to cut your intake of salt as drastically as your doctor will permit and to increase the water you drink to at least seven glasses a day. This will change the delicate balance of salt and water in the body, and your body will be able to throw off some of the water which an excess of salt in the system causes to be held in between the cells. This retained water and salt, along with trapped impurities, is the real culprit in cellulite bulges. Please do not imagine, though, that cellulite (or any kind of fat) can be massaged away.

Massage is a beautifully relaxing and stimulating treat for the body. But no massage can "break down" fatty deposits beneath the skin; there just is not that kind of pressure in the human hand. Don't count on the masseur's hands, but on your own brain and discipline if you want to get rid of fat.

CHAPTER SIX

Brazil?
With My Hair? Never!

My HAIR WAS ALWAYS A BIG PROBLEM FOR ME. I was born curly and I would have done any "bassesses" to have it straight. I guess that translates best into English as meaning I'd have done anything, *anything,* although in French the word is always a little tongue in cheek.

As a little girl I suffered because of my hair, and the more people would tell me how lucky I was that I wouldn't have to have permanents when I grew up, the more I hated them. The people, and my hair.

As soon as I was old enough to open a drawer and find a scarf I wore it day and night, to the despair of my mother.

Later my life became conditioned by my worst enemy, humidity, and a few little rain drops would make me do all kinds of things, like racing across a busy street during a red light. I had to wait for my eighteenth birthday to be allowed to have my hair straightened and what happened then was a disaster. It all broke off.

That's not the worst I did to my hair. I recall years later in Sardinia one summer when my best friend Marisa Berenson and I used to iron each other's hair. We spent a lot of time at that. We used a hot laundry iron and took turns putting our hair on the ironing board, literally ironing it. That's a recipe for straightening that may be highly successful, but is definitely not recommended.

It took a long time and a lot of experimenting but I've finally learned how to control my hair; although it really is not the simplest way, I manage. Since my hair is very strong and full, when it's really long its own weight pulls it down and keeps it straighter. I keep it clean and healthy and I brush it often. When I take my bath, I wrap my hair around my head to keep the humidity from getting at it. This helps to straighten it, but it also makes it flat. So, after my bath I make a couple of jumbo rolls high on my head with bobby pins and leave them while I'm putting on my makeup. Then I backbrush it vigorously just before I get dressed to give it the height and fullness I like. When I'm at sea or walking in the rain in the country, I just tie it back or push it back high on my head in a roll or a chignon of sorts and I forget about it. Now, since curly hair has come back, I often just let it curl.

I remember the first time I refused to go to Brazil on a holiday. I was sure it was going to be steamy hot and I just wouldn't go. When I finally did go, a few years ago, my hair had grown in and I had learned how to manage it. Brazil was hot and humid and my hair curled, but I was tanned and didn't care too much. I looked fabulous, had a fabulous time, and realized how silly I had been to think that happiness was having straight hair.

I guess my attitude about my hair isn't much different from that of most women. No matter in what part of the country or the world, when you put two women together in a beauty salon, one invariably says, "I wish my hair were curly like yours." To which the second woman replies, "But I've always wanted straight hair, like yours."

That really doesn't matter so much. What does matter is that you have to understand your hair and, like everything else in beauty, accept it and make it work for you. An attractive head of hair is very important to a woman because it is, after all, a frame for your face. But I don't think a woman should be too involved with hair fashion. Keep it healthy and clean and well cut in a style that works well for you. If you fuss too much with it against its nature you probably won't succeed anyway. When the rains come curly hair will surely frizz again and straight hair will go limp. Forcing your hair against its will with permanents or straightenings, gluing it down with heavy wave sets or lacquers encourages breaking and split ends, and no matter what the style, that looks awful. The easier your hair is to manage the happier you'll be with it and the prettier you'll feel.

Whether you wear your hair long or short, the most important part is to have hair that smells clean and feels nice to touch. And it really should be free, and move, and have life about it. Hair is very personal and personally I like a lot of hair. I like to play with my hair, to toss it, to run my fingers through it.

Taking good care of your hair is really very simple, whether you do it yourself or have it done.

What is your hair? To begin with, the hair shafts you see are actually dead, no longer living. The hair on your head is soft and long in contrast to the stiff, bristle-like short hairs of your eyelashes and eyebrows, and the downy, unpigmented hairs on your body—more about them later. The hair follicles just beneath your scalp, maybe one hundred thousand of them, are active, living glands that are constantly growing and pushing out the mass you see as hair. A human being's hair grows steadily, with each individual hair follicle developing its own growth cycle alongside other follicles, replacing the old with the new, but without any uniform pattern. Unlike some animals we humans do not have synchronized waves of hair growth and shedding. Ours just grows and rests, grows and rests for variable periods of time, anywhere from two to six years. Your hair grows about three-eighths of an inch a month and as it grows out many also fall out, maybe ten, twenty or fifty a day. That's normal.

As with every other part of your body, you can't have

healthy, energetic activity in your scalp if you're ignoring proper nutrition. A balanced, nutritious diet is of first importance, a diet with plenty of protein because your hair is about 97 percent protein and it can only draw from your body supply. You should be getting the proper amount of protein from the fresh fish, poultry and meats, milk and cheese which you eat regularly. Soybeans and other legumes are excellent protein boosters. Fresh fruits and vegetables supply necessary iron to your hair while whole-grain breads and cereals help to maintain important Vitamin B requirements. The doctors and dermatologists I consulted seem to disagree about whether fats and oils in your diet can keep your scalp from becoming dry or improve dryness in the same way that they question the ability of the fats to zero in on specific dry skin problems. If you're eating well you're including some fats in your daily diet anyway. (Your hair thrives on water so, once again, the six or eight glasses of water you drink a day are important.)

Now, suppose that instead of losing a normal ten or twenty hairs a day your hair seems to be coming out in clumps. What if you're losing one hundred hairs a day? It may be due to a drastic change in your diet. A crash diet that completely leaves out any of the balanced food values you need would certainly affect your hair growth adversely.

The problem may also develop from a hormone change. I remember being so upset right after my son Alexandre was born because my hair fell out in huge chunks. My doctor reassured me and explained that it was a natural reaction from the hormonal imbalance my body went through during pregnancy and as soon as the imbalance righted itself so would the growth and condition of my hair. Of course, it all passed away in a few weeks. But I did learn that any hormonal imbalance, one created by going off the pill for instance, or one created by the natural body changes during menopause, may also cause temporary problems. After going off the pill the body will readjust itself. As for menopause, some women are treated with hormones to help them maintain a comfortable physical and emotional balance and that also helps to stabilize the condition of healthy hair.

Diuretics, diet pills and tranquilizers also affect your system, sometimes in unsuspected ways. If you're taking medication under a doctor's supervision and you're aware of the possibility of temporary hair problems you needn't be alarmed. Of course, if you notice that your scalp is excessively dry or flaking or itching, see your doctor or dermatologist.

The Care and Treatment of Your Hair

Keep your hair and your scalp clean. It is most important to clean away the accumulated natural oils, the dirt in the atmosphere that clings to your hair and the perspiration that causes matting and stringiness in hot months and hot climates. How often you shampoo depends on the climate you live and work in and how oily or dry your scalp is. Some women have their hair shampooed once a week at the salon. If your hair is oily this should probably be your absolute minimum timing. Too much washing with a harsh shampoo just stimulates the sebaceous glands in your scalp and promotes more oil. I have mine done about every five days. I've one friend who has very short, baby-fine blonde hair and she washes it every day to keep it fluffy and fresh looking. She uses a conditioned shampoo for the wash one day and on alternate days she uses only a conditioner which she massages lightly through the hair and rinses out thoroughly. I'm told that's a really good way to keep light, fine hair from getting murky looking without drying it out.

We used to think that frequent shampoos robbed the hair and scalp of natural oils but today there are so many really gentle shampoos available that I don't think anyone has to worry about that. Do use one of the bland, protein-enriched, herb-based, or one of the newer pH-balanced shampoos. Don't use detergent shampoos—never use detergents. They may

109

strip your hair clean but they also strip it of all the natural oils you spend so much time brushing into the hair to make it shine. And don't use regular soap because it leaves a film and you'd just be replacing dirt with film.

Most good shampoos these days are as carefully balanced as cosmetic products but in order to clean properly they're still somewhat weighted on the alkaline side of the balance sheet. A light acid rinse of cider vinegar brings out red highlights, and fresh lemon or a camomile brew will rinse off all the remaining residue and add glints of sunshine to blonde hair. Use about one-half cup and dilute it in a basin of water. Then rinse with cool fresh water again.

Speaking of water, always use lukewarm, not hot water when you shampoo. You want to open the pores of your scalp in the same way you do when you cleanse your face. Start with lukewarm water, go to warm water, and finally rinse with cool water or the cool vinegar or lemon rinse to close the pores of the scalp again.

Shampooing in the shower is easy and most effective. Rinse out the loose dirt first, then put a dab of conditioner on to do its work while you erase rough areas at your elbows and heels. Rinse or shampoo the conditioner off.

Now comes the drying and this is important. A good brisk towel dry with a thirsty terry towel is great for all but bleached heads. Even if they're maintained in the best of condition you should never be too rough on bleached or very fine, very thin hair. If you have delicate hair, wrap your head in a towel for a few minutes—it will blot up enough excess water.

I think the blow dryer is the greatest boon to hair styling but you have to be aware that heat is the absolute worst enemy of your hair. First make sure that you buy a hand dryer that doesn't overheat. Use it on a moderate setting and keep it a good distance from your hair. If you place the back of your hand next to your hair and adjust the temperature so it's comfortable on your hand, you're safe. Take a few minutes longer to dry rather than risk burning or drying out your hair. Letting your hair dry slowly by itself on warm days is marvelous but don't dry it directly in the sun if you color your hair. That's just destroying the artifice which your hairdresser has worked so hard to create. Sun is much harsher on the chemicals in colored hair than on natural hair. However, since the sun generates many different rays as well as heat it really isn't good for any hair. I've learned to wear a porous scarf loosely wrapped around my head, or a lightweight, airy straw hat when I'm out gardening or just lying in the sun, for part of the time anyway.

Never wrap your scarf too tightly. Don't wear a hat that's made of non-porous, non-breathing fabric or, say, a closed visor or cap when you're playing tennis or golf. The perspiration that results clogs the circulation of the scalp and, incidentally, fades color fast. Always rinse your hair with fresh water when you come out of the sea or a pool. Salt and chlorides are also on your enemies list.

I don't think it's a luxury to have a professional scalp treatment every so often even if your hair appears to be healthy. A professional scalp therapist can massage and condition your scalp and hair with expertise in the same way that a facialist takes the extra time to cleanse and moisturize your complexion to a glowing look. However, if your hair is somehow excessively damaged, if you have split ends or lots of breakage, there isn't too much the trichologist can do except recondition your scalp. I think you ought to cut off as much of that hair as you possibly can.

It's easy to condition your hair at home with simple, effective household products. Use a quarter cup of olive oil, castor oil, or mineral oil and gently work it through the hair shafts. Wrap your head in a series of steaming towels for about twenty minutes. Shampoo well and rinse, rinse, rinse. Both the commercial conditioners and home remedy kind act as fillers for the hair shaft and they do add moisture to the hair to make it thicker. They also leave a film, which is why the shampoo and rinse, rinse, rinse is so important. If you find your hair is too soft and unmanageable after you first condition it use a little water-thinned setting lotion for control. If you want to comb the conditioner through your hair, go easy. Your hair is at its most vulnerable whenever it's wet. It stretches easily and the strain of pulling the comb through stretches it even more. Use a big comb, one with widely spaced teeth, and be very gentle. You should be equally careful after shampooing or rinsing when you come out of the pool or sea. Never brush wet hair.

You can also massage your scalp yourself. An occasional massage and daily brushing are the finishing touches for the look of healthy hair before you get to styling. I remember on that vacation in Antigua, when I first noticed my body going soft, I was also having all sorts of problems with my hair. It was falling out, it had no shine, and it was totally unmanageable. You can just imagine what a wreck I felt like since I care so much about my hair. I did go to see a doctor as soon as I came back from holiday and he explained to me that it was all from tension and stress. I had been exhausted and I knew it. My hair knew it, too. I had some professional scalp treatments then but I knew I had to learn to take better care of myself in all ways. And a funny thing happened. One of the peripheral benefits of my daily body movements program was that my hair began to improve. Circulation is vital to good health in the scalp and the bendovers that I did, with my head hanging, were circulating the flow of blood upward to nourish my scalp. Since I back-brush my hair a lot for fullness, I often do it in the bendover position and accomplish two things at once.

When I massage my scalp at home, I press my finger pads against my forehead and work them in strong circles slowly all along the hairline. Then I just knead, from the hairline all the way back and down to the nape of my neck. That stimulates the circulation but it also brings the oils to the surface of the scalp, so then I do my brushing, maybe twenty or thirty times to work the oils through.

As for brushing, the simple fact is that you should invest in a really good brush. It will last you a long time with minimal care. Natural bristle brushes are great because of their smooth, rounded bristles that don't break the hair but there are also many rubber-based plastic brushes with round-ended bristles that are fine. Just remember to keep your brush clean. Work a little of your shampoo through it each time you wash your hair and after you brush.

I really don't think there are any rules about brushing. Certainly with proper washing these days we don't have to do a hundred strokes a day like our grandmothers did. The theory now is that all that brushing at once promotes too much of an oil flow. The main purpose of brushing is to stimulate scalp circulation and keep the new hair follicles active. Brushing, like massage, also stimulates the scalp's oil glands so, if your scalp is oily, you shouldn't brush too often. Tinted, thin and fine hair has to be treated with extra caution in brushing. The other reasons for brushing are to remove dirt, free tangles, let fresh air reach your scalp, and to work the oils down the shaft to give your hair lustre. Be gentle with your hair. A good way to brush is to place your head way back for half the strokes and then down for the other half. That changes the direction of the blood flow. Brush in all directions. Brush against and away from your part. Brush whenever you can, ten, twenty, thirty brushstrokes at a time, while you're watching the late news on television, whenever, so it doesn't seem a chore.

After you've seen to it that your hair is clean and as healthy and shining and alive looking as it can be, the only remaining important part is that it should make you more attractive.

Hairstyle

Take time, lots of time to evaluate the quality of your hair. Take lots of time to look at your face. When you really know what the texture of your hair is, you're sure to find a style that will suit your face and your lifestyle. Fashions in hairdos do change, but they seldom change drastically. As I believe for everything, I just don't think any woman should be a slave to fashion nor should she let herself be exploited by it. When you know who you are and what your best look is you may wear your hair the same way for twenty or fifty years while blunt cuts and layered looks come and go with waistlines and hemlines.

Even though I sometimes think it's difficult to be living in a world where there are so many choices, where there are no longer hard and fast rules, it's great when it applies to fashion and to beauty. You really don't have to wear bangs, for example, if your forehead is very high. You may choose to highlight that feature of your face and show it off. When you think of beauty as being the visual expression of your individuality, as an expression of who you are, you'll discover the hairstyle that's uniquely yours as well. I don't mean something freakish or exaggerated. Being natural, being yourself is the most important part of beauty.

Your regular hairdresser should really be one of your best friends. It takes a little time for him or her to understand the growth pattern and the texture of your hair, but once he does he can help you to find the most attractive styling. Know what *you* want and then listen to his appraisal of your face and the quality of your hair. Between you you'll find the look that works best for you, and he's going to help you keep the look.

The right cut is fundamental to any hairdo. A good stylist knows how to shape your hair so that it keeps its shape as it grows in. Try for a style that requires only blow drying or a light setting once a week for body and fullness. Certainly soft body permanents are a good investment if they help free you from fuss for months to come. If your hair lacks body and fullness, you can always use some setting lotion, or give yourself time with the rollers, or back-brush. They all help. As for straightening, you know my own experience, so all I can suggest is extreme caution if you really feel you have to do it. Spend the money and see someone who's really expert.

I'd rather see a woman with her hair short and nicely manageable than see her walking around at the market with her head packed in jumbo rollers. And I don't think she ought to be in them when her man is home either. I always wonder what that woman is saving herself for. A woman wouldn't walk out on the street with a white treatment mask on her face, would she? Well, the rollers are almost the same thing. If your hairdo requires all that time in rollers, I'd say forget it. Being attractive for a few hours some evening is hardly worth being that unattractive all day. Being yourself and being natural with a man is wonderful, but being downright unattractive with him is foolish.

These days there are so many professional products available for quick setting and quick touchups, the curling irons, steam curling wands, heated rollers and roller combs as well as the dryers. All this quality equipment is well-designed and carefully tested to be as safe as it is efficient. But, here again, everything depends on you. The electrical appliances for hair come with use and instruction booklets. Read them and follow them to the letter. If in doubt, always use new equipment for a shorter time or at a lower setting than suggested. Because the heat is applied directly to the hair and for a longer period of time, there is a greater potential for damage to hair from electric curlers than from the blow dryer. Be sure to follow the instructions carefully. Using papers with electric curlers is a good safety measure and not much more trouble. If you prepare yourself properly, you can come home from the office and be beautiful in very little time. Set your rollers or your hot iron to heating while you cleanse your face of your day's makeup. Then, unplug your rollers so that they can cool down a bit while you apply a light refreshing mask. While the mask works, set your hair. The bigger the roller the looser the curl, the smaller the roller the tighter the curl, and they'll both give your hair some body. Now, take your bath or watch television or do your household chores. Rinse your mask off, take the rollers out and let your hair cool down naturally while you start your makeup and underdressing. Brush, dress, and you can probably do it all in a half hour's organized time and be ready for dinner in or out, and be beautiful for *him*.

I believe that as makeup makes a woman more attractive, so

can hair coloring. I have my own hair rinsed with henna about every six weeks to bring out all the red highlights. Personally I like henna because it's a natural vegetable dye, which Arab women have used for centuries. It's the semi-permanent variety of color which does fade and wash out and it's a little tricky to handle, so I never do it myself. Bruno, my hairdresser, tells me that it's really healthy for the hair because it coats in that semi-permanent way and helps to prevent split ends. It can't be used too often because the color will build up —here's where your hairdresser or the best colorist around really counts.

I've known women who've colored their hair for years but no one ever knew because they just went a few shades lighter or darker. I suspect that drastic changes, from very dark to blonde for instance, seldom work because of skin coloring. If you were blonde when you were younger and then started fading or darkening, chances are that staying blonde is right for you. But I could never be a blonde like Marilyn Monroe—it's just not my type. Any extreme color such as bright red or platinum blonde is probably wrong for you in general as you get older because it just seems to call attention to your hair color instead of to you. If a woman is genuinely beautiful she can get away with being noticed that way, but most great beauties don't need to.

Even if you're very skillful and plan eventually to do your own coloring, I think you ought to go to a really good colorist at first. Talk about what you think you'd like. Listen carefully to what maintenance will be required. Once you start, this is one of the beauty programs that demands faithful upkeep. Try on a few wigs in different shades. I think nothing drives a haircolorist up the wall quicker than the woman who tells him she wants hair the color of wheat. Once you decide, if the change is dramatic, let your colorist go about it gradually. It's just great to have your husband and your friends tell you that you look marvelous without their really knowing why.

Most important, as you change the color of your hair, make sure that you change your makeup. You'll undoubtedly find an exciting new color spectrum to experiment with, perhaps moving towards vivids and brights or softening down to muted pales in your lipstick and eyeshadows. Have your eyebrows lightened or darkened just a few shades to blend with your new hair color—your hairdresser can do this. The makeup artists at my shop lighten brows with an oil bleach so the brow just looks more natural without any attempt to have an exact match.

Most color authorities say that the chemicals used on the hair in bleaching actually help the scalp to stay healthier. It makes sense that the peroxide in developers which is strong enough to bleach is also working as an antiseptic on the scalp. But those chemicals also take a certain amount of the "starch" out of the dead hair shafts, so a good salon will see to it that your hair is conditioned with each coloring treatment. You should pay extra attention to your at-home conditioning and use a special shampoo created for tinted hair.

These days there are many techniques for adding highlights to overall color. You can choose from shading, streaking, tipping, sun-streaking for blondes. In the hands of a professional these coloring techniques make your hair look so much more natural. But I really hate wildly streaked hair—you know, the kind that's dark at the base and has some grey and then some blonde. I think you should either lighten or darken the whole head. If you've a lot of grey, let it come in and just have the darker areas lightened a bit until your own hair is evened out. (Incidentally, when you start greying you may have to re-evaluate your hairstyle. Greys change the texture of hair—normally it gets coarser—and you may find to your delight that you can suddenly wear a hairstyle that you couldn't manage before the greys arrived.)

I don't think all women with grey hair should cover it. I really don't. Women turn grey at very different ages and *unless it affects you psychologically,* grey and white can be just as interesting as any other hair colors. But I'm not sure which is worse, the unfortunate yellow drab that grey sometimes becomes or the blue that's put in to disguise it. A blue rinse is meant to take out some of the brassiness and help to blend the gold-grey, but it must be subtle, used like a highlighter on the face. If we let our highlighter sit unblended, stark white, on our faces, we'd look terrible, and so do women with blue hair.

If you're clever with your hair and do want to try changing your color at home, however, there are two kinds of products available. A temporary rinse shampoos in, coats the hair shaft superficially, and then it washes away with your next shampoo. Temporary rinses are really effective for "trying on." If you like the change, or if you want to color some grey, the semi-permanent rinse will coat the hair shaft and penetrate somewhat but it will fade away and finally wash out after four or five shampoos. Permanent color cannot be removed without stripping, so don't go into that until you're sure you want it.

On Wigs and Other Helpers

I have a closet corner that's filled with wigs and hairpieces and falls that I once thought I needed. I still think they serve a purpose—they're fun for some exotic masquerade ball when I want to have millions of tiny curls or something like that. And once in a while when I'm traveling and just haven't had time for a proper set I use a hairpiece to fill in and fluff out my own hair from underneath. In other words, I think hairpieces are great for adding on and occasionally for amusement, to change your look a little bit. But I don't think you ought to wear a wig all the time unless you have to. They do make your head perspire and they mat the hair. You can really do a great deal of damage by clogging up the growth of new follicles in the scalp if you wear a wig all the time. And anyway, what's the point in taking off the wig at night and ending up with a matted mess before you go to bed?

There are other ways to save the day when your hair just doesn't look the way you want it to in spite of everything. Learn how to wrap a scarf around your head for a fashion look. I'm not talking about babushkas in the rain but the turban-like ties and knots that are so interesting. Have a special outfit or two with a specially selected hat, a sports outfit with a crocheted cap, a dress that takes a big summer straw. Save those costumes for the I-can't-do-anything-with-my-hair days. You'll disguise your hair problems and also feel psychologically fresh because your whole look is special.

I keep lots of my own scarves in the country so when I tie my hair back I can add a bit of color at the nape of my neck. You can also use a wardrobe of ribbons and barrettes as fashion accessories for your hair. They make you feel a bit "jeweled" and distract from the hairdo that went awry.

No matter where I am or what I'm going to do, I always add one more thing to make my hair attractive: my eau de parfum spray. I especially love the spray because the fragrance is light. I hold it almost at arm's length and spray and spray all around my hair and it just enhances the clean, fresh smell.

CHAPTER SEVEN

The Natural Wrap—
Your Skin

WHEN THEY USED TO TELL ME I had beautiful skin, I never paid very much attention to it . . . I thought to myself that I'd rather have something else beautiful. Then one day, because I was over-worked and over-worried, my skin wasn't as clear as usual. That day I realized how important skin is, or rather, I realized how important skin care is.

I think we all take better care of ourselves when we know what makes us tick, and I've discovered that I take much better care of my skin since I've learned about it. I think if we know what our skin requires to be healthy and radiant and especially what will happen to it if we neglect it, we just pay more attention. Certainly you cannot be beautiful without good skin. Skin is really the outer reflection of beauty, isn't it? Fortunately, good care and treatment not only keep good skin healthy, but they can really correct and contain many problems of the skin—dryness, oily areas, breakout.

It's a little startling at first to realize that your skin is your body's largest organ. Your skin covers your entire body, encasing all of the living tissues and other organs of your body. It serves you as a kind of information station, helping your body to adjust to environmental changes. It's your sensor, receiving all of the physical impressions of the outside world for you—the sensual feelings of warmth and touch for example. It acts as a barrier against dehydration and it can lower the body temperature to make you comfortable through perspiration. It protects your internal body from trauma and from the invasion of bacteria.

Although the skin is a highly complex organ, it consists mainly of an outer layer of epidermis and an underlying dermis, two distinct layers which are totally dependent on each other. The epidermis, or surface of the skin, cannot be glowing and beautiful and elastic and firm if the inner dermis is not properly nourished and if the inner layers are not in excellent working order.

So in order to have good skin, you must first make sure that it's receiving all of the nourishment it needs, with plenty of proteins to help the skin cells to keep renewing themselves. Dry, dead skin cells are continually being sloughed off the skin's surface, and they're continually replaced by fresh, young new cells. I really like to think about that because it always gives us a chance for better skin.

The skin on each part of your face and the skin on different parts of your body vary in thickness and therefore require different kinds of attention. For example, the stratum corneum, that first epidermal layer, is thickest on the palms of your hands and the soles of your feet. It's thinnest around the eyes, on the eyelids. I think most women are aware of that. But perhaps you're not so aware that your skin is also thin and extremely delicate on your cheeks and the forehead, on the abdomen and the elbows. Knowing that, you also know to be careful of too much friction or rubbing or stretching on any of these extra-sensitive areas.

In addition to a proper diet, our skin needs help in three very important ways, and that's where cosmetic science really helps. We must keep our skin clean, we must keep it moisturized, and we must keep it lubricated.

Every minute of every day our skin is being attacked by

outside forces. Pollution in all its forms—dirt, soot, grime— attacks our skin, creeps into the pores, clogs up the skin's breathing apparatus. Even when you're sleeping, unless you're in a highly controlled atmosphere, the air that comes in through the windows is probably polluted.

Those are just some of the unintentional impurities that affect your skin. But there are intentional ones as well. The makeup you use every day, although pure as can be when you apply it, cannot stay on your face forever without becoming an impurity. It must be removed regularly.

Climate robs us of moisture constantly. If the climate is hot and dry we need to be on constant guard. We need to "humidify" our bodies, our breathing, and our complexions. If the climate is cold we suffer from chapping, windburn, and often the same lack of moisture. It's a constant struggle to ward off the pollutants, a constant struggle to fight the environmental damage to our complexions.

No matter what type of skin we have we must cleanse it properly. Certain types require more frequent cleansing, of course. But the most important thing is that cleansing should be effective and simple. I really enjoy washing my face. Very few things give me so much pleasure as feeling really clean. I love splashing the water, and the coolest rinse at the end.

Years ago, when I was growing up, we thought that all we needed to clean our faces was a bar of soap, a face cloth maybe, and water. But today we've learned about the pH factor in the skin and learned to guard and balance it carefully.

Your skin is assessed on a pH scale ranging from an extreme acid condition at point 0 to an extreme condition of alkalinity at point 14. Most skins fall into position at 4.5 to 5.5 on that scale. Maintaining the balance of acid and alkalinity keeps your skin healthy; it helps to prevent bacteria buildup and therefore infection. The problem with the pH factor is that it changes constantly, and unless you're a scientist, a dermatologist, or perhaps an aesthetician (beauty professional) you'd never be able to balance the pH all the time yourself. Fortunately we don't have to worry about it too much because modern cosmetic science has made every effort to balance the products that we use.

Nevertheless, we can and we should prevent breaking down the acid condition of our skin by avoiding soaps and detergents for cleansing. Alkaline soaps and detergents break down the acid mantle, leaving behind an alkaline mantle which bacteria thrive on. When we're very young the balance rights itself in about half an hour. But as we grow older our skin gets tired of righting itself constantly and pretty soon it may even stop trying.

In addition, soaps and detergents leave a film, a residue on the skin. In order to remove the residue, many women resort to strong, alcohol-based astringents which can further damage the skin by excessive drying. Strong lotions can shock the tiny little capillaries on the cheeks, for example, and cause them to fracture.

One more very important thing about soaps and lotions: If you have a serious skin problem, you should consult a dermatologist and follow his advice for your diet and for whatever medicated products he prescribes. Medicated soaps and lotions used arbitrarily may appear to be beneficial because they are drying. In my shop on Madison Avenue and at our cosmetic counters around the country we see so many skins that have been dried out too much by medicated products. We see troubled areas where the condition has only been aggravated and irritated through medicated washings. Acne, for example, is not just a surface breakout—that's all we see, but the infection is much deeper.

Perhaps you think of acne as a strictly adolescent curse. The truth is that acne can occur at any age. The hormonal changes of adolescence are usually responsible for the problem, but any hormonal disturbance or change (pregnancy, for example, or using the Pill) can do it. Most doctors now feel that fried foods and chocolates are less guilty than we once believed them to be in acne cases. But iodine as found in shellfish is probably best avoided if you suffer from acne. If you do suffer from acne, you should be on your way to the doctor. A good dermatologist is the person to tell you how to care for your skin from the inside and the outside, and the only person ever to remove pimples, blackheads or whiteheads from your skin. Also, medicated lotions and soaps will not correct oiliness but serve mainly to help keep the oil ducts clean, the skin free of bacteria. Contrary to what many teenagers and adult women think, too much drying-out on the surface only increases oiliness. The best way to treat troubled skin is to see your doctor first.

The Proper Cleansing of Your Face

1. Remove your eye makeup with a special remover. Late in the day or in the evening chances are you have a buildup of a few coats of mascara. You have to work too hard in the delicate eye area to remove that mascara, the shadings and shadows, even with a good all-round cleanser. Choose a remover that's very efficient and try to use one that has good oils and proteins so you condition your lashes and protect the eye area at the same time.

2. Always wet your face first with lukewarm water to open the pores so they can receive the cleanser.

3. Use a well-balanced cleanser which is formulated to do the deep-penetrating and deep-cleaning job the skin requires, without drying after-effects.

I like my liquid cleanser because it's deep-penetrating and not drying. It has no soap and no detergent. I discovered that water is an excellent cleanser in itself, but it can only clean away water-soluble impurities. You need the combination of a cleanser that cleans the oils and oil-based impurities, plus water. I also think there's less risky tugging and pulling of the skin with a "water wash." But if you prefer a cream, just be sure to tissue it off very gently and rinse well afterwards with fresh water.

4. Always adjust the water from lukewarm to warm, back to lukewarm, then cool. The warmer water opens the pores, the cooler water closes the pores when you're finished. Never use water that's very hot or icy cold. Again, it might shock your skin and create unattractive broken capillaries. If you open and close the pores of your skin too quickly, they too go into shock and can become enlarged.

5. Apply your cleanser using gentle, upward, rotating motions around all the parts of your face. In addition to a light stimulation for the circulation of the skin, the upward motion helps to loosen the impurities from the open pores.

6. Rinse, rinse, rinse. With the water changing now from lukewarm to cool, rinse, splashing the water upwards.

7. Cleanse your face thoroughly at least twice daily, lightly in the morning, thoroughly in the evening before retiring. But as you'll see later on in the makeup chapter, I really cleanse my face thoroughly three times a day because I don't think we should put new makeup on for going out at night without first taking the old off.

And of course, I don't think we should sleep with makeup on. I could never, never. It bothers me that all those "intentional impurities" are still there when I know that the unintentional ones are going to pile up on top while I sleep. I hate the idea of mascara that's going to smudge and look awful in the morning. So, no matter what, I always cleanse thoroughly before I go to sleep.

The Skin Fresheners

After cleansing, many women enjoy a skin lotion or a stimulant. A good lotion should be light, free of alcohol, and soothing enough to use on the most delicate and sensitive of skins. If you don't wear much makeup during the day, you can use my freshener often for a light cleaning and a delightful pick-up. A good tonic or toner should have a very low concentration of alcohol which helps to keep the skin clear of impurities and to maintain the proper pH balance. An effective tonic helps to tighten the pores and to create finer skin texture. Oily skin types benefit greatly from frequent tonic applications. No matter how shiny, no matter how oily your skin is, don't use strong astringents.

The Treatment Products

Always apply your treatment products in gentle, upward, rotating motions. This assures that the treatment will penetrate the pores, and again, stimulates the skin's circulation. The only exception to this rule is in the application of protective Eye Gel. If you're at home and you're not using any makeup, you'll apply your Eye Gel after you've moisturized. Place a dab at the inner corner of the upper eyelid and rotate the gel with your fingertip outward toward the temple and then inward in the under-eye area towards the nose. There's less stretching with a clockwise motion for the right eye, a counter-clockwise motion for the left eye.

MOISTURIZING

Every skin needs moisture. Every skin benefits from water in the diet, from moisture inside and outside the skin. Every skin should be moisturized with a light, effective moisturizer after cleansing. Oil is not moisture. An oily skin can be dehydrated just as a dry skin is. Surface oiliness helps to hold moisture on the surface of the skin, yes, but the amount of that moisture varies a great deal, depending on your diet, on hormonal balance in your system, on pills or diuretics you may be taking. The oily skin has to be moisturized to assure sufficient hydration. I particularly love my Moisturizer because it's so light and absorbs so quickly and thoroughly. It's compounded of special humectants which help to hold the moisture in the skin and also help to attract moisture from the environment to the skin.

Apply moisturizer all over your face, around your ears, on the ear lobes, leaving only the delicate eye area untouched.

Place a few dabs at the base of your throat. That way you'll be certain to carry the moisturizer upwards to the chin and jawbone. Use smooth upward motions at first on the throat, "lifting" with the fingers of your left hand on the left side, the right hand on the right side. Then rotate lightly upwards in half circles until it's all absorbed. On the chin and jawline, tap the moisturizer in with the backs of your fingers to encourage additional circulation.

Don't forget the V of your chest. Even though you may use a body lotion as well, that V area suffers from trauma almost as much as your face, maybe more. Sometimes it's completely exposed to the elements in an open-throated shirt or blouse, sometimes it's all sealed off in a turtleneck sweater.

Moisturizer applied to your mouth gives it a lovely smooth look and feel and it's a marvelous base for your lip color.

FACE SCRUB

I think a cleanser should clean. Period. If the dead cells on your skin are not sloughing off well enough or quickly enough on a dry or normal skin, if you have very oily skin or have many oily areas, help your skin along with a face scrub. Even though my skin is mostly on the dry side, I use my Face Scrub two or three times a week, concentrating a little more on the oily areas. It penetrates deeply but is gentle and non-granular. I really don't approve of granular scrubs for the complexion because if they're used too often or not used properly they can be irritating instead of helpful.

If you use a scrub, any scrub, watch carefully to see how your skin reacts. If you see red or seemingly raw patches, either your scrub is too strong or you're using it too often. Don't forget that the dead surface cells of your skin are there to protect you. If we didn't have them, our skin would be traumatized all the time by weather. You want to help slough off the ones that are ready to come off naturally. That's all. So go easy.

THE FACIAL MASK

One of the nicest things you can do for your face is to give it a light, refreshing mask. A good mask helps to hold the moisture in your skin and "plumps out" all the tiny little fatigue and stress lines. In the chapter on makeup I mention the Refreshant Masque which I often use in the evening because I love the extra glow and radiance it gives my skin when I'm going out. But many women tell me that they like to use a mask first thing in the morning as a morale booster before they start the day. You only have to leave it on about five minutes, and then rinse.

NOURISHING CREAM (THE LUBRICANT)

The morning or midday or evening cleansing routine is always the same. Cleanse, moisturize. But at night, before going to sleep, many skins require an extra step, the added help of a nourishing cream to lubricate the skin while you sleep. I call mine simply Night. You can "wear" it at night because it absorbs completely. It's invisible. I really hate the idea of going to bed in a greasy, heavy cream.

A good night cream provides the rich lubricants that all dry skins thirst for. Use it often, every night if your skin is very dry. If your skin is only somewhat dry, or a combination skin, it will tell you when you need a lubricating cream. Your age will also tell you because the older you get the more you need to replace both moisture and lubrication regularly, faithfully.

Even though most women do prefer a nourishing cream at night, there are no rules about it. Very often when I'm working at home in the morning I pat some on and let it feed my skin all the rich extras while I juggle the telephones.

I think before outlining the four skin types and the individual treatment and cautions it might be a good idea to briefly consider what happens to our skin as we grow older. Maybe we just don't think about it enough. If we did, we'd all probably take better care of our skin when we're young.

As the years accumulate the rate of blood flowing to the skin slows down and therefore less nourishment reaches it. Production of the lubricants, the natural fats and sebum, is slowed down, so the skin dries. Scales form more readily but they slough off more slowly. The "character" lines, the laugh and smile lines around the mouth, deepen and suddenly they're not quite the pleasant personality lines we found so interesting when we were younger. Frown lines in the forehead, squint lines at the eyes if sight troubles develop, also "sit" deeper in the skin. As you'll see shortly in the chapter on the sun, pigmentation may have been heightened by intense ultraviolet radiation and brown spots and so-called "liver spots" become even darker.

As you grow older your skin loses more of its natural moisture, causing skin cells to deflate. The collagen that helps your skin hold its elasticity, like a glue, starts losing strength at the same time. All in all, there's less to hold your skin tautly in place. Gravity begins to pull at the weakening skin, pulling downward, downward, until the skin drapes itself into wrinkles as it falls to the base of your throat. It gangs up on itself in little "sacks" under the chin and jowls, or makes droopy-looking "bags" under the eyes. This aging process in the skin varies a great deal from woman to woman—and there is, of course, no precise moment at which aging begins for everyone.

You may have noticed that fat people often appear to be younger than their chronological age. The skin doesn't seem to age so quickly and, in addition, since the skin is plumped up all over, it really looks younger. While I don't think anyone would recommend an overweight condition, I think there's no question that an older woman looks better with a little extra weight for that reason.

Some people say we start aging the day we are born. Certainly the difference is evident between a baby's skin and the skin of a thirteen-year-old. That's one reason why I feel it's very important that my daughter, Tatiana, clean her skin properly even now, at the tender age of four. As far as I'm concerned it's the same as protecting her teeth with proper brushing. They're both good and important habits that will stay with her for the rest of her life.

Proper, regular cleansing, moisturizing and lubricating can delay the aging of your skin. Somehow I cannot repeat often enough that proper diet is the foundation on which your good health and your good looks are built and continue to grow. And remember that if you avoid getting too much sun, don't smoke to excess, if you avoid excessive alcohol and pills, you can add years to your skin's good looks.

O.K. I'm not really the lecturing type, so let's go on.

The Skin Types

The purpose of all treatment should be to ''normalize'' the skin. Ideally, we'd all like to have just the right amount of oiliness for the right amount of shiny radiance, and an even texture, neither too fine nor too coarse. Ideally, we'd look healthy and glowing without makeup. And when our makeup goes on, we'd like it to smooth on evenly, without ''soaking up'' or fading, without blotching. Knowing your skin type helps you to treat your face properly, to normalize and balance your complexion, perhaps to achieve your ideal.

THE DRY SKIN

Lacking a proper flow of the natural oils to lubricate sufficiently, the dry skin has an extremely fine texture. You may not be able to see the pores. It often appears tight, even drawn. It flakes easily. It is readily victimized by weather, burning and peeling in the sun, burning and chapping in the cold and wind. It is the most sensitive skin to the aging process because when nature starts slowing down the output of the oils, when your body slows down in its ability to hold on to moisture, dry skin shows the wrinkles and crepiness first.

The Normalizing Treatment for Dry Skin

Keep the pores clean, the skin free of dead cells so that the oils can rise freely to the surface. Dry skin is always slower to slough off dead cells and proper cleansing and stimulation will help.

Use plenty of water.

If you enjoy a lotion, use only the mildest freshener, not a tonic, never a strong astringent.

Use plenty of moisturizer to feed the dryness. After you've applied it, add a little extra wherever you feel your skin is most dry. Reapply moisturizer frequently.

Always use a nourishing night cream. Find additional time during the day to apply an enriching cream.

THE OILY SKIN

This could easily become a problem skin because the oil glands are putting forth too much oil, sending it to the surface of your skin and creating shine, often a greasy complexion, and trouble. The excessive oils clog up the pores and permit surface dirt and grime to hold on. The skin texture may be coarse, and enlarged pores are common. Blackheads and whiteheads develop easily in this environment. However, although the oily skin may be the most difficult to live with as a young woman, the condition can be corrected and contained, and the woman with oily skin who's miserable at twenty may be happiest at sixty. The oily skin is the last to show the signs of age, the last to wrinkle.

The Normalizing Treatment for Oily Skin

Cleanse thoroughly and cleanse often. If you're using a well-balanced cleanser there's no danger of drying out. You must keep the skin free of excess oil, free of the environment that bacteria thrive on.

Face Scrub is marvelous for you. Use it three or more times a week. Apply and massage gently with a face cloth to exfoliate dead cells.

Use a tonic with a low alcohol percentage. It, too, will help to keep the oiliness down without burning, without drying too much. Carry it with you and use it frequently during the day.

Don't use strong astringents or medicated products unless they're prescribed. If you use them because you feel they will dry up the oiliness, it's true. They will. And when they do, all the oil glands will work overtime to rush more oil back onto your skin's surface.

If blackheads or whiteheads develop, have them removed professionally. A good facialist, a trained aesthetician, or your dermatologist can do that for you and you won't risk the danger of infection.

THE COMBINATION SKIN

This is a skin that's hard to understand at first. Your cheekbones and forehead may be dry, even a bit flaky. Remember those thin-skinned areas? And yet your nose, the valley between your lower lip and your chin may all be oily, shiny. That's called the T zone in cosmetic language. Obviously your treatment and care need to be directed very specifically to achieve the balanced complexion you want.

The Normalizing Treatment for Combination Skin

Follow the procedures for dry skin and for oily skin for each area of your face separately. It may take you a bit longer but the combination skin can be normalized quite easily and it's well worth the additional effort.

Use a tonic more frequently in the T zone.

Use Face Scrub once or twice a week for the entire face. Then use the scrub an additional time for the T zone.

Baby the dry areas with extra moisturizer and nourishing cream at night.

THE NORMAL SKIN

This is a rarity, a truly beautiful skin created by a balanced oil flow to an evenly textured surface. It appears transparent, glowing with good health and healthy color. It is silky, velvety, soft to the touch.

The Treatment for Normal Skin
Treasure it!

Don't ever ignore your skin just because you know it's healthy and beautiful.

Keep it clean and keep it moisturized, always. As you get older the benefits of the constant moisturizing will grow along with your skin.

As you get older, add the nourishing cream more often to replace the richness your skin begins to lose.

CHAPTER EIGHT

On Care of the Body— the Nails, the Hands, the Feet

I JUST LOVE TO BATHE. I start my day with a tepid bath and a cool shower—it wakes me up. Then I end my working day with a really hot, steamy bath, again followed by a cool shower, because I relax and all my tensions are eased before I start my evening. But of course, the most important thing is cleanliness.

Our bodies are so wonderful. We have our own "air-conditioning system" which allows our pores to open up and release moisture during hot weather, in overheated rooms, when we're tense and under stress. The pores open and let the moisture (perspiration) out, and our body temperature is lowered as it evaporates on our skin. In the winter, our "heating system" works just as effectively to decrease perspiration and thus decrease the amount of body heat lost to evaporation.

Contrary to what we may think, perspiration as it leaves the body is primarily moisture, and usually in itself sweet, not pungent or unpleasant. But bacteria attracted to the damp environment of the skin quickly cause unpleasant perspiration odors. So we need to shower or bathe to remove the bac-

134

teria, to open and cleanse the pores and permit the natural, healthy flow of perspiration to continue.

If you feel strongly about permitting your body to perspire freely and naturally, you may use a deodorant under the arms, which simply helps to attack the odor-causing bacteria and keeps you smelling fresh. But many women prefer an anti-perspirant, which checks the flow of perspiration and also deodorizes.

Just as in washing your face, starting in a tepid, warm tub or shower opens the pores, and letting a little cooler water run afterwards closes them again. In between, the soap and a good scrubbing do away with the bacteria and all the impurities of the air that cling to your body.

When I take my bath in the morning I consider it a treatment for my body. I'm absolutely extravagant about a bath and I always have been. I love all the oils and emollients and salts and bubbles. Before we had so many different forms of fragrance I could put practically a bottle of perfume in the tub. Even though I know I'm there to get clean, I love all the luxurious, really sensual and pleasurable fragrances. So I start with the fragrance and let myself relax and enjoy it all for a few minutes. Then I "go to work."

I use a loofah, a slightly rough, fibrous sponge or bath mitt that produces a light friction on my skin. It stimulates the circulation of the skin, erases flakiness, and helps to slough off the dry, dead skin cells. If your skin is very sensitive try just rubbing briskly with a terry washcloth. At least once a week I use my Body Scrub, which really cleans deeply. It has little granules that work on those dead skin cells, and it also has special emollients that soothe and smooth my skin. After the bath I take a cool shower to rinse myself off. And I always take my morning bath without any makeup on so my complexion breathes too. That's my wake-up bath and a relaxing one, because even if I'm scrubbing away, I try to enjoy that time I have all to myself.

In the evening I take a hot, hot bath that works almost like a home sauna. I take all my makeup off and "steam" myself.

Some women like to put a good nourishing cream on just after they get into a steaming tub—the pores are open so the cream penetrates very quickly and is absorbed fully.

At night I do a few leg, ankle and foot movements in the water, rotating and stretching. That's also when I use the pumice stone to work over the rough spots on the soles of my feet, at the heels. It just amazes me how keeping after those lightly calloused areas, and moisturizing afterwards, keeps my feet in such good condition.

Moisturizing afterwards is the key to it all. I just massage myself all over with body lotion, from my chin to my toes, as soon as I come out of the tub. I always moisturize when my body is still a bit wet because it seems to penetrate and seal better. I also spray myself all over with Tatiana when I'm still wet because the fragrance lasts much longer that way. For women with dry skin and those tight, tight pores, it's particularly effective if you apply your body lotion and your fragrance when the pores are a little bit open and the skin is damp.

A do-it-yourself massage is wonderful in the tub when you have the time. Use the palms of your hands in pressing, circular motions all along your legs and arms. Use the tips of your fingers across your abdomen, the midriff area. Take the flesh of your arms, your legs, your buttocks between your fingers and knead gently in a press-and-release, press-and-release motion. You won't lose inches this way, but you will help to tone and firm your body, improve your circulation, and unknot tired muscles.

Body Hair

Historically, different societies have had differing points of view about body hair. Although people in all parts of the world still feel that the natural body hair is sensual, American women usually do not feel clean with body hair. We prefer smooth legs, arms, and underarms. The body is covered with a soft, light "down" that is usually hardly noticeable and we're not concerned with that. When that "down" is dark or heavy, however, it can be removed in a number of ways, as can unwanted hair in the underarm area, on the arms, the legs, and the face.

Bleaching, though temporary, is a gentle and effective way to disguise soft but dark downy hair on the face, the arms and the legs.

Shaving is probably the most common way to remove underarm and leg hair, although it is very temporary. If you shave you do have to keep after it all the time to avoid unattractive stubble.

Many women prefer the commercial depilatory creams which leave the skin surface smoother; this method of removal lasts longer than shaving. Always be sure to test a depilatory on all parts of your body. One may be just right for your legs, but too strong for your face.

Waxing, or epilation, is the longest-lasting method for temporary hair removal. Waxing leaves a beautifully smooth surface and it can last for weeks, up to a month or more for some women. The only problem I've ever found with waxing is that you do have to have a few days' growth before you can have it done.

Then there is electrolysis—"permanent" hair removal. I've known some women who've invested very substantial amounts of money to remove the hair on legs, back, arms, face. You do have a small percentage of regrowth eventually with electrolysis and you may have to return a few years later for another short series. As I mention in the chapter on cosmetic surgery, an electrologist should always test a small patch on your face first to see how you react before you go ahead with a complete clean-up. If your skin is sensitive, you may react with retractions, tiny fine-line scars that are sure to be more hateful than the hairs.

I think waxing should be done by a professional and so should electrolysis—you might do yourself permanent damage.

Nails, Hands, and Feet

Someone once said that a woman's hands tell everything about her. In many ways that's true. After all, no matter how covered up we are, our hands are almost always exposed. And we use them, consciously and unconsciously, all the time, for expressing our thoughts and our emotions.

Whether you have a weekly professional manicure or do your own at home, your hands should be soft and well moisturized all the time, and your nails well shaped with neat cuticles.

THE MANICURE

You need a softening hand lotion or oil, an emery board, an orange stick, a good, sharp pair of cuticle nippers or scissors, cotton, polish remover and a base coat, top coat and colored lacquer if you use nail lacquer. Personally I prefer my nails clean and trimmed and buffed to a natural shine. If you do, too, you need a good chamois-covered buffer and a colorless powder or cream for the lustre.

1. Remove the old polish carefully and completely with the orange stick tipped with cotton. Wash your hands to be sure all the remover is washed away—it can be drying.

2. I think it's a good idea to use your emery board to shape the nails before you soften the cuticles, especially if the nails are not too strong. Don't file the nails too close down into the corners and don't file them to a sharp point.

3. Soften your cuticles in warm, sudsy water or warmed lotion or oil. Make a *bain marie* by placing a small container with the hand lotion or oil into a larger bowl of hot water. That way the lotion will warm through and work more quickly and effectively to soften your cuticles.

4. Push the cuticles back gently with an orange stick or a wet professional manicurist's pumice stone. These stones are gentle and they help to smooth off rough spots on the cuticles and nail. Don't push the cuticles too hard and don't use a metal instrument, or you may find yourself with unexplained ridges in your nails in a few months.

5. Use your cuticle nippers or scissors for cleaning off the rough edges that remain, and for nipping away hangnails. Don't cut the cuticle. Once you start, the cuticle begins to toughen and the more you cut the more you'll have to continue the cutting.

6. Rinse your hands thoroughly, dry thoroughly, and then apply another coat of the warm lotion, working it all around the nails and the fingertips, all over the hand and up over the wrist. This is a good time to add extra lotion to your forearm and to those always-dry and thin-skinned elbows.

7. When your lotion is fully absorbed polish with a base coat, two coats of color, and a top coat. There is a school that believes the nails are better protected against chipping and nicking and breakage with the polish overlay. If you prefer, you can just add a dot of lustre cream or powder to each nail and buff, buff, buff.

If your nails are very brittle and break easily, or if they're weak and just won't grow, I think you should invest in a series of professional taping "treatments." If you go for a series, a month or six weeks of tapings, your nails have a chance to strengthen. The taping "supports" your nails and prevents splitting and breakage; they then have the opportunity to develop their own strength. I've seen marvelous results with this kind of professional manicure. I've even seen women who bit their fingernails helped to really healthy and lovely nails and hands.

When it comes to your nails and hands, here's one time when water is not good for you. In fact, the worst thing for your hands and nails is prolonged immersion in water. The thin skin on the back of your hands dries out and your nails are softened, weakened by water. Try to wear rubber gloves when you're washing dishes or clothes. It's a small nuisance to remember them, but one more good habit that will help your hands stay younger looking. And here's something I just discovered for myself: If you use a mask treatment on the back of your hands occasionally it softens and plumps them up the same way it does your face.

If you're a gardener, try to wear cotton gloves. I know that's hard when you're working with young plants or seedlings, but try. Fungus infections are quite common to gardeners' nails. If or when you can't wear gloves, rub your fingernails along a softened bar of soap. The soap under your nails will help to keep dirt out and keep you from having to dig too much when you clean your nails later. When you've finished gardening, a good, stiff, short-bristled brush and the soap get together and really do a cleaning job. And I still think the old-fashioned idea of hand lotion under your cotton gloves when you're gardening or polishing silver or copper works wonderfully. You keep your hands protected and also seal in all the emollients and moisture.

THE PEDICURE

1. Clip your toenails straight across, never into the corners. Don't round the toenails because they can become ingrown.

2. Use an emery board to get rid of the rough edges of the toenails. Work in one direction only and then sand down on the tips of the nails lightly.

3. Now soak in a foot bath of sudsy water for about ten minutes. Pumice the calloused or rough areas on the soles of your feet, the heels, the toes.

4. Dry your feet with a terry towel and rub briskly to help brush off some of the dead, dry skin.

5. Use a warm cream or oil in the cuticle area and push back gently with an orange stick or your professional manicurist's pumice stone.

6. Apply a coat of colorless polish or, if you prefer, use the same color you use on your hands.

These days we wear sandals so much of the time that our feet should be pretty. Unfortunately our feet, ankles and legs are covered up a great deal of the time. Nylon stockings and skirts allow our limbs to breathe, but opaque, heavy-denier panty hose, pants, and boots especially, close off all the air. We need to give our legs as much breathing time as we can.

Try to walk around bare-legged and barefoot whenever you can. Exercise your feet and legs whenever possible. Walk on your tiptoes across a room and then walk back on your heels. That helps to strengthen the arches, leg muscles and ankles. Change the height of the heels you wear. By switching from a high heel to a flat thonged sandal, sneakers or loafers you keep the arches of your feet and the calf muscles limber.

CHAPTER NINE

How to Wear Your Face Better, or the Secret Between Your Mirror and You . . . Makeup

IMPORTANT! Makeup should have one function only—to make you look better, to make you more attractive. Forget the "fashionable" makeup, think only of your face; do what will make it prettier, and only that. Don't hide behind your makeup. Make it work for you. It has guidelines to help you bring out your best features and play down the others the same way other aspects of fashion have. But unlike dressing, there are a few very specific rules, "musts" for makeup one should know.

Makeup also has a common-sense order about it, so you can learn to do much of it by habit. Practice makes you skillful. You may be a bit clumsy when you first start, but if you do it carefully, after a while you'll be able to do almost as well as a qualified makeup artist.

Makeup is a luxury, so it should be fun. You should have fun experimenting with your makeup, trying different eye shadow and lipstick colors. Sometimes you may want to be a little more dramatic for a special evening—and that should be fun! Making up is like telling yourself a secret.

Of course, the first thing, the most important thing, is to start with a clean face. There's nothing worse than starting the day with last night's mascara crumbling around your eyes. So of course, you've cleansed your face properly the night before, no matter how late. You cleanse it again and moisturize in the morning and you're ready to think about making up for the day.

I think it's important to leave your face without makeup for a while after waking up. Your face is still a little puffy, perhaps, so clean and moisturize and then let it go for a while and do something else if you can. I do my body movements, my telephone calls. Let your skin breathe a while before applying your makeup, even if it means waking up a bit earlier.

One of the girls who works for me on Seventh Avenue has a long bus commute into town in the morning. She says she knows all the men on the bus and she just can't come in without any makeup. Well, if you have to be in an office early and you want to look nice for the people around you, fine, but at least let your face rest while you have your breakfast.

Start your day with a light makeup, very light. Don't get all "done up." If you're going out to lunch or have an important appointment later on, you can add on and that will make you feel freshened.

When I come home from the office I take my makeup off as soon as I can. I almost always have appointments, interviews, someone in the living room, someone in my little office, and the children of course. I take my makeup off, do all the things I have to do, then I sit at the dinner table with the children. I know I've planned half an hour to get dressed and made up. Whether it's a very involved evening or something more casual, that's the time I give myself because I need it. Not more, not less.

Then I start. My makeup has been off for a while, and I take a bath—very, very hot so that the whole face is steamed clean. Afterwards I put so much cream on my body that you can't believe . . . but I happen to have a great result: the softest skin, so "they" say. When I have extra time I give myself a mask because the pores are already open from the bath and my Refreshant Masque closes the pores and holds the moisture in. It just plumps my skin up a little bit and makes me feel fabulous.

I spray myself a lot, a lot, a lot with my favorite fragrance, Tatiana. All over. I put on a little caftan or one of the long wraps that I use at home, rinse off the mask, and I sit in the sink. I do. I've broken more sinks . . . I sit in the sink, on top of a big square sink in my bathroom with my feet in the basin so I'm very close to the mirror with the good light, and I'm very comfortable. I also manage to put my two phones in the sink so that nothing, but nothing, could get me out of there.

Then starts the ceremony (because that's really what it is) . . . the makeup. I usually have my hair rolled up and wrapped around my head to keep it straighter, but it's a good idea to tie a scarf around your head if your hair is down. That way all you see is shape and bones. And then you look twice as nice when you let your hair free and psychologically you feel much prettier.

I really have fun making up. I have a good face for making up, good bones. I do the shapings, then the eyes. Then I put on mascara and I do something else. Then I put on mascara again and do something else. Then I put on more mascara and my whole face is completely made up. I put on my stockings, my dress, more Tatiana, and poof, I'm ready.

When you start making up, what you should do is look at you. Look at yourself and see what is the best thing about you, about your face. Your eyes are the best? Then emphasize the eyes. Your mouth is too small? Don't go against it by trying to make it bigger with lipstick. That's a terrible look. Leave your mouth small, nicely defined, but work on something else.

It's very often true that some women look better without makeup, but that's only during the day. Even then most women need something light for the eyes, and gloss or a touch of color for the lips. If you're lucky enough to be one of those women, you still have to wear makeup at night. In the evening you don't see the quality of the skin the same way. Even if your skin is perfect, even if it's glowing and beautiful, electric lights defeat you. They deaden the complexion, make it look drab. They rob you of color. And then, think of all the other women who are made up. In the evening you just can't play the natural kid bit, that fresh-scrubbed look.

Of course, I've said it now about everything—I've said that what makes you attractive is being yourself, being natural, being unaware. Even though makeup is important, you should do it all, and then forget about it.

You don't want to look like anyone else, any more than you want to be like anyone else. You want to look like you. Imitation may be the sincerest form of flattery—but it's flattering to someone else. Not to you.

Then, too, you don't want to exaggerate any feature noticeably. I think only truly beautiful women can exaggerate and they don't usually have to. It's just like someone noticing the color of a dress instead of that the color is great on you. No one should notice how your eyes are done or the color of your eyeshadow. They should just notice you and notice that you're beautiful, that you have beautiful eyes.

I think I should repeat here that if you have a very bad feature or a bad skin problem, then you may want to have a correction made. I discuss all of the possibilities in the chapter on cosmetic surgery and dermatology. But if it's just that something bothers you because it isn't your best feature, then do your makeup, learn to do the best you can, and forget about it. Constantly denigrating yourself, constantly wishing you looked some other way is demoralizing. It goes against everything you want to do to be happy with yourself, to accept yourself as a woman.

THE ORDER FOR MAKING UP

THE EYES—Protection and Treatment
      Lightening the Shadows
THE FACE—Foundation
      Shaping Colors for the Face
THE EYES—Contouring and Color
THE MOUTH—Contouring and Color
SET AND SEAL

How to Have a Better Makeup

1. Use light, sheer products. If you start sheer and light, then you can add more foundation for more cover if you need it. You can intensify cheek or shadow color when you want to.

2. Use brushes whenever possible. They give you more control of fine lines and you can always brush out color to soften and smudge hard edges. Use a sponge applicator with an eye-shadow powder, because it holds the powder, will not drop the grains on your eyes, and prevents flaking. Use the tip of your finger for smooth blending of larger areas of the face.

3. Always apply your makeup in clear, bright light and then always check it in other light. Take a hand mirror to the window to check your daytime makeup, so you're not overdone. Turn the lights down in your bedroom in the evening and check again for the night lights you'll be in.

4. Work with a magnifying mirror when you need to. There's nothing worse than clumps of mascara clinging to your lashes or brow lines that have gone awry. Then check

again in a regular mirror because that really is how others will see you.

5. Makeup is an illusion. The most important thing you have to learn is the principle of light and dark, shine and matte. Whenever you apply a light color or a shiny texture you bring the area forward. When you apply a dark color or a matte finish the area recedes, moves back. So you highlight your good features with light colors and with products that glisten and shine. You play down your less attractive features or areas that you don't want to be too noticeable by using darker colors and matte finishing. And then, as you'll see shortly, you contour and shape the entire face by skillfully blending the darks and the lights, the shine and the matte. I'll discuss that at some length for contouring the face and for shaping the eyes.

6. Always, always apply foundation and cheek color with a downward motion. Makeup is the exact opposite of your cleansing routine. When you clean your face you want to get into the pores. When you apply makeup you want a smooth finish. Makeup should stay on the surface of your skin, permitting the moisturizer and protectors to do their work underneath.

7. Leave yourself time to make corrections. That's why you powder or seal absolutely last.

EYE GEL—PROTECTION FOR THE EYES

The very first area to consider when you start your makeup is the eye area. In the same way that you moisturized your face for protection, you need always to protect the delicate under-eye tissues. It took cosmetic science a long time to realize that heavy creams could not be absorbed by the extremely thin tissue under the eyes.

There are approximately nine layers of facial skin, but the

layers of skin under your eyes are so fine that they are more like the equivalent of three layers of skin. You might consider the undereye skin as tissue paper or onion skin compared to cardboard. That undereye skin is so fine that heavy products don't penetrate, don't absorb, and a specialized product is required for protection. I use Eye Gel, applying a small amount directly at the *inside* corner of the *upper* lid and rotating it outward toward the corner of my eye and the temple, and then inward to the bridge of the nose, always using a gentle circular or oval motion. This reverse application causes less stretching of the undereye tissue. Of course you can apply your eye product to the undereye area only, but in this instance, my Eye Gel affords protection for the upper lid while also acting as a smooth base for the eye makeup to follow.

COVER FOR THE EYES

Before applying a foundation, examine your eye area for shadows, darkness, or puffiness. You know that extreme puffiness cannot be eliminated with makeup. Very dark shadows should be compensated for with a different makeup, darker coloring later on when you're shaping the eye. But if you have light shadows you can lighten them a little with a covering product. Don't just dab it on. You can start shaping and contouring right now. Don't use your finger to apply because the base of your fingertip is too wide for the control you want. Instead, using a soft brush, apply light lines of cover only where you need it, keeping in mind that the lighter, beige color will bring the undereye or the entire eye forward.

Unless your eyes are perfectly shaped, you want to lift the look. Applying a cover all around the eye in a circle is not what you're after. You'll end up with round, owl eyes. Instead, take your brush and make a downward stroke with the cover from the inner eye at the bridge of the nose, down and out, over the cheekbone. Now, skip past the very center of your eye and apply your second brush line of cover from the outer edge of the eye above the cheekbone and toward the temple. In effect you've created a V. Now blend and soften with your finger.

Contrary to what you may think, if your eyes are slightly puffy, or popping, you can use a light cover in spite of the fact that you may have thought it would accent the problem. Nicholas Guercio, our talented makeup artist at the Madison Avenue shop, explained to me that puffy or slightly bulging eyes most often have deep lines in the undereye area. By using cover in the line creases *only,* the entire lower area is equalized and you can then go on to shape, line and mascara that eye like any other.

Foundation

Now the foundation. I think the illusion of makeup can do many things. It can make a woman prettier in all ways, but primarily, because makeup should be used to *neutralize* and *heighten the color* of good skin, it helps to make a face look more alive. I guess I can't stress enough that tired skin due to improper care, lack of sleep, or poor diet cannot be covered over. Your own skin will show through almost everything worth applying, but how much nicer to have it glow through.

Foundation should be used to neutralize and balance the color tones of the complexion. You can't just decide that you'd like to have a delicately pale face and plaster it all over with an ivory foundation. You really borrow the artist's and the makeup artist's knowledge and skill by using color to neutralize. If your skin is sallow or olive you should use a pink foundation. The more olive your complexion, the deeper tone of pink you'll use. The truly light and pale skin of course can take an ivory tone, but if your skin is pale with ruddiness or high color, neutralize those particular areas with a peach foundation. Beige is the most neutral of colors, and a tan foundation will neutralize a dark-complexioned face, or a suntanned one.

Try it. Apply a small area on one side of your face and then back off from your mirror and study it. If, for example, your skin is a little bit sallow like mine, and you've tested the pink-based foundation but your skin doesn't look pink, just better, you've succeeded. If you see an obvious patch of color, try a foundation a little lighter or a little darker in the same family until you find the one that's closest to your skin and the least visible.

Learn to apply your foundation in downward strokes. Probably the most common complaint we hear when new customers come to our cosmetic counters is from women who don't understand why their makeup "fades." We explain that makeup fades far faster when it's applied upward. Many women treat their foundation as if it were a nourishing cream. They rub it in. Of course your makeup will fade, and it will also tend to blotch unevenly if it's applied in upward fashion. It's going to be lost in the pores, absorbed by them much more quickly. You should lay the foundation lightly on the outside of your skin in downward strokes.

Once you understand the concept of neutralizing your complexion, instead of coloring it, you'll realize that you do not have to apply foundation all over your face. On the contrary, you should apply it only to the specific areas that require neutralizing. You add different forms of color to the other areas. If you're going to highlight your eyes, lift and brighten your cheekbones, contour your cheek area, then leave them free of foundation. The less makeup you have on, no matter how sheer, the more your own skin texture can shine through, the more your pores can breathe. Apply foundation to the upper cheekbone and out toward the temple, in the chin area, about a quarter of an inch above the chin line, and in the center forehead. Don't apply foundation to your throat. First of all, the color will be different. The texture of the skin on your face and neck is different, and makeup on your blouse or rimming the edge of a turtleneck sweater will just make you feel soiled.

I prefer a light, liquid foundation and today we have a wonderful one, with marvelous covering qualities for all but the most damaged skin. If you have badly discolored areas, broken capillaries, enlarged pores, you might prefer a cream-based foundation. But I think if you do have those problems you should still not use too heavy a base; you should try to think in terms of distracting the onlooker from your problem areas by highlighting your attractive features. Plastering your face all over with a heavy oil-based foundation will just make it noticeably shiny, and powdering it down in hopes of concealing flaws will create an unnatural texture and work to the contrary. In addition, you're piling all that heavy makeup on, closing off your pores and further damaging your skin instead of letting it breathe and absorb the moisture it needs.

Instead of all that, use a light to medium liquid or cream foundation on damaged skin, and then follow the technique for powdering which I discuss later on in the section on setting and sealing. Lightly powder the areas of shine where enlarged pores and discolorations occur. The matte effect of the powder will recess your troubled areas and you can now go on to highlighting your good features.

For daytime, I usually prefer the most natural look I can achieve. Unless it is the middle of winter and I look especially pale, I use no foundation, just cheek color, eye makeup and lipstick. Cheek color is very important.

Once when I was asked to speak at a fashion show in Houston we opened the floor to questions and a woman drew a big laugh from the audience by asking me where she should apply rouge. She said she'd heard rouge should be used at the top of the cheekbones, but she wasn't sure where that was. Well, she was O.K. Many women have problems figuring out where to apply rouge and it is very important to the shaping of the face because it's both color and shine. The simplest way to determine where to start is to take your thumbs and press them under the bone of your cheek and gently lift. You apply your rouge on that cheekbone line.

Another frequently asked question is, how close or how far from the nose and the eye area should cheek color be applied?

If rouge is placed too close to the nose it draws attention to the nose. If it's too close to the eye area, too high, it makes the eye area appear smaller. Color always looks more natural on the outside of the face so that it frames the face. Place your finger straight up from your cheek to your eye and line it up with the outside of the iris, actually about a quarter of the way in from the outer edge of the eye. Start your color there. Pat the color on with your finger in a shape that will move from the outside of the iris, along the bone into the temple. Blend. By applying this way you "lift" the cheekbone and the eye area. Or try creating a sideways V with your cheek color. After blending out toward the temple bring the color inwards toward the center of your forehead above the brow line. We call this an "instant facelift" in the salon because it frames the eye so beautifully and naturally.

The cheek color you use doesn't really matter very much, just don't use anything too obvious. Primarily you're creating a reflection, highlighting. However, remember that you've neutralized your complexion, so if you want to you can use a brighter color if you're tanned, or want more brightness for the evening.

The next step is to really contour that cheekbone, complete the "lift." You may have noticed professional models and actresses who appear to have high, high cheekbones and beautiful, sculptured hollows below. A touch of a darker matte shading stroked below the rouge line creates that illusion. Draw a line of brown cream shadow on with a wet brush just under the rouge, under the cheekbone, and then blend and lift quickly outward while it's still nice and moist. If you prefer a powder for contouring—a blusher—use a brush and shake it out. There it all is again, the contrast of bright and dark, shine and matte.

The Eyes

The most important part of making up your eye is the shaping. Not color, not lid shadow color, but the shaping that highlights and dramatizes your eyes. You'll need shadow, cream or powder to start the contouring, highlighter, a lid shadow for color, and mascara.

When you start shaping the eye you should use a dark color. A brown is always good and it's the most neutral for daytime, so I'll illustrate the contouring with brown in mind. But depending on the time of day, your own coloring, perhaps a dress you want to complement, an evening mood you want to establish, you might choose any of a number of colors. Use a deep plum or amethyst color, a dark green, dark blues, or the greys: charcoal, pewter, a silvery-smoke tone.

Using a damp brush, apply the brown cream shadow along the top of the eye crease line, blending lightly upward and into the brow bone. Now, place a dot of highlighter at the inner corner of the eye, just above the tear duct. Place three more little dots of highlighter starting at the center of the eye and going up to the brow bone. Blend from the inner eye, across the top of the upper lid, and into the brow bone, until all of the color is gone and only shine remains. You can use a white highlighter as long as the whiteness disappears, though I really like my new Apricot Highlighter. It's even more subtle in blending and it adds a tiny bit of color for a sallow or olive skin. If you don't want shine, if you only want to lighten, then use cover instead of highlighter.

Here's a professional way to contour the eye if you like an extremely subtle look. It takes just a bit of practice and skill in the beginning but it prevents any possibility at all that you'll end up with a series of parallel lines. Start the eye shaping with a dampened fingertip and cover the whole eyelid with brown cream shadow. You can use the finger now because you're covering a larger area. Then, add your highlighter over that with the same little dots blended out of their color and into shine. Later on you can add a lighter brown lid shadow if you want to.

Always blend the cream shadow out to the end of the brow and think about whatever correction you may want to make for the brow line. The shadow should end where your brow line will end when it's penciled or brushed later. You can use a shadow powder for the upper lid, but if the lid has lost some of its elasticity it will appear crepier with powder. Also, most women who have oily skin think they *have* to use a powder shadow. But it will cake and also change color more readily as the oiliness gets into it, so the oily-complexioned woman is really better off with a cream that she can re-smudge a bit and keep soft when a correction is called for.

Now, the last thing you do is add the lid shadow color, in case you change your dress or change your mind. Don't use a shadow on the lower eyelid unless you've shaped the eye with makeup. Once again you're just calling attention to color, to the lid, and perhaps to an unattractively shaped eye. It's much better to stay all natural and even. It's better than one spot of color, one spot of texture that will only call attention in a bad way.

Don't use white or a bright color on your lids. No matter how pretty the color is, people are going to notice an eye shadow color, instead of noticing your eyes. People should see your eyes first, not your eyelids. I guess that sounds kind of funny, but I think more women make that mistake in making up than any other.

I've outlined the eye shadowing in the simplest terms, using one or two complementary color examples. But you might use three shades of color. Certain colors are best formulated as creams while others are richer, more effective as powder. In the evening you may prefer a frosted shadow. Of course you can use creams and powders and frosts together. Just stay in the same color family. Blend carefully. Be aware of the textures, the matte and shine effects you've created.

The main purpose of all your eye makeup is to create the illusion of beautiful eyes, alert, ''open'' eyes. A light dot of eye shadow, strategically placed, can help. Use a shadow at least three shades lighter than your lid shadow. The frosts are wonderful for this; a topaz, a white, a pink frost can be used anytime, even during the day, because you're just using a flake, a hint of the color. Place the dot on the upper lid in the center of the total eye. Place another dot in the tear duct area. And don't smudge. It's just a highlight.

Here are some complementary colors you might try.

Amethyst shadow ...... a dot of topaz (yellow complements)
Blue shadow .... apricot (orange complements)
Green shadow .... pink complements

If you're going to powder later on to set your makeup, you can interrupt now and powder your eyes very lightly with a soft brush. That way you prevent powder from trickling down on your liner and your freshly mascara-ed lashes.

Now, a soft, dark brown or black liner, smudged, and lots and lots of mascara. I prefer a pencil for lining the eye because I find it much easier to handle and because it smudges to soften the line, particularly for the day, when I don't want anything too obvious. You can use cake liners but remember that they dry to a matte finish and you have to be very adept at handling them because they can't be lightened or smudged afterwards.

When you use your liner, don't stretch the skin out to the side. If the skin is at all crepey, you'll have a crepey, bumpy line when you release the eye. And, if you stretch the skin, you'll end up with the line about a sixteenth of an inch above the rim. Instead, always apply your liner in two steps. Start from the outer corner of the eye and work to the center. Then pencil from the inside corner of the eye to join at the center. Obviously, that's for someone who lines the entire upper lid, and in a moment I'll get into different techniques for different eye shapes, but you'll still use your pencil the same way. Outer corner to center, inner corner to center. If you slant the pencil slightly you'll have less "pull."

Look at your liner head on in the mirror when you've finished. You don't walk around with your eyes closed and you want to create the illusion of an alert, open eye for someone looking at your normally.

Mascara is vital, so use it well and use a lot of it! When you apply your mascara to the top lashes, don't lift your head too much. Don't try to open your eyes up wide. You'll just end up mascara-ed all over. Instead, look straight into your mirror and lift your head slightly. That will lower the lid enough for you to get under the top lashes. Hold your brush horizontally and apply, and then reapply as often as you like, always drawing the brush from the beginning of the lashes right out to the edges. When you mascara your lower lashes and the corners, hold your brush vertically, at an angle, and just use the tip. Always favor the outside edges of your eyes when you're applying mascara.

I always use black mascara, as many coats as I have time for, and I think most brunettes favor black. But here's another trick that's great for blondes. Use black for the first coat and then do the building, the lengthening with brown. Another good way for blondes to get the intensity of color without too many coats, too much buildup, is to use a base coat of brown mascara and then just tip the lashes with black. Both techniques give you a subtle and very effective eye. Incidentally, a dark blue mascara has a delightfully soft quality during the daytime and is wonderful in the evening because it really looks black with night lights.

The Eyebrows

Most of the time, if your eyebrows are clean and nicely shaped, you don't have to do more than just brush them a bit. I think too much shaping, too thin a line is unnatural and ugly. Having your brows symmetrical, perfectly matched, is unnatural. Waxing under the brow gives you a nice clean surface for makeup and avoids the broken, stubbly hairs that tweezing often causes in the brow bone area. But eyebrows should be tweezed lightly wherever necessary.

Remember that old rule about never, never touching the hairs at the top of the eyebrow? Forget it. That goes all the way back to the twenties and thirties when the ideal brow was arched as high as it could be—arched high and highly artificial. Pluck out a few hairs wherever they're scraggly or too irregular.

Too much penciling also looks artificial. If you need to fill in your brows, or to darken them, try this. Instead of applying a pencil directly on the brow, rub your pencil across a stiff brow brush and then brush your brows that way. It's even more effective than a brush and powder, more natural.

Whatever you do, whether you wax the brow area yourself or have it done professionally, don't use wax for shaping. Fashions in eyebrows do change, perhaps almost more than any other part of a "look," and waxing will discourage the growth of your brow hairs, perhaps permanently. Use wax as an underbrow cleanup and always tweeze for the shaping or arching you need.

Before leaving the brows, I think it's important to repeat what I said earlier about lightening. If you're coloring your hair and you're blonde with dark eyebrows, just tweezing them thinner won't help, nor should you want them matched to your hair color. That might be too pale to give you any definition, and your brows should frame your eyes. Have your brows lightened professionally, just a shade or two, enough to make them look natural and compatible with your new hair color.

Now let's consider the shape of your eyes and how best to enhance them. I just keep saying over and over again that you should go with what you have. If your eyes aren't your best feature, then make them up carefully, watching the illusion tips that help to create subtle changes, and feature something else, your mouth maybe.

OVERLEAF

After you've filled out a questionnaire, here is an example of the treatment and makeup charts we create for you at our salon on Madison Avenue and at our counters at stores all over the country. It is an individual appraisal of your skin with recommended treatment and your own personal makeup.

This is my personal daytime makeup chart, using a light eye cover, cheek color, and the shaping of THE ALMOND EYE *with shadow and lots and lots of mascara.*

157

For   Diane _____

1. MOISTURE--- Night

2. FOUNDATION--- Beige/use only where needed

3. COVER--- With Brush

4. SHADING---Earthy Brown Cream Shadow

5. CHEEKCOLOR---Deep Earth

6. BASE EYE COLOR---Earthy Brown Cream Shadow

7. HIGHLIGHTER--Apricot

8. EYESHADOW---Brown Bisque

9. Pencil--- Black and Blue Pencil

10. MASCARA--- Black Top and Bottom

11. POWDER---

12. LIP COLOR---Russet Pencil
      Clear Mocha Lipstick and
      Japanese Red Gloss on top

Makeup by_____

To help you find the right colors for your own makeup I have designed three charts for all skin and hair types, including black skins. Lip and cheek colors are the most important "right choices" to make since they affect your overall makeup look the most. Eye colors offer more freedom since contrast is often needed for good effect. Enjoy experimenting with different looks.

160

Sunny Blondes and Redheads

	SPORT/ COUNTRY LOOK	DAYTIME CITY LOOK	EVENING	SUNTANNED
MOISTURE	Always	Always	Always	More than ever
FOUNDATION	None (or a little of your exact skin tone)	Ivory or Peach	Ivory or Peach	No—Beige if needed
COVER	No	If needed	Yes	No
SHADING	No	Lightly with shading powder	Yes	No
CHEEKCOLOR	Soft Mocha or Deep Earth	Soft Mocha, Deep Earth, Vermilion	Vermilion and Coral Powder*	Bronze
BASE EYE COLOR	Earthy Brown cream shadow	Earthy Brown or Khaki	Earthy Brown or Deep Amethyst	Earthy Brown or Burnt Sienna
HIGHLIGHTER	No	Apricot	Apricot and Gold	Gold or Apricot
EYESHADOW	A hint of Neutral Brown, Heather, Brownstone, Brown Bisque or Sandy Pink	Brown Bisque, Olive Frost, Mint Jade, Brownstone	The Browns and Topaz, Amethyst, Lapis Lazuli	Brown Bisque, Topaz for evening
PENCIL	Brown	Brown	Brown and Blue or color complimenting the makeup	Brown, Blue
MASCARA	Brown	Brown	Brown/Black Mixed Blue/Black Mixed	Brown
POWDER	No (only in excessively oily areas)	Lightly	Yes	No
LIP COLOR	Clear Mocha, Sienna Red, Nude Rose lipgloss	Russet pencil liner Lipstick: Mango, Nut Brown, Sepia, Russet, Persimmon, Coral Mocha, Japanese Red, Nut Orange Lipgloss: Warm Orange, Japanese Red, Clear Mocha, Sienna Red	Same and Clear Red and Red Berry lipstick and lipgloss	Russet Pencil liner, Sienna Red or Warm Orange lipgloss

* Cheekcolor: For evening we suggest cream cheekcolor (similar to your daytime color), strengthen by adding a touch of vivid powder.

161

162

Brunettes, fair skin, and Ash Blondes

	SPORT/ COUNTRY LOOK	DAYTIME CITY LOOK	EVENING
MOISTURE	Always	Always	Always
FOUNDATION	Ivory or Peach (but very little and only where needed)	Ivory, Peach or Pink	Ivory, Peach or Pink
COVER	No	Yes, if needed	Yes
SHADING	No	Lightly with shading powder	Shading Powder
CHEEKCOLOR	Deep Earth	Rose or Deep Earth	Rose and Raspberry Red‡ Red Clay and Raspberry Red‡
BASE EYE COLOR	Pewter cream shadow	Pewter or Deep Amethyst cream shadow	Amethyst cream shadow
HIGHLIGHTER	No	Apricot	Apricot or White
EYESHADOW	Silver Smoke or a hint of Heather	Silver Smoke, Star Sapphire, Amethyst*, Heather, Sandy Pink	Charcoal, Silver Smoke, Rose Quartz, Amethyst, Topaz, Aubergine
PENCIL	A bit of Brown	Black and Blue†	Black, Blue or color to match the shadow tone
MASCARA	Black or Brown	Black and Blue†	Black or Blue
POWDER	No (only in excessively oily areas)	Yes, but always brushed lightly onto the face	Yes
LIP COLOR	Rose Mocha or Nude Rose lipgloss	Russet pencil liner Lipstick: Fuchsia, Red Berry, Rose Mocha, Fawn, Plum Mocha, Nutmeg Rose, Glazed Rose, Claret Lipgloss: Rose Mocha, Cranberry Glaze, Boysenberry, Red Berry, Rosewood	All the colors listed for Daytime City Look plus Oriental Rose

There is no Suntanned category. Ash blondes become sunny blondes when tanned, brunettes with fair skin become brunettes with warm skin.

* Amethyst: Not used all over lids but only around the lashes at the corner of the eyes as an accent.

† Black and Blue: Blue is best for ash blondes as it livens the often quiet coloring of the face. It should be used carefully by brunettes.

‡ See footnote on cheekcolor, page 161.

| | *Brunettes with warm skin** | **Black Women** | | |
	EVENING	SPORT/ COUNTRY LOOK	DAYTIME CITY LOOK	EVENING
MOISTURE	Always	Always	Always	Always
FOUNDATION	Beige	No	Beige, Tan or Suntan	Beige, Tan or Suntan
COVER	Yes	No	Yes	Yes
SHADING	Shading powder	No	Earthy Brown cream shadow	Earthy Brown cream shadow
CHEEKCOLOR	Vermilion and Coral †	Red Clay or Deep Earth if skin is light	Red Clay or Vermilion	Red Clay and Raspberry Red, Vermilion and Coral†
BASE EYE COLOR	Earthy Brown	Burnt Sienna or Burgundy	Burgundy	Burgundy
HIGHLIGHTER	Apricot	No	Apricot	Apricot or Gold
EYESHADOW	Charcoal, Aquamarine, Topaz, Amethyst, Aubergine	Charcoal, Brown Bisque	Sienna Rose, Aubergine, Charcoal	Charcoal, Rose Quartz, Lapis Lazuli, Amethyst, Topaz
PENCIL	Blue or strong colors	Black	Black, Plum, Olive, or Amethyst (at the base of top and bottom lashes)	Black and all tones of Gold, Amethyst, Deep Turquoise
MASCARA	Black	Black	Black	Black
POWDER	Lightly brushed onto the face before powder cheekcolor is added	No (only in excessively oily areas)	Yes, where needed	Yes, but always light
LIP COLOR	Russet pencil liner Lipstick: Japanese Red, Red Berry, Clear Red, Bright Orange, Sepia Lipgloss: Sienna Red, Japanese Red, Red Berry	Russet pencil liner Sienna Red or Boysenberry lipgloss	Russet pencil liner Lipstick: Russet, Claret, Japanese Red Lipgloss: Japanese Red, Boysenberry, Sienna Red	Same and Red Berry lipstick and gloss

* For Daytime—See Diane's personal chart on page 159. It is ideal. For Sport/Country Look—Keep same, eliminating highlighter and shadow cover. Use foundation only if you must hide imperfections. Replace black and blue pencil with brown when suntanned. Still using Diane's chart, add coral cheekcolor and topaz eye shadow for evening.

† See footnote on cheekcolor, page 161.

The Shape of the Eyes

ALMOND EYES: I guess the almond eye is considered everybody's favorite and certainly it's an easy eye to make up. My eyes are basically almond shaped over high cheekbones, so I like them to appear to be all shape, with nothing obvious jumping out. After the basic contouring, I use a light brown shadow on the lid instead of another color. Incidentally, I often add a dot of Cheekcolor at the top of my brow and blend it into the highlighter. It just gives my cheekbones more lift.

I first outline the top lid from the inside corner toward the center of my eye, about half an inch, *underneath* the lashes. Then I line from the outer corner on the upper lid toward the center *on the outside of the lashes.* I leave the upper lid free of pencil from the center to the inside corner on top. I like a blue pencil inside the lashes on the lower lid all the way. Then I finish off with lots and lots of black mascara.

The basic almond shape, if it's well proportioned in the face, allows for quite a bit of imagination and experimentation and you can have fun trying different effects. Just remember that the longest, thickest, silkiest lashes are the best friends your eyes can have.

ROUND EYES: Draw a full line, from outer edge to center, from inner edge to center on the top lid, stopping right at the edge. For the lower part, apply your pencil on top of the lashes to create more fullness. You need less mascara on the lower lashes that way. Even though all eyes are improved with lots of mascara at the outer corners, the round eye is especially attractive when it's treated to fullness at the outer edges.

SLANTED EYES: Highlight your shape by lining just the outside corner lines, from the outer edges to the center of the eye, top and bottom. Leave the inside eye free of pencil. Apply your mascara only where you pencil.

SMALL EYES: Pencil-line the eye with a light brown or perhaps a taupe color. Line either the top or the bottom depending on the shape of the eye, but do not line the entire eye—that just makes it look smaller. Light eye shadow colors do more for you. Don't go too dark in the lid shadow, nor too bright.

LARGE EYES: This eye needs careful shaping because very often the large eye has too much eye white showing. A dark pencil liner is your most important shaping aid. Line the inside bottom lid with a dark brown or a black pencil, leaving the top lid free of liner. That minimizes the look of too much eye white. If your eyes are great, well shaped and large, and you prefer to frame them entirely, use the lower liner on the inside, and then lightly line on top of the upper eyelid, again with the dark brown or black pencil. It really works.

NARROW EYES: Apply your contour shading above the crease of the eye and blend quite high, but not into the brow line.

CLOSE-SET EYES: You cannot change the shape of your face, so you do your contouring and face makeup carefully, and then add a bit of cover or highlighter on the inside edges of your nose. Carefully evaluate your eyebrows. If they are too close, remove a few brow hairs near the nose so that your brows are spaced further apart. Complete your liner and mascara according to the shape of your eye.

WIDE-SET EYES: You want to recess the distance, so use a dark brown shadowing at the edges of the nose near the eyes, and pencil the brows in a bit closer to the bridge of your nose if necessary. Complete your liner and mascara according to the shape of your eye.

DEEP-SET EYES: Here's another time when many women make that most common of mistakes by trying to lighten too much. Deep-set eyes often have dark shadows in the recesses and a brown eye shadow, outlined with a darker brown or black pencil, creates a more subtle effect. By contrasting the brown shadow with the darker pencil line, the shadow appears

167

lighter without "jumping out" as a pale shadow color—a blue, an aqua—would.

The Nose

LARGE AND WIDE NOSE: Use dark shading on either side of the nostrils. Use a brush with a creamy dark brown shadow. Since ours is applied wet, it gives you complete control. Don't use powder under any circumstances because the texture will be obvious and you don't want to call attention to your correction. Add a light streak of highlighter in the center of your nose and blend, blend, blend.

LARGE AND NARROW NOSE: Lighten the sides of the nostrils and the outer edges of the nose with cover. Darken the center and blend smoothly.

HOOKED NOSE: Highlight underneath the tip of the nose and use a tiny bit of shading at the tip of the nose. If there's a bump, brush a bit of dark shading on that area to help recess it.

UPTURNED NOSE: Shadow the tip.

Other Problem Areas

THE JAWLINE: TOO WIDE, TOO BROAD. This is most often the square face. Start just above the area you intend to shade and apply parallel angled /// lines blending downward. When you start high in this fashion you won't end up with shading on your neck.

ROUND FACE: This is often referred to as a "moon face." Use parallel, vertical ||| lines from under the cheekbone, blending down to the edge of the jawbone.

DOUBLE CHIN: Do not attempt to disguise this by applying makeup in the chin area itself. Never try to shadow underneath. Instead, highlight on top. Highlight the front of the chin or use a bit of rouge on top of the chin.

RECEDING CHIN: A spot of highlight on the tip of the chin will bring it forward. Otherwise, the less done, the better.

SUNKEN, HOLLOWED AREAS: For the older woman who has this problem, a light color under the cheekbones will help to fill the face in.

The Mouth

The mouth should always be most desirable. It should be shiny, it should be colored, but never inaccessible. I always use a soft pencil to outline my entire mouth. I think every woman should use one, preferably a neutral brown color that blends with the lipstick. You don't want the lip line to show at all. I also think every woman should learn to use a lipstick brush, except for public touchups later on. You can't really create a clean, beautiful mouth with your finger or even with the lipstick itself.

A lip gloss is a marvelous finishing touch whatever color you use, and a first coat of gloss with the lipstick blended in is heavensent for dry lips. If you have excessively dry lips, you might just use gloss to the intensity you like and reapply whenever you need it. If, however, your mouth has "rivers," those little lines that run vertically upward or downward from the lips, stay away from color gloss or any lipstick that's too thin or too greasy. That color will run very quickly. Use a little moisturizer on the lips and around the outside and then always use a pencil to carefully outline and set the shape of your mouth.

THIN LIPS: Use bright, light colors to make them richer looking.

FULL LIPS: Control the fullness a little with a pencil and favor the darker, more muted color tones.

UNEVEN LIPS: Here again, of course, no one has perfectly matched lips. But if the bottom lip is much fuller, the top lip thin or smaller, mute the lower lip with a deeper color and use a few shades lighter for the upper lip. Be certain that the two shades are in the same family of color. If you line the lower lip it will help to make it look smaller. Leave the upper lip unlined.

SHORT LIPS: Line the bow of the mouth leaving the edges unlined. Bring a light lipstick color out to the edges.

LONG LIPS: You can either just line the corners of the mouth, or line the entire mouth, depending on the shape of your lips. Use a muted or even a dark color lipstick.

DROOPY MOUTH: This is a common problem for the older woman. The lips are usually narrow, particularly the lower lip. Using the dark brown lip-lining pencil, line only the corners of the lower lip, lifting the outer edges. Then blend with lipstick. The top lip is equally important. Just concentrate on the center, the bow of the mouth. Line the bow only, do not outline the entire upper lip. You can't lift there anyway and lining it will defeat the illusion.

The Finishing—Setting and Sealing

Now, depending on the time of day and what kind of a makeup you've applied, you may want to set it, to seal it so that it will last even longer. There are two ways to set makeup, depending on the quality of your skin, on how oily it is, and, sometimes, the time of day.

You can set your makeup with powder. You can use loose or pressed powder; I think the loose powder is best for setting because it has less grain. It's the grain of the powder that adds that unwanted extra dimension of texture to your skin. Older women should always be especially careful of powdering because the texture of powder adds years to your face.

Always use a brush to apply your loose powder. Dip the brush in the powder, and then shake it off, shake it down so the grains sift through. Dust the parts of your face you want to with the brush. You probably will dust the nose area, the chin crevices, the forehead, because that's where oil rises most commonly. By powdering only through the center of your face you leave your cheek color, highlighted brow bones, the shine areas contrasted to create shape. Of course, if your complexion is very oily, use a light dusting all over. Later on, when you use the pressed powder for a touchup, shake the powder puff out in the same way.

The important thing to remember is that all you're doing is setting your makeup. Years ago women used foundation as a color and then they put a "colored" powder over. But today we use translucent powder which has no color, so the makeup cannot change.

Sometimes, however, you just prefer a more glowing look. Try this. Wring out a cotton pad with water and dab it gently all over. Better yet, use a freshener on a cotton pad. It will make you feel fresh and will help to control oily areas without dehydrating them. Women with very dry skin, who shouldn't use powder for setting, might try this.

If you want a glowing look, use water or freshener to set and seal. If you want a matte look, use powder. Think about what you're wearing in the evening, though. If you're wearing a sequined or satin gown, a very shiny dress, you have to be careful not to look like circus lights, so matte your face with a light powder dusting. The opposite also applies. If you're wearing a "matte" dress, a jersey perhaps, add a bit of frosting, glitter, shine to your makeup. Learn to add or replace in your makeup whatever is being reflected or absorbed by what you're wearing.

I definitely think makeup is important, and even more important is knowing how to use it. Make yourself a present— consult a makeup artist and learn what you can do to "wear your own face better."

On Fragrance

I think the most fun I had in creating my cosmetics was in developing a new fragrance. Unless you've ever been involved in the selection of a perfume yourself, you cannot believe how many new perfumes I sampled before I made my decision. I knew exactly what I wanted but it wasn't easy to get the idea across to the chemists in words. I didn't want anything too heavy, too obvious. I didn't want a perfume that smelled like "mother's handkerchief." I didn't want one that was reminiscent of any other fragrance, even favorites. Nor, for that matter, did I want something reminiscent of another time, another era. I wanted a contemporary perfume, and I didn't want it to cost $100 a bottle because I think every woman should wear fragrance and I think it should be affordable. Smelling good should not be an extravagance.

I kept looking for the words that would express what I hoped we could formulate. Alive. Pretty. Up. Open. Fresh. Floral, without being cloying or too sweet. A little bit sexy, a little bit sensuous. How do you combine green gardenia and jasmine to match the words?

I just kept repeating that I wanted something that smelled good. That's what I think a fragrance should be—something that smells good. Something that makes you feel good.

And then . . . I'll never forget how it finally happened. I love to tell how we finally got it, after about six hundred—honest, six hundred—attempts. One day the chemists came into town with the next group of samples to submit. It was the day I was showing my fall collection at the Pierre. Bob Loeb, who then directed my cosmetic and fragrance business, had an idea. He invited the chemists to come and see the show. They came and they saw the girls move down the runway, often on the arm of an attractive male model. They saw how the girls moved, what the clothes were like. The ballroom at the hotel was jammed with press and TV people and enthusiastic buyers from all over. The chemists caught the spirit and the next time they came in, we had it. I named it simply Tatiana, for my daughter.

I don't think there's any mystery about perfume. Most women know about pulse points that are warm and help "float" a fragrance. But I do think the choice of a fragrance is highly personal, very individual. Just use one you like. Use it freely. Dab it, spray it, splash it. All over. Use it for yourself, because it makes you feel good, because you enjoy it.

Perfume doesn't make you sexy. The sexiness, the mystery, the glamor is in you. But more than anything else, perfume reminds you that you're a woman.

CHAPTER TEN

I Love the Sun! But . . .

SUN IS DRYING AND AGING. Sun makes your skin leathery. Sun causes wrinkles, scaliness, skin cancers and broken capillaries. Period. Right.

But I really love the sun. I love how healthy I look when my skin is tanned. I love my body bronzed all over. I love the warm, relaxed, sensuous feeling I get all over me when I lie in the sun.

I think you have to pay careful attention to all the dangers and the don'ts and then you should just go ahead and enjoy yourself in the sun. After all, the sun can really give you the most natural and healthy way to be beautiful.

You know, it's not "the sun" that's so bad for your skin but rather a tiny percentage of the rays. Less than one percent of the sun's rays, the ultraviolet rays, do all the damage. And the only barrier between you and ultraviolet radiation is the natural pigmentation in your skin. That natural protection is a layer of melanin that rests at the bottom of the outer epidermal layers. Every woman tans or burns differently depending on the thickness of the melanin layer in her skin.

The more fair the skin, the less melanin there is, and the

darker the skin, the thicker the pigmentation protection. Therefore, the most susceptible woman is usually the Caucasian, usually of Anglo-Saxon or Scandinavian descent. She has little or no inherent pigment in her skin. She also has little capacity to form more pigment after exposure to ultraviolet light, although she may freckle. If this is your general type you have to be exceptionally careful. If you're fair-complexioned and the blue-eyed descendant of blue-eyed parents, you are probably terribly susceptible.

The middle group is loosely considered by dermatologists to be darker-skinned "Mediterranean" types, and the third and least susceptible category is black women, who have the thickest, heaviest layer of protective melanin in their skin. Although some lighter-skinned Negroes may burn as readily as Caucasians, that thick layer of melanin in dark-skinned blacks protects and plumps the skin so effectively that an older black woman may appear to be far younger than she actually is.

Obviously there are variations within each group depending on your ancestral mix, but the guidelines are helpful. I also think it's important to mention that in addition to the unpleasantness and damaging effects of ultraviolet burning, each of the skin types or groups is susceptible in the same degree to skin cancer and broken capillaries as to sunburn.

Sunburn does not eventually tone down and turn into a tan. It may blister, it will peel or flake quickly, taking natural oils and moisture away with the sloughed-off cells. It will leave a reddened, sensitive, unprotected top layer of skin, which has to heal itself. When the new skin cells form they are so exposed that they have to toughen and thicken in order to protect you. The drying, aging, leathering process begins right then. I've met some women who've told me that they purposely burn because they think there are advantages to a "light peeling." Personally I think the light peeling or exfoliation of the skin is better left to the skilled hands of a competent facialist or your dermatologist.

Teenagers in particular often think that the drying out of a light burn will help acne. It may. But it may also encourage the spread of the infection. You'd better get an O.K. from your doctor instead of diagnosing and treating yourself.

There are women who tan easily and well. After building up their tan they feel safe to play tennis at high noon, unprotected by a sunscreen. The tanned woman, the dark-skinned, the olive- and oily-complexioned woman may still be courting dryness and skin cancer, or may suddenly find that she has a web of broken capillaries under the tan when it fades.

Excessive heat and sharp cold contrasts also cause broken capillaries, as you remember from the chapter on skin care. A really hot day and a quick plunge in an icy sea can do the same thing. Cool down a bit before you dive in.

The Do's

1. DO start your tanning in small doses, whenever and wherever you start. A few days of five- or ten-minute exposures will build up pigmentation slowly. Expose all sides of your body evenly in those first periods so you're free to stay in your bikini or tennis shorts for longer periods of time later on. Clock yourself. Don't cheat even a few minutes.

2. DO pay attention to the hour of day you're in the sun. The peak hours, between 10 A.M. and 2 P.M., are the greatest risk hours with high noon (solar time) the most treacherous. I usually play tennis early in the morning, before ten in the East. It's cooler and more comfortable then anyway. If you want to garden or just lie in the sun and read after three, you can still get good color and be safe without an intense sun beating down on you.

3. DO start your tanning as early in the season as you can. If you live in a climate where there's always sunshine, make sure you get a little often enough to maintain that pigmentation buildup.

4. DO find a product that will help to protect you. Many women who tan easily like to encourage their color with tanning lotion. But don't make the mistake of thinking that it is protecting you because it's oily, greasy, or buttery. Most tanning agents filter out only the tiniest fraction of the burning rays—their main job is to attract the sun to you.

A cosmetic product cannot create natural pigmentation; it can only encourage the buildup. Today there are many sunscreen products available which do exactly that. They screen out most of the ultraviolet rays and they're wonderful to use after you've taken your normal quota of direct sun. If you tan nicely, you should still wear a sunscreen when you golf, swim, sail, whatever. The almost total sunblock is an invaluable friend to the fair-complexioned woman who previously just had to stay out of the sun entirely.

Freckles and dark spots may appear all over your body, not just on your face. They're the visible signs of a genetic, unusual melanin activity in the inner layers of skin and cannot be removed easily—as you'll note later on in the chapter on cosmetic surgery and dermatological peelings. If you don't want them, avoid the sun entirely and always wear a sunblock when you're out. Incidentally, zinc oxide is a very effective sunblock.

Speaking of cosmetic surgery, dermabrasion and chemical peeling, I think it's important to state now, even though it's repeated in the next chapter, that you must follow your doctor's orders on sun exposure. The risk of incurring sun spots on newly exposed skin is at the highest. Your doctor will tell you for how many weeks or months you have to avoid any contact with the sun and he'll recommend an effective sunblock for your normal activities.

5. DO be particularly aware when you're exposing your entire body to the sun. It's not just your face which can be damaged or burned. Wrinkled, dry skin is far more common than we realize on the legs and arms. The throat and the back

of your neck are particularly vulnerable. The dermatologists' manuals are filled with cases of "farmer's skin" and "sailor's skin," instances where the back of the neck and the arms suffer severe symptoms due to prolonged exposure to sun and wind. Your chest dries out very quickly and your ankles are often unexpected candidates for overexposure.

If you're a true sensualist like I am for nude sunbathing you must be aware that your body is used to being covered most of the time and therefore has the least amount of pigmentation. You should GO SLOW when you first expose your breasts, your buttocks, your abdomen, in a bikini or in nothing. Use the lotions all over you.

Protect your mouth with moisturizer, a lip gloss, or plenty of unscented lipstick. Protect the delicate tissues around your eyes with a sunblock, always.

6. DO reapply your tanning lotion, your screen or your block often. Perspiration and absorption win out over your protector's effectiveness fairly quickly. Always reapply when you come out of the water.

7. DO cover yourself well after you've had enough direct sun. A long-sleeved caftan, *not* a filmy one, and an airy straw hat look great at the pool anyway. Watch out for your ankles if you're a fair, barefoot girl.

8. DO keep a mental note of any medication you may be taking. It can affect you differently in the sun. The doctors' offices were deluged with confused patients when "the pill" was first introduced. Strange liver-like spots appeared on women's faces. High blood pressure pills, diuretics and tranquilizers cause changes inside your body which may react adversely on your skin.

9. DO moisturize your face and your body constantly. An effective moisturizer, a body lotion helps to keep your skin

supple and glowing. "Moisturize" yourself inside as well. When you're outdoors, engaged in active sports, or just taking time for relaxing, you're going to perspire and lose water from your system. You can step up your usual intake of six to eight glasses of water a day considerably. Drink an occasional glass of grape, grapefruit or orange juice; a little natural sugar will keep your energy high.

10. DO keep yourself clean. All of the screens, blocks, even moisturizing lotions clog your pores. Even though perspiration may release some of the attracted dirt, sand, whatever, those pores need cleansing. Bathe more often. Cleanse yourself thoroughly and then reapply your moisturizer after you've cooled your skin down with a freshener or tonic. If you're staying inside, away from summer bugs and insects, then there's nothing that makes you feel fresher and more beautiful than an allover spray of eau de parfum, or lots of splash cologne.

The Don'ts

1. DON'T use perfume, cologne or a scented sun product in the sun. Painful burns and rashes are caused by photosensitive allergy to essential oils. Just a dab of perfume behind the ears or at the wrists can do it. Even the totally natural ingredients in some products cause photosensitivity, so you'll have to try and err until you find the right products for you.

You may find you're suddenly getting allergic reactions in the sun in spite of your careful screening of lotions and avoidance of fragrance. You might have a contact photosensitive reaction to the antiseptics in the detergent or soap you use washing dishes, to the oranges you squeeze for breakfast, the shampoo you rinse with when you come out of the water. If you're a gardener you can have an allergic reaction to a number of vegetables you grow, to the herbs you enjoy—dill and parsley for example. Wear gloves in the kitchen and in the garden. This type of allergy is extremely difficult to pin down, so if you don't locate it, consult your doctor or stay out of the sun entirely.

2. DON'T use a reflector, ever. You tend to hold a reflector so close to your face that you increase the risk of burn and peeling a thousandfold, no matter how brief the time or what the season.

3. DON'T think that you're safe if you're swimming. Ultraviolet rays penetrate water and attack your body even under the waves. Water is a powerful reflector, so your arms and head above water are under double attack. Count your swimming time in with your sunning quota. Dry sand and even grass are reflectors. You're safest under a shade tree or an umbrella on the grass, true, but if you're highly sensitive you may find that the reflected rays have zeroed in.

Incidentally, somehow I keep referring to summer sun or vacation sun. But I like to ski occasionally when I have time and I've learned that like water, snow is a dangerous reflector of radiation. The rays are always strongest in the summer when the earth is closest to the sun, at the equator, and on mountaintops. All the warnings apply to winter sports when the sun is high.

Don't ignore any of your precautions on a foggy day because ultraviolets can cut right through an overcast or hazy sky.

4. DON'T toy with home remedy cures or drug store creams and powders if you do get a bad burn. You might have an allergic reaction, which will only compound your problem. If you notice a rash or skin blemishes and eruptions see your dermatologist. Take a bath in lukewarm water. Apply calamine lotion or a bit of mineral oil to ease the discomforts of a

slight burn. A little baking soda in your bath will help to cool you down, draw the heat out.

5. DON'T fool yourself. If you're eighteen now and you're spending eight hours a day sunning improperly, it will show eventually. Suddenly one day, maybe not so many years from now, you'll see the wrinkles and the toughened scaly outer skin that the burning and drying built up and you will not be able to reverse it. You could moisturize and treat that ruined skin from the day it appears until forever and it will not, cannot be changed.

I've learned a nice makeup trick that works particularly well when I'm behind on my tanning, or when I arrive at a resort for a vacation and everyone looks great already. I make a little mix of my Cheekcolor with moisturizer. Then I slip a touch high on my cheekbones and down the front of my nose. Sometimes I paint a little around my shoulders and on the bones where I normally get extra high color. It gives me a real glow and that flushed look of a day in the sun.

CHAPTER ELEVEN

Should I or Shouldn't I?

(FACTS ABOUT COSMETIC SURGERY AND DERMATOLOGY)

D O YOU THINK MY NOSE IS TOO BIG?" "Do you think I need a face lift?" "Can they do something to my legs?" These are the kind of questions women ask me all the time. I guess we've all thought about changing or improving something. Some of us did it, some of us should do it, some of us will never do it.

But today cosmetic surgery, or reconstructive plastic surgery, is really quite common and popular in America. Chemosurgery, dealing with skin treatment through chemical peeling, and dermabrasion have advanced many new techniques for cosmetic corrections. I think it's great that there is so much help available and I think it's important that we talk about it openly and exchange information.

At one time, before my children were born, I considered my figure a problem of "less" rather than "more." I wanted to have fuller breasts and I was very serious about it. I don't know why. I guess I thought then that it would make me sexier, more of a woman. There are a number of different ways to augment the breasts and I spent a lot of time talking to different doctors. While I was there, as usual, I asked all the questions about the other things that could be done for me in the future. Well, I didn't have my bustline augmented. But I did learn a great deal.

As you know by now, what I think is really important, and I keep repeating it to myself, is to be the woman you are and to accept yourself—so basically, I should be opposed to the idea of cosmetic surgery. It's true that I've known many women who have dramatized a seemingly unattractive feature and made it an asset to their reputation for beauty. There's quite a famous model whose nose is really too long. But she makes up her eyes to perfection and carries her head as if she were a classic Nefertiti. Another fashion model has a mole on her face and instead of having it removed, she made it work for her. It became her "beauty mark," an immediate identification of her face in fashion photographs.

You can probably think of many television or film stars with less than perfect features who are considered beautiful. Of course, actresses are usually very skilled in the art of makeup. But they also project such confidence and assurance that their look becomes desirable, often even imitated. After all, there really is no such thing as perfect beauty. Throughout history our "ideal" of woman's beauty has undergone many radical changes.

An older woman I know has been talking for years about having her face lifted and getting rid of "all these tired, old wrinkles." But her husband is completely opposed. He insists that she's lovely as she is. She's really lucky. She knows who she is and feels secure because he really cares for her. I think she just talks about it when she's with other women—I really think she likes to tell us that he likes her as she is after thirty years of marriage.

But it also seems that somehow all men have a tendency to be opposed to plastic surgery, so the best way sometimes, if you really want to do it, is not to tell them.

You really can be unhappy with a large nose, or feel miserable because you neglected your skin and look older than you are. No matter how hard you try to adjust, no matter how honestly you try to accept yourself as you are, a not-so-still, small voice inside of you keeps nagging at your insecurity. If making the change will make you feel more attractive and more secure with yourself, then it doesn't matter what anyone else does or thinks. Do it for you.

When you're contemplating cosmetic surgery, the doctor, believe it or not, is of secondary importance. Honest. I mean that. In the beginning, you and only you are the one who can make the decision. No reputable doctor will decide for you.

Be very straight with yourself about what you want to change. Be very specific. Small corrections can make beautiful, happy changes in you. If it's bags under your eyes that bother you, you certainly don't need to have your whole face lifted. But don't deceive yourself. Perhaps the bags are just the most obvious part to you of the overall aging process. If this is so, lifting them won't make you look all that much younger or better and you'll be disappointed. Perhaps you really should consider a complete face lift. The more specific and certain you are about what you want, the more specific your doctor can be in advising you on what is possible.

When wrinkled or scarred skin is a problem, chemical peeling may ease and soften enough of the lines and blemishes to make you feel really freshened. There are liquid silicone injections that contour or "plump out" wrinkles. Perhaps one of these procedures could serve your purpose without surgery. Be prepared for the fact that more than one procedure may be required. You'll see why as we go on.

Frankly, this is probably the most important decision and one of the biggest investments you ever make for your face or body, in time and in money. I think you should see more than one doctor and have different opinions. After all, remember that you're dealing with medical science—the possible—not magic, the wish. You are not just wishing for a change, it can be done. You want it done efficiently, skillfully, and well.

Should I or Shouldn't I?

You choose a cosmetic surgeon or a dermatological specialist in a number of ways. A doctor's reputation. Your family physician may recommend one he knows, or he'll inquire for you. Your local hospital and state medical societies, the county or state medical school won't recommend any one physician, but they can give you a list of qualified plastic surgeons for you to investigate.

Many plastic surgeons specialize. The surgeon who specializes in eye lifts might recommend a "nose man" for your consideration. Your dermatologist could give you a few names.

Check with your friends, especially women who've had something done. Ask them the questions. Ask about their doctors. I've met quite a few women recently, and men for that matter, who've had their eyes lifted successfully, and they do talk about it these days.

You probably could learn a lot from a good makeup man or woman in your town. After their doctors approve, many women want help disguising lingering redness, or they want to learn entirely new makeup techniques. The makeup artists in my New York cosmetic salon see and talk to many women, both before and after.

You may have to travel to one of the big cities of America or to one of the European, Mexican, or South American clinics to find the man whose techniques and artistry you most admire. Think about it.

The major portion of a plastic surgeon's practice may have to do with the reconstruction and repairing of war-damaged or accident-damaged patients. The dermatologist's primary concern may be the treatment of abnormal skin conditions, the correction of severe acne-scarred skin. Years ago cosmetic surgery was considered a vanity and a luxury for the idle rich. But today we know so much more about the psychological damage a woman, or a man, can suffer from a physical fault or defect. Doctors, too, are far more sympathetic. At least, you want to go to one who is, one who recognizes your need as a legitimate one.

Incidentally, plastic surgeons do turn down patients. You

185

don't hear too much about that, but in this age of high medical insurance costs and malpractice lawsuits, a doctor may say no. He may recognize that a patient's psychological problems would never be satisfied by a new nose. If you think you lost a job or a husband because your nose is large, if you hate having been born with your mother's profile instead of your father's, you might start looking for a psychiatrist or an analyst to help straighten you out first. You can straighten the nose later on. You may even find you no longer "need" to.

Here are some of the questions you'll want to ask the doctors during your initial visits and consultations: Just what can be accomplished? (Since you've already made up your mind and you know what you want, you must be sure that he understands. Listen very carefully to hear whether your aim can be fully satisfied or only partially realized.) What anesthesia is used? How long will the operation itself take? You want to know how long you'll need to heal, how long before you'll be ready to brave the outside world.

You want to know where your operation or dermatological procedure will take place—hospital or office. I did learn that there are many, many differences in procedure from one good doctor to the next. For example, one doctor will perform a small operation, the eyelift, in the office, use no bandages, and he'll send you home a few hours later. Another surgeon may work only in the hospital, bandage your eyes for twenty-four hours, and your stay could be two or three days. These days the cost will be increased manyfold if a hospital stay is necessary.

The doctor should explain the possible pain, all of the discomforts, and the risks to you. But I want to say something that I feel strongly about right here. You often read about the dangers and the risks, the things that went wrong. A doctor who is skilled in his techniques does not plan to do bad work, nor does he want anything to go wrong. He does not choose deliberately to inflict pain on you. The tolerance for pain differs so widely from one person to the next that even if you ask your doctor if it will hurt, how much it will hurt, he probably can't tell how you'll react. In addition to the operation that's performed or the chemical that's sprayed on you, there are so many factors involved: your health and the state of physical well-being you bring with you; your emotional tensions and reactions—nervousness and fear can make one woman's slight stinging sensation another woman's screaming pain. As with many other things, we often hear only the trouble stories and that scares us away from the successes.

When you've chosen your doctor he will tell you what the possibility of risk is, and, in all honesty, if the percentage of risk is high, he'll recommend another procedure or a milder method. He'll tell you what the sensations will be. He'll help you along with medication. He'll be very specific about the type of discomfort you might have and advise you how best to ease it.

There is always a risk in any operation, and putting chemicals on the face or dermabrading the skin must be handled with judgment and skill. As I said, take time. Spend the money for the consultations in the beginning, until you've found the man you respect. You must feel confidence and trust. This is no time for markdowns or bargains. Choose a doctor who will give you time for the questions, but don't stay away from the chance to be happier with yourself because of lurid headlines of malpractice lawsuits. On the other hand, if you're fifty years old and you've happened on a doctor who tells you you'll come out looking twenty, *leave*. It can't be done.

There are two different categories of cosmetic corrections to consider. Plastic surgery can reshape, recontour features, and also "lift" and tighten the skin. Chemical peeling, dermabrasion, and the less familiar silicone injections can correct or improve specific skin problems, acne scarring, and wrinkling.

Cosmetic Surgery

You can have your nose made smaller or straighter, remove a bump, hook, crook. You can have your nose narrowed, widened, lifted, curved. Mostly the work is performed internally so there are no scars. If work is done on your nostrils, the incision is made in the crease and should not be noticeable. You probably will suffer dark bruise marks around your eyes and mouth for up to a month, but not necessarily. It may take from three to six months for the swelling to subside completely, but after a few weeks to a month the swelling will be obvious only to you.

This is one of the most familiar and popular of all cosmetic surgery operations and therefore, perhaps, it is the one that should be considered the most seriously by you. Changing your nose will also change the aspect of your cheeks, chin and forehead. You can't just put a perfect nose into any face. The perfect nose would end up just that, a perfect nose. What you really want is to make your face more attractive.

Don't permit yourself to think that you'd like to look like some celebrated personality or film star you admire. Don't bring a picture to the doctor's office and tell him you want to "look like her." You probably wouldn't turn out that way anyway. You're you. You should have plastic surgery for an improvement, because you want to look better and feel better, but you still want to be individually, uniquely, identifiably you.

There is more than one operation to correct the eyes. Undereye surgery removes fatty cells and some muscle. The baggy, droopy look is softened or disappears. However, an eyelift cannot change the color or tone of your skin. Yes, sometimes a bit of undereye skin, excess, is tucked away, which does eliminate part of the darkened circle, but it's not always possible. Too much tightening may make your eyes "pop." Too much tucking in of the lower lid may cause eversion, an ugly downturn of the lower lid. But, after undereye surgery you gain a new makeup advantage. Probably before surgery you just couldn't use a cosmetic cover without exaggerating the puffiness and wrinkles. Now, with a newly smoothed-out surface, you can use a lightening cosmetic cover under your foundation to tone the entire eye circle to your complexion.

There is also upper eye surgery to diminish droopy or overhanging lids. This is a fairly simple procedure because the incision scar rests unseen in the natural lid crease.

Of course you can have both eye operations performed. The successful eyelift is probably the smallest and least painful operation you can have with the largest reward. It can make an older woman look much younger, really freshened, and usually people don't suspect why at all.

You can have a receding chin built up, or a protruding chin diminished, and you can have your ears resculptured. But it's the face lift that most of us think about as we get older.

The term "face lift" is entirely accurate. The doctor makes an incision in a kind of crescent shape, starting back behind your hairline above the temple, reaching to the top of the ear. Then he works the incision down into the natural crease at the front of the ear, under the earlobe, up behind the ear, and back into the hairline. He then lifts and draws your "face," really the skin of your face, back from the throat, from the cheeks and temples, leaving only the ear untouched, and sutures the skin into place. The sagging lines alongside your mouth are lifted somewhat, the droopy jowls and crepiness vanish.

Years ago doctors performed the lifting process separately on face and neck. I remember once seeing a woman who had her face lifted and it did look much younger. But for some reason she was frightened of the throat surgery, so there she was with a really crepey "old" neck contrasted sharply against that new face. I doubt that any doctor today would perform that sort of operation.

As for the operation and aftereffects, you may have some pain and a great deal of discomfort because it is, after all, major surgery, but most of it is handled easily with medication. The risk of scarring must be taken into account, particularly for certain complexion types. Black women, women with dark and olive skins are likely to form keloids, raised scars which you see at the ear lobes of some women. By the time you're ready for plastic surgery you should be well aware of how quickly or slowly a cut on your finger heals, or how susceptible you are normally to blacks-and-blues when you're bruised. It's a good idea to discuss it with your doctor if you think you're a slow healer or are particularly thin-skinned.

The face lift is going to take time out of your life. You may not want to tell anyone. Since you will still be swollen and uncomfortable when you first come out of the hospital you also may not want to share this experience with your husband or your friends. I think you ought to realize it could be a somewhat lonely time. Don't kid yourself. Even though you were properly prepared by your doctor, even though you were absolutely sure you wanted to do it, you may suffer a bit of emotional shock. After all, you were cut open and sewn together. You're not altogether sure of what you're going to look like. Prepare yourself especially carefully for the uncertainty and it will help you.

A face lift is not permanent. Your skin will continue the aging process as long as you're alive and the crinkling and wrinkling will creep up on you again. Years ago, all the doctor could do was lift the skin and the lift didn't last very long at all. Today surgeons in many areas of the world are also eliminating some of the muscle action beneath the skin and the lift lasts many years longer. Obviously that kind of work demands the utmost in knowledge and skill. At best, at the moment, the most expert face lift will last about ten years.

You should certainly be aware of this fact, which may help you to decide at what age to have your first face lift. The older you get, the more elasticity your skin loses, and the more operations you have, the tighter that skin will appear on your face. You don't want to end up wearing a mask. So I don't think anyone can tell you when to have your first face lift. On the other hand, there is something to be said for having it done before you really appear to need it. Maintaining the continuity of looking attractive and looking younger is much more desirable than a sudden, sharp change.

Now for the body. There are operations that can remove the excess fat that you haven't been able, or willing, to diet or exercise off. The same operations lift sagging skin on the body and tuck it away. "Body tucks" are not uncommon on the upper arms, the inner thighs, the buttocks and the abdomen. You have to have scars, usually long, thin or fine ones, but scars nonetheless. Be sure you know where they'll be.

Sometimes I jokingly say that I cannot imagine any woman wanting less bosom, but I know that isn't so. Breast surgery can reduce size, but it will leave a scar, usually to the side and under the arms, so you have to know why you want to do it. You may be prettier in clothes, but . . .

Augmenting the breasts usually involves the insertion under the breasts of different types of implants, space-filling silicone bags, or bladders which are then inflated, or filled with gel or salt water. All are meant to approximate the shape and consistency of breast tissue, though the balance of just how hard or just how soft the ''new'' breast should be is often tricky. No matter which type of insert your doctor finally decides on, beware of liquid silicone. The large amounts that have to be injected to raise your flat chest to full are rightfully still considered extremely dangerous.

Equally important as knowing what cosmetic surgery can do is knowing what cosmetic operations cannot do. As I said earlier, plastic surgery cannot change the color or tone of your skin. It cannot remove deeply furrowed lines in the forehead, nor completely remove the deep lines that settle down at the sides of the mouth. Those lines may be somewhat softened so they may seem to have vanished, at least enough not to disturb you anymore. Cosmetic surgery cannot repair badly wrinkled skin, skin that's been all dried out by sun and weathering. Your skin has to have some moisture and some elasticity left in order to respond to the lift.

Dermatological Corrections

Chemical peeling, dermabrasion, and silicone injections are non-surgical procedures that can do a great deal for your skin and for certain types of wrinkling. Your doctor will recommend which process can soften your forehead furrows and mouth lines. He can remove or improve many types of acne-caused blemishes, surface pitting, enlarged pores. He may even use dermabrasion to force acne infection to the surface more quickly. This is not an end in itself because the acne then requires further treatment, but it is a new help for teenagers and other acne sufferers.

In the chemical peel, an acid or organic chemical is sprayed on the face or particular areas of the face in order to deliberately irritate the skin and cause a reaction much like a bad sunburn. Although a discussion in terms of layers in the skin is a little artificial, the light or mild peel usually refers to one that peels the epidermis, the outermost layer of the skin. Your dermatologist or even a highly qualified facialist can do this because the chemicals used are not usually strong enough to cause any damage. Your skin will be pink or somewhat reddened, and will usually be back to normal color within a week.

Some women believe that a mild peel every nine to twelve months keeps their skin younger-looking. Dr. Robert Berger, one of New York City's respected young dermatologists, with whom I consulted, suggested to me that it's difficult to draw a conclusion on this as a theory. It's not unlike many questions which go undocumented and unanswered in cosmetology. In theory, the woman who has annual peelings appears to have younger skin. In practice, the woman who has annual peelings is usually the same woman who avoids the sun, watches her diet, cleanses and moisturizes her skin carefully. She's a woman who has money, may have had her eyes or her face lifted. She's the woman who is concerned with herself—some might say overly concerned—but the fact remains that it would be difficult to determine whether it's the peeling or the overall care that keeps her looking often strikingly younger than her contemporaries.

The deep chemical peel involves stronger forms of the acids or chemicals, does more to soften wrinkles, to tighten enlarged pores, remove scars. No one, but no one but your dermatologist should do this one.

The chemical is applied to burn the skin and within a few days your skin will crust and finally start cracking and peeling. You may have some pain, but more likely you'll feel only a burning, stinging sensation as the chemical is applied, and a numbing sensation briefly afterward. You may suffer a slight allergic reaction with all the symptoms of a cold. You will be uncomfortable when your skin crusts over because of the lack of mobility. For the first few days you'll just look like you've had a lot of sun, heightened color, and then, about the fourth, fifth, sixth days, when the crusting takes over, you take cover. You can work that out during a business week, leaving yourself a quiet weekend for the worst of it.

You may have heard of peeling where a strong acid is applied and the face is taped afterwards. Dr. Berger thoroughly disapproves of this procedure; he informed me that although "with good luck the results could be as effective as dermabrasion," he had seen many cases where severe scarring and serious skin damage have resulted.

The varying degrees of chemical peeling can help many areas of the skin. The fine, light lines knowns as "crow's feet," if they're not too deep, and the "rivers" that run around the entire mouth can be eased, softened, apparently erased—temporarily. The neck can be freshened with a light peel. The most difficult problem is that of dark circles under the eyes; if they're very dark, here's where your doctor may recommend you see a surgeon for an eye lift, if you have the excess skin to be tucked away.

After peeling you should not end up with obvious color demarkations "spotlighting" the area peeled. When called for, the doctor will do the entire face. But if all that's required is one area, here's where the doctor's judgment, or artistry if you will, is most important. If he does the upper lip, he'll probably carry the peel down to the chin, for example. A difference in tone between the skin on your face and on your throat is usual anyway. You wear makeup on your face which contrasts slightly with an unmade-up neck, so you won't have a problem. It may take three or four months before that light pinkness blends with your complexion color, but it will.

Although there are some beauticians who may do a deep peel, don't take chances. Don't put your face into any hands but those of the best doctor for a deep chemical peeling.

Dermabrasion is generally a much deeper process. The doctor uses a tool attached to a rotary motor to plane the face. Back in the forties, I believe, doctors used a kind of sandpaper for superficial skin planing. Today that's been replaced by either a fraise—an industrial diamond adapted for the purpose—or a fine wire brush, much like a suede shoe brush, which seems to be most effective for deep acne scarring, the most common reason for dermabrading.

The skin on your face is exceptional in relation to the skin that covers the rest of your body. Things can be done to the face, and will heal, that cannot be done on the back, the chest, the abdomen, most of all the legs. So peeling and planing just can't be done on the body.

Discolorations of many sorts on the skin are often a nuisance rather than a serious problem. They spot and shadow and make the skin look splotchy, uneven and old.

So-called "liver spots" are not uncommon at all in the older fair-haired, fair-skinned woman who spent a lot of time in the sun when she was younger. As she ages, these spots frequently appear on the backs of her hands, the V of the neck, and the face. Fortunately these are readily erased, often permanently if she stays out of the sun, with painless, trouble-free dry ice treatments.

There's another skin discoloration called chloasma which the doctors see a great deal more of these days in young women than they used to. Chloasma is larger, irregular or maplike patches of dark tan color which are hormonally stimulated. These may appear during pregnancy and they occur frequently in women who take birth control pills. They appear on areas above the eyebrows, at the temples, on the upper lip, and they're difficult to get rid of, especially if the woman continues to take the contraceptive pill.

Broken or dilated capillaries on the legs can be treated by injection, or with a form of electrolysis which "sparks" or dries them off. There is a high degree of success predictable with electric needle treatments on the legs and thighs. However, when treating the face, your doctor should test a few of the capillaries in a less conspicuous part of the face to see how the skin reacts to the electric needle process. Unfortunately, many women get small scars known as retractions and they may not look any better than the spidery fractured capillaries you wanted removed.

Silicone injections have had extraordinarily bad press due to the horrible stories of some time back when go-go girls were having their breasts enlarged with silicone. And rightfully so. Silicone can only be injected safely in tiny, tiny amounts, and the large amounts that were used to inflate the breasts then were indeed dangerous—and still are for that matter. In addition, the silicone must be pure, and the women you read about were treated with adulterated silicone.

But there are reputable doctors who have been using small amounts of pure fluid silicone for more than a dozen years now in the face and the body with what many women consider fabulous results. Pure silicone does not harden, will not lose its contour, does not move around, and, so far as the medical material I've read indicated, affords no present dangers in small amounts.

When small amounts of the silicone are injected they "plump up" the hollows or valleys on a level with the rest of the skin. When it's done the right way, silicone can do a great deal to improve the appearance of normal, not too deep, acne scars, creases and lines on any part of the face and body, excepting the breasts. Forehead furrows, the "rivers" that run around the lips, even the side-of-the-mouth lines can be helped in this new, usually painless way. You can even have your cheeks plumped up a little bit above the bones and deepened hollows below filled in a touch.

Different doctors, once again, have different techniques for injecting. You may go just once or for a series of small treatments, and you won't feel more than a pinprick.

There's a nail care salon in New York which is a kind of conversational meeting place for women who talk about cosmetic surgery while they're having their hour-long manicure and drying sessions. They seem to know the name of every doctor in the world among them. Anyway, one of the women there has been having liquid silicone injections for ten years to date, mostly in her forehead furrows and around her mouth. You never know when she's been because she goes every year for a few visits and has just enough done to keep looking wonderfully young all the time.

In all cases, after you've selected the doctor or surgeon who best meets your needs and you've had the work done, follow his advice to the letter. He'll tell you when you can reapply makeup and when you can shampoo your hair. He'll watch for any kind of allergic reaction to a peeling. He'll warn you to steer clear of extreme cold, wind, and sun. He'll give you a medical sunblock to protect you.

I recognize all of this as a very big problem. Should I or shouldn't I? But I think plastic surgery and getting a better or more youthful skin makes so many women happy that I'm glad it's all available to us.

I think you should do it if you're emotionally insecure and you're convinced that looking better will make you feel better about yourself. The security of feeling more attractive can encourage your security as a woman. But don't allow yourself to think you can change a nose or get bigger breasts to win back a man you've lost. If you've lost him, that's not why you lost him. To continue to keep a man, to win a man, maybe. Yes. But only because you feel better.

Daily routine between 7:30 and 8:30 A.M.—*breakfast, newspapers and exercises.*

197

With Rex Reed.

Marisa Berenson.

With Governor Jerry Brown.

198

Laughing with John Schlesinger

*With Christina Ford
at a party.*

*Loulou de la Falaise, marvel-
ous woman and great friend.*

*With Henry Kissinger,
Barry Diller and Bob
Evans.*

*With John Fairchild
and actress Florinda
Bolkan.*

199

Talking business with partner and great friend Richard Conrad.

Filling orders in the shipping department.

In the showroom.

Diane: Princess, Mom, Dressmaker, Feminist

BY MARJI KUNZ
Free Press Fashion Writer

NEW YORK — Fortunately Bonwit Teller invited Diane von Furstenberg to do her public appearance in Detroit today. On Monday she had elevator operator duty in her plush Park Avenue apartment building where tenants (and not their servants) are pitching in during the current maintenance workers strike.

Still, it's one of those things you'd think a princess (by marriage) and business dynamo who earns $250,000 a year (at age 29) and happens to have an Oriental houseboy, Oriental maid, Argentine cook and English nanny on staff could avoid.

Diane wouldn't think of opting out. Stretched out barefoot on one of her peach satin sofas, under her own print trio of silk screened portraits, wearing one of her own jersey dresses, the Belgian-born beauty enthused, "Last week I was doorman.

"That's America. It wouldn't happen anywhere else. Everyone is equal," she went on, flexing her bared toes. "I've applied to become a citizen. This country has been very good to me."

The best evidence that America has been good to her is the distance she has come in five years from a novice designer with a suitcase full of samples to the cover of Newsweek (March 22).

SHE FIRST MADE headlines not on fashion stories but on society stories when she married, and then split with, Prince Egon von Furstenberg. Together, they were the darlings of the jet set for awhile, but she wanted more.

She started with a few printed jersey shirtdresses, a bit of jewelry designer Kenny Lane and the all-important approval of Vogue editor and fashion arbiter Diana Vreeland.

That and $32,000 seed money from her father launched a business that now has sales in the millions.

"This year we'll sell about $19 or $20 million of the dresses at wholesale," said Diane softly. "I can't imagine any Seventh Avenue designer is selling so many." But that doesn't include the eyeglasses and sunglasses, shoes, furs, tops, lounge scarves, sleepwear and Vogue cosmetics business. Or the book she's [writing] ... estimates...

Eye On Fragrance

Tatiana, or the real Diane von Furstenberg

By STEVE GINSBERG

NEW YORK — Two years ago, Alvin (Bud) Lindsay, president of Roure Bertrand Du Pont, was stymied. His chemist and perfumers were ... translating Diane von Furstenberg's fragrance into ...

Lindsay, whose firm had been the supplier for several of Estee Lauder's successful fragrances, enjoys the manufacturers ... has also worked with corporations, like Lanvin-Charles of the Ritz, whose Rive Gauche Du Pont developed.

"We read Diane wrong. Here was a beautiful black-haired, brown-eyed, sophisticated, sexy jet-set image. Ideally, Lindsay dispatched hundreds of ... Roure Du Pont's labs produced ... [I] though Furstenberg rejected ... with von Furstenberg helped him to finally find the ...

... on Furstenberg's fragrance finally gave her approval to a fragrance ...

It debuted in October 1974. Its ... lack of advertising. Its ...

... cantecaille, outlined

... turer has been "marvelous." Lindsay is equally enthusiastic in discussing the successful teamwork. He said:

"Diane von Furstenberg is a personality, not a company. She contributed a lot to her fragrance. She kept saying no but finally pointed us in the direction she wanted. It was more fun than making a fragrance for a corporate committee.

"The earlier our clients come to us and share in the creative process, the better. Many years ago, we started saying no one really needed, including the bottle, and came manufacturers got everything ready to fill that bottle. They realize they must have the right fragrance. A fragrance will sell on the first go-round but must have some ... but you need a good product for the second go-round.

Roure Du Pont's last product for the second go-round ... Unlike Tatiana, Rive Gauche was heavily promoted ...

Du Pont's lab facilities produce Rive Gauche ... Lanvin-Charles of the Ritz research and ... Rive Gauche account. "We were well aware of their conceptual ideas ...

Clippings.

THE ARIZONA REPUBLIC

Designing princess at Magnin

Designer, world traveler, business woman, mother and now author. These are the sum that is Princess Diane von Furstenberg, who will make a personal appearance in the Valley Wednesday.

She'll bring a collection of some 200 of her latest designs for modeling at I. Magnin before and after she commentates her own Designer Showcase luncheon at the Arizona Biltmore.

Featherweight packable dresses...

Diane von Furstenberg

Diane von Furstenberg creates the ultimate in dressing for autumn '75, surpassing her own outstanding wrap dress success ... a perfect example of what can be done with pure ingenuity and talent! A handsome performer and year round travel coat ... looking and feeling like leather, the beauty and practicality are genuine. No-care wipe clean and feather light polyurethane in battleship grey or chocolate brown in sizes 6 to 12. $170. Diane's famous wrap dress ... 100% acrylic jersey you can treat casually and wear endlessly. In green/grey feather print. Sizes 6 to 16. $84. Tatiana ... Eau de Parfum. 2 fluid ounces. $10. Feather jewelry ... brilliantly polished gold with overlay relief of silver. Collar. $40. Bracelet. $30. Earrings. $20. Tatiana silk print scarf. 25" square in brown, green or blue with grey. $10.

Jacobson's
PROCTOR SHOPS

Los Angeles Times

Thurs, May 15, 1975

Princess Launches Beautification Project

BY BETTIJANE LEVINE
Times Staff Writer

Diane von Furstenberg is a bankable name.

It sold $13 million worth of dresses last year.

It is inscribed on watches, costume jewelry, scarves, luggage and handbags.

And now, at I. Magnin exclusively, it is spelled out on a smoky mirror in the new Diane von Furstenberg cosmetics boutique.

Miss Von Furstenberg is risking her legendary name—and probably part of her personal fortune—by bringing out a new collection of cosmetics in this recession-riddled world.

But she's doing it because she says she knows she has something good to offer.

Editing Out Junk

"People still crave taste, especially in cosmetics," says the Belgian-born 28-year-old apparel firm...little printed...

FINISHING TOUCH—Diane von Furstenberg touch on one of her customers at her...

6 diane von furstenberg gives you safety in numbers 9

Bloomingdale's

The Montreal Star

'Title some advantage'

Diane von Furstenberg
—her fashion highness

By Iona Monahan

NEW YORK — Diane von Furstenberg, publicized jet-setter and beautiful person...

For your holiday shopping convenience Saks Fifth Avenue will be open until...

TODAY, DIANE VON FURSTENBERG PITCHES HER RAINTENT AT S.F.A.

SAKS FIFTH AVENUE
CELEBRATING OUR FIFTIETH CHRISTMAS

The Times-Picayune

SUNDAY MORNING, JANUARY 26, 1975

Princess Diane von Furstenberg Enters the Cosmetics Kingdom

By PATRICIA SHELTON

CHICAGO — A smart princess doesn't let herself get caught without a kingdom to call her own.

And Diane von Furstenberg, legally separated from her prince, Egon, of the Fiat family for almost a year...

More clippings and some ads.

MODEL'S CIRCLE
For Women Who Want to be Beautiful

Be Dressed

The Princess Diane von Furstenberg arrived in the United States in 1969 — a time when designers were having a field day dressing women in kinky-looking clothing. Trying to buy clothing that was not covered with cowboy fringe or decorated with Indian beads was a big problem for Diane. This was the "hippie" era — love beads, heavy suedes, boys looking like girls, girls looking like boys, looking and feeling like a lady — a way of dressing that she was not about to change.

Since she could not find what she was looking for in the shops of New York, Diane decided to design her own clothes.

"I was never an adolescent," Diane said. "I went from a little...

Newsweek

March 22, 1976 / 75 cents

Rags & Riches

Dress
Designer
Diane von
Fürstenberg

VOGUE

What is a Diane
Von Fürstenberg?

More than a designer. A woman. More than a woman. An idea.
More than an idea. A philosophy. More than a philosophy.
A totality.

The totally adds up to me: a new way of living and looking.
Elegant, easy clothes and cosmetics and fragrance and accessories that establish the truth of you. For you wear them, they
never wear you.

Diane Von Fürstenberg knows who and what you are and
where you're going. She believes fashion is freedom. Experience this lovely, liberating force in her supple, subtle, on-the-
move clothes, in her swift, efficient makeup and skincare collection as good as it is beautiful, in her fresh, openhearted new
fragrance Tatiana... to make you a woman of today.

What is a Diane Von Fürstenberg? Today's woman: tomorrow. Tomorrow's woman: now. The way we live now
more meaningful...

Diane Von Fürstenberg

*How does it feel to be a cover
girl? . . . Strange but nice!*

FORTUNE

April 1974

The Golden Edge
of Fashion

"If you're a woman and you're young
and social, nobody takes you seriously,"
says **Diane von Furstenberg**, 27. As
the wife of a German prince and daugh-
ter-in-law of an Agnelli, she is social beyond question; Princess von Furstenberg's jet-set doings are chronicled in
gossip columns almost day by day. But

207

In the cosmetic salon on Madison Avenue—personalizing beauty.

Making me up . . .

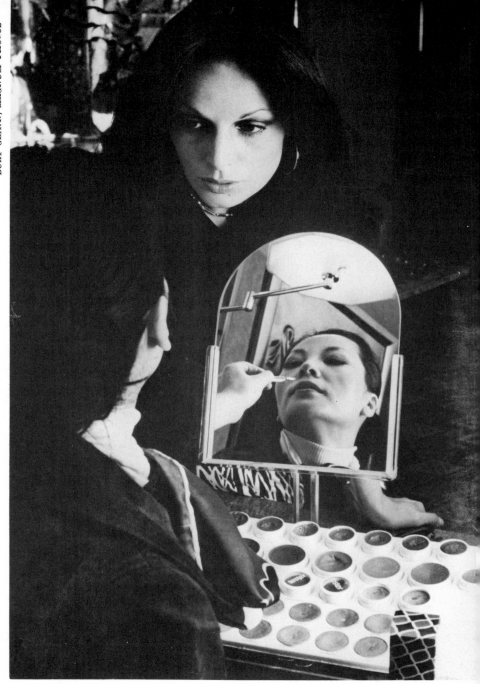

. . . and teaching the little "tricks" to clients.

In the snow with Alexandre and Tatiana.

ON WEEKENDS, ANOTHER PERSON.

The children, the fire and lots of books . . . my life in Connecticut.

212

With Barry.

Time to think,
  time to re-evaluate . . .
    long walks with Elvis and Skonk.

CHAPTER TWELVE

Time for Yourself—
Relax . . . and Sleep

Relax is a big word, a very big word. It is used for everything, everywhere. *Relax!* they say for any product they want to sell, for anything. It's become such a big word that they use it in every language and use it all the time—misuse, I should really say.

We all—or almost all—are under terrible tensions. I must say that I myself am terribly harassed by them. I am always late, always behind schedule, and have been for the last seven years! I have this good/bad habit of using time, so even if I'm under the dryer or waiting for an elevator I always manage to do something else as well. The result of that is an enormous productivity, but also an enormous tension, and I keep on hearing this voice: relax, relax. I've started to learn not to feel pushed and frantic and tight. But it is very difficult.

The key, I think, is to take time for yourself. You must set aside some part of every day or every week to think about yourself. To put your mind in order. To relax. To unwind. To be kind to yourself or to pamper yourself. To shut the whole world out. To do nothing.

You may find your way of relaxing with yourself is to do

something. I'll get into that in a minute. You may just want to close the doors behind you and laze in a bath for a half hour. But you must separate yourself from everybody, from everything, and be alone with yourself sometimes. Be solitary. Be quiet. Be still.

For me, the best way to relax is to do nothing. I mean nothing. Having a vacation for me is really doing nothing. I don't mean going to a movie, playing tennis, going shopping—just doing nothing.

My favorite way to relax used to be to take long walks all alone in the country. You think much better when you walk. If I go for a long walk in the country I come back and I think I'm Napoleon. I get high, really high, when I walk. I build up a whole world; it's unbelievable. I build and I build. When I come back I'm so energetic I can't stand it and I start writing and telephoning. I get some of my best ideas when I walk, so I call Dick Conrad, my partner on Seventh Avenue, and I tell him all my new ideas. And most of them work out very well. I get so much energy from the walk and afterwards it seems so easy to organize myself and go on with other things. But, is that really relaxing?

I also tried taking Friday off every week. Everybody in my office knew that I wouldn't be in that day. To myself I had decided that Friday would be my beauty day. Well, it failed, because, since it was supposed to be the free day, I managed to accumulate a lot of odds and ends, and it ended up being the busiest day of the week.

Silly things relax me, like watering the outdoor gardens in the summer. I disconnect the sprinklers and stand for an hour every evening at dusk watering everything by hand. That's my peaceful time in the country. The air is cool and fresh; I am surrounded by beauty and it completely relaxes me.

You may do your best thinking and feel happiest with yourself when you're cooking or baking, sewing, brushing your dog, painting a picture or painting a wall. Your time for yourself might be reading a book, clipping and pasting recipes, or giving yourself a manicure. But the real way to relax is to escape from your environment, to escape reality for a moment and not think about what you're supposed to do next.

Some women feel that a nap in the late afternoon is the best. Go ahead if you can. But when you take a nap, prepare yourself first. Before you lie down, think of all the things that you're going to do when you get up. If you're resting before going out for the evening, decide what you're going to wear or even lay your clothes out. Switch the makeup and the money you need to your evening bag. If you're going to cook dinner, think about what you're going to cook, how long it will take, then switch off the phone and forget about everything.

Of course, the same applies for sleeping at night. Again, sleeping is taking time for yourself and it's important to sleep well in order to be fresh and ready for the next day. Many women take the tensions of the day to bed with them and they just can't sleep. Many people fall asleep but don't sleep soundly and well.

I guess I'm fortunate. I always sleep very well. But I do prepare myself. Before I go to sleep at night, even if I'm exhausted, I go into my library and check my list of all the things I have to do the next day. I write down quickly anything new, cross things off.

And I could never sleep with makeup on. No matter what time I go to bed and in what state, I never, never sleep with makeup. It's a way to concentrate more on your sleep. You won't sleep worrying about a soiled face, smudged mascara.

I never worry about how little time I have to sleep either. If I'm having a really good time, I enjoy it and I don't worry about the "tomorrow-wake-up-time." Sleep is easier to make up than a unique evening. And besides, it is not so much how much you sleep but how you sleep. No matter how many or how few hours I have ahead of me, the get-ready-to-sleep procedure is always the same.

When I'm traveling, then it's really a matter of concentrating. When I'm on a plane to go to Europe, I take my clothes off, put on a loose dress, take my makeup off, and go to sleep. I imagine it's night. I say "Good night" to myself and I go to sleep. When I wake up, I wash myself and change clothes. I put on my makeup and when I leave the plane it's as if I had spent a whole night sleeping. I know it isn't, but the idea of changing clothes and relaxing completely makes me feel it's a new day when I arrive.

Here are a few simple suggestions to help you sleep soundly and well.

Don't eat a heavy meal before you go to sleep. Give yourself a few hours. Your mind may stop churning but your body won't if it's still digesting pasta.

Watch anything that tends to stimulate you. Even if you smoke, try to stop an hour before you go to bed. Don't drink coffee, tea, or too much alcohol.

Open the windows and let the fresh air in. If it's noisy outside, turn on the air conditioner.

Try the body movements for relaxing before you get into bed. The concentration and quietness of them really help.

Take a lukewarm bath and "collapse" in it. Make sure your towel is ready, your bed is turned down. Have everything prepared so you can just get out of the tub into the towel and into bed.

If you've really had a nerve-jangling day, turn on some soft music, read something light—but stay in bed so you can slip off into sleep when it comes.

You have to concentrate to sleep well. When you have problems or something is bothering you, instead of thinking about it at night, say, "Now I'll sleep. I'll think about it tomorrow." With a fresh head things are always easier. They don't tangle. Otherwise your mind is always completely embroiled.

Don't worry about not sleeping. That's almost worse than worrying about tomorrow. You can get along on less sleep than you think and worrying about not getting your seven or eight hours will only keep you awake.

Time for Yourself—Relax . . . and Sleep

No matter how much of a hassle a day is, you can learn to deal with stress. Taking time for yourself has many benefits besides the wonderful one of enjoying yourself. The effects of the time you take are cumulative. You just won't feel the push and pull as much when it comes. If you have problems chances are that you've thought them through during the time you took so that the problems are closer to resolution anyway. And being with yourself, talking to yourself also becomes a kind of habit finally. If you know how to talk to yourself, if you know how to relax, then you can pull back for a few minutes in a crisis situation and talk to yourself mentally, and relax. Whatever it means to you.

CHAPTER THIRTEEN

P. S.

I T'S TAKEN MORE THAN A YEAR to write this book. I'm thirty years old right now and I guess I've gone through a few things. I've become a woman and I'm aware that I'm a woman. I'm aware that I'm a mother. I'm aware that I've become a successful businesswoman.

I've spent many pages discussing how to be beautiful because it is important. I think that everything we do is for the outside world—for others. We try to be successful or we work to prove to the rest of the world that we are something. Everything we do is for show. We dress and we are beautiful, we decorate our houses for show. That gives us labels and identity so people will know who we are.

We create things so we can deserve love. In my own discovery of a woman, the woman I am, I've learned that I do it all to earn love. More important, I've learned that finally it's the part that isn't really anything, the other side that doesn't show, that is usually loved. It's the things that you're not even aware of yourself maybe, what you're afraid to give because you're afraid to be hurt, afraid to open up too much— that part is often the nicest, the most desirable part of you.

P. S.

That part, your vulnerability—not the outside, not what is so
evident, not what shows—is what a man truly loves.

We are all alike. We all do the same things. We were born,
we grow, we make love, we die. And I believe that we all need
love. Unless you're going to share life, unless you're going to
talk about it, about what you do, about living, it's not really all
that much fun. Very simply, I need a man. I couldn't live without a man. I can't live without a man because I need love and
the warmth and caring for somebody and doing things for
somebody and being beautiful for somebody. We all need love
so badly. That's why we have to find one person and give it all
to that one person.

I think women today are almost too perfect. We play the
cook, the mother, play psychiatrist for a man, please him at
making love—but that's what makes life more fun. I think we
shouldn't ever overplay one role. I think every part of life
should be a small part. It's only a part, not the whole you, so
you try to keep all the different persons separate. Since we
are women, born women, with all that's demanded of us, I
think we want it that way. Since it's there, let's enjoy it and
play all the parts.

It may be very difficult. It is very difficult for me because
my business keeps me very busy, because I have to deal with
so many problems every day. I have to be strong. I have to
prove my point. It's not always easy to switch from one role
or one side of myself to another quickly. It's not always easy
to relax at the core, to come down and permit the vulnerability to come through. And that is often difficult for a man to
cope with.

As time goes by priorities change and keep changing and
still will change. I've learned that the most important thing is
to try to keep the very necessary priorities up front. I try to
keep as close to the base, to the very basic values, as possible. I
think the further we go, the older we get, the harder we should
try to be warmer, to be more tolerant, more indulgent of
others, more responsive. I think the further we go the harder
we should try to understand and to free our vulnerability, to

trust so that we can give and receive love honestly. You can't give until you can trust that someone is not going to hurt you. I'm learning that I now feel more confident in trusting someone.

No matter how much I've learned, every day is a new adventure for me. Every day I discover that what I learned before is not definitely right, not necessarily true, but I grow richer through these experiences. I grow richer in experience and richer in my feelings. And I think that that is the true sensuality and the true joy of being alive and of being a woman.